What readers are saying about the Independent Publisher's Book Award-winner, *Under the Same Sun*

"Kobras does not disappoint in this sparkling, fresh sequel to *The Distant Shore*. Walk with Naomi on a still beach. Drink in the atmosphere of love and peace. Give yourself the gift of a classic romance.

You will be so glad you did!"

~ Donna Carrick, author of IPPY Award-winner, *The First Excellence*

"The author has a fantastic sense of place. As the story moves from the west to east coasts of the US, to northern Europe, to Italy, you can *feel* the changes in climate and culture. If you have fondly experienced any of these places, you are anxious to return, and if not, you are dreaming of your future journeys…

The personalities of Jon and Naomi are artfully reflected against the changing scenery…You are convinced that their relationship is one that *should* work. You are pulling for them all the way, and you cheer when they grow and succeed."

~ Becky B., Amazon.com

"She expertly stitches events and feelings together to form a tapestry that one can almost reach out and touch…She writes with layers, much like a quilt. Each sentence another stitch in the written quilt, the story.

Mariam's beautiful sensory descriptions of each new venue allow her readers—even the most frugal of us—to feel as though we've traveled the world with Naomi and Jon. Whether we are dancing on a lakeshore in Geneva, shopping at Harrods in London, or decorating their house in Brooklyn, we are there. We can see the area, feel the smooth wood of the Steinway, or the rough cobblestone road, the local aromas waft around us, as the sounds mingle with those of our real surroundings."

~ Nita Beshears, www.DevotedtoQuilting.wordpress.com

"Mariam continues to pull me in with her wonderful story of love and the world of rock music. This is a compliment: her story is like the addictive soap operas that you fall in love with: you love (or hate) the characters, root for them, and cry with them. I can't wait for the final installment!"

~ Molly Campbell, goodreads.com

"There is a poetic feel to Ms. Kobras's writing that really draws you in. Jon's rock star life and Naomi's beauty are envied by many, but the characters are very real and their vulnerabilities are laid bare. You begin to see that all the glitter and glamour of rock star living is not as it seems. A compelling read and highly recommended."

~ Eliza Green, Amazon.com

"Kobras left me feeling I was leaving old friends when I finished the book…There are writers who tell a story and writers who take you into the story. Kobras takes you into the story, and with her descriptive powers, leaves you with vivid images of the places to which the characters travel, and the feelings of the characters. Further I found several passages which were very thought provoking. Ms. Kobras has fast become one of my favorite authors. I'm sure I will reread both books with regularity and am looking forward to the next book Ms. Kobras releases."

~ addicted to romance, Amazon.com

"Kobras has created an effective mix of romance and suspense in *Under the Same Sun*. The portrayal of what it's like to be stalked is genuine and frightening, and readers can feel Naomi's vulnerability. As Kobras reveals who the stalker is, she also shows us how modern high-profile marriages withstand realities like being apart, crazed fans, and more. Naomi and Jon are very believable characters too who react in credible ways. They're both flawed, but both of them are at the core good people who know that they need each other. Romance fans will be richly satisfied with *Under the Same Sun*."

~ MMK, Amazon.com

"Interesting, multi-layered characters that make you laugh at times, and shake your head at others…Beautiful settings, wonderful descriptions make you a part of the scene. I traveled around the world within this story and often felt like a bird sitting on the window sill watching the story unfold!"

~ Santos, Amazon.com

"A page turner from the moment I started it…It's a smooth transition from the first book. In the continued story of Jon and Naomi, it dives deeper into their lives as it reveals more about who they are, where they came from, the differences between their families, and the depth of their commitment to each other. There is so much detail in the characters, it's like being right there in real time. When I finished the book, it left me hanging and wanting to know what happens next! Never had a favorite author until now."

~ MarathonMom2three, Amazon.com

Song of the Storm

Books by Mariam Kobras

The Stone Trilogy
The Distant Shore, Book I
Under the Same Sun, Book II
Song of the Storm, Book III

The Rosewood Guitar, Jon's Story, coming 2014

Song of the Storm

by
Mariam Kobras

Book III: The Stone Trilogy

Buddhapuss Ink   Edison NJ

Cover Art *The Other Room* @ 2007 Eric G. Thompson
Author Photo by Sarah Fulford
Cover and Book Layout/Design by The Book Team
Library of Congress Control Number: 2013939882
ISBN 978-0-9842035-7-4 (Paperback Original)
First Printing July 2013

PUBLISHER'S NOTE

To contact the artist Eric G. Thompson or learn more about his works, go to:
www.ericgthompson.com

Buddhapuss Ink LLC and our logos are trademarks of Buddhapuss Ink LLC.
www.buddhapussink.com

For Keith Peterson and MaryChris Bradley—they know why.

chapter 1

SHE HAD MEANT to tell him in Vegas.

But after the incident with the fan group, Naomi had followed Sal back to the hospitality area where she huddled on a couch in the corner.

She sat, her back to the wall, and watched as a couple of girls refilled the platters, preparing for the concert's end when they would all come in, loud, sweaty, exhilarated, calling for food and drinks.

Sal stood, clearly waiting for her to say something, but she could not find any words.

Jon hadn't seen her behind Sal and Russ, watching him as he leaned against the wall in the hallway just inside the huge security doors, well surrounded by guards, his head lowered and his hands folded, waiting for the ladies, composing himself, becoming the figure they wanted to see: the star, their icon.

The music had begun out in the auditorium, slow and not too loud; she had heard an announcer's voice asking the audience to take their seats, the murmur of the crowd as it settled down. LaGasse beside her had shifted slightly when the door opened to admit the fan club, more guards just behind them, their faces deep in concentration.

They had been through this ritual at every tour stop, a well-rehearsed moment, a bow to publicity.

Yet this time it had been different. There were seven of them, all sighing in awe when they saw him.

Jon had straightened, smiling, greeting them politely, and allowing a few snapshots. He had signed their tour books, answered a few questions, and wished them a pleasant evening. After a few minutes Art had stepped forward and signaled, and Jon had excused himself, saying it was time to take to the stage. Then it had happened.

One of them, a woman about her own age—blond, ample, with cheeks as round and red as apples—had said, "Too bad what happened at the Oscars. I would have loved to comfort you during that time."

Sal, quite swiftly, had taken Naomi's arm and tried to pull her away, but she had shaken him off.

Without another word Jon had turned and stalked away, his shoulders drawn up in anger, while the women were asked to leave. Security had nearly pushed them back into the auditorium, shutting the heavy doors behind them.

"NAOMI," SAL WAS saying, waking her from her thoughts, "don't waste a minute on it. It's not worth it. You know they lose their heads when they see him up close."

Of course she knew, but it was different being confronted by it in such a manner and seeing Jon's reaction.

"I have to go, Sal."

"Yes, of course. He'll be waiting to see you there." There was relief in his voice, displaced immediately by disquiet when she shook her head.

"Not out there." She waved her hand in the general direction of the music. "I need to go back home, now."

He blanched visibly under his tan, but before he could ask, she got up. "Come on, let's go and take a look. And then I'm off."

"What's going on?" Sal called after her, but she was already on her way, following the lure of Jon's voice and the song the band was picking up just then.

A huge security man pushed the door open for her, and Naomi entered the auditorium.

No matter the country or city, the feeling was always the same.

She went to stand next to Art and Russ at the computers at the side of the stage. Jon saw her. His face lit up, and with a movement of his hand the song took off, soaring all the way to the domed ceiling, his voice carrying it away across the thousands of listeners. He had turned slightly toward her, as if he was singing to her alone, flirting with her until she smiled back at him.

She stayed until he introduced the band and then launched into his most famous song, the steamy rock rhythm like the beating heart of a huge beast and Jon its toy, giving himself up to it.

It was hard to turn her back on him, but she patted Art's shoulder and walked out, leaving a bewildered Sal behind.

JON SAW HER leave but thought nothing of it. His mood had lightened considerably, the uneasy moment with the fan group forgotten.

The music seemed easier suddenly, no longer a job that had to be done to please a crowd. He caught Sean's grin and smiled back, hitting the strings of his guitar with a flourish and dropping his pick into it with the rapid movement. Jones, his lead guitarist, held out another one to Jon, laughing at him, shaking his head at his boss's antics, and it was party time on the stage, a jubilant celebration of his songs.

They sang three encores, his voice hoarse and tired from singing before he waved a final farewell.

Sal was waiting for him with a bathrobe, towel, and a bottle of water.

"Naomi," Jon whispered between sips.

"She's not here at the moment." Sal cursed his personal bad luck.

Jon stopped in his tracks, right there in the hallway, the equipment crew streaming around them on their way to the auditorium to take down the stage.

"Jon. Please let's go to the dressing room." Sal literally pushed him forward.

"How can she not be here? She was out there a few minutes ago."

Russ came up behind them, Art in tow, a bright smirk on his face. "Wow, that was a first. I've never been asked for an autograph before. And what a nice, charming lady that was! Didn't even ask for you, Jon. She just wanted one from me, said she enjoyed so much how I came across on that video from the last tour. Jon, you're losing it!"

Jon was still staring at Sal.

"In the dressing room," Sal repeated.

A couple of assistants peeled the sweat-soaked shirt from Jon, and he wrapped himself in the bathrobe. Sal put a cigarette in his shaky hand when he held it out.

"So where is Naomi?" Jon repeated after taking a couple of deep drags, "She was there during the concert. She didn't hear what that woman said, did she, Sal?"

"She heard." Russ had come inside, closing the door on the noise. "But she didn't react. Just went back to hospitality with Sal."

"Yes, she was relaxed." It wasn't entirely true. Sal saw Jon's blinking cell phone on the table. "Here." He handed it over. "You have a message, it seems."

Jon took it and read the brief note she had sent just minutes ago.

"She says there's an emergency with the plumbing at the house," he said slowly, "and she had to go right away."

Sal sighed in relief. "Oh well. Then you can relax, right? We all can. Come on, Jon; you need to eat something and rest now."

They left him after that.

Jon remained alone, and the silence sank in on him like a fine white mist. His ears were still humming after the noise of the past two hours, his body still feeling the rhythm. He missed her. For the first time in a long time, he was without Naomi after a show, and he missed her sitting on the edge of the dressing table, legs dangling, while she watched him come down from the hype, undress, take a shower, and gradually change back from the star into himself. After a moment's hesitation he tried to call her but got her voicemail, so he stepped into the shower. For a long while he stood in the hot deluge, easing the exhaustion from his muscles, thinking of the episode with that fan, cursing Sal's insistence that he go through this process again and again.

And the nerve.

Jon balled his fists against the ugly beige tiles of the bathroom. Naomi, shot down, nearly dying in that hospital room from her wounds while he had been beside himself with fear and anger; and he had to take that comment from a stranger without losing his smile. The memory of that day was still so vivid, and it curdled in his stomach as he got dressed.

He turned to hold out his hand to her when he was ready, his mouth open to tell her to come along now, the others would be waiting for them; but there was only empty silence. For a moment he stood, staring at the space that was hers in every dressing room at every venue, that corner of the table, and how he loved seeing her there. Before the shows, when the makeup artist came in to get him ready, he sometimes slapped her rump playfully and told her to get off so she wouldn't be in the way; but she never budged, stating she wanted to watch Ralph turn him from her husband into that idol the other ladies were dying for. The eyeliner, that got her every time. He smiled at the memory of how she would literally creep closer when that moment came, her face a study in bemused fascination, and how he would give her a hooded stare as soon as Ralph was done. She blushed every time.

And she would walk with him to the stairs at the back of the stage where they would be waiting to put the monitors on him and check the microphone one last time, help him into his jacket, and pat down his hair; but it was always Naomi who touched him last. Maybe she would just smooth down the lapels or brush over his sleeve, but it had become a ritual he relished.

The hallway had quieted down when he stepped out. From the auditorium came the rough sounds of the crossties with the lights and speakers coming down, the hammering and scraping of the stage being dismantled and returned to the huge shipping containers.

A circus, that's what they were when it came down to it.

Jon was tempted for a moment to go and have a look at the now empty hall with the debris of the concert to catch the feeling of a performance well done, but he stopped and turned to the catering area.

Naomi had insisted they add Las Vegas out of sheer quirkiness, he knew it. Just when he had vowed never to return, never to appear in one of the flashy places here, she had asked him to so she could see him perform in that setting, this once; and he had given in.

And now they were here, and she was gone.

Sal pressed a glass of orange juice into his hand and urged him to eat something, but Jon didn't feel hungry. He sat at the table with them, listened to their comments on the night and the ladies in the front row in particular, but didn't touch the food Art offered him.

"Maybe we should stop those backstage visits with the fan clubs," Russ said.

This caught Jon's attention, and he looked up in time to see a glance pass between Art and Sal.

"Yeah." Sal had a beer in his hands, which made Jon wonder why he was given juice instead. "But then the crowd here is always more hyped than anywhere else. They come to the concert after having partied all day long."

"That's true." Art sat down, his plate heaped with steaming curry. It looked a lot better than the pasta he had been given. "And some think if they say something outrageous, it will catch your attention, Jon. They'll take any chance to get you to notice them."

Jon went to get himself some of that curry.

"Too bad about the emergency at the house," Sal went on. "Naomi wanted the show here so much. I think she would have enjoyed it a lot. The craziness would have tickled her."

They hadn't spent much time at the ostentatious luxury suite provided by the hotel, just long enough to make her deliver an amusing monologue about the private swimming pool and the three bedrooms, each equipped with a bathroom large enough to house a football team. Naomi, looking out the huge window at the panorama of the glittering city and the mountains in the distance, had noticed the roller coaster on top of the Stratosphere Tower and pointed, as excited as a schoolgirl, and asked if he would take her on a ride. He had loved to see her eyes alight with joy and adventure.

"You want a roller coaster ride, babe?" he had asked, and then had offered her one, right there on that big bed. The memory of that tussle made him smile now as he picked at his cooling food.

"I suspect your thoughts are somewhere else." Sal had a huge helping of dessert in front of him.

"Yeah." Jon wanted to be alone. He wanted to burrow into the sheets where he and Naomi had lain together, inhale her scent and imagine she was there beside him.

The suite greeted him with silence.

The maid had been here; the curtains were drawn and the AC was turned up too high for his liking. There was a basket with fruit and champagne on the table, and the bed was freshly made, with pristine sheets and a fancy wrapped candy on the pillow. Dismayed, he stared at it, his fantasy blasted away.

Her travel bag was gone. She hadn't brought along a lot of clothing in the first place, arguing that she didn't need much since the whole thing was about him and not her. Jeans and a few shirts would be enough.

He pulled the phone from his pocket and tried to call her again, and this time Naomi answered.

"Babe," Jon said, breathless to hear her voice, "where are you?"

"Just boarding the plane."

The noise in the background told him she was still at the airport.

"Naomi, please tell me you're not using a regular flight?" The thought alone made him break out in a sweat.

"Jon. Stop worrying. I'll be fine. LaGasse is with me. I'll just pop over to New York and do what has to be done and join you as soon as I can."

He could hear her talking to someone else, the cool voice of her guard in the background, the chime of a speaker.

"Don't go, Naomi. Wait for me, I'll come to the airport, and we'll go together. I don't want you going all by yourself."

"No." She sounded distracted. "Don't, Jon, really. Have to go now. I'll call you. Don't worry."

From the corridor he could hear the others—Art, Sal, Russ and the band—getting out of the elevator, their laughter loud and exuberant after a successful night, and he opened his door. They stopped in their tracks, the entire group turning. It was almost comical how their attention focused on him immediately.

"Guys," Jon said, "I'm not tired yet, and I have a huge fridge filled with booze. Anyone game for a round of poker?"

chapter 2

IT FELT STRANGE to be on the bus without her.

Jaded, that's what he was after all the years of touring. Jon had realized it shortly after they had started out. New places, new hotels, strange cities meant nothing to him anymore. His attention centered on the venue where they were to perform, the food and the comfort of a bed, but he had left the sightseeing behind him a long time ago.

With Naomi, though, everything had changed. There had been moments when it felt like having an excited child with him, she enjoyed it so much. He loved her enthusiasm, even her impatience to get out and see the places where they were; he even loved how she made the bus stop on the road for a break when something caught her fancy, such as that ice cream shop in the middle of nowhere outside Atlanta.

And now, without her on the way to Phoenix, he looked out at the landscape drifting by while most of the others slept and wished she was there to see the wide, empty space of the desert. They passed a lonely diner with an old-fashioned, garish neon sign, some dusty cars parked in front like tired horses tethered outside a saloon, and Jon smiled. She would have wanted them to stop there. She would have asked the driver to stop, even if it was only for a cup of coffee.

His head leaned against the window as he watched the building vanish behind them, a wave of sadness washing over him.

It just was no fun without her. It was his job, and he was doing it well, but the joy had gone out of it.

Sal came to sit beside him, a pack of cigarettes in his hand. "We should have stopped back there. I've become used to having these frequent breaks. Damn. Naomi would have loved that one."

"Yeah."

"Plumbing can be such a nuisance."

Jon turned to look at Sal, but there was only regret for a lost smoke on his face.

"Did she say when she would join us?" Sal produced a lighter from his jeans pocket.

"You're not going to smoke on the bus, Sal." He was itching for a cigarette himself by now. "No, she didn't. And I'm thinking, after Phoenix, I'll fly over to New York and have a look myself."

Sal thought about this for a moment before replying. "We only have three days before the show in LA. It would be a tough trip for you."

"I can sleep on the plane." A gas station was coming up ahead. "Tell the driver to stop, will you. I need coffee."

The others stirred when the bus slowed and pulled into the lot.

"You could be in New York by early morning if you leave around midnight, but you'd be beat." Cell phone in hand, Sal got off before Jon. "You want me to ring the office and have them order a plane? Or do you want to travel commercially, like she did?"

"Nah." The air was so dry and hot it stung in Jon's nostrils. "Get me a jet; I want to sleep." He walked a few steps away to be by himself in the silence of the late afternoon. The sun was dipping westward toward the horizon, the light nearly liquid gold with a tinge of orange—a picture postcard view. He could almost see her standing there, turning to share her impressions with him; and even while she spoke she would be shaping her words so they would turn into a song in his mind. And then, yes, he would reach out and she would come into his arms, and they would absorb the moment together.

"Done." Sal handed him a paper cup of coffee. "Right after the show." He sipped his own. "Jon. You don't think it's an excuse, and she fled because of what that woman said, do you? I mean, come on. You get stuff like that every day."

"No. Not really. She didn't sound upset on the phone. Just"—he'd been about to say *disinterested* but caught himself just in time—"worried about the house, I guess." It was lame, and he knew it.

Sean and Russ were coming over to them.

"Hey, Jon," Sean called, "Maybe we should go back to that diner we passed. Apparently, they make the best ribs in the state."

"That's what it means to be us." A wide grin appeared on Sal's face. "Always on the lookout for food. What do you think, Jon?"

Jon shook off his brooding mood. "Why the hell not. Let's go, people."

THE CONCERT IN Phoenix was routine.

The audience loved him. He gave them a few lively encores, even told them he would stop by again on his next tour, whenever that would be, and he gave a few autographs to the ladies hanging around the backstage door when he left. Russ had been at him to eat something before he went, but by then he had been too impatient. The impetus was too strong now; he wanted to go.

"You are as crazy as ever," Sal told him in the limousine. "Naomi can take care of herself. Good grief, Jon, she lived without you for so many years. She can surely manage for a few days."

"She wasn't my wife then." By now he was really hungry, and he cursed his decision to go without dinner.

"Damn right she wasn't your wife, the poor girl, and still her own mistress. You sit on her, Jon. I mean, we all know you're a control freak, but, man, give her some space!" Seeing the expression on Jon's face, he quickly drew back and took a breath to continue, but Jon replied, "I'm not sitting on her, Sal, and you of all people should know better. But the fear never goes away."

"You'll see, everything is fine and she'll yell at you because you came running after her," Sal said when the car stopped beside the little jet. A cute flight attendant in a red uniform was waiting beside it, smiling brightly at them.

Jon grinned. "Yeah, probably. But maybe it will be good if I'm there to help with the plumbing problem."

Sal's shout of laughter echoed through the hangar. He waited until Jon had vanished into the plane and it began moving toward the runway before he got back into the limo and returned to the hotel.

SOMEONE HAD BEEN thoughtful enough to order a dinner on the plane for him, and as the sizzling steak was put before him now, he felt grateful that the people working for him really cared that he was well. Exhaustion from the concert flooded his bones while he ate, a pleasant drowsiness that he knew from experience would make him fall asleep in the comfortable couch the moment he put up his feet.

Jon looked out the window, but there was only darkness below. He would, he decided, stop on the way from the airport to their home and pick up fresh croissants. They would have breakfast on the terrace and take care of any problems together, just the way it was supposed to be. And then she would come back with him for the last leg of the tour, only a few more shows along the West Coast before they could return to New York for good and at last settle down in the new house, the one she had given him as a wedding present, the same one he was rushing to now.

The thought pleased him, and his mood got even better when he realized she might still be asleep when he arrived and he could crawl into bed with her and wake her up with his kisses. With this delightful image in his mind he wrapped himself in the blanket and closed his eyes.

THEIR HOUSE WAS right on the Promenade, a big mansion in a large garden by Brooklyn standards. It was well hidden behind old trees, a high hedge, and a gate. A deep balcony looked out from the second floor toward Manhattan. As a young boy he had dreamed of the room behind it being his studio so he could step out during breaks for a cigarette and have that grand view before him, but now it was their bedroom. He liked that even better, and he couldn't wait to get settled after the tour.

There were voices.

Jon pushed the gate open a little so he could look into the yard without being seen himself.

Naomi was standing in the doorway, in a bathrobe, and she was laughing at a man, a tall, blond stranger maybe a couple years younger than himself. He was holding her hand, talking in a low voice, and she replied, her face glowing.

"Don't worry, my dear," he was saying to her, "all will be well. You need to tell him soon though. He needs to know."

His blood turned to ice when Jon saw her embrace him, kissing him on the cheek. She let go of him again and wrapped her arms around herself against the cool air. "I will tell him, don't worry. Just as soon as I fly to Los Angeles to rejoin the tour."

"Naomi, I don't want you to go to California. You are safer here. Forget the tour."

Her answer did not come right away, but when she spoke, Jon

stepped back, dizziness whirling in his head.

"Ok. I'll call him. Though I have to say I'd rather tell him in person. This will be complicated. He won't accept it easily. Jon loves me, Julian. He loves me very much."

The stranger chuckled. "Clearly, but I'm sure he will know how to deal with this. Don't worry. And if it gets too rough, I'm always here to talk to him myself."

The street was nearly empty of people. A single car drove by; a block away a woman came outside to pick up her newspaper; a jogger flitted past on the Promenade.

Jon dropped the bag with the croissants in the gutter and fled. He caught a cab at the next cross street, his mind a hive filled with screaming, tortured wasps, his breath a chain of thorns ripping apart his chest. The driver was staring at him through the rearview mirror, waiting for instructions, but all he managed was "Go," and a wave of his hand in the general direction of Manhattan.

Mindlessly he stared at the river below as they crossed the bridge, at the bright sunlight skipping over the water and the ships leaving glittering trails, the gulls cruising on the spring breeze. From the radio came Indian music, strange, garbled words sung to the intriguing rhythm of a drum. The driver's fingers tapped the steering wheel as he whistled along under his breath.

"What," Jon cleared his throat. "What is he singing?" Anything to get his brain working again.

The man glanced at him again through the mirror. "Love song. He is saying his love is like a river that flows endlessly and to please not build a dam to stop it."

That made Jon grin mirthlessly. "I've changed my mind. Take me to LaGuardia."

There was no sense staying in New York. He would be better off in LA now, with his work and friends, and the turmoil of the next concert at the Hollywood Bowl.

He refused to think about it. He tried to push the picture of her embracing that blond stranger out of his head, but it didn't work. It was stuck in his brain like the after-image of a flashbulb—blinding, painful, stark in its outlines—and it hurt.

A plumbing problem, indeed. Bile rose in his throat at her choice of an explanation while he wondered if it had been intentional, a cynical hint at her real reason to go. There was no surprise at the terrible hurt he was feeling, and that was even worse than the thing itself. She had never needed him as much as he needed her—Jon knew this only too well; he was the one always fighting for their love, and she had permitted it, ever ready to run. And now, here, he had stepped into the realization of his nightmares and was running himself. For a moment he thought of turning back, storming into the house and demanding an explanation, but he couldn't find the courage to do it. For a while, just a little while longer, he wanted the illusion that he had maybe misinterpreted the scene, seen something different than what it seemed, and she would show up at their Malibu mansion in a couple of days, or even at the concert, and all would be well. She would be there, and he would hold her, and life would go on.

chapter 3

JET-LAGGED AND DRAINED, he arrived in LA.

Glad their housekeeper had left for the day, he walked straight up to the bedroom, where he opened the door to the huge roof garden.

October, and it was so much nicer here than in New York. Leaning against the balustrade, he lit a cigarette and looked out at the ocean over the treetops bathed in the gold of a clear autumn afternoon. A few surfers were playing among the waves, their neoprene-clad bodies as black and sleek as seals, and he thought he could see dolphins farther out. The air was filled with the scent of flowers, as tangible as pearls of fragrance, and felt warm on his tired skin.

He had one night to collect himself and get back into shape before he would have to face the crowd at the show, and here, in LA, he would have to deliver his best. They knew him too well; it was like performing for his own family, and they would see right away if he was hiding something, even if it was a broken heart.

The house felt strange without Naomi: empty, quiet, deserted. Going down the stairs to the kitchen, Jon thought he could hear the echo of her voice, see the shape of her body as if she were there but somehow caught in a parallel dimension, just out of reach. A bud of anger bloomed slowly in his chest and pushed the pain into the shadows behind his heart.

The bottle of Bourbon in his hand, he picked up the phone and dialed the number of her cell phone.

"Darling," Naomi said, "I was just about to call you. Are you in LA yet? How are you?"

Her tone was so loving, tender.

"Yeah. I'm here." He pushed the empty tumbler around on the counter. "When are you coming back?" The moment he said it he hated how needy he sounded.

"Jon, there's something we need to talk about."

Some of the Bourbon missed the glass. "Really, is it important?"

"Yes, very. What's wrong with you, Jon? You sound weird."

The alcohol burned in his constricted throat. "You leave just like that, you hardly call, and you expect me not to sound weird, Naomi?"

Her breath caught, almost like a sob. "I'm sorry, love. I meant to talk to you before the show in Vegas, but then...but then you walked off after...after what that woman said."

"Oh, so now it's my fault. Great." It wasn't what he'd meant to say at all, and he cursed his stupidity. "If you have something to say to me, come here and tell me to my face. I don't want to hear it over the phone. Why am I here by myself and you so far away when the concert at the Bowl was supposed to be a celebration of everything we've been through? Damn the plumbing, I want you here, now!"

"Jon!"

"Don't, Naomi. Don't pull the helpless card on me. Come back to me. I'm not going to ask twice." He emptied his drink in one big gulp and poured again.

"Jon, I have to tell you something; won't you listen?"

Something in her voice caught his attention, but he pushed it aside, too hurt to bother. "Then come here. Come here. I'm not going to talk to you on the phone."

There was a long pause. Jon could have sworn she was crying softly, but he didn't care. By now, with all the alcohol in his empty stomach on top of the exhaustion of the long flights, he was well beyond worrying about her feelings. When he closed his eyes for a moment, he could still see her in the arms of that blond man—his wife, the love of his life, embracing someone else.

"Okay," Naomi said. Then, after another ragged breath, "Can you call the office and arrange a plane for me?"

"Naomi." The bottle was empty and no other within reach. "You managed to get yourself on a flight from Vegas to New York on your own quite well. You will manage this, too. Just get here. Because if you don't, this thing ends now. I'm tired of going after you. I'm sick of having to find you and bring you back. If you think this is a romantic game, I have to tell you it's not; it's a pile of crap and nothing else. Take a commercial flight for all I care. But if you're not here by tomorrow night, that'll be it. And…"

She hung up on him, just like that; he didn't even have the time to finish his tirade. Furious, he slammed down the phone and made his way to the living room, where he dropped onto the couch. Misery was replacing the anger, a desolate, bitter misery that made him want to throw something at the wall and drink even more, but he didn't have the energy to get up for a new bottle. The stark words he had said to her roiling in his head; he dropped into a restless, uncomfortable sleep.

HE THOUGHT A sound had woken him, but the house was quiet and quite cool. The sun hadn't risen yet. The light outside was gray with early dawn, the trees still and dreaming in the twilight. His neck felt stiff from the awkward angle in which he had fallen asleep, and his bones were as weary as battered driftwood. Jon made himself climb off of the couch and go upstairs.

The roof garden door still stood wide-open.

They had spent so many hours here under the vine-covered trellises while she recovered from her injuries. It had been like an Oriental garden, filled with flowers and scents and the laughter of their friends. Often enough there had been music, too, when they had played and sung for her while she reclined on the broad day bed with the silk quilts, listening, smiling at him, and holding his hand.

So beautiful, and it tore his heart to see the place deserted and neglected now, the life gone out of it with their departure.

Jon plucked a dead jasmine blossom from one of the potted bushes and crushed it between his fingers, hoping to find the sweet perfume; but there was only a memory of it left, like the imprint of a moth's wing on a leaf.

He would forgive her; if she came back now and told him it had only been a brief affair; she had needed a break from him and his exhausting life. He would forgive her and put it down to the emotional strain. Of all people, he knew how it felt to find release in a quick encounter with a stranger; he had done it often enough.

And, Jon thought as he dropped his clothes on the carpet on the way to the bathroom, he would teach her he was enough for her, only he, no other.

Shaved and showered, he felt better, more like himself. Cynically he recalled the croissants he had dropped onto the street the day before.

He wished he had brought them along. There wasn't a lot to eat in the fridge, not even milk. Amparo, their housekeeper, hadn't expected them for another day and hadn't done any shopping yet. All he could find were some frozen pizzas and containers of unidentifiable leftovers. At least the coffee tin was full, and, opening another cupboard, Jon wondered why there was more than enough booze in his house but he had to go hungry despite having a wife and a housekeeper.

A key rustled in the door. Relieved, Jon dropped the pizza back into the freezer.

"Amparo, we have no bread," he called, walking toward the entrance. "Nothing! Not even a slice of ham! Can you go and get some breakfast?"

Naomi looked down at the half-eaten doughnut in her hand. "You can have this," she offered, and held it out to him.

"You're here." It came out stupidly, and she gave him a tired smile.

"Yes, Jon, I'm here. Of course I am. You wanted me here, so I came."

There was no luggage, just her favorite red purse, which she had dropped on the kitchen table to pick up his coffee cup and drink from it. Jon followed her, the doughnut in hand, its icing sticking to his fingers. He put it down next to the old puddle of Bourbon.

"You said some very unkind things to me last night." She was in jeans and one of her old felt jackets, much too warm for California but just fine for New York. Under her eyes were dark shadows, and she was terribly pale.

"What did you want in New York, Naomi?" There was no sense in drawing it out. He wanted to hear it right away.

Her shoulders came up in defense. "First I need to change. I'm smelly and sweaty."

Jon followed her upstairs and watched as she opened her wardrobe. All her lovely evening gowns were there, the rainbow collection of silk and lace and velvet, most of them from her favorite Lebanese designer. He had wanted to give her the life of a princess, and here was the proof. The Rolls he had bought exclusively for her was outside in the garage, her jewelry in the safe; and despite it all she still preferred her old clothes, the ones she had brought along when she had come away with him from Norway.

"You're angry at me, Jon, and I can hardly bear it. I don't know what I did to make you so angry." As if nothing had happened, she began to undress right there in front of him. "I need a quick shower."

Seeing her made Jon swallow, hard. He wanted her, and he hated himself for it.

"I'm not angry at you." And here was a big fat lie. He sat down on the corner of the bed and waited.

"I went after you," he said when she came back, wrapped in a towel, drying her hair with a second one; "I left Phoenix right after the show to be with you in the morning when you woke up."

"Oh." That was all, and it did not even come out guiltily.

His hands balled into the quilt. "I bought us croissants. I wanted to find you asleep and wake you up, wanted to surprise you, but, well, you surprised me."

Naomi stopped rubbing her locks. "You were there?"

"Yes, I saw you." Jon jumped up and began to pace the carpet. "I saw you, in your bathrobe, like you had just climbed out of bed, and you were…" He could hardly say it. "You were kissing someone. He was leaving our house, and you half naked, you kissed him. And then you tell me you have something to say to me. I'm not totally stupid, and I can figure out what that might be."

Incredibly, mirth dawned in her eyes. Naomi, her hand over her mouth, did not reply.

"Yeah, and there you stand," Jon threw at her bitterly, "and you know you've won. You've turned me around and brought me to my knees; you know I'm a total fool about you and would do anything to make you love me, and now you're going to tell me you're leaving me for that blond jerk."

"Jon."

He waved her away. "Don't. Don't try to explain. I know what you're going to say. My life is too much for you. The tour brought it home to you. What that woman said, it hurt you. You want out; not even my love for you is enough to keep you with me. And"—dramatically, he laid his hand on his chest— "I'm not going to fight for you anymore. Twenty years are enough, Naomi. If you want to go, go."

"Jon, that man is my doctor."

It took a moment to register. "What?"

"That blond jerk's name is Julian, and he is my new doctor. Kevin recommended him. I went to New York to see him, and I didn't tell you because I didn't want to upset you. He came to the house yesterday morning before going to work to spare me another trip downtown. He took some blood. Look." She held out her arm to him. There was a small bruise on the inside of her elbow, about the size of a lentil.

"He said his nurses are better at drawing blood, but he saved me hours of hanging around the hospital." Her brows drew together. "Hours I thought I'd rather spend with you."

"But baby…" His anger evaporated to be replaced by worry. "But why do you need another doctor? You were fine; all the time on the tour you were fine." Something else occurred to Jon. "And I made you come here! I threatened you. And you needed to stay there for more tests? Is it something to do with your injury? Are there after effects? God, Naomi, I'm the biggest piece of crap in the whole wide world."

"Sometimes, yes," she agreed with a shake of her head. "Sometimes you really are. Those were really mean things you said to me, Jon."

"Yes." He wanted to sink into the ground. He wanted the sea to flood the room, tear him away and drop him somewhere on a lonely and cold reef far away from any other humans, somewhere he could hide his mortification.

Naomi took fresh clothes from the wardrobe, this time not jeans but a pretty yellow cotton dress with a square neckline.

"He said he didn't want you to come here." The shame of having overheard those words shook him.

"He said that, Jon. Yes."

Jon noticed with surprise that she had trouble closing the zipper of the dress. It was a tight fit.

"You've gained some weight," he said, moving closer to help her. "That's a good thing. You lost so much after the shooting."

"Yes." She brought out flat shoes.

"Naomi." Again her shoulders came up, but he ignored it. "Why didn't he want you to come to me? Are you okay? Is everything all right?"

With a deep sigh she sat down on the bed, in the same spot where he had been only a short while ago.

"Jon, I'll tell you something. I'm really, really sad right now, and also quite furious at you. So you saw me hug a stranger. You listened to what we said to each other and were terribly suspicious. I can see why. But instead of coming inside and facing me, instead of asking me right then and there what it was all about, you chose to fly back here on your own and nurse your anger. And then you yell at me over the phone and won't even let me explain. You forced me to come here right away, and I did, out of fear you'd never let me near you again; and you know you could do that if you wanted, wife or no. I love you, Jon. I love you so much I flew through the night to tell you why I had to see a doctor and why I did it the way I did, but now that I'm here I just don't feel up to it. Instead, I feel like I want to punish you and let you wonder and worry and sweat some more, even tonight during the concert." She held up her hand in a weary gesture when he opened his mouth to reply. "You are going to pay for this big-time, Jon, rock icon or not."

"Whatever you want, baby, it's yours. Just please, tell me what's wrong. And you are right; I should have stormed in and grabbed that sleek jerk by the lapels."

She laughed, despite herself. "He is not a jerk, Jon. He is one of the best..."

"Babe, yes, best what?"

But she shook her head. "Oh no. You can squirm some more. And where is that doughnut? Did you eat it?"

Jon stopped her when she tried to walk past him. "No, this is serious. If you want to punish me, fine. But please find another way. Please, Naomi. You know," It would sound soppy and she would laugh at him, but he had to say it anyway. "You are the light of my life, my reason for living. I was beside myself, seeing you like that. I thought, God, I imagined you in bed with him, imagined you making love to him."

There were tears in her eyes. "You idiot. This is all I get from you, after what we've been through?"

He let go of her.

"Jon, if I had an affair, do you think I'd have it in our house? In the house I gave you for our wedding?" She drew a deep breath to collect herself. "This is such a bitter moment. I can't take you anymore."

Over and over she would do this to him, have him shaking with fear; and now, trailing after her back to the kitchen, Jon racked his brain, trying to set things right again.

"Where is that freaking doughnut," he heard her mumble and stopped in his tracks.

"Naomi!"

"What? I'm starving and I want to eat something. Not particularly doughnuts, mind you, more like fried eggs. Or potatoes. Fried potatoes. With corned beef and eggs. And jalapeños."

"You aren't pregnant, are you?" Jon could hardly say it.

She whirled around. "What if I am? Do you even care?"

This made him angry all over again. "How can you even think that? Why in the world didn't you just tell me?"

Her eyes blazing, she threw the rest of the doughnut at him. "You arrogant…I wanted to, remember, I said that on the phone. I wanted to tell you in Vegas, but you just walked away after that dowdy matron simpered all over you. I had booked the flight well before then."

Jon bent down to retrieve the sorry doughnut from where it had landed on the tile floor. Sticky little pieces remained behind, which he tried to wipe away with his bare hand, but he only succeeded in spreading them farther.

"This is not how I wanted it to happen," she said, her voice wavering. "I dreamed of this, of us making a new child, and how I would tell you, how there would be a wonderfully romantic moment, just the two of us, and how I would see the joy in your face. I tried. And you ruined it."

"I'm so sorry, my love." Sheepishly he washed his hands before turning to her. "I messed up again, huh?"

Very slowly she looked up at him, her eyes tired and sad. "Go buy us some breakfast, Jon. I'm totally exhausted; I'm going to bed now. I just want to crawl under the blanket and forget this whole mess."

HE NEVER DID this, never.

A baseball cap pulled down on his brow and sunglasses over his eyes, Jon drove to the deli where he knew Amparo sometimes bought takeout food for them when time was too short to cook or one of them wanted something special. The store was filled with people, most of them getting coffee on their way to work, but no one looked his way as he strolled down the aisles, pushing a shopping cart. Milk—somewhere he had heard pregnant women should drink lots of milk so he grabbed a few cartons, and fresh smoothies, and fruit.

Waiting in line to be served at the hot counter, it struck him. He was out shopping because his wife was having cravings, because she wanted fried potatoes and meat for breakfast, and probably dill pickles. A sudden, hot rush of elation flooded him, and for an incongruous instant Jon had the overpowering urge to tell the man in front of him that he was going to be a father. He had missed out on seeing Joshua grow up, had never seen him as a baby because Naomi had left him and raised their child by herself, but this time he would be there every moment.

He could hardly wait. He could hardly wait for her to grow big and lush with the pregnancy, and he dreamed of going out for her in the middle of the night to get her weird combinations of food and then rub her feet while she ate them. They would discuss names and buy baby things.

It was his turn. The clerk stared at him, brows drawn together, but didn't comment or ask. They were in Malibu after all, and he wasn't the only celebrity in the neighborhood.

A girl. Jon wanted a girl; he wanted it with all his heart. He would pamper and spoil her, raise her as a princess, give her everything to make her life a fairy tale. And Naomi, he thought with a grin, would give him hell for it.

The car, he realized when he got back to the Porsche, no more cruising around in a sports car. She needed the safety of the limo. The shopping bags on the seat beside him teetered dangerously when he took the turns just a little too fast.

The cool dawn had turned into a beautiful, mellow fall morning by now, with the fronds of the palm trees along the road rustling in a laid-back breeze and some lacy clouds dancing over the hills. There were many cars around him with their tops down, some of them blasting music at the world, and from one of them he even heard one of his own songs and the announcement for his show that very night. With some regret the speaker added it was sold out, had been for quite a while, and the only way to hear him live would be to camp out somewhere in the surrounding forest.

Back at the house he stood for a moment, looking up at the proud, old facade with its balconies and the large porch, glad once again that he had held on to the property through all those long years. It was a huge mansion, much too large for the two of them, but it was the most beautiful spot in all of LA. No other garden on the beach was this large, this rambling, and he had never been in one with its own cedar grove. Naomi loved the wildness, and the arbor with the stone bench where they had spent many enchanted evenings. There was no swimming pool, it was true, and he sometimes missed that; but she didn't want one. She wanted the shadows of the trees and the unkempt beauty, and Jon was willing to give her anything to make her happy.

It was quiet inside the house and yet different, as though it now was awake and breathing, with Naomi back.

She was curled up under the quilt, deep in slumber, her lips slightly open and her face soft, her hand wrapped tightly around the corner of the blanket. For a minute he considered waking her so her breakfast wouldn't get cold but then left again and retreated to his studio to prepare for the concert.

NAOMI WOKE TO the tinkling sound of the piano.

After their long time on the road it felt surreal to be back in her own bed, in the house she had come to love so much.

She could hear the gentle roll of the surf and smell the mixture of scents that were firmly connected with this place: the tang of the ocean, the spiciness of the cedars, the perfume of jasmine. She closed her eyes and knew she was safe.

The wardrobe still stood open, and from her comfortable nest she gazed at the row of evening gowns, so many colors, so much precious material, and among them, pristine, never touched, covered in a plastic sheath, the replica of the cream dress she had worn to the Oscars in spring. Her designer had given it to her a few weeks after the shooting; he had come all the way from Lebanon to present her with it, offering his commiseration, but she had barely been able to look at it. The original had been destroyed by the bullets and the torrent of her blood. She knew Jon had seen it. She had watched his face when Sayed had unpacked the new one, saying she might one day like to wear it when everything was over and forgotten and realized she would never, ever, put it on. There would be plenty of new gowns, but that one would never see the light of day.

A car pulled up to the house, tires crunching on the gravel drive. A moment later she heard Sal's voice from the terrace below and Jon admonishing him to shut his trap. They retreated inside, Sal still talking, his volume distinctly lower now.

Her anger was gone. It seemed as if sleeping in her bed had lifted it away and left only the pleasant feeling of anticipation and a gnawing hunger behind.

Amparo was in the kitchen, grumbling over the shopping bags Jon had dumped on the counter and then forgotten. She pulled out the container with the now-cold fried potatoes.

"You want to eat this?" she asked doubtfully. "It doesn't look very appetizing."

Naomi thought they looked delicious, fresh or not, and just what she wanted, but Amparo would hear nothing of it. She would make her fresh food, she said, and please to take her coffee and go sit in the sun until it was ready.

Sal and Jon were in the studio, discussing the set list for the concert and what time they should leave for the soundcheck at the Hollywood Bowl, and where they would go for dinner later and who would be allowed to come.

"No fan clubs, Sal," Jon was saying. "Not before, not after. I'm done with them for this tour."

"You can't, Jon." Naomi recognized the tone very well; Sal was going to push him. She stopped outside the door to listen.

"Not on your life. I don't care, Sal. Leave me alone."

"We're in LA, Jon, your home turf. They expect to meet you. And you know they want more than a cool nod. These are hard-core fans."

"No," Jon said in a cold, steely tone, and underlined it by banging his coffee mug on the piano, which protested with a soft, melodious ring. "I'm not going to risk putting Naomi through anything like that again. God, it cut me to the core, and she must have felt even worse when that tart said that."

"Maybe she didn't mean it that way at all," Sal offered, but he didn't sound too convincing. "Maybe she just wanted to commiserate."

"Like hell. You know what she wanted. And I do too. The same thing they all want."

"There used to be a time you liked it. Often enough one of them would share some space with you after the show."

She heard Sal light a cigarette and Jon say sharply, "Go smoke on the porch. No smoking in the house."

"What?" But Sal left the studio and entered the living room to see her standing there, one of the smoothies Jon had bought in her hand.

"Oh, you're here." His eyes wandered from her face to the fruit drink and back again, his brow wrinkled.

"Outside," Jon shouted. "I'll clobber you if you smoke that in here!"

"Wow, someone is in an evil mood." With a shrug, Sal walked out on the porch and slumped down on one of the couches.

"I'm not!" Jon smiled when he saw her but didn't try for an embrace. "Hey, babe. Did you get a good nap? Did you have something to eat yet?"

Naomi sighed. "I had a good nap, but Amparo wouldn't let me have what you bought. She said it was cold and messy, and she is making a fresh breakfast now. And so I have to wait for food and, it seems, beg for a kiss. The day is not going so well."

He moved closer, hope lighting his eyes. "I wouldn't dare to rush Amparo with the food, but I could help with the kiss."

There was no difference. It felt like always, being in his arms, as if the past two days had never existed and her nap had washed away all doubt and grief. Jon's grip around her tightened, his body warm and strong against hers.

"My love, I feared you wouldn't let me hold you for a long time to punish me," he whispered against her lips, "such a dire thought."

She pushed him back enough so she could look at him. "No, I won't punish you. I'll let you get away with it this once, because I'm so happy."

And she kissed him.

chapter 4

SAL HAD BEEN anticipating this day for a very long time, and now, seeing them together as they stood outside the house and waited for the van to pick them up, he wondered how Jon felt. Naomi seemed as serene as a cat after a large bowl of cream.

Jon had pulled out a cigarette and was smoking, a few steps away from them. He was humming to himself while he gazed up at the trees of the garden gently swaying in a warm breeze. The weather was perfect for an outdoor show: clear, and not too hot.

It surprised Sal that they didn't seem to see the meaning of it all, how it had been just like this all those years ago when she had left him.

He remembered it quite clearly.

Jon had been restless, pacing the driveway, nearly oblivious of them, and she had been pensive, as if she meant to say something but didn't have the courage to do it. They had gone to the Greek Theater, and she had retreated to somewhere up in the top rows of the huge auditorium where she could watch the soundcheck while Jon filled the valley with his voice. Later she had sat beside Russ at the mixing table, but there had still been that air of withdrawal around her.

And then, of course, there had been the party, the drug bust, the chaos of that night and the disillusionment of the gray, cold, dawn when they had found her gone. Sal shook himself out of this depressing memory when the huge gates to the estate swung open to admit their transport.

Art gave them his brightest grin as he jumped out. "Hey, it's a great day for a party onstage, eh? Baby Girl, it's been a long time since you last saw your man rock this place; are you looking forward to it?"

To Sal's surprise she gave Art her sunniest smile and embraced him. "And how. I remember he broke two strings on his guitar the last time we were there. The fresh air gets him overly excited."

"I can hear what you're saying, you know," Jon growled. He tossed the butt into a flower container and came over to put his arm around Naomi's waist.

"This time I'll tie you to a chair to make sure you don't disappear again. Or maybe I'll just take you on the stage with me and hold on to you through the entire show."

"I won't run this time," she promised softly, leaning into him, her hand on his chest. A small secret something passed between them, more than a glance and less than a kiss, excluding everyone else without a second thought.

"All right, let's go." It came out slightly gruffer than he had meant it, and without another word Sal climbed into the van and nodded to the driver.

"And I won't let you," he heard Jon say. "Not ever again, you know it. Today's concert will be all for you, and there won't be anyone at the house tonight but you and me."

Of course they knew, Sal realized sourly. Of course they saw the significance, and as always, they had their own way of dealing with it. Watching them now as Jon helped her into the van and then sat down close beside her, his hand on her knee, he had the eerie notion that they were not even really here with him and Art in this reality but in a dimension they had created only for themselves where communication by word was not necessary at all, as if anything others overheard was only a small extension into this world.

"What do you want me to sing for you tonight?" Jon asked. "Any song you want to hear?"

Naomi thought for a moment. "No, not really, as long as you don't flirt with the front row too much."

He laughed at her. "Baby, that's my job. You know it. Don't be jealous. You know I love only you."

"I'll listen to only you."

"Yeah," Jon breathed softly, leaning toward her, his eyes on her mouth.

"Enough cooing already," Art tossed in. "You're making me sick with all that sweet talk this early in the day. Jon, there's a meeting with the local fan club two hours before the show; those ladies need more than a handshake, and you know it. I've ordered some coffee and cake for them. And after that there will be a short press conference. There's nothing like a show at home, is there? Oh, and there will be a party later, right?"

Naomi sighed.

"You can party all you like," Jon replied, "but it will be without us. We've just returned from New York and we're jet-lagged."

Art turned around in his seat to look back at them. "I wonder why you always have to be so difficult about these things, Jon. These people are your customers, and you want them to buy your albums, don't you?"

"No party. I'll do the rest if you insist, but no party. Not tonight." The tone of command was back in Jon's voice, and Art gave up.

THE SUN HAD passed its zenith by the time they drove into the compound behind the huge amphitheater in the hills. At the back entrance the ritual of unloading the trucks was in full swing. From the stage they could hear the first test runs of sound and the amplified voice of Russ shouting instructions at the crew through a microphone.

Following Jon inside, Naomi wondered if the same person was responsible for all the backstage areas all over the world, they looked that much alike. For all the glamor of the shows later, these hallways were stark, unadorned, functional at best, some even downright dingy.

There was, as always, a very nice hospitality area, but she knew this was more Art's doing than anyone else's. The band and crew needed a lot of food, good food too, and no one wanted to risk a flare of temper from Jon before he had to go onstage.

She hesitated at the door to the dressing room set aside for his personal use. It did not look like the one she recalled from back then; this one was a lot more comfortable. Jon was moving around in it as if to make himself familiar with it, touching the things on the table, looking through the row of shirts on the rack, humming to himself.

"Jon."

He looked at her. Naomi stood, her hands folded and her face serious, waiting for him to give her his attention. She had stood just like that back then, nearly in the same posture. He remembered it so well. Even back then, for a brief instant, he'd wondered if there was something she wanted to say, but it had blown over, his mind on the concert and not on her at all.

"Jon, there's something I have to tell you." The words she should have spoken but never had. Ever and again she could do this, send fear rushing up his spine like a needle of poison.

"Jon, I'm pregnant. I'm pregnant, Jon. We're going to have a baby." She even looked like she had then, wearing a similar dress, only her hair was a lot shorter.

Jon closed his eyes. The feeling wasn't fear at all, he realized, but something altogether different: deeper, more painful, and yet also more exhilarating. He understood that she was doing now what she should have done back then, when instead she had carried away the secret of Joshua with her when she left him. She was trying to give him back that day with this, and he loved her for it. Smiling at her, he took a step in her direction.

"My love, that's wonderful." Anything would have sounded lame; there were just no words to describe what he felt. "I've so wanted a baby; I've been dreaming of this, of us, more than just lovers but a family, something that will last forever. Because, Naomi, no matter how difficult the rest is, I want us never to be apart. Not for a day. I know I can take on anything if you are with me, and I'll always care for you, and love you."

She looked at him thoughtfully but didn't reply. Jon had the urge to search for his cigarettes, her steady gaze made him that nervous, but he held out his hands to her instead.

"You're wondering," he said, "if I would have said this to you back then when we were here and you were pregnant with Joshua. And the answer is yes, I would. Then I would have swept you off to City Hall and married you the very next morning." A grin tugged at his lips. "Hell, maybe I'd have asked if there was a priest in the audience when I walked onto the stage and made a huge spectacle of marrying you right then and there."

"You are never serious." Naomi sighed. "You are the biggest goof on Earth."

There was a knock on the door, accompanied by Sal's shout that he needed to get moving.

"I have to go." His hands came down on her knees and pushed up her dress so he could stand between them, very close, their bodies touching. "But first I need a kiss. You don't want me to go out there in need of an embrace, do you, and all those other women only too ready to give it?"

"That's blackmail. You are shameless." Her arms wandered around his neck. She gasped softly when he pressed against her, hands tightly on her hips.

"So no more lovemaking for a long time, right?" His lips touched hers, but he did not allow the kiss yet.

"I asked. Julian said to go right ahead."

Jon rocked against at her at those words. "That doesn't seem right somehow. Someone giving you permission to have sex with me. I think I need to meet this Julian guy. The nerve, telling you to go right ahead." He loved how she clung to him and returned his kiss, the terrible discussion of the morning forgotten.

"We could do it right here and now," he suggested, but Naomi laughed again and pushed him away.

"Yes, with Sal banging on the door and all of them waiting for you. I'd feel like a hussy."

Reluctantly he let her go and watched as she put her dress in order. Her hand on the door, Naomi turned back to him.

"But tonight, Jon. No party, no people; and this time, the house and the bedroom will be locked, and you will be only mine."

"On your life, baby," he called after her, his spirits soaring at what life had given him, and followed her out and onto the stage.

SAL WAS ON the point of going back to knock on Jon's door once again when they emerged. He could have sworn he heard Jon whisper, "Hussy, yeah," but it seemed so out of context he decided to ignore it.

The band was in full swing when Jon joined them, Sean on the keyboard playing a wild and hardly recognizable variation of one of his less famous songs and singing himself. His rather soft voice was drowned out by the bass and the guitar, but he didn't seem to care at all and only smiled when Jon took the microphone from its stand and jumped right in. For a moment all the attention turned to him, the work crew stopping what they were doing to listen.

They had been together now for so many years, and still Sal watched in awe how Jon could transform himself, and those on the stage with him, into a perfect musical unit the instant he took over. It seemed as if the melodies flowed from him and infected the others.

From the corner of his eye he saw Naomi climb the stairs between the rows of seats. The contours of her legs were quite visible through the muslin of the yellow skirt. She stopped about halfway and turned, raising her hand in a graceful movement to shield her eyes, and looked back at them.

Slowly, mindful of Jon's reaction, Sal followed her, his hands in his pockets, trying to appear as casual as he could. Naomi waved to him but resumed her ascent until she had reached the top of the bowl where wooden benches stood in the shade of the trees on the crest of the dell. Here she sat down, her arms on the backrest before her, and gazed at the white shell covering the stage. Sal waited a moment before he dropped down beside her.

"This is one of the most beautiful places I've ever been to," Naomi said. "Just look, Sal. They built it like a church, and the stage is the altar where the music is offered to the gods. The sound here is so awesome, as if it collects in this bowl in the hills so it will rise to the sky all the clearer and stronger."

Sal drew his brows together. All he could see were the rather arid slopes around them, studded with evergreens and tired brush, and in the distance, the Hollywood sign shimmering in the heat of the afternoon. When the soundcheck was interrupted for a brief discussion, he could hear the roar of the highway just behind the shell, and he thought it was one of the most unromantic spots on Earth.

"I remember," she went on, "the last time I was here it was so hot the bowl seemed like a puddle filled with hot light, and the air was as thick as tepid seawater."

"But the memories of that day are not very pleasant otherwise." It was still hard to look at her directly, and he wondered if he would ever be able to without his fantasy running away with him.

She gave him a soft smile. "Oh, the day was all right. The night gave me some headaches."

"Oh Lord, not just you." To his surprise, he found he could talk about it. "That was the worst night of my life."

Her gaze wandered away from him and back to where Jon, his guitar in his hands, had begun on the hard, fast beat of the "River Song," one of his most famous pieces, a signature tune. Now, in the bright afternoon sunshine, it sounded light, almost like a dance rhythm. But tonight, when Jon would use it to open the show, he would transform it into a steamy invitation, the bass drums and congas like the heartbeat of a wild mating act.

She bit her lip. "That day my life seemed to end. For a long, long time, everything stopped. I didn't even think I'd ever draw a breath again. When I left Jon that morning, I left everything that meant joy, love, and living."

Once again Sal found the conversation going in a direction he didn't want at all. "I meant, it wasn't really fun being around him after you left." It was weak, pointless, a repetition like a mantra, and not what he wanted to say.

She was so beautiful. Despite her forty years her skin was flawless, nearly translucent, and her mouth had the most inviting shape Sal had ever seen. Her figure had filled out again after the many months of recuperation, and he liked to see her like this: healthy, glowing, her old self. The yellow dress fit well on her—it was even a bit tight around her waist and chest—but it gave him ample opportunity to enjoy her cleavage.

"And I think you need to know," she was saying, "because many things will change now. I'm just glad that it's the end of the tour."

He realized he hadn't been listening at all, but staring again.

"Yes," Sal said stupidly. "Of course. One more show in New York and then on to the musical."

Naomi blinked at him. "Okay." She drew a deep breath. "If that is all you have to say to it, then okay. I was afraid you would be worried when it is totally unfounded."

Their attention was once more drawn to the stage when Sean began the slow, fragile intro into the "Secret Garden" song.

Her head went up and she moved forward. Her love song to Jon, written when she had been barely more than a teenager, and it still wove that web of invitation and intimacy around them, even across the space of the amphitheater.

"I hope it's a girl," Naomi said into Sal's thoughts and rose, her hand unconsciously coming to rest on her stomach for a moment. "We haven't even talked about that yet."

"What?" Even as he asked, Sal knew he didn't want to hear.

Jon's voice drifted up to them, soft and low on the words she had given to him, the melody playing around them like a caress.

"Weren't you listening, Sal?"

"Yes, yes." He marveled how his ears could be so much smarter than his heart to ignore what she had been telling him.

"I was listening. Congrats, right?" He needed a cigarette very badly.

Naomi was looking at him thoughtfully. "Thank you." She paused, shifting uneasily from one leg to the other. "I know, Sal; I'm really too old and not exactly healthy, but it is such a gift. Please don't throw warnings and objections at me. I want this very much. And I promise, it will not get in the way. If I have to I'll stay home and let you do the musical without me."

A bitter laugh rose in his throat, but he chewed it back down. "Yeah, right, as if he would ever allow that to happen. He'd rather call it off than be at the theater every day without you."

"That's not how it's going to be, Sal. I won't let him."

Her head tilted and her lips slightly pursed, she gazed down at him, waiting.

"You aren't old. It's nothing these days for a woman of forty to have a baby, and this isn't even your first. You'll be fine." It was the best he could come up with, seeing her like that, still as slim and lovely as ever. "I bet he's really happy."

Instead of an answer she gave him a radiant smile and began walking down toward the stage where Jon was singing again, and this time it sounded to Sal like a jubilant celebration of life itself.

He watched her slow descent and Jon's reaction, watched the smile spread across his face and his hand come up to wave to her, and her response, the kiss she blew across the space between them. With every step she took away from him, and toward Jon, he felt a little piece of him die.

JON, IN A fine mood, was torn between giving yet another encore and leaving the stage to finally get Naomi to himself.

He loved this venue more than any other in the world. The sound was fantastic and the surroundings so dramatic, with the trees on the hills outlined against the sky and the glimmer of the city highlighting the few passing clouds.

Maybe, he thought as he paused for a drink of water and a change of guitars, it was even the knowledge that he would be in his own bed afterward and not in a hotel.

The ladies in the front row were calling to him, asking for their favorite songs, begging to be let closer to the stage, and he smiled down at them. There were one or two who, in other times, might have tempted him for a night's adventure; but then he looked over to where Naomi was sitting with Russ and Sal, and his mind returned to ending the concert.

"Just one more," he said into the microphone. "My wife is watching, and she is signaling that dinner is waiting. I have to go, folks. Nothing worse than an angry wife." With a wave at the audience he added, "The guys out there know what I mean."

Laughter rippled through the amphitheater. One girl, a lovely blonde in skimpy shorts, had come right up to the security guards and stood, her saucy breasts pressed against the outstretched arm of one of them. She had invitation written all over her face, and it made Jon grin. This one, he knew, would have been in his bed. In another life, before Naomi had returned to him, he would have signaled to Sal, and he would have brought her backstage. Maybe he wouldn't even have taken the time to take her anywhere else; or even change out of his stage outfit: she would have gotten the whole package, him, the star, on the dressing-room couch. A fast, satisfying few minutes, an autograph on a CD booklet, and a quick good-bye.

As suddenly as he had appeared on the stage with the intro, he left it again, nearly jumping down the stairs at the back of the stage and right into Naomi's arms.

"Let's go," he said, and she didn't argue.

Not even Sal was fast enough to stop them.

THE HOUSE WAS dark and silent.

Jon took care to lock up before he led her upstairs to their bedroom, and shut that door firmly behind them too.

"Here we are." His words dropped into the stillness like pebbles.

Naomi had the weirdest sense of displacement, seeing him like this, still in his stage clothes, his face sweaty and made up. He was Jon, and he was also the star who just a little while ago had mesmerized the thousands in the audience.

"You need a shower." Her voice shook a little.

"I thought you liked the eyeliner. Doesn't it turn you on?" He grinned insolently as he began peeling off his shirt, stepping closer to her.

"I want my husband in my bed. I'm not going to sleep with a sweaty pop star."

"You're getting all of me, baby. And you can't back out now. See, you wanted me to lock all the doors and I did. You're all mine now." But he did go into the bathroom and turn on the water. "Care to join me?"

"No. I'll wait."

She was in bed when he returned.

All the playfulness left him at the way she looked at him.

"I know," Jon said softly, "I know I have to keep you awake until dawn so you'll believe I'll be here this time, and not in jail, when the sun rises. And so I don't have to come back to find the house deserted and you vanished."

"It will not be deserted. Stop talking, Jon."

He recalled how it had been then, how wild they had been and how furious their lovemaking just when the cops stormed into the bedroom. And here now, so many years later, she was still giving him the same sultry glance, inviting him with the same small smile.

"I love you. I'm sorry about what happened then." He had said it so often before, and yet it somehow never seemed enough. "We should not have been apart. We should have been together all our lives, not separated for a moment. I can hardly bear when you are away for a few days. Without you, I go to pieces."

It occurred to him how ridiculous he probably looked, naked, his hair still dripping, while she was comfortable under the quilt.

"You always go to pieces when you don't get what you want, Jon." She said it so drily, he forgot what he had been about to say and just stared.

"Come to bed." Naomi patted the sheet. "Don't make me wait any longer. I've come all the way from New York to be with you, and now you stand there and drip water on my lovely Aubusson carpet."

And how different, he thought, loving her, how utterly different this was from those encounters with strangers. Hearing her whisper his name, her lips against his, her caresses tingling on his skin, washed away the last of the stage hype and gave him back the peace he needed so badly.

She fell asleep in his arms. Jon could feel her weight shift when she drifted off, her body going soft and her fingers relaxing on his chest, and he tightened his embrace so she would not slip off his shoulder. He lay awake despite the exhaustion of the concert and waited until the gray light of dawn crept up in the sky. Only when the sun cast its first rays over the treetops did he allow his eyes to close, secure in the knowledge they had survived the night together this time.

chapter 5

IT WAS RAINING in New York.

Sal cursed the weather the moment they got off the plane and stood on the tarmac, already homesick for LA.

Morosely he watched the rain falling on the puddles of water swirling the colors in them into different patterns with every new drop.

Naomi was back in her felt jacket, her cheeks tinted by the blustery wind, hair blowing. She was impatient, repeating that she needed lox and a bagel right away; and Jon stood, shaking his head, smiling at her, promising he would take her to the best diner in town, just please give him a moment to get things sorted.

"As if there aren't enough people around to do that for you," she complained, but it did not sound sincere.

She knew as well as everyone else in their group how much Jon valued being there with them when they all arrived at a new place. He always wanted them to feel like a small traveling village, even the intern carrying the clipboard. This was what made the long tours bearable, their closeness.

One more show, just the one at Madison Square Garden, and then this life would end. Jon insisted it would, but Sal had a hard time believing it, even with the baby on its way. They had been doing this for nearly a quarter of a century, and he could not envision Jon settling down for longer than a couple of years.

But then, with Naomi back, everything had changed.

There was a discussion going on between them about croissants that had ended up in a gutter. He couldn't make any sense of it at all, nor why Jon was teasing her about some blond man he would ask over for breakfast if she kept being impossible. Naomi gave him her most impertinent shrug and replied that she would have to put on her bathrobe first, and skipped aside when Jon tried to reach for her.

The house would be waiting for them, that wonderful, white mansion on the Brooklyn Promenade, renovations and furnishings finally completed. It had been a beast to secure, so close to the street and the public eye. They had bought the property next to it—thankfully not as large and expensive—to house their guards and extend the garden.

Everything, Sal thought, reaching for his cigarettes, everything she wanted, Jon would make possible.

He watched them drive away, a second car with their guards following, and climbed into a van with the others to go to their hotel in Manhattan.

"Naomi's father has offered us a house in Brooklyn, close to the Master's," Russ said as they drove over the bridge. "I'm right glad I don't have to go house hunting in New York City. What about you?"

"I have no idea." For the first time Sal had to admit he was a bit scared of the future. Maybe, just maybe, it was time to accept other clients and stop working exclusively for Jon and Naomi, but then again it was far too interesting to be part of their life. He could not imagine doing anything else, or being too far away from them, from her.

"I'm thinking of finding a loft," he replied. "Something hip and cool that will attract the ladies."

"Solveigh wants a real house. She wants a yard and a view. The Norwegian in her is coming out with the kid."

She was still in her hometown with her parents, safely tucked away for as long as they were touring.

"How is Marisol?" Sal asked, and it made him smile how Russ beamed at his interest.

"I swear, Sal, I never thought I'd love being a father so much. Marisol is the sweetest little doll, my little angel. And being married to Solveigh is everything I'd hoped it would be. I miss them so much."

Sal's attention drifted away from his happy ramble as he looked out at the skyline of the city and the buildings along the waterline. He wondered if it would be possible to find a place to live right there, with a view of Brooklyn across the water so he could have the illusion of being close.

"Look!" He pointed, interrupting Russ's monologue. "That would be cool, living somewhere on the river. You'd catch the morning sunlight."

Russ stared at him in confusion, but he went on stoutly, "That will be the only time of the day when we see daylight anyway. We'll be stuck in that theater for hours on end."

"There's no need for you to be here all the time, you know," Russ said slowly. "In fact, there is really no need for you to be here at all. You could very well return to Los Angeles and do something else for a change. Why would they need a manager now? Once the musical is up and running they'll probably take a break."

"Yes." Sal had no idea if he was allowed to tell, but it nearly burned his lips. "They will settle down and not do anything at all, I'm afraid. Naomi is pregnant." There, now he had spoken the word, and it felt like a stone dropping from his mouth.

"Seriously? Wow, what great news!" Russ again took off on a speech about the joys of fatherhood until Sal was ready to throw him out of the car and down into the river below. "But is she healthy enough?"

That question woke Sal from his boredom.

"She lost half a lung; and even though she seems healthy, a pregnancy is harsh on the body, and she is what, almost forty? Wow, I hope they thought about all that before."

"It's not our business," Sal interrupted him gruffly. "I'm sure they did."

Russ fell silent, exchanging a meaningful glance with Art, who had been listening.

"It is their business," Art agreed, his face for once without his usual grin..."and totally none of ours. And you should stop that discussion right here. We tend to forget that Jon is our boss, guys, but this is a very good moment to remember it."

They settled back like chastised children, their hands on their knees.

SHE WAS CLOSE to tears, but Jon didn't budge.

"It's only a bloody soundcheck, love," he repeated, "and you've seen so many of them. Please, Naomi, get some rest and let LaGasse drive you over later. I swear you'll not miss a thing. I'll even wait on the make-up until you are there. Please."

"But I won't see it empty, without the audience, or get the feel of the place, and the excitement."

He looked at her where she lay on the couch, wrapped in a cashmere throw against the fresh air coming in through the open patio door. She was very pale and seemed tired, but her face was a study in obstinacy and almost made him laugh.

"I swear, no eyeliner without you."

That made the corners of her mouth crinkle, and he sighed in relief.

The house was beautiful now. She had picked a totally different style here than they had in Malibu, with deeper colors for the rugs and curtains, and English furniture. The place had a very European flair. From their bed they could look out at the Manhattan skyline, an incredible luxury, and he was very satisfied with the space she had set aside for his studio.

"I didn't know it would be like this," Naomi said into his thoughts. "Jon, I didn't mean it to be like this."

He had to go. The van had driven up a while ago, and he knew Sal would be waiting, ready to come inside and drag him away. "You just need to be careful for a few months, baby. I want you safe and well."

There was no housekeeper. Amparo had returned to LA to be with her family and look after the other house, but she had offered to send her niece, Lourdes. She would be arriving in a couple of weeks, but until then they were on their own, and he was scared Naomi would try to do too much.

"Jon, I'm not going to spend six months lying around like...like..."

"And you won't. But we just got off the plane yesterday after flying back and forth across the continent. God, Naomi, even I'm tired! Stop arguing already and let me go. Will it help if I come here myself to pick you up later?"

She took a deep breath and sat up. "No."

The bell rang.

"And you are standing there not even kissing me. This pregnancy thing is totally turning you off me."

This made him laugh. "Yeah right, you greedy thing. Like I didn't give you enough last night. Don't make it so hard on me. You know I won't be able to leave if I kiss you now."

"Jon."

He wanted to stay right there with her on the couch, spend the rest of his life holding her in his arms, breathing in the scent of her hair and shutting out the world, but the bell rang again. Very reluctantly he drew away, planting one last kiss on her lips. "Three hours, my love. I'm so glad we managed to bring the Rolls. You will be safe in that car."

Naomi slapped the blanket in a futile show of fury, but Jon shook his head at her. "No discussion about that. I'll see you later."

THEY WERE LATE, and Sal was angry. Driving downtown, he gave Jon a harangue about rush hour in New York. The traffic going up-town to Penn Station was bad indeed, but no worse than usual; Jon even enjoyed being surrounded by the yellow cabs and the noise.

"We could have a burger before we go inside," he suggested, peering through the tinted pane down into a sports car with its roof down and at the pretty girl driving it, her dress pushed up on her legs.

"Not on your life. We are running late as it is." Sal didn't even look his way.

Their car pulled into the backstage area of Madison Square Garden, past the security detail and the row of their trucks. A small group of fans had found their way inside, cordoned off by guards; and they were now milling around, gazing toward them expectantly.

"Drive right up to the entrance," Sal ordered the driver, who sped up a little to get past the people and then hit the brakes in an attempt to swerve around a girl standing right in front of the door. She managed to jump to the side just in time, but she hit the wall and slumped down against it.

"Damn it all!" Sal shouted. "That's just what we need, an injured fan!" He got out, Jon on his heels.

For an eerie moment, before anyone moved, they were all alone with her, inside the ring of security.

Jon swallowed his unease, the memory of the Hollywood shooting so clear in his mind. She was looking at him in a very still, dazed way, her hands pressed against the building behind her, long, black hair falling over her shoulders, lips trembling, her eyes a study in shock.

"Are you hurt?" Sal asked, "Are you okay?"

She shook her head, still staring at Jon.

"Speak up; do you need an ambulance?" Sal stepped closer to her to take her arm in an attempt at support. Jon's guards had reached them now and tried to take over, but Sal raised his hand to stop them. "Are you hurt? I'm sorry, we didn't see you, and you shouldn't have been here at all anyway."

"I'm okay," she answered in a weak voice.

Art appeared in the entrance. "What's going on? Why are you so late?" He looked from one to the other. "What happened?"

Jon moved forward. "Right. Sal, bring her inside. Sit her down and give her a glass of water. Call an ambulance. Take care of this, you hear me? Don't let her walk away."

"Yes." Sal knew what he meant without needing to hear it. To the girl he said, "Please come with me. We'll take care of you."

Reluctantly she allowed him to take her elbow and lead her inside. Jon and Art followed them into hospitality, where Sal sat her on a chair in a quiet corner, well away from the band, who had congregated for a snack before going onstage. Art was cursing under his breath, phone in hand to call for medical help.

"We didn't really hit her," Jon said. "It was close, but she got out of the way in time. She had no reason to be there. Stupid chick."

A surprised snicker escaped Art. "She's a pretty enough little dish. Sal seems quite upset."

Jon had been thinking the same thing, watching Sal fuss over the girl, who sat, her hands clamped in her lap, looking around with a mix of confusion and fear. "Give her something to eat," he ordered, and left.

THE SILVER BANGLES on her arm chimed when she raised her hand to push the hair out of her face and take the glass Sal offered. She was still shaking a little but seemed to calm down after a sip.

"We can get you something else, if you want," Sal suggested. "A cup of tea? An ambulance will be here in a moment. What's your name?"

It took her a moment to respond. "Maya."

Almost furtively she looked around, as if she was only now taking in where she was. A spark of life seemed to return to her face when Sean came closer, nodded toward them, and helped himself to a sandwich from the buffet.

"Are you hungry?" Sal waved toward the food. "Can I get you anything?" He realized he was repeating himself and felt stupid. From the stage they could hear Rodney test the drums, someone counting into the mike for a first check, routine things; but her head swiveled in the direction of the noise.

"I have a ticket." Her purse sat on the floor beside her, and she bent to pick it up. "I only wanted to see you all arrive. Jones gave me an autograph. But I really wanted one from Sean."

This made him grin. "Not Jon?"

"Well," A blush crept up her neck, "I didn't think I'd be that lucky."

Two medics came in, led by Art, and Sal stepped aside for them. Sean was sitting at a table, his plate heaped with pastrami and pickles, and observed the proceedings with amusement.

"Nice one, Sal," he said around a big bite of meat. "This has never, ever happened before. The last concert of maybe forever, and you run over a fan? Hilarious."

"We didn't run over her, all right?" Sal stole one of the pickles. "We almost did. Nimble little thing, she jumped aside pretty fast. I'd fire that driver if he was one of ours. I only hope she doesn't have the guts to sue us. This could end nasty."

Art dropped on a chair beside them. "Sal, we can't let her walk away. First we have to make sure she'll not bring down hell on us."

"And what do you suggest we do?"

The medics were taking her blood pressure and feeling her neck and shoulders.

"Well, give her the VIP treatment. Let her meet Jon, watch the soundcheck, make her sit with us during the concert. Take her home afterward." Grinning evilly, Art tried to sneak a slice of pastrami from Sean's plate and earned a slap on the hand.

"Get your own food," Sean told him sharply. "What's wrong with you guys; there's a whole table of it, and you need to poke your fingers into mine?"

"Yeah I'm too lazy to get up." With a huge yawn, Art leaned back in his seat. "Man, I'm so glad this tour is over. Sue has the patience of an angel, but she's fed up with being alone. We've been discussing what to do now." He shrugged. "Not that we have much of a choice, eh? It's either find a new job or move here."

"I'm moving to New Jersey. We bought a house down by the shore. Wife didn't want to live in Brooklyn," Sean said, and got up to refill his plate.

"Bring me some of that pastrami, will you?" Art added a winning but not totally convincing smile to his request.

He wasn't sure why, but Sal wanted them close together, just in case.

He was still wondering what that case might be when the medics came over to pronounce their work done, the patient unharmed and well enough to be sent on her way.

"I'm getting a loft," he announced, moving away from the table. "Just so you know. A real Manhattan loft in an old warehouse. Haven't looked yet, but I want a really cool place. On the water too."

The girl was still in her seat, her eyes darting around as if she was waiting for something to happen.

"Maya." Something in the way she turned her head and looked up at him made Sal catch his breath and glance over his shoulder, certain Jon had walked back into the room and her attention had focused on him, the resemblance to Naomi was that strong. She was a lot younger, it was true, and didn't have her poise; but there had been something in the movement that turned his heart over and made him take proper notice of her for the first time.

"Maya," Sal said again, tasting the rhythm of the unusual name on his lips, "Would you like to stay and watch the soundcheck? Is someone waiting for you outside? Were you with anyone?"

"No, I'm by myself." A small smile flitted over her face. "No one wanted to come. The tickets are so expensive, and my friends think I'm out of my mind because Jon Stone is so old."

He bit back a sharp laugh. "Right. Don't tell him that to his face, he'd hate to hear it."

"To his face?" She rose in a fluid movement, a strip of tanned skin showing around her midriff where shirt and jeans didn't quite meet.

"Well yes, if you happen to run into him later. He doesn't like to hear he's old. Because he isn't of course. None of us are, yet. We feel quite young. Youngish." He was prattling, and he knew it. Prattling like a geezer from Florida trying to impress a pretty young thing.

Like he actually wanted her to stay for the soundcheck and be in his way, and the others would have an evening of fun over it. "None of us is over fifty. So we aren't old." There, he had talked himself into painful embarrassment, mirrored in her black eyes. "That's not old these days."

Maya, her purse clamped to her chest, giggled.

"I'm shutting up now." Defeated, Sal pulled up his shoulders and gave her a lopsided grin. "So come along, I need to go inside and tell the famous Mr. Stone what to do onstage or he'll look like a total idiot."

chapter 6

HE SAT HER in the front row, pressed a can of Coke into her hand, and told her not to move. For good measure, he asked Russ to keep an eye on her and see to it that she was comfortable and didn't get in the way. Returning to Jon's dressing room, he had a mental picture of himself in Bermuda's and a shirt that said "Daytona Beach" on it, possibly with a straw hat to protect his balding head, in search of a drink and some attention.

Jon was on the phone, talking to Naomi. He gave Sal a brief glance and turned his back on him. "Yes, love. No, it's great. I have to go now. Sal is here and giving me his most murderous look. Put on something nice; we'll go out for dinner after the concert. Any idea where would you like to go?"

Sal rolled his eyes at him.

"One more." Jon sighed on their way back to the auditorium. "Just this one, Sal. It's so hard to believe. I'm really excited about trying something new. Our lives will completely change; are you aware of that? God, I'll miss the California weather. I'll miss the beach and the Malibu house."

"You have a rather nice house here." It sounded a little more morose than Sal had meant, and to lighten it he added, "You're not letting the that house go, are you? You can go there any time you want."

Jon stopped him just outside the huge fire doors leading into the hall, his hand on Sal's shoulder. "You know you don't have to stay if you'd rather be in LA, Sal."

"Hell, no, you'll have to listen to me whining about the weather here, but I'd never pass up seeing this happen."

They entered together to see Russ talking to Maya, smiling at something she had said. The band had stopped playing, waiting for Jon.

"It will be a fun ride." Jon jumped up the stairs to join them, leaving Sal to himself.

Maya's attention had turned away from Russ to the stage where Jon was now in command.

Sal, so used to the ritual of a soundcheck, tried to see it through Maya's eyes.

Jon adjusted the microphone stand in passing, barely glancing at it, before he moved on to where his guitars had been set up in the order he would use them, the tray with picks just beside them. Russ had bitched about it after Vegas, saying Jon needed more of the things than even Jones, who was a far better player but never dropped them, and their income would be much higher if he took better care of them.

They were still in their street clothes, most of them in jeans; Sean even sported one of the tour t-shirts, Rodney with a baseball cap drawn down over his eyes against the glare of the spotlights. The light check was well underway too, the fog machines diffusing the colors of the beamers nicely all the way up to the ceiling of the huge hall. It would be a good show.

And Jon.

Sal, watching Maya, had an inkling of her emotions. She was staring. Staring at the star as he got ready to do his job, so unglamorous, once again dropping a guitar pick to the laughter of his band and cursing loudly.

"Good thing Naomi isn't here," Art called from his place at the computers. "She'd give you hell for all those "f" bombs, Jon."

"Go to hell," Jon replied good-naturedly, testing the guitar he had chosen and tuning it. "Let's get this thing rolling."

He stepped up to the microphone and started to sing, just like that, his voice was soaring through the space, conquering every corner.

Sal could see Maya's face quite clearly, the dawning rapture and delight in it, the smile on her lips, the movement of her body toward the stage. Her excitement made him grin. The accident was her great good fortune; she was getting what no mere fan ever got. As hard as he tried, Sal could not remember Jon ever having asked anyone inside for a soundcheck who was not at least family.

Then, looking again at Jon, it came to him that indeed there had been one instance.

Just one, and many years ago, in Europe, when Jon had first met Naomi and dragged her along, afraid she would disappear.

He glanced at Maya. Naomi had been younger by a few years on that hot, summer day in Geneva. How that memory still stirred his soul. Jon had been so possessive, so scared of losing her, he had even taken her up on the stage with him to make sure. Until she had gotten fed up and came down to sit with him, Sal, in the front row and watch from there. Just like Maya was doing now.

Russ left to join Art at the controls, and Sal sat down next to her.

Her attention was on Jon, who started a new song, broke off again to change guitars, and began again from the start.

"Do you do this often? Bring girls inside?"

The answer froze in his throat. He had to breathe a couple of times before it would come out.

"No, never." He couldn't remember exactly what Sean had replied to Naomi way back then, but it had been something similar.

"Tell me about yourself." And that, he knew, had been exactly what he himself had said to Naomi.

"There's not much to tell."

Nausea. Yes, it definitely felt like nausea, and dread.

Not Naomi, and yet so similar. The same long, black hair, clear dark eyes; but her complexion was duskier, almost as if there was Oriental blood in her. Not Asian, but maybe India or Persia, something like that. She didn't have Naomi's perfect figure, and she was a bit taller. Her hair was loose, not as long or curly as Naomi's had been but just as black, and he wondered how it would look in a braid, falling over her shoulder; and again his memory made a somersault back to Geneva and the way he had stared then, stared at that fat braid on Naomi and the way it had forced him to take notice of her body, so close beside him and yet so forbidden. No one tried to take what Jon had claimed, and he had made it abundantly clear that she was his.

"I live in Brooklyn," Maya was saying, "with my family. My father owns a deli, and I work there. I took the day off today to come here and see…" She waved towards the stage and Jon. "To see the concert."

"A deli?" He was not interested in that part at all.

"My father is from Pakistan," she went on. "People like Indian food."

Naomi's tale had been so different. She had talked about yacht clubs, ski trips to the mountains, and attending a university.

"Yes. My mother does most of the cooking. She is American." A small laugh escaped her. "I mean, she is…I guess you'd say Anglo-

Saxon. Sounds stupid. Oh well, she is blond."

Sal guessed she was in her midtwenties, which would make her older than Naomi had been then.

She was looking at Jon again, absorbed by the music and the man, letting him weave his spell around her even without the trappings of the show.

"I've liked him since I was twelve or so," Maya said into his thoughts. "There was this song on the radio, and that voice just caught my attention. I think I was peeling potatoes or something, in our kitchen."

It was more than Sal could take. He excused himself and asked if she wanted him to bring her coffee and maybe something to eat, but to his surprise she rose too.

"I think I'll go with you, if you don't mind, and eat something back there." Again, that wave of her hand. "Backstage?" She tilted her head with a smile. "God, this is exciting. I can hardly gather my thoughts. No one will ever believe me."

"Then we'll have to make them believe, right?" Sal held the door for her. "So first we'll get you a backstage pass."

Her surprised gasp pleased him enormously.

JON, COMING DOWN from the rehearsal for a quick snack, saw them sitting at a table in the corner, deep in conversation, and was relieved to see her well and quite obviously entertained by Sal. The girl was wearing a backstage pass on a lanyard around her neck. She touched it frequently, as if she could hardly believe her good fortune. And Sal, the most restless and alert of them all on show days, was reclining in his seat, legs crossed and his arm slumped over the back of his chair as if nothing else mattered at all.

"On the East River," Sal said. "Yeah, with a view of the water and the sunrise, that's what I thought. I'll have to look around. Maybe I'll take a stroll down there in a couple of days, find a nice place for lunch, and look at some places."

She thought for a moment before she replied and Jon didn't catch her words, but Sal laughed and answered, "Oh, now that's a really good argument. Well, I'll make a suggestion: why don't you come along and show me the place you mean? I don't know New York that well. And yeah, we could have lunch together, if you like."

Jon was sure he had misunderstood. He stood by the buffet table, a plate in his hand, and savored the moment: an hour before showtime, and Sal was not pushing him to do anything. No fan clubs, no press, no city mayor. Of course it wouldn't last, but he had a few minutes of grace without having to lock himself into the solitude of his dressing room, and he had that girl to thank for it.

"Naomi is here." Art had come up to him without his noticing, so engrossed had he been in the tableau of Sal and the girl. "Security called, the car is entering the backstage compound just now."

The day fell into shape. In a moment everything would be the way he needed it to be. Jon set down the food and hurried toward the hallway, Art on his heels.

"Careful, Jon. There may still be fans outside." Art's red curls bounced as he tried to keep up with Jon's long strides. "You might run into a gaggle of screaming girls."

"But my girl is out there too."

The sunlight blinded him for a moment when the guard pulled open the heavy doors to let him through, and the noise and thick air of a hot New York afternoon hit him like a wall. Rush hour, and it seemed as if an ant hill was in alarm and some of the stragglers had been lost right here under Madison Square Garden and were now milling around, waiting for a leader. They all turned toward him when Jon stepped outside, as if they had been waiting for this moment all their lives, which, he thought wryly, might even be the truth. He felt the crazy urge to call out "I'm not your leader!" to them, do something totally incongruous and liberating.

Naomi's Rolls glided up, and the cordon of security opened for it. The fan group surged forward, hopeful to get closer, but there was no chance for them. After the Hollywood shooting Sal had tightened safety into a near ridiculous regime.

"You could give some autographs, if you feel like it," Art suggested, but Jon shook his head.

There was some truth to it, Jon admitted as Art opened the car door for Naomi; it did look a bit as if the queen of England had come and now deigned to visit him for a backstage chat before the show.

Only the woman climbing out of this monster of a car was a lot more beautiful than any princess he had met on his tours, and she was smiling at him like none of them had ever done.

"May I come in now?" Naomi asked. "I cheated and left a little early."

His love for her clutched his heart and squeezed it until he thought it would burst like a ripe peach.

He turned his back on the spectators to shield her from their greedy eyes and cameras. "Come inside, darling."

She cast a glance around him, assessing the crowd. "They are waiting for you."

"Yeah. Let them." A few moments of peace, of having her to himself before the circus of the show started, that was what he wanted now, not polite exchanges with excited strangers.

"These backstage areas really look the same everywhere," Naomi stated as he led her through the corridors to his dressing room. "I wonder why they all have to be either white or dingy gray. It's as if someone wants to show the artists there is a sordid side to their life. What a letdown." And added when he opened the door for her, "See? Same thing. It's big, but why in the world is there never a window in these rooms, and why are they always so bare and unfriendly?"

"There's a couch," Jon offered, amused by her monologue. "And I'm sure it has seen a lot of action and some people had a lot of fun on it."

She whirled around. "That's downright sordid. Now I'll never sit on a couch in a dressing room ever again." Her finger came up to point accusingly at the rather nice piece of furniture in the corner. "And maybe there's even some of you on it?"

"Ah, don't go there!" He pulled up his shoulders in discomfort. "I'm sure this is a new couch. Don't remember it from earlier. No, this is definitely a different couch."

"You're impossible. Why have we never talked about the furniture in all the other dressing rooms we've been through?" A different thought seemed to occur to her, and a malicious grin appeared on her face. "I wonder where we made this baby? Hey, this kid may well be the result of a dressingroom stint."

"You stop right there. I'm sure it's not. No, it can't be. Surely we made it in a nice hotel room. God, but you have a way of making me feel ashamed, Naomi."

This was why he needed her, Jon understood; she would neatly take off the pressure of the upcoming show and send him out on the stage with a grin on his face, his mind still on what they had been bantering about just a moment before.

"But I like the thought," she went on, unperturbed. "A groupie baby. You, the star, and me, your…"

"Stop now."

"Your little chick for the night. Maybe…" Moving to stand beside the table in front of the big mirror, patting the gleaming surface invitingly. "Maybe even on a table much like this one. Let me do some math. It could have been Amsterdam, or Frankfurt."

"Stop." His hands came around her waist and lifted her up, the makeup rolling around dangerously behind her.

"We made this baby in just such a dangerous moment, I'm sure of it. Door unlocked, Sal prowling outside, and we…"

It was too much.

Her thighs were warm and firm under his touch when he pushed up the dress, and her mouth came open willingly.

"You asked for it," Jon whispered into her mouth. "Now you can deal with it."

SAL KNEW BETTER than to knock on a door that Jon had closed behind him.

It didn't matter that time was running short or that the local fan club was waiting outside, the ladies dressed to kill and bearing presents for their star.

"I take it the wife is here?" he asked, and turned on his heel when Art nodded, a sour taste of bile in his throat.

Walking into their house in the morning for a meeting with Jon and seeing her come down the stairs in a bathrobe, hair still wild, and imagining she had been in his arms only moments before was one thing, but knowing they were together in that room was something else entirely.

"Man, Sal," Art called after him, and he shouted back, "What? Time is running; the fan club waiting, and he's taking a time-out with the lady. I'm so glad this touring business is over, and he'll have to learn to look after himself!"

Sal had left Maya in the care of Sean, but when he returned to the hospitality area, it was empty. Furious at himself, he stalked back into the hall to find her sitting on Sean's piano bench, her hands clasped between her knees, listening to Jones practicing while Sean was putting his music in order and talking to her.

Sal stared at the tableau, his anger melting into something like despair at seeing her with the band, chatting with them as if she belonged there already.

He was going to play it out. He was going to give himself the feeling of helpless loss that had gripped him back then in Geneva when Naomi had stepped into their lives and for the first time ever he had allowed the withered bud of love in his chest to bloom.

She looked his way when he waved, but unlike Naomi she did not clamber from the stage but chose the stairs to come down to him.

"It's nearly time. The doors for the audience will open in a short while, and we have to get out of here. Come along."

Sal had a memory of walking away from Naomi that afternoon in Geneva, leaving her where she was sitting in the front row as soon as Jon ended the rehearsal and jumped down to join her. He had looked back once to see him take her hand and hold it, and she had not pulled back. Of course she had not pulled back; it had been Jon's hand, after all. The star's hand, the one every girl wanted to touch.

"You still want that autograph from Jon?" he asked. "Come on; let's go find him."

The door was open now, the makeup artist laying out his equipment on the table. Jon stood in the middle of the room while a couple of assistants helped him into his shoes. He was humming a merry little tune, as relaxed as could be, fussing with his cuff links and pulling down his sleeves.

Naomi was nowhere to be seen.

"Well, hello," Jon said when he saw them. "And there's the accident girl. How are you now, my dear?"

Maya stared.

"Don't be afraid; no one will bite you." Jon gave her his most charming smile. "Is there anything I can do for you?"

"She wants an autograph," Sal replied for her. It came out a bit more bitingly than he had meant it, but Jon ignored his tone.

"Certainly. Go get one of the tour books, will you, Sal? I'd be happy to sign it for you. Oh, and since you're at it, maybe a couple of t-shirts. But take the nice ones."

"Of course." He hated to leave Maya behind with Jon but did as he was asked.

When he returned, Naomi was there, sitting on the edge of the dressing table as always, feet dangling, a bottle with juice in her hand, chatting away with Maya, who was still standing just outside the door in the hallway. Jon, in the chair now, had his eyes closed and legs stretched out while makeup was applied to his face.

"The eyeliner," Naomi was saying, "it tickles me to death. And it makes me wonder what his fans would say if they saw him without it."

"Just because my eyes are shut, it doesn't mean I can't hear you," Jon growled, and grabbed her ankles when she put her feet on his knees.

"But I am a fan. And I'm here, I'm sure, because Sal is scared I'll try to sue Jon's pants off for nearly running me over. You're all falling over yourselves because you're afraid of a scandal."

Silence descended. Jon peered at her around the makeup artist. Naomi, bottle halfway to her mouth, gave her a small, appreciative grin; and Sal cleared his throat. She had dropped the sentence as dryly as if she had been telling them the time and was now returning their quizzical stares with a shrug. "Not that I don't enjoy it. Thank you for caring; you could have left me out there and said it was my fault. Which it was. I think it was totally nice of you to bring me inside." She threw her hair back over her shoulder, the movement pulling up the hem of her shirt again to show a tawny, smooth stretch of stomach.

Sal saw Jon's gaze drop and his lips purse in appreciation. He held out the tour book and a pen to him.

"Well," Jon said slowly, "I'm glad you see it that way. We sure didn't mean to hurt you. It wasn't your fault and it wasn't ours. Security didn't do their job properly, but they weren't our people."

Signing the cover with a flourish, he added, "Maybe you should consider taking Madison Square Garden to court."

That made her giggle again. It was, thought Sal, like the sound of water over pebbles—soft, melodious, low—and he liked it a lot.

"We will ask you, of course, to keep to yourself how I look while they are getting me ready for the stage," Jon said into his thoughts. "And that my wife loves to make fun of me. And you are not to tell anyone how much we all eat."

It had been delivered in a charming, light tone, but it was more than just a request, and Maya nodded.

"Normally, I go to meet the fan clubs by myself." Jon rose. "But if you want you can come along."

He seemed even taller in the stage outfit than he already was. For this evening he had chosen a cream shirt and his usual black slacks, and he looked every inch the rock icon.

Sal saw it reflected in Maya's and even Naomi's expression, saw the lust for him on their faces. With Naomi it was a fleeting thing, replaced by amusement in an instant, but Maya lowered her head and stepped aside to let him pass.

He was tamed, it was true, deeply in love with Naomi, but that didn't keep other women from wanting to be his prey.

Art joined them on their brief walk to the backstage doors, where the fan club would be waiting.

Just before they turned the last corner, Jon stopped to touch Naomi's cheek gently. "Baby, you don't have to be there. You don't have to listen to it all."

"But I've always been there, Jon. At every stop, every night, even if you didn't see me." Her arm came up around his waist.

"I can't leave you alone with all these girls. There might just be one who catches your fancy."

"Never!" He held her in a tight embrace. "You know that won't happen. Only you really don't have to watch me being treated like a trophy and smiling like a fool."

"But there might be cake, and Maya and I can eat some while you work."

Jon groaned but released her reluctantly. "Okay, so come along and watch the spectacle. One last time." He straightened his shirt and took a last calming breath. "All right then, showtime. Let's kill the beast."

chapter 7

EVERYTHING FELT DIFFERENT. It looked the same, yet the atmosphere was strange.

When Sal stepped out of his room into the hallway of the hotel that had been secured for them, he found suitcases in his way and half the band ready to leave even though it was only the middle of the morning.

"Can't wait to get home," Jones said in passing. "Three months' break before we start the rehearsals for the musical, and man, I'm more than ready for some downtime."

They had done it so often over the decades, their lives had developed into a cycle around the touring, and it had turned them into the family-like, tight unit they were. Sal, staring at the suitcases morosely, felt for the first time something like fear at the change coming toward them. He could hardly imagine a sedentary life, least of all here, in New York.

"I need coffee," he grumbled, and went into the dining room set aside for their private use. Sean was there, alone at a table, staring out the window at the traffic, an untouched slice of toast and a boiled egg on his plate.

Sal sat down with him.

"So." Sean nodded toward the bustle outside. "New York. I wonder what summer will be like here. I've heard terrible things. And not a beach in sight."

The waitress came over with a fresh pot of coffee. Sal didn't feel hungry. In the gray light of morning, the prospect of moving here looked even more dismal than it had the night before, in the atmosphere of the show. He flinched when a police car tore past outside, its siren blaring.

"There are beaches, I know," Sean went on, oblivious to Sal's black mood, "I know there are. There must be; we're on the Atlantic, right? I've heard of Coney Island."

"Don't think you want to go there," Sal said absentmindedly, his eyes on a couple of girls walking past, their long hair fluttering in the breeze, voices loud enough to be heard through the partially open window, "They have rollercoasters there, I've heard."

Sean blinked at him and took a bite of his toast. "So you're going to look for an apartment today?"

"A loft. I want a loft. And not one of these new-fangled things that just call themselves loft. I want a real one, in an old warehouse, with one of these lifts that open horizontally." He could see it in his mind: a huge space with rough brick walls, a high ceiling showing the steel beams, and windows overlooking the river. It would be a beast to heat in winter and probably not in the best neighborhood, but that was what he wanted.

"You could get a bike," Sean mused, "and ride to the theater every morning. You'd probably be very fit in a few months."

"Hey, I am fit, okay?" Sal fletched his arm muscles to prove it. "I'm quite fit for my age. You, on the other hand, my friend, with nothing to do but play your keyboard all day long, you are quite flabby around the middle. In a couple of years you'll be nothing but a middle-aged daddy."

Sean tossed a piece of eggshell at him. "Shut up, you old geezer. You're just in a rotten mood because you don't want to live here, and you're afraid of the changes coming our way. You don't really have a job now, you know. Jon doesn't need a manager for this."

"Like hell he doesn't." He hated how Sean voiced his own misgivings so easily over a half-eaten egg and the crumbs of his bread. Jon's offer to return to Los Angeles still echoed in his ears; and now, hearing nearly the same words from Sean, he wondered if maybe it had been a subtle way of telling him he was no longer wanted.

The coffee churned in his stomach at this thought. He would have to have a serious talk with Jon soon.

"No worries, Sal, I was kidding you." With a grin, Sean raised his cup to signal to the waitress. "Nothing will change. Jon will still be Jon, even if he changes his line of work for a year or so. He needs you to keep away the everyday worries and take care of the business for him. I'm surprised; normally you aren't upset this easily." He gave him a sharp glance. "Or is it the new family situation in the Stone family? Is that what's eating you?"

"No." The reply had come too quickly; Sal knew it from the smirk on Sean's face. Stoutly, he went on, "I'm meeting Maya for lunch today."

"Who?"

"Maya. The girl from last night."

Sean put down his knife. "That young thing you nearly ran over? The fan? You're meeting her for lunch?"

"That's what I said." He hated how Sean could always make him sound stupid. "She offered to show me a few places where I might find a loft."

"She's a real estate agent, then? She seems a bit young for that."

"No, she isn't." Sweat itched on the back of his neck. "She works at her father's deli or whatever. I thought it would be good to make sure she doesn't get ideas after the glamour of the show has worn off."

Sean reached for a second egg. "You do that, Sal. Make sure the glamor doesn't wear off." A chuckle escaped him when Sal threw down his napkin and rose to stalk out of the room.

He had told her to meet him in the lobby; and now, after seeing off the staff and the band as they got into the bus that would take them to the airport, Sal wandered around aimlessly in the empty hallway, the doors to the rooms open and maids cleaning up. Seeing the bedding and towels of the troupe strewn on the floor like debris washed up on a beach made him feel lonely and depressed all over again. The image of a lone astronaut came to mind, someone stranded on a space station with a lot of robots after everyone else had died off, the last human in a lost world in the darkness of space.

His own room did not look much better. A young, blond woman was busy cleaning his bathroom; and he retreated again, oddly embarrassed by seeing this intrusion into his privacy and then irritated by his own squeamishness.

A cigarette between his lips, he stood on the sidewalk just outside the entrance and watched life as it hurried past him in all the guises of a Manhattan morning.

NAOMI LAY, HER face resting on her hand, looking out at the towers of Manhattan shimmering across the river in the early light. Jon let his fingers trail over the smooth curve of her shoulder and down her arm. Her body was warm against his, soft with sleep.

She stirred and pulled the cover up to her chin. "I want to lie here all day and not move at all. Just lie here, watch the sun wander across the sky and watch it play across the skyscrapers, and listen to the music of the city. Every city plays its own tune. Every place does. I'm surprised you can't hear it."

Jon lay back on the pillows, his arms crossed under his head.

"They even have a different rhythm. Halmar was so sedate, like the tolling of a large bell in a space of silence, it's echo more a vibration than a sound, as if it wanted to underline the stillness. London is like a song from the sixties—it skips and has such lightness to it—and LA..." She turned around so they were face-to-face. "LA is the hum of an electric guitar and the rapid beat of percussion. But New York, New York is like a modern symphony. There's everything here, from the harp to the chorus with four voices, from the snare to the piping of a flute. It's as if it soaks in the melodies from all the other places and weaves them together. I could just sit here and listen."

The blare of a ship's horn tore through the air.

She never ceased to amaze him. He reached out to her, and she came into his embrace, her head under his chin.

"I love you," Jon said softly. "I love you more than my life, and with every drop of blood in my body. The fairies shaped you from stardust, just for me. Without you, nothing has any meaning. We should never have been separated, not for a day. The world was off-kilter when we weren't together."

"You are so maudlin this morning." Her fingers twirled his slightly too-long hair into curls. "I wonder how I can use that to my advantage. How about a little trip downtown? We could look at baby stuff, and some maternity clothes for me. Oh, and Jon." Naomi sat up. "We should go to the hotel. You should see the band off. You are always there with them after the concerts, and just because we have a house here you shouldn't desert them today. Really."

"Why do I have the feeling," Jon replied, "you will come up with an endless supply of reasons to go downtown today? You just can't wait, can you? You think New York City belongs to you now."

"Well, it does." Struggling against him was useless. She ended up flat on her back with him looming over her. "I'm in love with it. I love its music, and I love its face."

"You're supposed to say you love me." His voice went dark and slow with the sensual threat. "Not some bloody city, least of all New York.

Loud, dirty, dangerous, expensive."

"Except for the dirty, all of those apply to you too." Laughter welled up in her voice as she tried to free herself from his hold on her hair and the weight of his body.

Jon inhaled the warm scent of her skin, his arms tightly around her. "I'm not loud," he said. "That's a lie. But I know how to modulate my voice for singing. There's a world of difference between the two, my dear. And dangerous?" His hips moved against hers. "Yeah, I guess I'm dangerous. In a certain way."

Her lips parted invitingly, and he teased the corners of her mouth with his tongue, drawing a soft moan from her.

But Naomi pushed against his chest. "Jon, seriously. We should go to the hotel and see the gang off. At least you should go."

"Ah jeez, the first day after the tour, and you are worse than Sal, throwing me out of bed at the crack of dawn."

He obeyed and cast aside the quilt. It was quite warm in the room despite the early hour and the open balcony door.

"So you want to look for baby things, darling?" He stretched, facing the spectacle of the sun playing over the buildings across the water. The good feeling of achievement echoed in the soreness of his muscles, the hum of the music from the night before still in his mind. There would be reviews to read later, only this time it was also the end of a tour, and so a special day. In the past they had met for breakfast and a chat at his house in Los Angeles the first morning after returning home—he, the band, Russ, Sal, and Art—one final time together before they took a break from seeing one another nearly every minute of every day for so long. One after another, they would drift away until only Sal and Art stayed behind to smoke one last cigarette, drink a final cup of coffee, and sum up what they had achieved.

And invariably, he had always ended these meetings with the question "And now? What are we going to do now?"

Jon, squinting at the mosaic of light reflected from the high-rise windows, recalled these moments with bittersweet regret.

"You're right," Jon said out loud. "Let's go meet the troupe for breakfast. You're right, as always."

HE NEEDED A new car, Jon complained on their way uptown. One he could drive himself, and got an angry stare from Naomi in return, who was reclining in the deep leather seats of the Rolls in an attitude of distaste and boredom.

"Don't start," he said when she opened her mouth to reply. "Don't give me another rant about how much you hate this. I want you in the safest car there is."

"This car, Jon, is like an invitation to anyone evil. Oh, look, there's someone wealthy and important; let's hijack it! I can't even drive it myself; it would scare me to death to maneuver this monstrosity." She gestured to the two people in the front, her personal guards. The woman, LaGasse, had been hired after the shooting; next to her sat Alan, her driver, with whom Naomi had hardly exchanged a word. "I need others to take me wherever I want to go."

"So you do." Jon hated the recurring discussion about security as much as he hated the idea of her going anywhere unattended, unprotected, and the possible, dire outcome. They had been through enough with the shooting at the Oscars and her abduction only a couple of months ago.

"I want you to be safe, Naomi."

Naomi sighed. It was a useless battle.

"And with the baby on its way," Jon went on, "I want to make sure you're really comfortable and secure. This is the best the market has to offer."

"Like a harem girl," Naomi mumbled, but Jon ignored it. "So you're going to get a new toy car? What do you think it will be?"

He had left his Porsche in Los Angeles, saying it was older now and belonged there.

"Nothing sporty," Jon replied, taking her hand as they walked up the steps. "Something civilized. Maybe a Jag. Haven't had one of those in a long while. Would that meet your standards, baby? That should be stylish enough for you and cool enough for me."

"And why can't I have one of my own? I want to drive myself."

Her played petulance made him laugh out loud. "As if you give a damn. Come on, enough with the stupid car discussion."

The hotel lobby was quite busy. A group of German tourists was about to leave, the carts with their luggage standing in line close to the entrance to be transported outside; people milled around them, sorting out their belongings, piling shopping bags with famous labels on top of suitcases, chatting in their foreign, harsh language. Naomi understood quite a lot of it, and she overheard one of the women comment on them, ask the man next to her if that was Jon Stone, what did he think, and his low reply not to bother anyone and not stare and just move on. The stranger cast one more furtive, wistful glance at Jon but did as she was told.

"We're late, it seems," Jon said. "You're right; we really should get a faster car." And added, after a moment of looking around, "Oh, not totally. There's Sal."

He tugged her forward but Naomi dug in her heels, a sound of disbelief escaping her at the tableau presenting itself to them.

"Baby, what?" But he had seen as soon as the question had popped out and stood staring, himself.

A long time ago, nearly a lifetime, this same scene had played itself out in a hotel lobby far away in Geneva when he had met Naomi for the first time; and here, with different protagonists, it was being repeated.

Jon was speechless.

There was Sal, his long-time friend and manager, sitting on one of the couches, his hands folded over his knees, looking toward a girl approaching him across the space of the lobby, a young girl with long black hair down her back, dressed in jeans and a cream shirt. He rose to greet her, taking a few steps forward, and she walked right up to him, sunglasses in her hand.

"Wow," Naomi whispered, "I feel like I'm in a movie about our lives. This is very awkward."

"Yes." Jon cleared his throat. "Only I wish it wasn't Sal playing my role. I think I deserve a younger, better-looking actor."

This made her giggle, and she hid her mouth behind her hand. "Who is that girl, Jon? I mean, her hair is nice, but mine is curly. At least they could have put some effort into that."

"I think…" He had to start again, the moment was so eerie. "I think that's the girl from last night. The one we nearly ran over. Yes, I recall there was some talk about a lunch meeting today."

Sal was giving the stranger a smile and held out his arms for a second before he pushed his fists into his pockets and laughed under his breath, rocking on his heels in a show of embarrassment.

Jon wondered if he had looked that sheepish and ridiculous way back then when Naomi had stood before him just like that. Quite cynically he noted how the expression on his friend's face had changed,

how his sharp features softened into the gentleness normally reserved
for Naomi.

"You said you wanted to go and look at baby stuff." He took Naomi's
elbow, and she followed readily when he led her back outside. "So let's
go and do some Saturday-morning shopping, like everybody else."

Back in the car, Jon sank into the seat, stunned. "When we met in
Geneva," he said slowly, "you came up to me just like that. But I know
I was alone. I had sent Sal away. I told him I wanted to be alone when I
met whoever had written those songs for me. I'm sure he wasn't there."

Naomi looked down at the rings she was wearing, the big diamond
and the wedding band, and turned them on her finger.

"Sal is in love with you," Jon went on. "He has been from the moment you sat down beside him in Geneva during that rehearsal, all
those years ago. I could see it from up on the stage, could see him staring and his face going all dreamy while you talked to him, the bastard.
It was the reason why I broke off the soundcheck; I was so afraid he
would make you leave with him, and you would be lost to me before
we ever had a chance."

She laughed softly, but Jon shook his head. "No, I'm serious. I was
scared to death. And the fear never went away completely. Sal is like my
brother, and I'd hate to send him away; but Naomi, watching him stare
at you was sometimes hard to take. The only reason I never said anything was because he never, not once, became offensive." He paused
to gaze at her thoughtfully. "Or did he? Naomi?"

"No, you silly bastard." His stern question made her laugh. "He is a
proper Lancelot. He is a faithful servant to his king, which, of course,
means you."

The corners of his mouth twitched. "I'm not sure that thing between
Guinevere and Lancelot was all that chaste, my dear. But I'll be as good
as Arthur and not dig too deep. At least I have the blissful certainty
that my wife loves me and not one of my knights. Or do I?"

"Jon!"

"Yeah, you say that now, but baby, I can still see you hugging your
Julian guy on my very own doorstep, and in a state that would have
made Scarlett O'Hara blush." Grinning, he fended her off when she
slapped his shoulder. "Seriously, you practically flowed into his arms;
and I stood there, that stupid paper bag of croissants in my hand, like

a stray dog in the cold of dawn, and had to watch a stranger kiss you."

"Oh, shut up! You're such a baby." Naomi was glad for the screen separating them from LaGasse and Alan. "That was a very chaste kiss on the cheek. In fact, it was only the idea of a kiss, and given in gratefulness for the good news." That gave her an entirely different idea. "Jon, we should go tell your mother. Kevin must be bursting with the news and can't spill it because he's also my doctor. Let's go now. We'll be in time for lunch. Call her."

"And your shopping?" He pulled the cell phone out of his jeans pocket.

"There is plenty of time for that. There's always time to shop."

When he had made his call, Jon turned thoughtful again. "We joke about it, but what is going on, I wonder? That girl is a kid. And she was nothing to remember, don't even recall her name. Why would Sal be that interested in her?"

There was no answer. Naomi was looking out the car window as she always did when they crossed the bridge.

When the car stopped outside their destination, she said, "I have a feeling we'll find out soon enough."

HELEN OPENED THE door. "Well. What a surprise. Have you run out of food?"

From where they stood on the sidewalk, if she stepped back a little, Naomi could see the high walls of their own property, only two blocks down the street, right on the Promenade. It was a good feeling to be this close to family, and it gave her a sense of home. There was little traffic here, the Italian restaurant on the other side, owned by an old school friend of Jon's, the red-and-white awning flapping lazily in the warm breeze. The old houses sat serenely in the sunshine, proudly showing off their yards. She could see herself raising a child in this neighborhood.

Jon's mother looked down at them quizzically. "You really like to stand out there and stare down the road, don't you? I wonder what's so special."

And, Naomi thought as she entered the brownstone, she could see herself taking their child to school every morning, the same one Jon and his siblings had attended and where his sister—Valerie—was a teacher now. It was within an easy walking distance and, thanks to Jon's generous sponsorship, was a very well-equipped institution.

They followed Helen into the roomy kitchen.

"I don't have much in the house to feed you. The others won't be coming home until tonight," she said in her usual tart tone, looking them up and down suspiciously. "What brought this on? I would have thought you'd sleep all day after having been on the road for so long."

"We could get some pizza," Naomi suggested, hungry again. She would need new clothes soon.

"I'll go." Jon turned to leave, but Helen held him back.

"Don't be ridiculous, Jon. I'll make you some sandwiches if you people are that hungry. There's some pastrami."

Naomi, sitting at the huge oak table in the center of the kitchen, nursed the coffee Helen had put before her but didn't drink it. The scent was torture and made her stomach growl furiously.

"So," Helen went on, her back to them while she inspected the contents of the fridge. "Did you just want some food? I'm happy to feed your faces, of course. It's a nice surprise to have you here."

Jon, still standing in the door, savored the moment. He caught Naomi's small smile as she lowered her head over her cup, waiting for him to announce their news, and he loved her for it, loved how she gave him the chance to live this out now after having raised Joshua on her own.

"Mother," he said, the famous voice shaking, "you're going to have a new grandchild soon."

Not even when he had told her he had sold his first song, won his first Grammy, or received an Oscar had Helen's face shown the joy that spread over it now. In fact, Jon couldn't remember ever having seen a smile quite that radiant on his mother's face before.

"What a blessing," Helen breathed. "What wonderful news. You deserve this happiness more than I can say."

Small and dainty as she was, her embrace still nearly smothered Naomi. "And I am happy too, of course! Oh, how wonderful!"

The usual briskness returned to her tone. "Not to say, of course, you haven't done well with Joshua; he is a fine young man. But a baby! I just love the smell of newborns' heads. And you will be so close! I can see my little grandchild every day if I want and not be presented with a teenager, like with Joshua."

"Yes." The old hurt, and how neatly it could be unpacked over and over again. The pain surprised Jon, but he bit down on it.

"When? How long? How long do I have to wait?" Critically, Helen eyed Naomi's waist. "You are still very slim. I can't see a thing."

"There is some time yet. Well before the premiere." Naomi patted her stomach. "I think I will grow fat from my constant hunger before the baby bump shows."

"Right! Your lunch!" For good measure Helen added another dollop of mayonnaise to the sandwiches. "We must have dinner together tonight and invite the family over! Oh, goodness, Kevin will be so excited! I bet he'll want to check you from head to toe."

"He already did."

That drew Helen's attention away from the food. "And?" Her brow drawn, she looked from one to the other. "How stupid of me. I should have asked first, before starting to plan a dinner party. Are you well enough to be pregnant?"

Naomi nodded. Yes, she replied, she was well enough, and no, it would not be too large a strain on her body. She repeated all the doctors' injunctions and predictions, how she would tire easily and be out of breath with half her lung gone after the shooting, that her heart would suffer from the strain and they might not allow her a normal birth if she was too weak by then. But yes, she could have the baby. Apart from her injuries, she was as healthy as a horse.

"But," Helen interrupted sternly, "I can just hear that huge *but*, my dear. You are supposed to tread very carefully and look after yourself. No jet-set life for you in the near future."

Naomi wanted to drop her head on the table. "You treat me as if I'm an invalid! I'm only pregnant! I've done this before you know!"

"No one had shot away half your lung and a good portion of your innards then. And you were a lot younger. You are an invalid." No one else had ever put it quite that bluntly. "What?" Helen shrugged at her stunned face. "I'm only saying what everyone knows, Naomi. My wonderful son here, he is so scared of you he would never tell you to your face; but you were dreadfully wounded, and it will never go away. I'm as happy as a lark about getting a new grandchild, but I don't want to lose a beloved daughter to get it. So are you telling us the truth? Did they really say this is safe?"

"Yes!" Naomi pushed her coffee spoon away. "Kevin had me come here right away; I had to leave Jon in Vegas and fly all night and go right into the hospital." She stopped, recalling that lonely flight across the continent, her heart full of apprehension and hope. Even now, her ears rang with the harsh disappointment in Jon's voice, the doubt and fear, all of it piled on top of her own anxiety. Her sigh came out as a ragged little breath. "You can ask Kevin yourself."

Defiantly she took a sip of coffee. "And anyway, it's too late now to think about it. I'm not going to give up my baby to save my own life."

Silence dropped like a black velvet curtain.

Jon, his face ashen, lips in a tight line, gazed at her, while Helen poked at the bag of bread, her eyes averted.

"Nobody," Naomi said, "nobody is going to tell me what to do with myself. If this is too much for you all to take, I'll just go back to Norway and have my child there. And come back when it's over. We wanted a baby before I got shot, and I want it now just as much. I'm taking the risk. And there is no way you're going to make me give it up."

"Oh, nonsense," Helen tossed at her before Jon could even open his mouth. "What utter nonsense. Of course you will stay here with us. Stop this talk about running from Jon again, Naomi. You have family here, and we will take care of you." She paused as another thought occurred to her. "And your own family? Have you told your parents?"

Naomi pulled up her shoulders.

"Baby," Jon took the coffee from her, prying the cup from her fingers against her resistance and a moue of protest. To Helen he added, "Not yet. We've just returned from the tour."

"Well." In a show of briskness, Helen threw back her silver hair. "There's really only one thing that's important now. What to cook for dinner? You are the pregnant one, Naomi, so what would you like? We have reason to celebrate, I think."

It took Naomi a moment to put on a smile.

"Let's have steak," she said, her voice shaking a little. "I love watching Jon try and light the grill."

chapter 8

IT WAS CLEAR to Sal that she'd never been to this part of Manhattan.

They had taken a cab down to where he thought he wanted to live, with a clear view of the Brooklyn Bridge and the river, close to shops and restaurants and some nightlife.

"There is this tourist place," Maya said on the way, "Seaport something. But I have no idea if there are apartments anywhere near."

"Loft," Sal replied, "a loft. I want an original, reconstructed loft with a lift that opens horizontally." To emphasize his words he flapped his hands up and down but pulled them back again immediately, hugely embarrassed by his own inanity.

She was giving him a steady, inscrutable gaze without commenting , her hands holding her purse tightly clasped on her knees.

"In an old warehouse. By the river," he finished lamely, and she nodded. "Well, if you say there's a tourist place down by the river, we can go there and have lunch, right? And maybe we'll see something. A Realtor's sign or whatever."

The taxi was stuck in traffic between a meat truck and a bus. Their driver had rolled down his window to let in some fresh air, but all they got was a blast of exhaust fumes and the noise of running motors.

"I lived here for a little while." Sal waved at the street. "A long time ago, and in a different part of town. One would think I'd know my way around better. It's not as if Manhattan has changed a lot." Through a gap in the skyscrapers he could get a glimpse of the World Trade Center. "Those," again he pointed, "always tell you where you are." Maya glanced in the indicated direction. "I have a friend who has offices up there. He owns an agency. Been there a number of times."

"Of course." The corners of her mouth twitched sardonically.

Defeated, Sal gave up.

Maya shifted so she could look straight at him. "What do you normally do the day after a concert? I would have thought you would sleep in. Rested up."

"Yeah. We sleep in a bit." The cab moved forward marginally. Sal wished for a cigarette very badly, but there was a NO SMOKING sign dangling from the rearview mirror. "But not too much." He wondered how much to tell. "While the tour is ongoing, we have a pretty strict regime. Otherwise we wouldn't be able to see it through."

She waited for him to go on, so he said, "The traveling. We try to rest as much as we can on the planes and buses, but generally there isn't much time for anything else. It's a lot less glamorous than you think."

"But you stay in very glamorous hotels."

"Oh, that." Sal shrugged. "Yeah, sure. It's something you learn to do early on, as soon as you can afford it. The longer the tours get, the older we get, the more we try to be as comfortable as possible. You have no idea how much a good pillow is worth. Some of us take our own along. There's nothing more important than a decent night's sleep." He was babbling again, and he hated himself for being such a sorry sod. "And good food."

Their latest road escapade came to his mind, when they had turned the bus around in Arizona to go back to that diner for barbecued ribs. Like a horde of apes, like they had not eaten in three days, they had swarmed the place and made the locals flee. No one had recognized them or even bothered to look properly as they crowded around the open grill at the back of the building, cans of beer in their paws, nearly slobbering over the cook's shoulder.

"But the cities. The fabulous places you get to see."

Sal didn't reply. He didn't say how after a few weeks on the road, everything seemed to blur into one big circus, and all they wanted was to get the show done and drop in their beds afterward only to climb on another bus or plane the next morning bound for another destination and another venue packed with fans. This time it had been different, with Naomi aboard; she had enjoyed the travel so much. It had seemed as if she needed to see the world to find her own life again. He had been so afraid for her, weak and wan as she had been when they had started out, but the longer the tour lasted the stronger she had become as she soaked up the energy and adventure. He had watched Jon's desperate efforts to keep her safe, never letting her go anywhere without an escort, and his exhausted relief when she came back from her forays into the strange towns loaded with shopping bags and full of stories.

She had given them the slip in Hamburg, leaving long before any of them had crept out of bed the morning after the concert, leaving even LaGasse behind, and returned with her braid gone. Sal's heart had nearly stopped when he had seen her, her hair in short curls around her neck. For some reason, he'd never been able to figure out, Jon had been with her when she came back to the hotel, and they had been in ridiculously high spirits.

"Some cities are better than others," Sal said lamely. "Sometimes we go out for dinner."

HE LIKED THE place.

It was as lively as the street where he lived in Los Angeles, shops and cafés lined up next to one another. There even was an indoor market from which the smell's of fresh fish and bread drifted out onto the street, and it was right on the water.

They walked to the end of the pier, past the big sailing ship moored to it, and looked across the river at Brooklyn, the bridge to their left. A barge was passing under it, slowly chugging downriver, a flock of gulls circling over it. A water taxi zoomed past, almost flying across the surface.

When he turned back toward land he could see the buildings of Manhattan rising like a mountain chain before him, the World Trade Center the highest peaks, their sides glinting in the sun like glaciers.

On the corner of the street were a few buildings that looked like old warehouses, and one had a real estate sign outside.

To Sal's amusement there was a huge billboard plastered to its side advertising Las Vegas, with an invitation to come and visit his home-town, and he took that as a good omen.

The door opened when he tugged. On the ground floor was a small office, no more than a cubicle, with a young woman typing busily on her computer. Her face lit up when he asked about lofts, and she led them to the back of the hallway where a lift was waiting. This had been, she explained, a warehouse and had only been recently restored. Sal's heart beat a little faster when the lift opened, just as he had imagined, horizontally.

"We have a fabulous penthouse," the woman said, "with a terrace and a really grand view of the river. Is that what you are looking for?"

He nodded, entranced and a little overwhelmed by his good luck. She turned a key in the elevator, explaining that this went directly to the top floor.

They stepped out into a large space. The dark wooden floor shone softly in the sun streaming in through huge windows; there was the faint, pleasing smell of new building materials. The sounds from the street below seemed far away.

It was for sale, he heard the agent say, not to let, and to please have a look around—she had to make some phone calls and would be outside.

The place was much larger than he needed. The big living area with the open kitchen led out directly to the roof garden, offering a wide view of Brooklyn and the mouth of the river. The far end of the space was elevated and separated from the rest of the big room, in a niche with high windows. The roof garden wrapped around two sides of the building. Right across the street laid the three-masted sailing ship, almost close enough to touch.

"This will cost a fortune," Maya commented.

He had forgotten about her. She was still standing near the elevator, unsure what to do, and watched him move through the loft. For an instant Sal had no idea why she was here, why he had bothered to bring her along.

"Yeah. I bet it won't be cheap." Other than the built-in kitchen there was no furniture, a drawback. But then again, if he went about it carefully and did not sound too needy, maybe he could get some help from Naomi. Maybe he could entice her to come have a look, and maybe even take on the task of decorating it for him.

He stepped out onto the terrace. Across the water he could make out the docks and above them the line of trees along the Promenade. Somewhere, hidden among the greenery, was the big white house, the one Naomi had given her husband for a wedding gift. As he stood, leaning on the brick wall enclosing the patio, the idea of getting a telescope flitted through his mind.

No one would really wonder about that, with the vista this place offered. He would be able to shrug it away and say he loved watching the ships, and everyone would believe him, even Jon.

"How much?"

The agent smiled sweetly at him and, after reeling off some more sales slogans, named a sum that made Maya blanch and Sal nod.

HE TOOK HER to lunch at a small Chinese restaurant right on the pier where they could sit near the water.

Maya hadn't said a lot, and now, a steaming bowl of noodles and shrimp in front of her, she stared down at it, the chopsticks between her fingers, silent again. He liked the way her hair fell over her shoulder and how he could peek down the neckline of her blouse just a little bit. Her skin had a soft, golden sheen and looked silken in the warmth of the sun.

"You don't talk a lot, do you?" Sal refilled her glass. She had ordered water, no cocktail, no wine, and he had refrained too, good manners winning over his wish for a drink.

Her head came up. "I don't know what to say to you. I'm guessing you're taking me out to make sure I haven't changed my mind about last night. You don't have to be afraid; I won't take you to court. I'd have to be able to pay a lawyer for that."

She picked up a shrimp and held it quite deftly between the sticks. "And anyway, you can't watch me all the time, right? Or you'd have to make me move into your new loft with you and drag me along wherever you go."

He choked on his water.

Maya was looking at him, her large, black eyes, waiting for a response, a trace of challenge in her expression, the earlier shyness gone.

"I want a drink," Sal said. "Would you like one too?" and almost coughed in surprise when she nodded and ordered a glass of white wine from the waitress.

"So tell me about your life," he suggested. "What do you do besides working for your father?"

"I'm boring. There is not much time for anything else. If you run a deli with your family, you work all the time. It was hard to get out today. I owe my sister big-time." The shrimp wandered into her mouth.

"But you must have something you do just for yourself?"

"Not much." She lowered her eyes to her food and poked at the cooling noodles. "There isn't much. We get up early, open the shop, work all day, and then I go to bed." Maya shrugged. "That's pretty much all of it. I don't get out too often."

"Couldn't your father hire someone?" It was a rather intrusive question, he realized, but she laughed.

"Oh, he wouldn't. He likes it this way. He says the money stays in the family, and he doesn't have to pay insurance for a stranger. And it's time for me to get back now too."

This statement disappointed him unaccountably. "That's too bad. I had hoped you would join me for some shopping. I need furniture and all kinds of stuff for the loft now, and my taste is, let's say, undeveloped."

She gave him a crooked grin. "I know nothing about decorating a house. I don't even have my own room. You should get a professional to do that for you."

Sal had no idea where his sudden resolve came from. "No. I'd rather we did it on our own. Way more fun. Come on; take the rest of the day off. We'll grab a cab up to where the nice shops are, and you can help me decide what to put in that huge space. What do you think?"

"I think," Maya answered slowly, "you are quite out of your mind and saying these things to dazzle me." She leaned forward on the table. "Sal, really, I'll give you a written statement that I won't sue you or Jon or anyone for last night. Only please stop being nice to me because you feel you must."

Surprised, he leaned back in his chair. "That's not what I meant. And I'm not being nice for any other reason than wanting to share your company." He was drifting into babbling again, and it made him wonder why she had this effect on him. "I'm happy about my good luck in finding just the place I wanted on the first try, and now I can't wait to see it furnished. I hate the idea of letting someone else do it for me. I want it to feel like my home and not like a designer's dream of a New York loft." A flat-out lie, and he hid the shame of it by studying the menu. The decorator he had hired to do his Los Angeles flat still calls him with suggestions. "The most important thing in any place that has more than one room is a good coffeemaker. That's the first thing to get."

They could see the building with his loft from where they sat; in fact, leaning back a little, Sal could see his roof garden and the green awning over it. He would be able to step downstairs for any kind of breakfast he wanted.

"You don't need a coffeemaker," Maya was saying. "Everything you could possibly want is right next door or here on the pier. You don't even need a fridge."

He watched as she picked at a piece of carrot carved into a flower at the side of her plate.

"I didn't ask you out because of last night. I asked you out because I enjoy your company and like talking to you."

Before he went on, he lit a cigarette. She had no idea, he knew, how unusual this was for him, or for any one in their group. They didn't go out with strangers. They didn't even meet with people outside their business often, too careful of getting the wrong kind of publicity and too weary to watch for traps all the time.

For the first time since Jon had announced his change in career over a year ago, Sal could see a bright side to it. Life would be easier. There would be freedom of a kind they had not allowed themselves, too circumspect about Jon's career and consequently their own. Some of them were married, some in a steady relationship, like Art; but some were single and missing something.

"We don't often do this." Sal signaled for the bill. "We don't invite people outside the group into our lives. It's a dangerous thing to do, for many reasons." When there was no response, he went on, "We have to protect Jon, in more than the obvious way."

But he did not go on to explain while he signed the bill.

"Okay." She rose, that purse he had come to deplore by now in both hands in front of her body again. "I'll go with you. But I'm warning you, I know nothing about chic interior design. My taste will probably shock you."

HE HADN'T DONE this in a long time.

It felt strange to walk through the streets with a girl on a Saturday afternoon with nothing in mind other than looking at couches and coffeemakers, and buying ice cream from a street vendor. For some reason that Sal could not quite grasp, they had ended up in Chinatown. The smells of food and herbs were intoxicating and made him realize their lunch had probably been a bad choice; they would have gotten much better fare here. He couldn't remember when he had last had more than a few hours to himself in New York. Naomi had called him here once, on the spur of the moment, when she had found the house and wanted him to negotiate for it, but since then he had not returned. There had been no reason to. His home was Vegas, and his job was in LA. Except when they were touring. Everything, all the changes in their lives, the reason he had just spent a few million of his hardearned dollars, were Naomi's fault.

Sal, standing by as Maya stopped at a store display filled with glazed ducks, chewed his lip. A mix of desperation and anger welled up in him, mingling with the feeling of amused fondness at Maya's fascination with the Chinese foods.

"Your taste in furniture is not shocking at all," he said. "I liked what you liked."

"I've never eaten that." She pointed at the ducks. "I wonder how they make them so red and glossy."

"Oh, next time, then." This statement surprised Sal, said so easily and without thinking. With a deep breath he repeated, "Next time we'll come here and try that duck. Maybe tomorrow?"

But she shook her head. "Not tomorrow. We're doing a barbecue feast tomorrow, and I have to help."

"So let's meet on Monday."

Maya gazed at him, her head tilted and her lips pursed in thought.

"Not Monday? You name a day, then," Sal offered.

"Wednesday," she replied slowly, "is my day off."

chapter 9

STAN WAS WAITING for them outside the theater, a huge mug of coffee in one hand and his cell phone in the other, yelling into it in the manner Naomi remembered so well. He waved at her when the car stopped, a broad grin spreading on his lean, unshaven face.

"So," Jon said softly, "it begins. A new era in our lives. From here on, we really step forward together. It's a bit scary, and so exhilarating. I wonder if they will accept me in this new role."

"You are the one who wrote this musical, Jon." She gently touched his wrist. "You got some really important people to invest a lot of money in it. They believe in you, and I do too. Stan believes in you, and he should know."

"Yes." He was still intimidated by what they were about to do, and that was a feeling he was not used to anymore. "Our money is going into it as well. If this doesn't work, we will be a lot poorer."

Naomi laughed at him. "Yeah, sure. We'll sell the bloody Rolls then. That almost makes me want the musical to fail."

"Don't say that! You're making me sweat!"

She climbed out of the car, right into Stan's shout of welcome.

"The day is here, at last, the day everything will change for Broadway. Good-bye, English composers of worthless music; here comes the Master himself."

His voice was so loud it carried straight across the traffic and turned heads on the other side of the street. "Everything is ready for you. Do you want coffee? A cushion? A personal servant? A Thai massage? Just say it; it will be yours!"

"Good grief, shut up, Stan. You are the wackiest guy in all New York, I swear, and that's saying something." Jon looked down the sideway to the alley with the backstage entrance to the theater, and the long line that had formed there. It vanished around the corner of the block like a chain of colorful puppets. A ripple went through them when he was recognized, and there was a swell of murmur, Jon turned his back on them, his hands in his pockets, to look up at the facade of the big building.

There was no real need for them to be here, but Naomi had insisted. She wanted, she had said, to be there when the casting began, and maybe even sit through the entire procedure, soak up the atmosphere, and experience the development of the musical from moment one. Jon had pointed out to her that the moment was long past: it had been when she had conceived the idea and written the first lyrics, way back in Norway, just after their wedding, but she had shrugged him off. This was different. This was the realization of her words, and she wanted to be part of it.

"It's the first time something I've written will be put on a stage," she had said, and he had laughed at her across the breakfast table and called her a silly girl.

"Baby, the things you've written, they were on a stage more than twenty years ago. I took them to the stage. Or don't I count anymore?"

"That's different" had been her mumbled reply. "You're my husband, and those were songs; I wrote them for you."

But she had been unable to explain, and he had not asked again.

Now, standing outside the theater, he understood.

They were handing it over to strangers; others would sing the songs they had created together, and they would have to watch and hope for the best.

He had very rarely done this. There had been two or three pieces at the beginning of his career that he had sold to other singers, but he'd never cared for the way they had been performed and had refused to do it again. And this, this was even bigger.

"And, my dear," Stan was saying to Naomi, "we even bought a new coffeemaker just for you. I'm that thrilled to have the privilege of staging your musical. What an incredible event, a gem coming to Broadway, something that should have happened decades ago. Jon, you were never meant to perform yourself. You were meant to be the great composer of musicals and movie soundtracks."

"There's a good number of people out there who really love my voice and my concerts," Jon growled. "We'll have to see if you can make me as much money as I did by myself, Stan."

"Money, money, always you go on about money." Stan held the doors for them. "Go to Vegas as a resident and grow old and fat there if it's about the money. We produce art. You will feel it, Jon; you will know the difference. This is shaping a piece of life on the stage, not dazzling a couple thousand women who are more interested in how tight your trousers are than in your singing. You have never worked in your life, my friend. Now you'll learn what it means to put something onstage."

Jon rolled his eyes at Naomi behind Stan's back, and she bit her lip to keep the laughter down.

They entered the auditorium to the sound of piano music and some shouting. The hall lay in darkness, just as it had the first time they had been here, with a table set up somewhere in the fifth row, illuminated by a desk lamp.

The stage itself still lay in shadows; a few people were working on and around it, setting up microphones and sorting cables. On a ladder, cursing loudly, a young man was trying to adjust a spotlight.

"You use mikes for a casting?" Jon asked, stopping halfway down the aisle. "That surprises me. I make my background singers do without them first."

Stan gave him a toothy grin. "Jon, you haven't changed your background singers in twenty years. How would you know anything about casting?"

Jon sighed in defeat. "It doesn't matter at all what I say, does it? You'll always find something to bitch about. I give up."

A girl with a clipboard came up to them and asked if they were ready to begin.

With that question Stan put on a cloak of brisk seriousness. He took Naomi's elbow and directed her toward the table and asked Jon to sit down too, to ask for anything they needed, and here was his assistant, Paula, who would be at their beck and call, but to please let him do his job now. From the table he took a wireless microphone and spoke into it to test it, walking up and down the aisle, his head lowered and shoulders hunched, breathing in concentration.

Naomi settled down to watch the proceedings. She felt like an impostor. For an instant something like panic rose in her, and she had the eerie feeling someone would walk up to her and ask her what she was doing here—she had no place in this theater—or else get her butt on the stage and show what she could do. This made her sink into her seat in a useless attempt to hide, but it was too late.

Someone had opened the backstage entrance. Sounds from the street drifted in: the honking of cars, the ubiquitous police siren, the background carpet of voices, laughter, life. She even thought the smell of hot dogs had crept in, and it made her stomach twitch.

A group of girls came in from the side of the stage, led by a young man in red trousers rolled up to reveal well-developed, hairy calves. His bouncy curls danced around his face as he collected application folders from them and handed out number badges in return.

"My name is Wilfred," he said to them in a clear voice that carried well into the space of the theater. "I'm the choreographer. If any of you does not have classical-dance training, you can leave now. We don't have time for amateurs, and it doesn't matter how good a singer you are if your dancing is crap."

A low murmur ran through the group, a shifting of stance, but no one left.

The folders were handed over to Paula, who laid them down on the table next to Naomi.

Stan came to sit beside her. For a few minutes he leafed through them, shuffling photos, scanning bios, his glance flitting back and forth between the people onstage and their documents.

"Right," his voice boomed over the microphone, "let's get started. This is the first round of casting, and you'll do as Wilfred tells you. Will, let's roll."

"That was a pretty terse announcement," Jon murmured so only she could hear. He was sitting behind her, well away from the light, his arms resting on the back of her chair. "And Wilfred? Who would call his child Wilfred? This is going to be better than I thought."

She had the feeling of slipping into a movie, and it made her wonder about the lives of the young people standing in an orderly line along the white tape, some nervous, some collected, the concentration clearly painted on their faces. A few even seemed to enjoy the procedure. There was a pretty, perky blond girl in cut-off jeans and a tight tank top, her hair in saucy pigtails, excitement sparkling in her eyes, her fingers twitching in time to the music coming from the piano, feet tapping the rhythm. Beside her stood a boy in shorts and a t-shirt, his arms folded in something like boredom while he stared at the ceiling. They caught Naomi's eye, but they were not what she had envisioned for the characters she had created when she had written the play. In fact, there was no one in this group she would have picked, but she knew she would not have any say in the choice.

Jon chuckled into her ear. "I knew this was all a big spoof. Dancing, dear God. We should have stayed at home."

"Shut up," she whispered fiercely. "If you keep this up Stan will throw us out, and I want to see this."

"Babe, you've seen so many of our rehearsals, is this any different?" His fingers caressed her neck and sent a shiver down her spine.

"You're only jealous because for once you don't get to be boss." Naomi gave him the coffee from the table when he stretched out his hand for it. "You hate being a spectator and not in command, that's all. This will be a good exercise for your inflated ego."

"You are so cruel." Jon sighed. "Am I not here with you? Am I not letting Stan toss insults at me?"

He didn't fool her; she could hear from the tone in his words that he was watching the proceedings on the stage intently and was only teasing her.

"It's different." Naomi tried to say what she was thinking. "It's different because you are not doing it yourself. When you take my lyrics and make songs from them, I know you'll also sing them just the way I wanted them to sound." She turned around to look at him. "But this feels…" Her hand fluttered as she searched for the right words. "This is giving it away, and that means giving away control. Putting my trust in strangers to do the best with my work. I have no idea what they will make of it. You and I, we created this, and now others will twist it any way they like."

"That's not going to happen." Jon's brow drew together. "It may seem to you as if we are only bystanders, but that's not true. Do you really think I'd give away my work like that? Or yours? The contract we have is many pages long, Naomi, and a whole building of lawyers has worked it out. Trust me, Stan, or whoever wants to touch our project, will have to strip nearly naked before he can even open the folder with the music sheets. Or the textbook. I don't give away my music easily. And part of that deal is our presence, and our opinion."

She looked back at the stage. "So I can say if I don't like someone? Or say if I do?"

More relaxed, Jon leaned back again. "Sure, baby, you can say anything you like. If you're not pleased with the way things are going, I'll buy the frigging theater and we'll do it ourselves."

Stan shot him a furious glance. "My mike is open. You do have a carrying voice, don't we know. If you keep this up, you might as well join that rabble on the stage."

"Nah, Stan," Jon drawled, "you know I'm better than anyone up there anyway. Your bloody stage would be empty."

"You are the most arrogant arse in the whole wide world." But Stan grinned as he said this, and added, "Yeah, you're probably right. Are you sure you don't want to play the lead role yourself?"

"Absolutely. For once I want to sit in the back row and bitch."

Stan picked up the microphone to tell the group they could leave and thank you very much. They left, grumbling a bit, and he tossed their folders into a big box beside him.

"You're not accepting even one of them?" Naomi felt a huge wave of relief washing over her.

"Nope. Not one of them has the presence I want on my stage." He signaled to Wilfred, who walked off to bring in the next group. "It's not just the voice or the dancing. They have to have that special something to be good enough for this. Ideally, it should be enough for them to just stand there. You know right away. Well, I do. They just have it." With a malevolent glance at Jon he added, "Your guy, he has it. And it's not the pretty face or the great butt. It's the aura, the magnetism, the spark of life."

"Well thanks, honey." Jon smirked at him. "We still don't have a date."

"Shut up." Stan returned his attention to the stage, and Jon laughed.

Naomi had been to many opera performances, concerts, and shows with her parents, and there had been a good share of backstage experience with Jon and his band; but this was vastly different. She knew the stage sets were even now being built somewhere in New Jersey, in the theater's own workshop, and they would be going there soon with Stan to have a first look.

She was astounded by the songs some of the applicants had chosen for the casting.

"I'd have thought," she whispered to Jon at one point, "they would pick musical songs. Who are they trying to impress, singing current hits that can't be performed without proper backing?" and sighed at his tired grin.

"I have no idea. Sad, isn't it? Even a bit disheartening. Broadway has nothing better to offer?"

"Will you two shut up?" Stan hissed, the fair skin of his face turning bright red with anger. "You are so distracting. I'm not supposed to be in a good mood for this, and you make me want to laugh all the time."

Naomi sank back in her seat, properly chastised, but Jon leaned forward again. "Let me do this then, Stan. I'm properly pissed now and feel like folding some innocent kids."

"You're not going to do this; you have no idea what I'm looking for. You can buy me lunch later, but stop mocking my job!" Stan took a deep breath before he returned his attention to the stage.

"I'm not mocking," Jon said, laughter in his voice, "just having some fun. Thank you for making me do this, Stan. I never knew I'd love sitting back and watching so much."

Wilfred, up on the stage, was having the group try dance steps that made the wooden floor resonate in a speedy rhythm.

Dust motes swirled in the beams of the spotlights, the melodies Jon had written for the musical filled the air, and Naomi's heart beat faster as she watched the slim bodies move to them. She knew she was seeing the ghost of their work, the raw bones of the show that would be presented in a few months to the public.

This time Stan kept back a handful of girls.

Things became even more interesting when Wilfred brought in a dozen young men. Naomi could feel Jon's reaction, sense the movement of his body as his attention woke.

He hummed along with the melodies of his own songs, performed more or less convincingly by eager young voices, tapping the beat on the back of Naomi's seat with his palms until she put her hands on his to stop him.

"Go and sing yourself if you need it that badly," she said, "but stop jolting me. The baby will start step dancing before he even has legs."

Jon came forward to put his face close to hers. "He? You think it will be a he? I want a girl. I want a little you, a girl I can spoil and pamper without your lengthy discussions and objections. A little lady with a black ponytail, my little princess."

Naomi leaned into him, her cheek against his. Jon's arm came up around her shoulder, pressing it gently, holding her.

"I don't want to worry, Jon. Please let's not worry, okay? I know what's in store for me. I want this more than my life."

Yes, and that was exactly what he was afraid of.

Jon, with her breath stroking his jaw, did not reply for a moment.

The talk he had with Kevin, his brother, rumbled in his head. They had been standing in their mother's kitchen, ostensibly to get more beer from the fridge; and Jon had asked, his chest constricted with fear, his hands unable to open the bottle. From the yard he had heard the sound of Joshua's laughter and his delighted outcry as Naomi told him about his soon-to-be-born sibling, sounds of a happy family, a life coming full circle; and Kevin, his face clouded with anxiety, had stood before him, shaking his head.

"You will have to watch her very carefully" had been his dour prediction. "You know your wife. She wants to live a normal life with such a vengeance, Jon; but she is ailing, and older, and very fragile. Don't let her will to do this fool you. The next few months will be hard on her."

"She is not old."

Kevin had taken a deep gulp of beer before replying. "Not old in that sense. Dammit, Jon, you know what I'm saying. A few months ago she was nearly dead. She was dead, a couple of times; they brought her back. All I'm saying is, be careful. Take it really easy. And don't let her tell you she's all right when you think she's not. Call Julian or me right away. Take her to the hospital immediately." He had laid his hand on Jon's arm to emphasize his words. "This is not about having a baby or not, Jon. This is about keeping Naomi alive. She will be fine for a while, until the child gets big. It will be a strain on her heart. She might have to go on bed rest the second half of the pregnancy."

Back outside with their family, he had seen only joy. Joshua, who had come down from Harvard for the weekend, had been tossing name suggestions at Naomi until she laughed and told him to stop and wait until they knew the gender.

Jon had swallowed his anxiety, seeing them together, the love of his life and their grown son, and decided to make things as easy as he could for her.

"I'm hungry," Naomi said into his thoughts now. "Do you think we could just slip out and find something to eat?"

"I'll get something for you. What do you want, darling?" he replied, and had to bite down a grin when she began listing what she was craving.

chapter 10

MAYA HAD BUILT herself a little corner on the roof, right behind the chimney, where no one would see her right away.

Over the years it had turned into a little garden with pots she had collected from the trash behind the flower shop next door. She had managed to coax a number of discarded roses back to life and even planted some tomatoes, their fruit hanging among the furry leaves like the promise of summer, exuding their tart fragrance even now and making her mouth water.

Karim, in a bout of goodwill and a rare moment of comprehension, had built her something like an awning a few years ago, saying he could understand her need for a refuge from the boisterous family. He had watched her with a trace of envy as she brought up an old mattress, blankets, and cushions, even some candles in old jars, and placed them ever so lovingly around her nook as if to mark her boundaries. He left her alone, even chased away Selma when she tried to join Maya, saying her older sister had a right to some privacy.

Through a gap between the taller buildings around theirs she could see the river and even some of Manhattan, and if she leaned forward a little, she could catch a glimpse of the World Trade Center—beacons of a different world calling her.

Maya liked to be up there at dusk when it seemed the constant noise of the street below turned into a softer hum, the smells of the daytime turned into their own memory and were overpowered by the scent of her flowers as it was released by the cooler temperatures.

She sat, her back against the sun-warmed bricks of the chimney, and looked toward the town across the water, recalling her last meeting with Sal and how she had asked herself why she was doing this as they strolled back to his hotel. From time to time she had glanced his way as he walked beside her, looking around at their surroundings as if he needed to reacquaint himself with New York, as if every corner was bringing back memories from an earlier time. Once or twice he had seemed on the point of remarking on something but then stopped, and she had been too shy to ask him what he had been about to say or what he was thinking.

Their talk had been an easy chat. They had not touched on topics that were beyond the everyday, and not once had he mentioned Jon or anything connected to him.

She couldn't figure out what he wanted.

At some point she had confessed that she needed to buy shoes, that buying shoes had been her excuse for being able to meet him at all, and he had grinned and taken her into a store she would never have dared enter on her own.

"Here" had been his words, "I know Naomi likes to come here. What are you looking for?"

Too embarrassed to speak, she had tried on the wonderful creations placed before her and walked up and down on the expensive cream carpet in heels she would never have picked on her own; and just when she had been about to find an excuse to leave, Sal had said, "Pick whatever you like. Consider it a gift for helping me find my loft. You deserve a reward."

She had blushed furiously, seeing herself in the black heels with the red soles and the perfect fit, and started to decline; but he would not hear it.

"It's either that or I'll give you a check and you can buy them yourself. You've earned it. Stop fussing. Nothing is free, my dear." Sal had enjoyed it, that much was obvious, and she had been unable to resist.

He had been so pleased, his joy had taken away her qualms. She had even consented to go to a bar with him after that and let him buy her a drink, some pink concoction with a fancy decoration on the rim of the glass, while he had sipped Bourbon and laughed at her awe.

"Meet me on Wednesday," he had begged when they parted at the subway station. "We can have a fun. What would you like to do?" and smiled when she answered, "Today was a lot of fun; it's not important what we do."

And it had been true.

On the train she had opened the shoe box and turned the shoes over in her hands, wondering if anyone in her family would recognize the brand and realize she would never have been able to afford them herself. The woman sitting across from her had raised her eyebrows in admiration and smiled, and Maya had felt a rush of pride at owning something so precious and being able to show it off.

Now, in her corner of the roof, she put them on again.

They were a far cry from the ballerinas she normally wore, and she had no idea where she was going to wear them.

From below she could hear the voices of her family as they gathered for dinner, the clinking of plates and the usual blare of the radio. The unmistakable smell of Pakistani cooking drifted up through the open door, mingling with a whiff of garbage from the containers in the backyard and the aroma of pizza from the Italian restaurant a few doors away.

Maya leaned her head against the bricks and closed her eyes. She wondered where Sal was now, and Jon, and Naomi.

She imagined them in a cool, clean place, maybe a restaurant on Fifth Avenue, where they were being served by elegant waiters, wine sparkling in lovely crystal glasses and soft music playing in the background. Naomi would surely be wearing shoes just like these, and pick whatever she wanted from the menu without looking at the prices even once. Later she would be driven home in her limousine, gliding through the night with Jon by her side, and not getting sweaty and grimy on the subway. And then she would have him all to herself, be in bed with him, lie in his arms; and Maya tried to imagine how that would be, hearing his voice whisper endearments while he lay close and the world was shut out.

Her mother's call woke her from her reverie. Hastily she took off her new shoes, returned them to their box, and went back inside to join them for dinner.

KARIM WAS LESS than pleased, and he showed it by dumping a bucket full of olives in front of Maya, informing her she might as well spend the evening pitting and halving them if she had decided to be away yet another day.

"I will not pay you," he said. "Don't expect to be paid if you are not here. What's wrong with you? Are you up to something?"

Maya took the small, sharp knife he was holding without comment and picked an olive out of the bucket. She hated her father's obsession with the things. Often enough she had told him it was no big deal to buy them without the pits; but he insisted they tasted better this way, and he could write *homemade* on his menu without qualms.

A large bowl on her knees, Maya sat between her mother and Uma on the couch and watched with them the talent show they were so fond of. It was hot in the room. The windows were open, but there was not even a sigh of wind to freshen the air. Angie had made samosas and placed them on the table together with a choice of pungent dips. Karim, in his armchair, was busy cracking and peeling pistachios and feeding them to Selma, once in a while popping one into his own mouth. The plastic covering on the couch stuck to the back of Maya's thighs, making a sucking noise every time she shifted, the vinyl tearing away from her skin like old plaster. Her fingernails were soon grimy from the black meat of the olives, and she stared at her hands in trepidation, wondering if she would ever be able to get them back into shape before she went to meet Sal the next day.

Her mother reached across her to pick up one of the samosas and dip it into the chili sauce. She took a bite and tried to push the rest into Maya's mouth, but she turned her head away quickly.

"Leave me alone, Mama," Maya said. "I'm not eating that."

"What, you're not eating this?" Karim asked. "Since when is your mother's food not good enough for you? You used to love samosas."

"Yes, but I'm not hungry." To divert his attention she poured him more Coke.

"There's something going on here." He drew his thick, black eyebrows together to scrutinize her. "You are away from home much too often, and you hide things. Those shoes, they are totally useless for work and much too fancy for you. Why did you waste your money like that?"

"Because I liked them, and I wanted them." Maya did not return his gaze but stared stubbornly at the bowl in her lap.

She had gotten into a major fight with Uma when she had brought home those shoes. Right after she had returned from the roof for dinner, she had put them down on her bed; and when she came back from washing her hands, Uma had been prancing in them through the kitchen, mindless of the dirty floor and the fat sizzling in the pan.

"Look, high heels! Maya, will you be going to nightclubs in these soon?" Uma had cried, and Maya, without a word, had gone up to her sister and slapped her face. She had not reacted to her mother's out-raged questions but pushed Uma down into a chair and taken the shoes from her by force, wiped their soles on her skirt, and stalked away into their room, slamming the door behind her. No one had dared follow her, and she had spent the evening curled on her bed, sobbing without really knowing why.

Angie had tried to talk to her the next morning, but Maya had refused her attempts.

"I'm thinking of finding a different job," she said now. "I'd rather work at a clean store downtown than sell curries all day long."

"Are you saying my shop is dirty?" Karim sat up straight. "Our shop is not dirty, and your mother is the best cook this side of the East River. People come from New Jersey to buy her curries!"

"I didn't mean…" Maya sighed.

Angie, beside her, picked up another samosa and popped it into her mouth.

"This is your home," Karim went on. "It makes enough to feed us all and keep up this house. Not everyone owns their home on this street, my dear. We are homeowners. Why in the world do you want to work somewhere else? When your mother and I are too old to work you, and Uma will run the deli, and then you can introduce hip new stuff like vegetable juice or cupcakes. But I warn you; everyone sells those, and if you really want your place to be a success you need to specialize." He nodded to himself, well pleased with his little speech, and returned his attention to the TV.

Maya looked down at her mother's bare feet on the threadbare carpet. Her ankles were swollen from standing in the kitchen all day, her heels dry and cracked, and Maya could not remember seeing her in anything but flat sandals or comfortable shoes ever.

Uma, on her other side, was barefoot too, but her feet were dainty and slim, with well-varnished nails and perfect skin.

Thinking of it now, Maya had to admit she had looked rather good in those black high heels, and she had walked well in them too.

"Oh, look, it's your lover!" Uma crowed.

It was an old clip, one she had seen before a number of times; she could even name the concert where it had been taped.

Karim picked up the remote to turn up the volume. "That's the one you went all the way to Madison Square Garden for? He's old."

Maya wanted to scream and pull her hair. "He's not old."

Somehow, after having seen him during the soundcheck, Jon seemed different to her. Beyond the lighting and the stage clothes she could see the person, the one who had talked to her and worried about her well-being. It was as if her vision shifted and overlapped, showing her two things at the same time that were totally unrelated and yet only made a complete image when perceived together.

"He's not old," she repeated under her breath, but no one paid attention.

MANY THINGS SEEMED different to Maya when she came down into the shop the next morning.

She had lived here her whole life, spent every minute she was not in school with her father, helping him, proud of herself when he allowed her to serve her first customer, in a state of bliss when he let her stand behind the hot counter on her own for the first time, feeling important when he told her to work the tables on the sidewalk just outside the storefront. He had given her a cute red apron and a matching hair clip, lecturing her about hygiene and that no guest wanted her hair blowing in their food, and she had braided her thick, black strands into a tight rope hanging down her back.

But that had been seven years ago, after she had just turned sixteen, and the money she earned had seemed like a wonderful privilege. Her parents had not sent her to college when she finished high school; in fact they had encouraged her to join them full-time at the deli, and that was her life now.

Seeing her father as he unloaded crates filled with artichokes from the van and Uma, cooking the first urn of coffee for the day before she went off to school, made her realize how much she had come to hate their existence over the past couple of years.

Only minutes ago she had watched Angie start her daily job of cooking, her ample body wrapped in a sack-like green dress and her hair bound together with a dismal rubber band. Mounds of onions and garlic had filled the cramped space with their aroma, the little jars with spices lined up on the table looking like multicolored fairy dust in the morning sunlight.

"You've met someone," Angie had said without turning around from the stove. "That's why you are so eager to go to Manhattan. Isn't that so?"

Maya had stopped at the top of the stairs, on the point of walking downstairs, and looked at her mother for a moment but hadn't replied.

"I'm not stupid, Maya."

Without a word Maya had left.

"Are you off again, then?" Karim greeted her. He looked critically at her clothes. "A bit overdressed for a Wednesday morning, eh?"

She was in her only really nice summer dress, the one she had bought at an expensive Brooklyn boutique a year ago in a moment of protest, uncertain when she would ever have a chance to wear it.

"And you want to go off in those shoes? Are you sure you can walk in them at all?" His eyebrows came up, seeing her in the high heels.

She did not tell him she had simple sandals hidden away in her purse, and nodded stubbornly.

Thoughtfully, Karim put the basket of oranges he had been about to carry inside down on one of the tables. "I'm thinking you've met someone. You've fallen in love, and you are ashamed to tell us because it's some nifty banker guy from Wall Street, and you think we're not good enough."

Shame burned her face and neck, and she hung her head but she did not reply.

"At least we run our own business," Karim went on. "We are independent and can do as we please. Your mother and I built this, and we are proud of it. You should be too."

With a sigh, Maya set down her purse. "But Papa, can't you see? You work day and night; Mama is in the kitchen all the time, all by herself, hot and sweaty; and in the evenings you are both dead beat and too tired to even think. All you do is hang in front of the TV for an hour, and then you go to bed. And you do it every day, every year. We've never gone away for a vacation, never been to the opera or a free concert in Central Park. I can't remember when we last went to the zoo! I'm afraid of living like that, being trapped in this street and this house for the rest of my life. There is so much else out there, and I want to see it! I don't want to spend my evenings watching stupid talent shows and pitting olives."

"Ah, that got to you, didn't it?" He grinned briefly but then brought out a grimy handkerchief to wipe his sweaty brow. "It's honest work, Maya, and nothing to frown on. Your mother is a great cook, and I love running the store. We like to chat with our customers; we like this daily life you seem to hate so much."

"But Papa." Maya had no idea how they had gotten into this discussion, and she was getting desperate. Sal would be waiting.

"Papa, I have no education. I'm not even a good cook. The prospect of running the store scares me. I'll be twenty-four next month, and I have nothing but pitting olives and serving korma to strangers." Fighting tears, she pointed at their house, wedged as it was between the others. "I don't even have a room of my own."

"What's wrong with your sister that you don't want to share with her? What's wrong with us that you don't want to live and work with us?" He waved a friendly greeting to their neighbor who had just stepped outside to open his flower shop.

"There is nothing wrong with you." She swallowed hard to keep down the anger and hurt and picked up her purse. "It's just not enough, not enough for me."

ALL HE HAD to do was drive across the bridge, make a few right turns, and he was standing outside her house, just like he had done often enough in Los Angeles.

The cab dropped him off on the street lined with old brownstones right at the corner of the Promenade. For a moment Sal stood, gazing at the scene across the water, and wondered if she spent a lot of time looking at it as the light changed on the reflecting surfaces. He could picture her, maybe in a silken, lacy nightgown, just out of bed, the warm scent of sleep still on her and her hair wild around her face, enjoying the sunrise; and he tried to push Jon out of that image, tried not to see him standing behind her, touching her skin, kissing her.

Sal crossed the street. The high gate was firmly closed, the wall and hedge seemingly insurmountable, the cameras on its crest staring down at him like dragons' eyes. No one was going to enter Jon's new castle without being vetted first by security, not even Sal. In a way, this was worse than the mansion in Malibu, which lay nestled in its own park among fellow estates.

Inside the walls, he was surprised by the sudden calm. There were no oleander and jasmine bushes, no palm trees, but the greenery was just as verdant and lush as her garden in Los Angeles. Sal had no idea how she had done it in the brief period of time.

A new maid opened the door to him. Sal thought she bore a

resemblance to Amparo, their Malibu housekeeper, but she was younger and a lot shapelier. She threw him a pert, assessing glance before leading him into the living room, where she told him to wait, she would inform Mr. Stone.

This made him chuckle sourly. "Mr. Stone," he mumbled.

Since they had been back from the tour he had not been inside their new house, the one he himself had wrangled from its old owners over too many cups of a musty brand of tea and biscuits that had curiously tasted of figs. He remembered how this room had looked then, dark and stuffed with aged furniture, the carpets threadbare and the hardwood floor dull. The elderly couple had been only too willing to sell, and he knew he could have gotten a much better bargain, but Naomi had insisted. She had not wanted them cheated out of the valuable property.

And now it was hers. Everything was new, shiny, graceful, a far cry from her small, simple apartment back in Norway.

Sal wondered if she had called on her family for the paintings decorating the hall and living room. He was certain they were originals and each of them an expensive museum piece, Canadian artists all. He didn't care too much for the stark depictions of northern landscapes but knew Jon had developed a liking for them since he had lived with Naomi in her little fishing town.

Staring at the chilling portrait of an iceberg, he wondered about that, and about the change that had come over Jon. It was a wonder to see him so much more outgoing, happy and easy with his life.

"Hey, Sal," Jon greeted him as he walked in. "You're up and around early in the day. What brings you here?"

A spike of jealously stabbed him as always when he saw his friend like this.

Sal hated the unconscious boasting in his negligent appearance, hated how Jon dropped on the couch, in jeans, shirt open, his hair wet and uncombed and his feet bare, a sight to make fans swoon. It made his bile rise. Jon was forty-seven, and still as handsome as ever. It was too much for a man to bear.

"I'm here to tell you about an offer." It came out a little gruffer than he had intended, but as always he had the image of them together hovering at the back of his mind: Naomi, in Jon's arms, maybe even just before Jon had come down to welcome him.

"Oh?" Jon took the coffee the new girl was offering him. There was not a lot of interest in his tone.

"Yes." Coffee was handed to him as well.

"I'm quite busy at the moment." There was a sound from the hallway, and Jon turned toward it, his attention for Sal gone.

"Not too busy to do a little composing, I should think. No one needs you at that theater. You're really only there for fun's sake." Sal felt anger rising in him and bit down on it. "I know, I know, the tour is only just over, but you should have a look. It might just be the right thing for you. And it would pay off rather handsomely."

Jon looked at him.

"There's this writer," Sal plodded on, "and his book is going to be filmed. He asked for you to do the soundtrack, and the movie producers have approached me. It would be something totally new for you. It's a fantasy novel. It might be a nice challenge. The imagery will be astounding. And anyway"—he added milk to his coffee—"this is what you want to do from now on, right? No more touring, no more concerts."

"I never said that," Jon replied carefully. "I never said never, just not for a while. For a long while."

"Yeah, I got it." He wanted to throw something at Jon. Something sharp, hard, and heavy, if only to make him button his shirt and stop showing off his nicely muscled chest and stomach. "But it's a very good book, the author a very famous man, and the movie a certain blockbuster. You could be in. We could be in. I'm sure there's room for a couple of songs, which means you could work with Naomi."

"I always and only work with Naomi, Sal." Delivered in an amused drawl that made Sal even more furious.

"Well, you didn't always. Come on, will you have a look?"

Jon shrugged. "Is Harry going to produce the movie? Or someone new we have to get used to?"

"You've met. Roger has made many blockbuster movies." He went on to list some of them but realized he was losing Jon's interest fast. "So will you consider it?" he asked instead. "It could take us to the Oscars again."

And this, Sal knew instantly, had been the wrong thing to say. Jon's brow clouded, and his lips pressed together in a thin line as he glared at his manager. "The Oscars," he growled, "are not a subject that's well liked in this house."

"The Oscars?" They both looked up at Naomi. Sal's breath hitched in his throat, seeing her in a scarlet silk kimono that made her skin glow, her hair gathered untidily at the back of her head.

"We're going to the Oscars?" she repeated, and planted a brief kiss on Sal's cheek. It tingled through his entire body.

"Sal is pushing another soundtrack at us." Jon reached out to her, and she sat down with him, putting her legs up on his lap, the kimono slipping dangerously. "And of course he thinks there's nothing we want more than to do this. Sal, no one gets an Oscar this close after the last one. Also, I'm sure Naomi never wants to see that place again. Nor do I."

"I do!" Naomi said. "Totally. Don't blame the poor Academy Awards for the shooting. It wasn't their fault at all. And I liked being up on that stage. Let's do it!"

"Oh, for God's sake!" Jon's voice sounded pained. "Let's have a look at the damn book first and decide if we want to take it on at all before we discuss winning an Oscar. Are you sure, Naomi? We've only just come home from the tour, the musical production hasn't even started, we're going to have a baby, and you want to take on something new? You're worse than Sal."

She shrugged. "I've started something new anyway. I've started writing a novel. You can't expect me to sit around and get bored."

Jon's lips twitched, but he didn't comment. Instead, he laid his hand on her bare legs, stroking them slowly, and Sal had to pretend to be looking for a refill for his empty coffee cup.

"Why don't you come to the theater to see how it's going?" Naomi offered.

He refused to turn around. The sight of those fingers on her thigh was too much. "Nah. I'm meeting someone later. Busy decorating my new place."

"You found a loft?" Of course she would remember him telling her what kind of place he wanted.

"Yeah, right on the water." He gestured toward the open patio door. "Over there. I'm meeting Maya today to find some stuff for it."

"Maya?" Jon freed himself from Naomi and got up for more coffee.

Sitting up, she pulled the kimono together.

"Yes, the accident girl. I'm meeting her for lunch and some shopping. I still need a bed and some stuff for the living room." He knew only too well how they would react.

"Oh, is she an interior decorator?" Naomi took a sip from the cup before he could snatch it away.

"No, she isn't." Sal sighed, but they did not pay attention.

No one, Naomi was saying, had forbidden her to drink coffee while she was pregnant with Joshua, and he had turned out just fine, to which Jon replied that he would have Lourdes hide the tin from her if she didn't stop. Naomi slapped the cushion beside her, eyes blazing, and opened her mouth to respond, but thought better of it and settled back down.

"Much better, baby." Jon went to the kitchen and came back with a big glass of orange juice. "You should be drinking milk, you know."

"And you know," she shot back, "I hate milk. No milk for me."

"Milk would be good for your bones, and the baby's."

"My bones are just fine. Give me that coffee!" Imperiously, she held out her hand, but Jon took a step back, shaking his head. "I want a child, not a coffee bean on legs," he said.

Sal left. They didn't even hear him wish them a nice day.

chapter 11

"SO TELL ME about the pregnancy thing," Jon said.

He loved the way the bedroom looked now, with the settee by the big window so she could sit there and look out at Manhattan. It was a small sanctuary, a retreat, and he wondered why she had not claimed one of the many rooms of the house for herself.

Naomi gave the rose-and-cream cushions a critical glance and rearranged them before she sat down on the sofa.

"There's nothing to tell, Jon. I'll get fat and slow and cranky, and my ankles will swell up. And then we'll have a baby."

"But aren't there things to do? Don't we have to do stuff?"

"Like what?" She hid her grin behind the pillow she'd been holding in her lap.

Jon felt stupid, and quite helpless. "Well, stuff. How am I supposed to know? Like, buy baby things, I don't know. Is this all we do, wait until the kid pops out?"

"Pretty much."

He could see the mirth in her eyes and hear the hiccups of laughter from behind the cushion. "Isn't there something I'm supposed to do? What's my role in this? Please be serious for a moment, Naomi. I want to do everything right. You know I've never been through this before!"

Naomi took a deep breath. "There's nothing, Jon, really. When I was pregnant with Joshua, I worked up to the last day. No one treated me differently, and I even had to get my own pickles from the kitchen. Remember, I was on my own. Nobody pampered me. And it was fine." The light mood blown away, she hung her head and plucked at the seam of the cushion. "No, it wasn't fine. It was terrible. It was lonely and sad and I cried a lot. I used to sit on my couch and stare out at the bay and the snow and wish I wasn't alone." She looked up at him, tears in her eyes. "I missed you so much. I'd just left you, the pain was fresh and raw, and I was carrying your child. It was terrible."

They had been over this so often, and it still made his heart weep.

"Well, this time you won't be alone." It was the best he could manage. "I'll not leave you for a single moment."

That made her smile, the moment of sadness gone. "That sounds like a threat. I'm sure I'll want a break from you, pregnant or not."

"You know," Jon said thoughtfully, "Other than the time in Halmar, we've hardly lived together properly. We've never had a home and just lived. There was always something going on. We were traveling, or apart. It's scary, the thought of living together, in one house, day in, day out, and totally exhilarating."

"You will be bored soon enough." Naomi pulled up her legs and turned to look out the window. "You will be bored by a quiet life, by me, by the view. Just wait and see. You'll get restless before Christmas. Me, I'll live here on this couch and admire Manhattan and write."

"And I'll be downstairs, in my studio, writing my music. And listen to you pacing and wanting out." He sat down beside her.

The house was silent. Lourdes had left to get settled into her own apartment; they were alone. A slow, tepid breeze blew in through the open balcony door, nothing at all like the fragrant air of Malibu. Jon found himself wishing for a place by the beach.

"We'll live like any other married couple in Brooklyn. Slouch around in jogging pants and slippers and grumble at the mailman. And I'll go out in the mornings for fresh bread and the newspaper." In fact, the longer he thought about this, the better he liked it. "Maybe we should get a dog." Sitting down beside her, he grabbed her ankles and pulled her feet onto his knees. "And not one of those small silly lapdogs but a big, manly beast that would look good walking beside me when I go out for cinnamon rolls."

"You'll soon be pushing a baby buggy when you go out for cinnamon rolls, Jon. You don't need a dog."

Leaning back against the pillows, she told him about the checkups she would have to go to and how Julian had told her to rest, rest, rest, and come to the hospital at the slightest feeling of discomfort or any sign of pain.

"He is a bit worried," she said without looking at Jon, "but I know everything will be okay. I know it." Her hand came to rest on her belly. "I've done it before, and I refuse to give in. If I did, Jon, then the shooting would forever dictate our lives, and I'm not going to let that happen. I've put it behind me; the last shadows were driven out when Parker abducted me and I realized I was in mortal danger. I'm not going to let it rule my life, nor yours."

The abduction, he remembered his fear well. That night, only a couple of months ago, had been one of the worst of his life, nearly as bad as those days he had spent sitting by her bed in the ICU after the shooting. The drive across New York and then down into New Jersey to find her had nearly torn him apart. Always, always the guilt remained.

"Then," Jon replied slowly, "maybe you shouldn't go to the theater anymore. Maybe you should really stay put and rest. It's not as if Stan needs us. I can go and show my face from time to time, but you should stay here."

"Not on your life, Jon Stone!" She slapped his arm. "I want to see it! I want to go there! This is my dream, my script! It's all I ever wanted, and now that it's being realized I'm not going to miss it!"

The sun fell through the open window and onto her hair, highlighting it, giving it a warm, red glow. They could hear children's voices from the Promenade, the lazy hum of a plane approaching JFK, a bird chirping in a tree, and the steady song of the city from across the river.

"All you're saying to me today is no. Do I like that?" Jon tickled the soles of her feet. "No, I don't. I don't like it at all. So tell me, where did we make this baby?"

A sweet blush crept up her throat. "I think we made it in Italy."

Surprised, Jon let go of her. "I don't know a whole lot about pregnancies and babies, but that means you're three months. Shouldn't something show? Shouldn't there be a bulge?"

Again she laughed and held up the cushion to cover her mouth.

"Stop laughing at me, dammit; it makes me feel even more stupid!" He tried to take it from her, but she held on and laughed harder.

"But you *can* see it, Jon," Naomi said between gasps of air. "You praised me for putting some weight on. I didn't put on weight. I'm pregnant!"

"Yes. Yes, you are." As often as they'd talked about it by now, he could still not wrap his mind around it. He recalled seeing her kneeling in that church high up in the hills above Positano where her cousin Ferro had been painting a mural of the Annunciation and lighting a candle to the Virgin. It seemed as if her prayers had been answered instantly. "Why didn't you tell me earlier, Naomi? You must have known earlier, right?"

She didn't look at him. "I wasn't sure. All the traveling, all the upheaval, sometimes strange things happen to a woman's body. And I didn't want to say anything before I'd seen the doctors. There was a possibility, well, there was a chance..." Her words dwindled away.

He didn't want to hear it, didn't want her to say there was still a danger of losing the baby. Sitting here with her, in the lull of a late morning while the warmth of the fall sun dripped into the room through the window, Jon realized he didn't even want to think about it. The musical, the work at the theater, even the ideas he'd been harboring for a new album, all these paled in the face of this enormous thing, the birth of a new child. Kevin's dire words rang in his head like a terrible bell.

"I'll just have to take very good care of you," he said. "Pamper and spoil you even more." His hands wrapped around her feet. "And, Naomi, no more secrets, I beg you. Please tell me up front, okay? No more overnight flights, no more trying to spare me. We're in this together."

"But, Jon."

He started shaking his head, but she went on. "Jon, there was a real chance they would tell me I couldn't have the baby. I wanted to spare you that. I didn't want you to know. I didn't want you to have to make that decision. I know how much you want another child, and..."

"Shut up."

Surprised, she looked up.

"Do you even know what you're saying, Naomi?" Jon's voice sounded rough with hurt. "Do you realize what you're telling me? You were going to go through this on your own, once again, on your own, cutting me out of your life, when this is something that concerns both of us like nothing else? Why, please, why do you keep doing this?" She opened her mouth to reply but he held up his hand in a weary gesture. "Please. Don't. I don't know what I have to do to make you understand that I'm very capable of taking on the responsibility of a family. You still don't trust me. You still carry a residue of that drug raid around with you, when I left you alone. You still do."

So many years later, and it still wasn't over. The guilt settled on his shoulders like leaden armor: hard, unforgiving, heavy.

Naomi leaned forward to touch his wrist. "Jon, listen to me." She waited until he raised his head. "Jon, that's not it at all. Why do you think you have a say in this? It's my body!"

"Because, you dumb chick, because I'm your bloody husband. That's why." He wanted to shake her, shake those stupid ideas right out of her. "Haven't I told you, haven't I shown you over and over again that you can trust me and rely on me? What will it take for you to finally let me into your life? What makes you think I'd leave you alone if the doctors would have told you to have an abortion?"

"But you are, Jon," she said softly. "You are in my life. You are the only person in the whole wide world I trust without reservation, and you should know it." It took her a moment before she could go on. "There would never have been an abortion. I can hardly speak that word, let alone think of going through it. There would have been no way, no way at all that I'd have given up this child." It took her a couple of deep breaths before she said, "It's not your decision, Jon. You don't get to decide who lives and who dies, me or the baby. That's my decision alone. And I'd have decided for the baby, and for you." A small, sad shrug, then: "But it doesn't matter now, does it? We can have it all. You can have it all: the baby, and me. We can stop this discussion now." A tentative smile appeared on her pale face. "We've been through enough crap, Jon." Her smile grew mellow, a little sad. "When you walked into the door of the Seaside, when you found me in Norway, I knew right away that I wanted you back. I wanted you back, and nothing else mattered. I'd have jumped into the sea then and there if that's what it would have taken to get you back. I'd have willingly died for just one night in your arms. I knew it wouldn't be easy, and yet I wanted you back. I knew we were in for a lot of trouble. You're always trouble!"

For just a moment he gazed at her, torn between exasperation and amusement.

"Life with you wasn't easy when we were young, and it's not easy now," Naomi went on with a sigh.

"What do you mean, it's not easy?" Jon pushed her feet from his legs and jumped up. "I'm trying to make it as easy as I possibly can, and I've even given up touring! Hell, babe, I've changed my entire life for you!

Look at me; I'm here, am I not? As domesticated as can be, I'm even smoking outside!"

She giggled. "Yes, yes, and no more girlfriends and no more Hollywood parties—I know, you silly man! Sit down and let me finish!"

"Like hell! I'm not going to sit here and listen to you telling me I'm difficult to live with!" In a dramatic gesture, he laid his hand on his chest. "I flew all the way from lovely, sunny LA into the permafrost of Halmar to win you back. I lived with cold feet and pickled fish for months just to win you back! I learned to speak that friggin' language so I could at least buy my own cigarettes, and I shared that tiny apartment with you! Don't tell me I'm not easy to live with!"

Helpless with laughter, Naomi reached out to him, but he stepped back. "No, I'm not going to let you smooch me into compliance! Tell me why I'm not easy to live with!"

"Because you're who you are, Jon!" She balled up the cushion and threw it at him. Jon caught it and tossed it onto the bed. "Because you insist on carting me around in that monstrous car, and I have to drag along two bodyguards; but you know all that! Because your music has always been your first love, and everyone, even me, has to step aside for her. Because you're as famous as Elvis, as rich as Rockefeller, and as popular as Kennedy; and I have to share you with the entire world. Oh God, there are so many reasons why life with you is not easy, but not one of them is your fault! Please come back and sit with me?"

"Nah, I won't."

"Jon, you are acting like a child! Come here!" Imperiously, she slapped the couch.

"Naomi." Serious again, Jon sat down. "I'm still gnawing on this bone that you've thrown me, the fact that you wouldn't have told me if there had been reasons for you not to have the baby. You would have gone through this nightmare all by yourself again. I want you to stop making these decisions without me. I want you to stop thinking you have to do this on your own! We are married. We do these things together; we make these decisions together!"

She crept onto his lap and curled up in his arms when he put them around her.

"I'm telling you, there was no decision to make. I wouldn't have had an abortion," Naomi softly said. "Not for anything in the world. No matter what they would have told me. I'd not have killed your baby. I didn't do it back then, Jon, with Josh, and I wouldn't do it now. That's why I didn't want you to know before they said it was okay. "

"I wouldn't let you be in danger. You're more important than any baby in the world to me." The tips of his fingers traced her hairline, followed the curve of her chin, and came to rest on her collarbone. "I've told you often enough, I need you. You are my heartbeat, and my every breath."

"You have to promise me," he heard her say against his chest, "you have to promise me, Jon, that I can die before you. I don't think I could take a single day without you anymore. Don't leave me behind alone. Promise. Not ever. Promise."

The pain of his love for her stuck in his throat. "I promise," Jon replied. "I promise I'll survive you for an hour. That's as much as I could bear. That's the limit of it. I'd probably inhale your last breath and drop dead right after."

She shifted. "Oh cool, are you telling me I'd exhale toxic fumes? Seriously, Jon. First of all, I'll be at least a hundred years old when I die. Which makes you even older. And my last breath will be a whiff of rose scent, and it will definitely not kill you."

With a sigh, Jon lifted her from his lap and got up. "Well, I hope we won't have to worry about that for at least another fifty years or so. And in the meantime, I think we should go and get some lunch. I'm starving; what about you?"

Naomi nodded. "Yes. Jon, my parents are back from their trip to Europe. We should go meet them and…"

"Yes." He still felt uncomfortable at the thought of facing her stern father, but it was not as bad as it used to be. Pushing his hand into his pocket, Jon touched his cell phone, a slim, silvery thing that elegantly snapped open at the flick of his thumb. Olaf had sent it, together with a pink version for Naomi, just after she had been safely returned from the abduction. Jon recalled only too well Olaf's mild disdain at his outdated, slightly battered phone and how he had hated being patronized by his father-in-law.

"Yes," he repeated, "we should go and tell your parents. They have a right to know."

chapter 12

NAOMI LOOKED AROUND as she walked through the lobby of the hotel,

It felt strange to be here, in the same place where she had run into Parker, where the abduction had actually started. She had insisted on taking the front entrance instead of driving into the garage and using the elevator. She wanted to retrace those steps and relive that moment.

Jon, holding her elbow, murmured that she was torturing herself for nothing, but Naomi shook her head.

She couldn't. She needed to face this, and drive out the last demons of the past.

"If that's how you feel," Jon muttered as they waited for the elevator, "Then you should put running from me on your list, because that's what starts all the trouble. You, running away. Every time."

"I didn't run away from you." Naomi wiped some fingerprints off the brass plate surrounding the elevator buttons with the sleeve of her jacket. "I called you on the phone to tell you where I was going, and why. That's not running away."

"But you didn't give me a chance to join you. You left me all alone there in Vegas."

"Oh, good grief, Jon." His plaintive tone made her grin.

"No, it's true. I mean, just imagine!" They were alone in the elevator, and he turned toward her, his hands raised in a dramatic gesture. "I was on that huge stage, in that huge venue, and there were all these people in the audience, their eyes like saucers after a day at the slot machines, their stomachs full to bursting after gorging at all those buffets they'd raided; and there I stand, singing my heart out, and the only one who cares takes off and leaves me there to rot."

He looked just the way he had when he had walked into the Seaside that day, just one and a half years ago. Just like that, and it almost made her wilt with desire. Jon had a penchant for black leather jackets, and, she had to admit, she had never seen a man who wore them with such panache. On him they looked natural, as if they had been invented for him. There was no gray in his hair yet; it was just as black and thick as ever, and his face hardly had any wrinkles except around the corners of his eyes, where laughter had etched them into his skin.

"You're my husband," Naomi said, her voice hushed and slow with the wonder of it. "You, the only man I've ever desired. You'll be mine until the end of time. I'll not let you go."

"Yeah, babe." He held her against the mirrored wall, his hands firmly on her waist. "You have such a talent for making these grand speeches in hotels. You can say what you want, but you're your father's daughter. And yes. I'm your husband. And I'll not let go of that privilege easily."

She squirmed when the elevator doors hissed open, but Jon ignored it. His kiss was breathtaking, deep, almost like an act of love all in itself, consuming her.

"There," he said, amused satisfaction in his voice when he felt her knees give way. "That should satisfy your need for dramatic scenes in elevators for a while."

Lucia opened the door. She took one look at Naomi and clasped her hands to her chest. "You're pregnant."

Jon, watching them, wondered how she was able to tell. Naomi had not changed yet. It was true, her waist was a little fuller, and she looked healthy in a way she hadn't in months; but that was all. It made him realize that for him, a pregnant woman was someone with a very big belly, someone near birth, and it made him happy in a special, quiet way. Here, now, with his own wife, he was experiencing the entire process.

He followed them inside, for the first time since that day after Naomi's abduction when she had faced down her father and wrangled one of the family's hotels from him, the one in Positano. Even then, watching his father-in-law, Jon had suspected that Olaf had been using that hotel as bait for Naomi, knowing very well she would not be able to resist. There had been that special smirk on his face, the same one he could see on her when she thought she had beaten the world.

The penthouse was filled with light. It seemed to stream in through all the windows, from all sides, and float in the rooms in clouds of gold.

The furnishings and decor had changed since they had last been here. There were books lined up on the shelves and paintings on the walls by artists he knew quite well by now. In the hallway and library he could see Canadian art, but when they stepped into the large living room, he stopped in his tracks.

This style he knew only too well. Propped against a wall, ready to be hung, were two paintings by Ferro—Naomi's cousin. Jon had never seen an artist with his understanding of beauty, his grasp of light. They were landscapes. Jon had seen them before, the day Ferro had taken him to his studio high up under the roof of his father's palazzo, and he felt a twinge of regret at not having bought them himself.

It was almost like being back in Italy, back in that little church on the hillside meadow, and finding Ferro there at work on his murals.

Even though they were in a penthouse at the corner of Broadway and Columbus Circle, even though he could hear the drone of the Manhattan traffic and smell the city, he felt as if he had been returned to that peaceful, quiet place. He had loved it there, loved the perfume of the flowers and the cool, musty scent of incense inside the building. That day, in that spot high above the sea, Naomi's view of herself had shifted, and she had begun accepting herself as an artist, had begun to let her creativity flow, and write in earnest.

The memory of her distress before that made Jon want to turn around and search for Olaf to punch him in the face. His fault, it was all his fault. Everything was his fault, and his friendliness now could not change what he had done in the past.

It had been so easy to find investors for the musical, ridiculously easy. And Jon was certain it was not the fact that he was the composer. Naomi had delivered a brilliant script. The lyrics she had written flowed with his music from the first moment, as if by being married, their creative spirits had become one. His melodies had embraced her words just as he embraced her; they were one.

"We brought these back. Ferro said something about a painting he did of Naomi, but he didn't let us see it. He said you, as the owner, had the right to see it first." Lucia regarded Jon, her head held at a graceful angle that reminded him a lot of Naomi. "He also said he was bringing it over himself so he could see where you want to hang it."

"Actually," Jon replied, stepping closer to the paintings, "I was thinking of talking to a gallery about showing his art."

"But Olaf has done that already." Pointing at the hallway, Lucia added, "Let's go share your news with him!"

The silliness of it all hit him when he saw Olaf sitting at his huge desk. Lucia had led them into his office, and they were waiting for him to finish a phone conversation.

"No," Olaf was saying, "not the Gulf Coast, look for something in the Keys. Doesn't have to be a hotel, you could get a big mansion that we can convert. Just make sure it's on the water. And only stone or concrete buildings. We don't want it swept away by a hurricane." He glanced at Naomi. "Fine. Your mother just walked in. I'll say hello to her for you. Bye now."

A twinge of uneasiness pulled at Jon's stomach, but before he could comment, Olaf rose from his seat.

"You are pregnant." He pointed at Naomi's stomach. "Wonderful!" A smile spread on his spare, narrow face. "What a wonderful, great thing; what good news!"

Jon felt stupid. He tried to see her through her parents' eyes, tried to see if she really looked that different. She was in jeans and a loose, square-cut cashmere sweater. Her hair had grown out a bit, the thick curls nearly touching her shoulders. Just last night when he had held her in his arms, Jon had begged her not to cut it again, to let the long curls he loved so much return. Naomi had smiled at him sweetly and promised she would but to let her sleep now, please. Entranced, he had watched how she pulled the quilt all the way up to her ears and snuggled down beside him, her eyes closing even as she burrowed her head into the pillow.

His wife, pregnant with his child.

Quietly, so he wouldn't disturb her, Jon had lain, chin propped on his hand, watching as her breathing slowed and her contours softened in sleep. He had closed his eyes for a moment, wondering if she would be gone when he opened them again, gone like a mirage, like a dream that seemed to linger after waking: but she was still there, her lips slightly parted, her fingers gripping the edge of the quilt.

Jon had gently reached for them, pried them from their hold, and held them in his own. Like that, he had at last fallen asleep.

"WE MUST CELEBRATE," Olaf said into his thoughts; "I will take you out for lunch. Where would you like to go, Naomi?"

"Well," she replied, hooking her arm through her mother's, "I was thinking of taking you to the theater so you can see what we're up to there. But lunch? Lunch sounds great. Can we go to Carnegie's? I want a really big pastrami sandwich."

Jon groaned, but Olaf's lips twitched into a smile. "Ah, you're just like you were with Joshua. Meat and pickles. No sweet stuff for you."

And this, Jon realized, was something else he had not thought about.

Olaf and Lucia, they knew. They had been there for her pregnancy with Joshua; they knew what she would look like soon, what she would crave, and how she would feel. For an instant he felt the bite of jealousy, but then gladness took over, and a fine measure of relief. She had done it before. She would be all right.

"Jon." Olaf came around the desk to clap him on the shoulder. "I think this calls for a cigar, a really special one. Come with me."

There was a room next to the office, something like a library, a gentleman's smoking salon, a relic from another age when wealthy people changed into evening clothes for dinner. Except for a couple of Chesterfields and small side tables there wasn't a lot of furniture, but there were lots of books. Most of them were leather-bound, the titles stamped on the back in gold.

The view from the large window was glorious. All the buildings of lower Manhattan stood in line for the owner of the Carlsson empire.

"I have this habit." Olaf gestured at the shelves lining the walls. "If I like a book and can't get a good hardcover copy, I have it bound for me. Paperbacks are so vulgar, don't you think? And leather, it's so much nicer to hold in your hand, and it smells so good too."

Jon nodded, remembering how Naomi had dropped that book about Ahab's wife in his lap, calling him an illiterate punk. No paperbacks for her, either. She was more her father's daughter than she would admit.

From a wooden box on one of the tables Olaf removed two cigars. "What did the doctors say?" His voice sounded as calm and cool as ever, but Jon could see the tension in his posture.

A plane glided past high above, its wings glinting in the sun. Jon could hear the soft drone, and he wondered where it was bound. "They told her to take it easy and be careful. They said the second half will be hard on her, and she will have to rest a lot. Her heart..." He couldn't go on. He couldn't say those words, couldn't repeat what Kevin had told him, not to Olaf. The burden of guilt for the shooting came to rest on his shoulders, a suffocating, heavy, terrible weight.

"Yes." Olaf's jaw tightened. "Her heart." The cigar's wrapper crackled softly as he rolled it between his fingers. "Naomi was always healthy before. She wasn't very happy with her life, but she was healthy. As fragile as she looks, she was as strong as a horse."

Jon nodded. There was nothing to say.

"So now," Olaf went on, "now she is pregnant; and, knowing my daughter, I have a feeling she wants to have this baby more than her own life. I'm quite sure she is doing this because she thinks she owes it to you; am I right? She thinks she owes you a baby after having kept Joshua from you."

He grinned, but it was more like a shark showing his teeth than a gesture of friendliness.

"We had many talks about it," Jon conceded, "and yes, you're right. But there's nothing I could do about it except…well, except." There was no way he was going to admit to his father-in-law how madly in love he was with Naomi, in fact even more than before. It seemed, Jon mused, that every day they were together, the bond grew stronger, his need for her more urgent. Somewhere in his mind he heard the hum of a new melody stirring with this feeling, and he wondered if he'd find the words himself or if he would have to turn to Naomi for them.

"You are useless, both you and your wife, my daughter." Olaf reached for the box of matches lying on the table. "Useless, like children. Starry-eyed. With all this wild love and your thoughtlessness, you stumble from one dangerous situation to the next. The shooting wasn't enough; you needed an abduction, and now this—life threatening, serious, dangerous."

"Believe me." Jon shook his head when Olaf offered the lit match. "Believe me, we want nothing more than a quiet, peaceful life. We're trying very hard to have that."

Olaf snorted. "Like hell you are." He blew out the little flame. "Jon, I like you a lot better now than I did before, seeing how you are a lot like me, tougher than I thought, and in fact a very good businessman. But it's sad to see that your brain stops working as soon as Naomi enters the picture. You're a besotted idiot, that's what you are. You're a wuss where my daughter is concerned; she has you wrapped around her little finger. You're like a fly in her spider's web, and the first thing she sucked out of you was your brain."

"Yes." His heart grew lighter as Jon listened to Olaf's verdict.

Olaf's lips twitched. "Yes. So you don't even deny it."

From the living room, they could hear Lucia's laughter, and Naomi replying.

Jon turned toward the door. "Well, I don't really like being called a wuss." His hand on the doorknob, he added, "But I do admit my heart turns to mush at the mere thought of my wife. Don't worry, Olaf. I'll take good care of her."

"Jon."

The tone made him stop and wait.

"Jon, what if her body can't take it? What if you have to make a decision? How will you deal with that?"

He didn't want to hear it. He didn't even want to think about it, or see it as a possibility. "I don't know. I'm praying it won't come to that. But you can be sure, Olaf, I'll let no harm come to Naomi." The words made his heart break. "I will not let her come to harm. This I can promise."

"That's a pretty cynical promise," Olaf said, "seeing as she's been almost killed twice since becoming your wife."

AS JON HAD expected, Olaf was not impressed with either the theater or the casting process. He sat in the third row with the same bored attitude he had shown at the concert in Geneva only a few months ago.

"So," he drawled, "you found investors for this folly of yours, I take it? I hope you're not throwing my daughter's money away here."

Something in Jon snapped. It wasn't a violent, sudden snap but more of a slow, gentle breaking, like soft bread coming apart in his fingers.

Turning toward the stage, he watched as Wilfred herded another group of young actors onto the stage. They had been at it for two weeks now, against Stan's bitter protest. Insane, he'd said, utterly insane and totally unheard of, but Jon didn't care. He didn't care about their résumés either. He wanted to get an impression of the personality and of how they presented themselves in the limelight.

"You never know," he'd told Stan, "how someone will suddenly bloom when presented with the right song and setting."

To which Stan had replied that he'd been in the business long enough, thank you very much; he knew exactly when he'd hit gold, and if Jon would shut up and not interfere anymore, he'd find what he was looking for in an hour's time.

"Don't worry about your Carlsson millions," he said to Olaf, "I wouldn't ask for money from you if I was down to my last dime. I'd rather stand in Times Square with just my guitar and live on what people throw into my hat than ask you for anything, ever, Olaf. It's hard for me to imagine anything worse than owing you." On the point of turning away, he added, "And my wife, Olaf, she doesn't need your money either. I can provide for my family without charity from you."

"Charity, good grief." Impatiently, Olaf slapped the back of the seat in front of him. "You and Naomi, you're always so dramatic. I was about to ask if you needed funding or if there's a way to buy into this venture, and you jump down my throat."

Naomi had walked up to the edge of the stage, where she was talking to Stan, watching the group intently. Her hand came out, and Stan, with a bark of a laugh, laid the microphone into her palm.

Intrigued, Jon moved toward her, forgetting Olaf almost instantly.

She was holding the thing nearly in the same reverend way she had held onto her Oscar statuette, and it made Jon smile. He'd never seen her with a microphone before. So many times he'd asked her to go onstage with him, sing a duet, even record a song, knowing she had a lovely voice.

Before they had met, before he had met her in Geneva and plucked her out of her life, she had been studying at a conservatory, had been trained to be a singer; but she had given it up, like everything else, for his sake.

"You." Naomi's voice sounded a little uncertain, but it echoed nicely through the theater. "You, with the red hair and the blue sweater."

A girl stepped forward.

Jon's heart skipped a beat.

Sophie had never worn that shade of blue, stating with disdain that no redhead in her right mind should try to set off the color of her hair by wearing turquoise. He remembered only too well how he'd once, only once, been shopping with her when she needed a gown for some kind of party, and he had suggested one to her, a lovely, gossamer thing in peacock hues. She had laughed at him and, as always, bought a black one. He had refused to take her out in black, and she hadn't wanted to go on her own either. They had spent the evening at her apartment, not talking much, having sex, until Jon had up and left her. Alone, he had driven through the city and out to his little beach house, where he had poured a large drink and stood staring at the pictures of

Naomi, the only things in that place that were kept clean and in order.

Sophie, and he had ditched her cruelly with a phone call from the airport the day he had finally found out where Naomi was.

Sophie, who had lost her mind over it and shot Naomi at the Oscars and who had died herself that day.

Even then, Jon realized now, sauntering toward Naomi, even then he had picked things that Naomi would have liked, that he would have wanted to see on her and no one else.

"Please let your hair down," Naomi said.

The girl complied, reaching up for the braid coiled on top of her head in a fluid motion. She had the thin, fleshless elegance of a dancer, with bones shimmering like alien parasites under her translucent skin.

"Your name?"

Jon grinned. It wasn't that Naomi sounded unfriendly, not at all; but her tone was so brisk it bordered on the impatient and so cool it almost made him stand up as straight as the kids on the stage.

"Eva," the girl replied, and Jon nearly sighed in relief. The spooky moment was over, and she was just another pretty, red-headed actress. His attention returned to Naomi.

"Do you know what we want you to do here?" Her arm resting on the edge of the stage, she was looking up.

"Of course." The hair came down, a wild tumble of red and gold, all the way to her hips.

Seeing those curls nearly broke Jon's heart. Naomi's had been that long, as black as night, fat tendrils to wrap around his hands and body when they were in bed making love. On a whim, she had cut them off in Hamburg. She'd slipped out on her own to go to a salon. He had hardly recognized her when he saw her later that morning.

"Well, then." She gestured toward the piano. "Get the music and let's hear you sing."

Eva obeyed without hesitation. She whispered with the pianist for a moment, cleared her throat, and declared, "I'm ready," before launching into the "Mermaid Song."

"Why that one, dear heart?" Jon laid his hands on Naomi's shoulder, standing close behind her. "Why a redhead?"

She leaned into him. "Because I think the fishtail costume I want will look great on her, Jon." Putting the microphone down, she turned into his embrace. "Green, blue, purple. I want the fishtail to look like peacock feathers. Brilliant, beautiful, dazzling." She gestured at Eva. "And golden fish scales up her spine, flowers in her hair. She will be beautiful up there."

His breath curled up into a knot. She knew. She always knew. She shared his visions as if she were a part of him. She made the universe stand still in these moments of creativity. Without taking his eyes off Naomi, Jon reached for the microphone.

It was so easy. The moment he opened his mouth, the song drifted from him, his voice soaring, mingling with Eva's sweet soprano, setting it off beautifully. Startled for a moment, she blinked and missed a beat, but then she found the words, gazing down at Jon in open admiration. But Jon didn't see her. He was singing to the woman in his arms.

chapter 13

SO FAR THERE was only a mattress on the floor and a coffeemaker in the kitchen.

The loft looked almost as empty as it had four weeks ago, when he had made Maya go furniture shopping with him.

He had taken her out for lunch in Chinatown and introduced her to Peking duck. Pleased, and quite intrigued, he had watched her try to figure out which spices had gone into the plum sauce by letting it melt on her tongue, her chin propped on her hand, her eyes half closed.

"Star anise," she had mumbled between bites. "Definitely that, but what else?" Popping another morsel into her mouth, she had added, "Garlic, that's for sure. Oh, I love this. I love how the meat is all crackly and spicy and the sauce so sweet and velvety!"

Sal had asked her what kind of food they served at their deli, and she had closed up, her eyes shuttering like windows in the face of a storm. There hadn't been a good reply either, and they had parted soon after, strangers again, the moment of fun and ease blown away by his innocuous question.

He had watched her as she walked away in those high heels, her hips swaying gently, hair fluttering in the autumn breeze. For an insane, wild instant, Sal had been on the verge of going after her, calling her to come back to him, spend the rest of the day and maybe even the night.

Frightened by this sudden impulse, he had drawn back and pushed his hands deep into his pockets when she had turned around to wave at him before descending the subway stairs.

It hadn't been that her smile died; it was more of a drying up, like the withering of a bloom.

HIS BACK MADE a funny sound when he rose from the makeshift bed on the floor, and he winced. His Boy Scout camping days seemed to be over for good.

The chalk marks on the floor made him grin as he padded over to the kitchen counter to start the coffee.

Maya had put them there, saying it was the only place for a bed in this loft, even if it was two steps above the rest of the room. A four-poster had been her decision, a huge four-poster with billowy, white curtains that would move in the breeze.

Sal had pointed out that there would be no breeze, just the drone of the heating or the AC, and she had gazed at him thoughtfully.

"But how," she had asked, "will you hear the sounds of the city and the river, and smell the air?"

And Sal had stared, first at her and then at the room, seeing that bed in his mind, seeing exactly how the windows would be wide-open and he'd be lying there at night, listening to the sirens and the ship's horns calling to each other.

"I need art," he had replied, "some paintings, some sculptures, and music. A stereo and a TV."

Maya had tilted her head and looked at him. "You seem like a lost boy. What did you own, how did you live?"

They had talked about it before, but now, this time, he had explained that his apartment in LA was really no more than a transient accommodation, something where he could go to at night and sleep.

"I'm always busy." He had shrugged, digging in his pocket for his cigarettes. "There wasn't a lot time to get domestic in LA."

"And now you have time?" Her brows had come up at the smoke that drifted across the room, meandering toward the patio door. "Now you want to settle down, and you pick a loft?"

"Yeah." Without her having to say it, he had gone outside and stood in the drizzle of the cool day. "I think I want to settle down."

THERE WAS NO coffee.

He'd forgotten to go shopping again. Sal realized he hadn't done much the past few weeks except sleep and eat, and the place looked it.

Dirty laundry was lying around, used takeout containers littered the kitchen sink, and the fridge was empty.

He needed a housekeeper, or at least a cleaning woman, and quickly.

None of them had ever bothered to look after themselves. There was too much living to do, too much work, too much partying, and too much touring.

Jon's needs had dictated their lives, and now that he had retired, Sal found himself at loose ends. So far he hadn't even gone to the theater to see how things were coming along, waiting for Jon to call him, ask him to join them; but there had been only silence.

Jon didn't need him anymore.

Sal didn't even dare go and visit them again, or drop in to see Naomi, the way he had always done in Malibu.

Everything was different. It felt as if the drawbridge to her castle had been pulled up, as if Jon had built a wall of thorns and nails around the house and her, it was that quiet, that still.

Dolefully Sal peered into the coffee tin. It had been good, bought at a small store for an impertinent price, but it had been worth it.

Maya had picked it, and even told the barista how she wanted it ground. As always, he had watched her do things, watched her move and talk without ever touching her, without ever attempting to. Not even here, alone in his new home, had he tried anything.

It seemed as if she was too precious, too special, not one of the girls he normally seduced and left behind.

On an impulse, he put the tin on the counter and went to get dressed. It was Sunday, not too late in the morning, it was raining, and he was alone, all by himself in a town where he didn't want to be, in an apartment that was empty, cold, and way too still.

Out on the street there were hardly any cars. From the highway he could hear the constant sound of traffic, but down here on South Street, it was quiet.

His hands in his pockets and a cigarette between his lips, Sal made his way up to Water Street. For a few minutes he stood on the corner, his toes touching the curb, then raised his arm to hail a cab.

Atlantic Avenue, he knew that much. Not too far from the river. A deli—there couldn't be that many Pakistani delis over there.

He would find it.

As always when he went across the Brooklyn Bridge, Sal gazed down at the green edge of the Promenade and the spot where he knew her house, Naomi's house, was hidden among the trees. He wondered if they were home, having coffee in the conservatory, whiling away their time in the studio, or maybe she still was in bed, dreaming, sleeping.

Even though she was so close now, no more than twenty minutes away, it seemed to him that the East River was more of a barrier than the Atlantic had ever been. It was so hard to envision them in that house, living a quiet, domestic life away from everything that had meant anything to Jon before.

Sal battled the urge to tell the cab driver to turn onto Hicks and go back toward Pierrepont. He could see himself getting out on the corner of Montague and walking down toward the Promenade. Walking past those lovely old brownstones and looking up at their windows, maybe even dropping by Russ and Solveigh's new home, only a couple of blocks away on a small street with the name of a fruit.

"Where on Atlantic?"

The driver's question made him snap back to reality. "Here is fine."

Once more he stood on a street corner, lost in this city, only this time on the other side of the river.

Sal couldn't be sure, but somehow Atlantic Avenue felt different from a street in Manhattan. There was the tiniest hint of provincialism, of slowing down and Sunday-morning sleepiness. A couple of shops were just opening; at a café on the other side of the road, some girls were busy taking the chairs off the tables and distributing menus.

Mindless of the traffic lights, Sal walked across and into the café. The scent of fresh coffee was almost overpowering. Homesickness sliced through him. He felt alone. Alone, and old in a way he never had before. His bones creaked in a weariness he'd never known, as if with the slowing of his life, his body had remembered its age.

Fifty. His lips refused to speak the word, and his tongue was in a gnarl over it; but here it was: all he had to do was turn around twice, and that number would be calling his name.

"Coffee," he managed when the barista looked at him expectantly. "Make that extra-large, black, no sugar."

There was no one else around.

"I'm looking for a deli," Sal said, which earned him a puzzled glance, so he went on, "a Pakistani deli. Family owned. It's supposed to be here somewhere."

"Oh." The girl put a lid on his paper cup. "It's down on the next corner. Ansari's. They make really good curries." She gestured vaguely to the left. "And their samosas are to die for!"

With a nod of thanks and his coffee, Sal returned to the coolness of the November day. Now that he knew where it was, he could see it.

A blue awning flapped in the breeze, the name faded, hiding the windows in its shade. There were a few trash cans pushed sloppily against the wall, beside the iron rail of the basement stairs, and a stand displaying fruit next to the entrance. The door was closed, and from inside no movement, no light could be seen.

A million places, Sal had seen a million places like this one. For some strange reason, he had expected more. He had thought that her home, the home where Maya lived, would be more glamorous, more stylish, something funky and fusion-like, and not this shabby little grocery store on a street corner in Brooklyn. She had such sure, good taste and such a talent to pick the nicest and most expensive pieces.

He had asked her, over their last lunch, why she always carried that ugly black purse, always the same one—he was sure she must have others; but she had shaken her head, again with that trace of sullenness, and replied that she hated fakes. She would not be caught with a fake naked and dead in Central Park.

"Fake?" Sal had stolen a piece of duck from her plate, and she had slapped his hand.

The meat had stuck in his throat at her response. With a disdainful shrug, with the same gesture he knew so very well from Naomi, she had said, "I want the real thing. If I can't afford a real Gucci purse, I'll not get one at all. No fakes for me."

He had offered right then and there to buy her one, just for fun, just because the weather was nice; but she had declined huffily, stating that she would not accept any presents from him, thank you, and he'd better wait and see. Someday she'd walk into that shop and buy it with her own money.

AND NOW HE understood.

Slowly, Sal pushed open the door to the deli.

Music greeted him. The warbling Bollywood tune made him feel slightly dizzy and brought back some of the manager in him. He knew the composer; they'd met at a Hollywood movie premier. He'd rather liked the small man with the impish grin. Of course, as always, the conversation had turned to Jon—his talent, his project, his voice, and finally, whether there was a chance of a collaboration, of working together on a movie score or some other project.

Sal shook himself out of his memories.

There was a nook with a few tables for guests, and he made his way there, sitting at the one closest to the window. From here he had a good view of the street, and the inside of the deli. It wasn't the cleanest place he'd ever seen, and it was certainly not fancy. The owner either had no interest in or no knack for making it look inviting and tasteful; and yet, in its own slapdash way, it had a charm all its own, a bit reminiscent of older, crazier days, as if it was run by an old hippie.

A movement in the back caught his attention. The awful fly curtain moved, its orange, red, and purple beads rattled softly; and there she was, Maya. Sal had no idea why his heart dropped the way it did or why he sat up straight, clearing his throat like a teenager.

She looked so different in her Indian garb, a knee-length blouse worn over wide cotton trousers, with a matching shawl over her shoulders. Her braid swung down her back, her feet in cloth slippers, and on her wrist an array of colorful bangles chimed as she moved.

The menu in hand, she came over to him, distracted by something, and didn't even glance his way until she stood beside his table.

"You look very pretty in that," Sal said.

Every drop of blood drained from her face. It was, he thought, a trite and totally boring observation, but that was what happened: within a second, she was as pale as a ghost.

"What are you doing here?" It was nearly a hiss, frantic and hasty, and for an instant he thought she was going to slap him with the menu.

"I want breakfast." He was enjoying himself more than he had expected. "I had a hankering for something exotic, so I came here. So. What should I eat?"

Maya cast a nervous glance back toward the curtained doorway. "Sal, please, you can't be here. If my father sees you..."

"Nah, I'm staying." With a grin, he leaned back in his chair. "You wouldn't come to Manhattan to see me, so I have come here to see you. Breakfast, please."

She didn't respond.

"And what a great idea," Sal went on. "I think I'll do this every day now since there isn't anything else for me to do and my loft is still not furnished. You promised you'd help, remember, and then you walked out on me."

From the back, they heard voices, a man's and a young girl's, some shouting from upstairs, and trampling on the stairs.

Maya pressed her lips together, dithering. Then she replied, "If you let on that we know each other, my father will kill me. So please, Sal, if you care for me at all, don't say anything."

"Tea," he said out loud, and took the menu from her. "And what do you recommend?"

She rolled her eyes and walked away.

The curtain rustled again and parted for a man around his own age. Sal guessed that he had once been a very slender young man, with fine bones and a narrow face, but now he had run to fat and resembled a caterpillar with his rolls of flesh and double chin. His black hair was glossy and very curly, too long to be well-groomed but not long enough to be a serious statement. Just like Maya, he was in traditional clothing, only on him it looked as if he was wearing the pajamas he had slept in.

His face, though, was friendly enough, and when a little girl of maybe five burst through the curtain, he opened his arms to catch her in an embrace.

"Tea." Maya put down the glass rather forcefully, spilling a little on the Formica tabletop. "I'll bring your breakfast in a moment."

"When can I see you?" Sal quickly asked, on the verge of grasping her hand.

Without a reply she left.

Her father was looking his way, inspecting Sal briefly, nodding a greeting; but he did not come over. Instead, he turned to Maya when she came to the counter and talked softly to her. She shrugged and then flipped her wrist in such an elegant and disdainful way that it made Sal want to go over, grab her around the waist, and kiss her. Shocked by his own impulse, he gazed out the window. A couple in their thirties was walking past. The man was pushing a baby stroller. His wife was eating a bagel, laughing at something he had said. They looked so serene and happy that Sal sighed.

Brooklyn was not the best place for him. He could just imagine them like that: Jon, with his new baby, and Naomi, smiling at him, popping a piece of bread into her mouth, just like that. So close, just a few blocks away, and yet they lived on a different planet now.

"Samosas." She slammed down the plate with the same verve as the tea a moment earlier and stood beside him, waiting.

Sal eyed the golden brown triangles and inhaled their spicy aroma. "What's in them?"

"Potato in one, meat in the other. Lamb." Again she rolled her eyes at him. "You can also have some pakoras if you want, but it's a bit early for curry."

"You look so cute when you're angry, I never realized. Why don't you sit with me and have breakfast too?" He felt flirty, and he knew he was falling in love. It had been a good idea, coming here, the best idea since he'd come to New York.

"You are insane. I have to work, and my father would kill me." Maya pointed at his food. "Eat, and go."

"I'm not." The samosas were delicious. Sal sighed with bliss as the paper-thin crust melted on his tongue and the flavor of the filling invaded his mouth.

"I'm not going anywhere until you've agreed to meet me again. I want to see you all the time." It came out a bit mangled with the potato bits in the way, but she understood.

"You're insane." With a furtive glance toward her father, she added, "Why, Sal? It's not as if we're dating or anything. I think it's wrong for you to stalk me like this, coming all the way here; it's indecent. I'm not your girlfriend!"

He took a sip of the tea. It was a mix of black and mint, liberally sweetened, and the perfect supplement for the hot food.

"Yeah. Maybe that's a mistake."

Something in her face changed. It was not that she looked older, or younger, or in any way different at all; but suddenly there was a softness, a tiny crinkling in the corners of her mouth, a general mellowing. She picked up the menu, fiddling with it, thinking.

"I'm off at four. Come back then. You can buy me dinner."

When she walked away, there was a swing in her hips that hadn't been there before. Sal was sure of it.

chapter 14

"A DAYBED," JON said, "or at least a comfy couch. Please, Naomi?"

She looked up from her computer, her fingers still resting on the keys, a distracted expression on her face.

"A couch?" Jon repeated patiently.

He loved it. He loved how this big room, the one she liked to call his studio, was really a mirror image of her apartment in Halmar.

Day by day she had brought in a little more of herself, pieces of what she needed to feel at home and comfortable, and he had let her, had allowed her to transform it into what it was now: another living room, with a grand in it, just like in Norway.

There was more than enough space on the third floor, practically unused by them so far, where he could spread out for serious work.

"You can't sit in that window seat all the time. It will soon get uncomfortable, and I'm afraid you'll catch a draft once it gets cold. So can't we buy you a couch? Or a chaise?"

She set aside the laptop and rose to stretch, her arms crossed behind her neck.

There it was. The bulge, the gentle swell of her belly, and he had to resist the urge to get up and run his hand over it just to feel the change in her body.

"Yes, a couch would be nice," Naomi said. "You are right about the draft. It is a bit cold here." Rubbing her back, she came over to him. "So we have a reason to go shopping? Can we go now? Can we have lunch somewhere?"

"You are so crazy. You and this city, what is it with you? We don't have to go out to buy a couch, for crying out loud. I'm sure we don't have to go anywhere for that; we just call an interior decorator and let them suggest something. You jump at any excuse at all to go into Manhattan."

Well-being. He couldn't find another word to describe it. The peace he had longed for so badly—the quiet, gentle life—here it was at last;

and it had come so fast and easy, almost as if, deep inside, they had known all along how it would be, how they wanted it, and the moment they had stepped through the door to this house, here it was, waiting for them.

"I'm thinking of calling Jane."

Jon reached out to her and pulled her onto his knees when she was close enough, listening to her.

"I want to call Jane and ask her to read what I've written. I want to know if it's good enough to go on or if I should start knitting again."

"So call her. We can take her out for lunch. I'm sure there's some nifty publishers' place somewhere in downtown where they all congregate, all of them dressed in black and taupe, looking important and snotty. I'm betting the drinks are really good too."

He cupped her belly with his hand. It felt like touching the smooth curve of a taut ball, something hidden deep inside of her with only part of the surface showing, a secret, a miracle.

"What have you written?"

She squirmed a bit. "I don't want to tell you just yet. You'll take it from me, with all your love and curiosity, and you'll tell me what you think, and then it will change because of your influence, and I don't want that to happen; I want it to be mine for a while, mine alone."

That only made him want to know even more. "But surely you can tell me what kind of book it is? Crime? Sci fi? Or romance? What are you writing?"

"None of those." With a blush, she tried to get away from him, but Jon held on. "It's just a novel. A story about people."

"But where did you get the idea? What made you decide to use this idea?" As always, he was intrigued by the way the creative process worked for her, so different from his own. Jon could feel her shrug.

"If I can pull it off. I've never written a book, only your little ditties. I know nothing about writing a book, about structure, or dialogue, or anything."

The tips of his fingers traced the bones of her shoulder, the smooth skin of her neck. Rose perfume lingered in her hair, in the wool of her sweater.

They had been shopping; she had needed new clothes badly, and everything was too tight now. How he had relished that, how he had loved to watch her try on maternity things. Jon had no idea if she did it intentionally or if it was an unconscious reflection of her imagination, but she picked brilliant colors.

No hiding in fashionable black or gray for Naomi; she wanted bright blues and violets that made her skin shine, and again he had been reminded of that peacock dress Sophie had refused so rudely.

"You have to come to the hospital next time," Naomi said into his thoughts. "Julian wants you to see the ultrasound. You can see the baby now, Jon."

"Yes." And how bitterly he had regretted that he had not been able to go along the last time, but there had been a meeting with the investors, and they wanted to see the famous face in person.

"You'll love it. You can actually see it move." She patted her stomach. "Like a little fish in a bowl, waving at Daddy."

"Daddy." He had to swallow. "Stop calling her it. She's not an it."

"You don't know it's a she yet."

"If we had a couch," Jon said, "we could sit on it now, snuggled up and comfy, instead of perching on the piano bench like teenagers squished into the backseat of an old car. Really." He loved how quiet it was in the house. The silence was like a down comforter, enveloping them despite the grandeur of the city across the water. It was almost as good as being in Halmar, in her little apartment, in the hotel, where there had been nothing but the water of the bay and the mountains in the distance. This was what he wanted. Quiet. Peace. A slowing of his life. And Naomi. He had it all.

"I could cook you lunch. We don't have to go out. I'd love to cook you lunch," Jon offered.

They had found that they didn't like having Lourdes around all the time. For some reason it was different here, having a housekeeper in the house. It felt cramped in a way it never had in LA. She had her own apartment in the same building with the security people, just the way Jon wanted: close, yet separate. He had learned how to put his small empire in order, and it worked very well.

"We have this huge house," Naomi replied. "It is so huge, Jon. We could put up our families easily, and we spend all the time in this one room, just like in Halmar. It's insane."

"Oh, I don't know." He lifted her from his lap so he could get up. "It will change soon enough. Once the baby is born there will be a nurse, and a nanny, and we'll have to have Lourdes here more often to do the chores. Life will be a lot livelier."

Only when he was halfway to the door did he realize she hadn't followed him but was still standing beside the Steinway.

"What? Lunch? You said you wanted to call Jane?"

"I'm not going to hand over my baby to a nurse, Jon. I raised Joshua on my own, without you, and I'm sure I can raise this one too."

"Baby." With a sigh, he went back to her and took her hand. "Baby, you don't have to. Maybe you even won't be able to. Please, let's think about it when the time comes, okay?"

"You talked to Kevin." Quite roughly, Naomi pulled her fingers out of his. "You talk to Kevin behind my back, and you make plans for me without asking me what I want. I'm right, am I not?"

Jon cursed himself and his thoughtless remark. Kevin had told him to break it to her gently, knowing so well how she would react, and knowing she would refuse this. "Yes. No. It came up. He thinks you'll need all your strength to get well again after the birth, and you should take care of yourself first and let someone else get up in the night to look after the baby. I think he has a good point. And please, for the love of God, can we please not have a fight about this right now?"

A deep crease appeared between her eyes, and her lips pinched together in a thin line. "Jon, I love you. I love you more than my life, more than I can say. In fact, I adore you, and everything about you. But please, please, don't reduce me like this. I'm your wife, a person, and not only this mother-thing you want me to be right now. Women all over the world have babies all the time, and I'm no different! Just because I'm married to you, and you're the father, doesn't mean this baby needs royal treatment. Stop fussing like that!"

"I'm not fussing, dammit!" Her outbreak had taken him completely by surprise. "I'm taking care of you, the way I'm supposed to, right, as a good husband and father. I know I missed out when you were pregnant with Joshua—we've been over that more times than I can count—and so I want to make sure I do it right this time. And I'm telling you, if Kevin thinks you'll be better off with a nurse, we're getting a nurse."

Her fist came down on the polished top of the grand, bringing out a fine ring from the strings. "And what if I don't want that? What if I don't want a stranger holding my baby at night? What if I want to do that myself?"

"Oh, good grief, Naomi, let's go and have lunch." Again he held out his hand to her, but she hid hers behind her back like an obstinate schoolgirl. "Come on, I'll take you downtown, and you can meet your publisher friend and talk shop."

And even though they were in deep waters again, on the brink of a bitter discussion, he could not muster the energy to feel annoyed or angry. In fact, he loved it. He loved the idea that he was having a fight with his wife, and he didn't have to fear that she would walk out on him again.

"Well, I want to hire her myself," Naomi muttered as he helped her into a jacket, "Seriously. I want to decide who we have in the house."

"Of course, darling." Anything, anything. He was ready to do anything at all to make her happy, he was that happy himself.

On the doorstep, breathing in the wet, slightly musty fall air, Jon looked around. The leaves were brown and dead, the flowers wilted. A deep, dark sky hung over Brooklyn; it was dusky despite being mid-day.

"Thanksgiving," he said, the thought popping into his head. "We should throw a big Christmas dinner. We should ask everyone over. Your family, mine, all our friends. Jane, too, and maybe even Stan."

Naomi put her arm through his. "And we need Christmas decorations. For the entrance, for the house! Yes! Let's do it!"

It didn't feel real. It still didn't feel real, somehow. It still felt as if he was walking in a dream, that everything was too good to be true, and he would wake up at some point and be his old, sad self, the lonely, drunken man in the empty beach house in LA.

But here she was, her face raised to him, with a smile and a gentle glow in her eyes, waiting for him to say something, reply to her; and Jon, helpless with love, caught her in an embrace and kissed her right then and there, and he didn't give a damn if there were paparazzi hanging around or not.

The car was being brought around by LaGasse, and she was holding the door for them, patiently waiting in the drizzle.

"Let's go buy a doll," he suggested, "a pretty doll in a pink dress. Maybe that'll make up the baby's mind and she'll pop out a girl."

Naomi sighed.

"And we should start thinking about a nursery. Where do you want it? How do you want it? What do we need?"

That made her stop on the garden path. "You know, less than you'd think. Joshua had a cot next to my bed, I changed his diapers there too. His things were in a couple of drawers in my wardrobe, and that was it. We didn't need more. The living room was his playground. We…"

As if she needed to separate herself from him to call up that memory, she took a step back and stood with her purse like a shield in front of her stomach.

"We lived a small, quiet life, day by day, the same routine, the same people, the same things to do. Joshua grew up in that hotel lobby. He learned to walk there, and he learned to ride his bike in the parking lot behind the building. We never went anywhere at all. You didn't miss much. It was boring, and very still."

"I didn't miss much? Are you out of your mind?" Gently, he took her face between his hands to plant a soft kiss on her lips. "I missed you. I missed you beside me in bed at night and with me during the day. I missed your voice, your touch, and the sound of your laughter. I missed you like I'd miss my heart, if it were ripped out and hidden away in a box somewhere. That's how much I need you."

"Maudlin!" She freed herself from his hold. "Maudlin, Jon Stone, and you aren't getting any better with age. Now, I'm going to have lunch with my publisher friend. And you, you should go check on Sal. I have the distinct feeling something fishy is going on over there. He never stays away this long if he can find an excuse not to."

She was right. Jon, waiting for her to climb into the car, realized she was right, and he hadn't even noticed, he had been so caught up in the slow, peaceful life they had carved out for themselves. He hadn't missed Sal and the others, who were still busy settling down and finding their bearings, and he hadn't gone out of his way to see them. Russ had dropped by a couple of times, getting more excited the closer the day came when Solveigh and the baby would join him. Sean had called to tell them he was not going to take up their offer of an apartment close by after all. He had his heart set on the New Jersey shore, and to hell with the commute. It resembled, in a gray, disheveled way, the California shore, and he wanted to live there. Jon had, in return, asked him if he had been smoking something or if he'd lost his marbles during the tour, but Sean was certain. It had to be New Jersey. What was good enough for Springsteen was good enough for him.

It wasn't funny, and when Jon had told Naomi about it she had blanched, recalling the nightmarish hours she had spent on that New Jersey beach after Parker had abducted her.

"Yes," he replied, "I'll do that. I'll call him and have lunch with him, while you meet Jane. And then we can go shopping for a doll." He patted her knee. "Make sure you take her to one of those places where all the publishers hang out. You want to get a feeling for the business, don't you?" Then he grinned. "I think you'll stick out. Don't these artsy New York people all wear black or taupe? You'll look like a bird of paradise among them in that bright blue sweater."

She shrugged. Jane, on the phone had mentioned a restaurant that wasn't too far from her office. Naomi had never been there or even heard of it.

"I wanted to take her to the Russian Tea Room, but she said I had to see where the publishing world flocks together. I'm not sure I'll feel at home there."

"Well, you don't have to. Have lunch with your friend, talk about your writing, and get out of there."

How normal. How confusingly normal their conversation was, this talk about meeting friends for a meal, of deciding where to go afterward, just like normal people.

Jon, leaning back into the seat, allowed himself to relax. Maybe, just maybe, it was going to work after all.

Maybe he was getting all that he had always hoped for now, a little late in life, but cherished all the more for it.

His hand once again found hers where it was resting on the leather and clasped it. She returned the pressure and held on.

chapter 15

THE PLATES WERE huge, the arrangements fanciful, but the portions so small they made Naomi want to weep.

Dolefully she stared at the minuscule steak and the three tiny potatoes before her and wished she had not wanted to see the place where the New York publishing world went for their business lunches.

The drinks, she had noticed, were not small. And they were carried past their table often, more often than food.

Jane was watching her with an amused twinkle in her eyes as she poked at the mushrooms in her risotto.

"It's nice," Naomi said in an attempt to be kind, "nice decor. And the desserts look great. A nice place."

Four bites and the steak would be gone. She knew it. And she would get up hungry and have to ask Jon to take her to Carnegie's for a sandwich.

"Yes, nice. And over the top. But here you can see who rules the publishing world." Jane was wearing the diamond bangle Jon had given her to show his gratitude. It went well with the black silk turtleneck she was wearing. She looked different now, sleeker; and there was a thoughtful, alert edge to her that she had not shown earlier, at her own home. There was not a lot left of the slightly confused woman who had opened her car door to Naomi on that night when she had been abducted.

"I read what you sent me." Putting down her napkin, Jane raised her hand for the waiter. "You're a good writer."

Naomi shifted uncomfortably. "But?"

Amused, Jane pulled up her eyebrows. "But? Are you expecting a 'but'? There's no but. Or, if there is, then it's, 'but where's the rest of the story?' Because I want to see that too."

A couple of very well-dressed men walked by, talking loudly in a manner that let the world know they were powerful, successful, that they pulled strings and the world danced.

"Yes. I'm still working on it. You know I only just started, but I wanted to know if it's worth the trouble at all, if you think I should go on or maybe start knitting." She felt like a child, lost in this new and weird environment. "But I'm not sure how I feel about it. And so…"

"Yes, yes." The waiter came, and Jane asked for the dessert menu. "You want an opinion. Well, I'll give you one, as a friend. Don't buy any yarn. Chuck the knitting needles. Write your story. It's compelling, and you have a great way with words. No knitting for you."

It was said so matter-of-factly, so calmly, without even looking her way, that Naomi put down her fork to better digest the words.

Cheesecake, Jane was telling the waiter, and fresh strawberries, and coffee, decaffeinated.

"And when you're done writing, and you've edited your writing, send it to me. And then we'll see." Jane was looking at her like a bird, her head held at an angle of curiosity, her lips slightly pursed. Her fingers were fiddling with the short curls behind her ears, but she smiled. "How very strange. I've never yet met an author in the middle of the night on the parking lot of a fast-food joint. And barefoot too. It will make an interesting bio."

At the table beside them was a group of five people, three men and two women, chatting about a book they were about to publish.

Naomi had the distinct feeling that one of the women was the author. She was giving herself away by the way she sat, her hands folded in her lap, her head swiveling from one to the other, listening but rarely joining in the conversation. She seemed a bit like a waif, unsure of her place, uncertain if this was really the spot she was supposed to be in at this particular moment in her life. Her clothes were nice enough; she had obviously taken care to dress and groom for this lunch meeting, but she still had the slightly frumpy air of someone from somewhere else, someone who had been taken out of her normal surroundings and transported into a different world.

"I don't want to be published because I'm Jon's wife," Naomi said, and Jane's smile drifted off into an ironic grin.

"Oh, that wouldn't happen, trust me. Not with me. If I accept your book it will be because it's worth publishing, and not because there's a famous name on it. I have that much self-respect," she replied quickly.

"But I can tell you now that you have a very special way of saying things. That novel you're writing, it's so tightly interwoven with the city. I like how the man's story is so wrapped around his love for New York, how they intermingle, the person and the place." Again she gave Naomi that bird-like regard. "You love this place, don't you? It comes through in every paragraph."

"Yes." The steak was gone, as Naomi had feared, in less than five bites, and that just didn't seem right. There was an empty spot in her stomach that wanted more meat and not frilly potatoes, or cheesecake. "I love it here. From the very first moment, I've loved New York. It's as if it hums in me, resonates. I know it's crazy, but that's the way it is. When we first came here, when Jon first brought me here, it felt as if the city had been waiting, as if it spread out its carpet to welcome me; and there it was: the lights, the sounds, the traffic like blood coursing through the arteries of the streets."

Embarrassed, she stopped, only to find the eyes of the author from the next table resting on her thoughtfully.

"It's a dirty place." Jane's sane, dry voice woke her from her confusion. "Dirty, loud, and crowded. That's all it is. And I'd rather leave today than tomorrow." She sighed, nudging her plate. "But I love my job. And yes, you're right, there are moments of grandeur when you come up out of the subway station in the morning and the sky shines over the skyscrapers. Yes, I'll grant you that."

"It feels so alive." Strange, it was strange to defend the city to a native. "As if everyone here has a purpose, is living with a vengeance, as if they are here because they want to be, not because chance brought them here. New Yorkers are the most alive people I've ever met."

Jane signaled for the bill, but Naomi shook her head. "No, this is my treat. I wanted to meet with you. I wanted to hear your opinion."

For an instant Jane gazed at her. Then she said, "No. I'm paying. I'm taking a future author out for lunch. That's a good thing."

Naomi leaned back in her chair, taking in her surroundings once more. She was alone with Jane, alone in a place she'd never been; and the talk was not about Jon, not about hotels, not about anything but her own career and her own wishes. Her eyelids fluttered as she tried to wrap her mind around that vast, new concept, and she felt a little giddy.

"So here's what you're going to do," Jane went on, pulling out a credit card. "I want you to finish the first draft before your baby is born. Can you do that? How long do you think the book will be? And do you have a title yet?"

Yes, Naomi again said, she had a title, and it almost made her cry to talk about it. She cursed her hormones, swallowed some coffee, and went on to tell Jane about her protagonist, about how he liked to come home from work and sit down at his piano to play and sing movie and show tunes from the '40s and '50s. His favorite, she said, was "Secret Love," the song from *Calamity Jane*, and so the title of her book would be a line from that song.

Jane, her fingertips on her lips, nodded. "I love it," she said softly. "I love it a lot. The more we talk about this, the more I'm convinced this is going to work." With a glance at her watch, she rose. "I have to get back. Let's talk again, okay? Keep in touch. Send me what you have. And remember, I get first shot at your manuscript; don't you dare take it somewhere else!"

OUT ON THE pavement, Naomi pulled on her gloves. "Is it really this easy, Jane? Is it this easy to get a book deal? I always thought that was the Holy Grail for a writer, and almost as unattainable."

It was raining, already growing dark though it was only three in the afternoon. The lights of the cars cast wondrous shapes on the wet asphalt, the cracks in the surface like scars on ethereal bodies.

"It is." Jane was wearing a red velvet scarf, a sharp and intriguing contrast to her otherwise black clothes, and it made her look less stern, less like a member of the intellectual scene of Manhattan. "It's very hard. But you took a shortcut, right across the parking lot of that burger place." She shrugged. "Sometimes these things happen. They are meant to happen. These stories are the ones that sound like fairy tales and keep the illusion going that it can happen to anyone. Only, of course, it very rarely does. We had a one-in-a-million chance meeting. Now, don't dither. Get that book written."

On the point of turning away, she added, "I know, that was a terrible night for you. You must have been beside yourself with fear and worry. And even now, I can't imagine what that man might have done to you! And to think, you lived through it. And your poor husband."

"It was so strange." The car was there, LaGasse getting out to wait for Naomi. "All those hours I was with him, while Parker, the man who abducted me, drove around in New Jersey with me, down to that beach and then to that burger place where we met. I felt so displaced, as if nothing mattered, as if it wasn't really happening. I cried, and I was scared when he took my wedding ring from me and threw it in the ocean; but on the other hand, it was as if nothing mattered anymore. Only then, when I realized I had to go to the bathroom and made him stop, did some will to live return. You see..." She gestured at LaGasse to wait. "Jon and I, we had the most awful fight that afternoon, and he walked away from me. Just got out of the car, in the middle of the city, and walked away, without once turning back. And I thought everything had ended. So when I met Parker in that hotel lobby, on my way to see my parents, I didn't care anymore. It seemed as if there would be no future." Jane's steady regard made her shift uncomfortably. "It's so unreal. I keep thinking of that night, and it's as if it happened to someone else, as if it were a movie that I was watching, not as if it had happened to me. And now I see you again, and in a totally different context, and I realize it must have been real. Because that's how we met. I was at your house. You made me tea and fed me cake. You gave me that pink elephant."

Again Jane gave her one of her soft, smart smiles. "I've always maintained that a really good writer is, first and foremost, someone with a very keen sense of observation and a really good memory. You have both. Let's meet again soon, shall we? And we'll pick a place where there's more on the plate and the surroundings are less intimidating."

Naomi laughed. "Well. I have my own hotel just up the road. And I can promise the food will be just as good as it was today." This, at least, she could say with conviction. This was something she knew.

Behind them, the group from the neighboring table stepped out. They were still talking, and the woman author still looked slightly out of place.

Naomi watched Jane walk away and vanish into the crowd on the sidewalk, her slight figure mingling with the gray of the dusk and the movement of the people around her.

Naomi had not asked. She knew the name of the publishing house, of course, but she had not bothered to look up the address; and here she stood now, wondering into which of the tall buildings Jane was headed, and how her office looked, if she had a grand view or just another wall outside her window.

Getting into the car, she wondered what it would be like to come here every day, live and breathe the fast rhythm of the city. So different, it was so different from the peacefulness of Halmar, and yet it made her feel at home, and wanted. She loved the wet, musty smell of the rain on the streets and the noise of the traffic as it picked up for rush hour. Deep in her heart she wished she could spend all day sitting in a café, close to the window, observing life as it flowed past her.

HER CELL PHONE rang just as the car turned onto the bridge entrance ramp.

"Where are you?" Jon asked, and went on to say that if it wasn't too much trouble he wanted to be picked up right now, and for his part, he wouldn't mind if they went straight home and didn't spend any more time in Manhattan that day. His words came out clipped and cool, as if he had to restrain himself, as if he had listeners around him and didn't want to say what was really on his mind.

"It will take a while," Naomi replied. "The streets are crowded. You sound like you need a drink."

"Like hell I need a drink. I need five drinks. But not here, and not—" He broke off. "Just come here, okay?"

Worry rose in her throat like sour champagne. "Is everything okay, Jon?"

"Yeah. No. I don't know." A bus rumbled by, drowning him out for a moment. "Later."

And that, too, was unusual, that he did not ask her how she was, if she wanted anything. Bemused, phone in hand, she asked LaGasse to turn around.

He was standing on the curb, the collar of his leather jacket turned up, a cigarette between his lips, squinting across the street, his brows drawn together. His hair was ruffled from the wind, damp from the rain. He looked so much like he had the day he had walked into the Seaside that Naomi's heart turned over.

The cigarette landed in the gutter, and he pulled the car door open and dropped onto the seat beside her.

"I can't believe it." Jon shook droplets off his sleeves. "Sal really is dating that girl."

Confused, she stared at him, waiting for an explanation.

"The accident girl," he went on. "Don't you remember? The one we nearly ran over before the show at Madison Square Garden? That one! He had her in tow just now, brought her to lunch, would you believe it;

and she sits there like a sheep, like his prized possession, that atrocious purse of hers clamped on her lap. The poor mite, she had no idea what to do with the caviar Sal ordered or how to eat it. I felt so sorry for her; why is he doing this?"

"Maya?"

"Yeah, whatever her name is. That young thing, the one we saw with him in the hotel lobby. I had no idea he was still seeing her. What an insane thing to do." He drew a deep, angry breath and tore open the zipper of the jacket. "I'm not sure what to think of it. I don't want her around. He'll have to…I don't know. He's never done anything like that. He's never confronted me with strangers like that, strangers outside the business." His fist hit the leather of the seat. "Dammit, I don't want that kind of intrusion, least of all from a bloody fan we nearly killed!"

There was no need for him to go on. Naomi took his hand and knitted her fingers through his.

"You can't very well tell Sal who to date or not, Jon," she gently said. "There's no way you can do that."

"Like hell. But I can tell him who not to bring to a meeting with me. I don't have to let him show me off to impress some chick."

The muscles in his shoulders were still tense, hard against her cheek when she leaned on it. Sadness seeped into her, clouded her vision like the mist on the windowpanes, and she pushed her arm through Jon's, listening to his rant as the car crept back toward the bridge through the traffic.

"He must be so lonely," she interrupted at some point. "He must feel so lonely, if she's the only company he can find."

"Lonely." Jon pulled her close, but it was more a reflex than real tenderness. "There are thousands of women who'd take him on in LA, literally, and he's had them all. There must have been one, surely…" His words dwindled away.

The ramp of the bridge loomed up before them in the darkness, the arches like steeples of a church ruin, like gates into another world.

His lips on her temple, Jon held her, and Naomi closed her eyes to listen to the rhythmic thumping of the wheels as the limousine ran across the metal ribbons connecting the slabs of concrete.

"Well, he can't have you," he said, his voice gravelly with feeling. "He can't have you, ever. So he'll have to look somewhere else. You are mine, and mine alone. If he thinks that girl is a good substitute for you, he's an even sorrier jerk than I thought. She's not anywhere close to what you are."

That made her sit up. "Close to what I am, Jon? What am I, then?"

"Mine." It came out with conviction, and quite vehemently. "Most of all mine. And yes, mine, because you are you, wonderful, lovely, talented. And mine."

"Not even back then, when I was younger than Maya is now? When we first met, and I was barely more than a teenager?"

"But my beloved, how often do I have to tell you? When you walked into that hotel lobby in Geneva, when we first met, it was like a star had fallen from the sky directly into my arms. How can anyone at all, any woman, be the same? No, Sal is the sorry bastard in this game. He can play out his fantasy in every single hotel all over the world; he'll never get what I have. He'll never have you."

And that, she had to admit, was the bitter truth, the sad end of all wisdom.

chapter 16

SHE HAD STOLEN a napkin.

They hadn't noticed, Jon and Sal, and no one else had cared. In fact, it hadn't been a real theft at all. She only noticed once they were out on the street. The linen cloth had been clamped in her hand; and too embarrassed to speak up or to return inside and take it back, she had hastily stuffed it into her purse.

Sal had wanted to take her out for lunch; she had loved the idea and was excited about his choice, too. She had dreamed of seeing this place from the inside, imagining the rich people who met there, imagining Jon there.

And then he had walked in. All by himself, his hands in his jeans pockets, as if it meant nothing, as if it was the most normal thing in the world.

Jon Stone, and he had barely glanced at her, almost not acknowledged that she was present at all. It had made her wilt, his cool, dismissive politeness, as if she was no more than an invisible assistant, one of the waiters, one of the flowers in the vase adorning the table.

And the food. Caviar, yes, she knew that. It had been served in little silver bowls nestled in a bucket of ice, together with little pancakes and sour cream. She had no idea what to do with it until Sal showed her. The tiny globules exploded on her tongue to release the scent of seawater and fish, and then a curious sensation of nothingness, as if she had swallowed rancid air. There had been champagne too, but Jon had barely touched that either and watched Sal's good appetite with bemused patience. He had ordered an omelette, stating that he didn't feel like caviar right now, and it had come with smoked salmon and fried, shredded potatoes, not exactly hash browns but something similar, lighter, golden.

Maya had gazed around at the surroundings: the red leather couches and elaborate table settings, the curlicue ceiling, and the people. She felt almost as much out of place as she had the night of Jon's concert when they took her backstage.

They had talked about Naomi briefly, and how she was having lunch with a friend, a New York publisher. Sal had smiled, his hand on Maya's, and said that he was sure something good would come of that; he could hardly wait to attend the book launch. That smile, the one he did not direct at her but at the thought of Naomi, had been tender, very gentle, matching his tone. Jon had changed the subject quickly, chatting about traffic, the weather, about the funny sound the engine of his new car made when he drove across the bridge, and that he wanted to buy cigars later; he hadn't had any in the house for ages.

"Cigars, now?" Sal had asked, raising his eyebrows. "You're going to smoke in the house with Naomi pregnant?"

At that Jon had sat back, given Sal a blank stare, and fallen silent.

There hadn't been much conversation after that, and shortly later she found herself on the sidewalk, napkin in hand.

KARIM, AS IF he knew, as if she deserved to be chastised, had set her the task to pick through the crate of kiwis. The prickly orbs scratched her hands and ruined her fingernails, but she didn't care. Her heart was light, and she could hardly wait until the afternoon, when she would be free and could return to Manhattan.

She loved the loft. She loved the way the smooth, huge expanse of dark hardwood floor gleamed and smelled with the scent of orange oil, so different from the sticky mats in her mother's kitchen. She adored the new furniture. Sal had bought all the things she had liked, amused by her enthusiasm, and even encouraged her to pick expensive pieces, saying he would be living there from now on, and he wanted it to be nice. It had felt wrong at first, awkward, as if she was committing to something, as if this was more than helping a friend decorate his new house; but Sal, noticing, had waved her misgivings away.

"Look," he had said, "I don't give a crap about these things. I'd buy whatever I saw first, and it would look like a wild jumble from a garage sale. You seem to know what goes together, so I'm more than pleased to leave it to you."

He had, though, picked the coffeemaker. Bemused, she had watched him do that, as if it was a very important thing, as if it made a huge difference.

And yes, he had explained later, it did make a huge difference indeed.

There was nothing as wonderful as the taste of that first cup of coffee in the morning.

FROM THE STAIRS, she could hear her mother's voice, and a moment later she entered the store, carrying a huge pot of steaming curry that she placed on the counter. With the back of her hand she wiped her forehead and pushed back her sweaty hair. Her gaze fell on Maya.

"You look as if you're ready to leave again," she said.

Maya put down the fruit she was holding. It was unripe, hard and rough, a murky green thing. She wondered how to describe the shape. It wasn't a globe, and it wasn't an egg. It was something all its own: willful, different, difficult.

"Yes." She didn't turn around, waiting for her mother's next words.

"So tell me," Angie went on, coming over to her, "since your father is out of earshot and we have a moment to ourselves. Tell me about the boy you met."

Boy.

"He's not a boy, Mama. He's a man. A grown-up man. Very nice, very courteous, very funny."

Angie took the kiwi from Maya's hands and rolled it between her fingers. "A man? What are you trying to tell me, Maya? And how did you meet him? You aren't dating someone you just met on the street, are you? You're more cautious than that?"

They could see Karim standing out on the sidewalk, talking to a customer. His shirt was flapping in the breeze; he was not wearing a jacket despite the cold. Every time the hem lifted, a roll of stomach became visible: brown, hairless skin hanging over the belt of his trousers.

"I am cautious." She was done with the crate. One of her fingernails was torn, and she had cut her thumb on the wood. Resentment flared up in her chest, a bitter yearning to be back with Sal, in the clean, cool surroundings of the loft, with people who talked about books and music, fashion, and new restaurants.

"You could bring him here and introduce us."

"No." Maya glanced at the table where Sal had sat a few weeks ago.

"We would like to meet this man you're going out with," Angie pressed. "You're our daughter, after all."

Something in Maya burst. She had to take a few calming breaths before she could reply in a civilized manner.

"Mama," she then said, "I'd really like to know what you consider to be the right people. Really. Please tell me."

Angie, her brow furrowed, waved at Karim. "Your father was talking about that the other day. He thinks it's time you got married to a nice boy from the Pakistani community. I can't see anything wrong with that. It would be much more fitting than you running around the city."

One of the fruit clamped between her fingers, Maya nodded. "Please tell me, Mama. What year do you think we live in? Which century? You were a hippie; you married a freaking foreigner when that was so not done. A dark-skinned one too! You didn't give a damn about convention or your parents' consent. And you picked your own life! And now you want to find a husband for me? Like in the Middle Ages? Am I dreaming?"

"We have the business to think of." Gently, Angie pried the kiwi from Maya's hand and returned it to its brothers. "We have this house, this shop, and your younger sisters to think of. It's a lot."

"But it's not my lot." In an effort to calm herself, Maya squeezed her eyes shut until she saw tiny yellow dots against the black background of her lids.

"I know you want me and Uma to take over someday. And maybe even Selma. You have this vision of a small family empire, of a chain of delis, a Paki Dean & Deluca or something; and it's a great idea. Only you never asked if I wanted that. You never asked what *I* wanted."

Angie gazed at her.

"Look at you, Mama." Maya plucked the ribbon of Angie's apron from where it was tangled in the waist of her skirt. "Just look at you. You are a beautiful woman. You have the loveliest hair I've ever seen, so golden, and thick, and curly. Your complexion is as pastel as marzipan, and you do nothing but cook, cook, cook. You spend your entire life in that hot kitchen, no air conditioning, no break, nothing. Do you really want me to lead this life too?" Tears stuck in her throat like sour lumps of dough. "I want beauty, Mama, and freedom, art, music, space! There's so much more out there!" She swallowed against the resistance. "I know you and Papa love this life, even though I'll never understand why. But I don't, Mama, I don't. I want out; I want to live my own life!"

"Your life."

Karim was waving good-bye to the customer and stood, his hands on his hips, looking up and down the street.

"Your life," Angie repeated softly. "You have no idea what you even mean by that. You're a dreamer, Maya; you always were. You even believe your Jon Stone, that singer, is a real person, a person you'd like off the stage, don't you? You think if you met him, he'd be your friend, or even more, and you'd have a place in that life he leads."

Maya's jaw dropped open.

"But those people live across the water in Manhattan, and you live here; there's no room for you over there. You're not one of them, Maya. You have to stop dreaming."

"I have never in my life…" Maya had to stop and start again. The words were a wild jumble on her tongue, unsorted, raw. "I've never heard such nonsense before. Why would you even bring Jon up in this conversation?"

"Jon, huh?" Smiling softly, Angie peeled off the apron. "Jon. So is that your big secret? Are you stalking Jon Stone? I've heard he has settled here in New York to produce that musical of his, so is that what you're doing, hanging around outside the Fifth Avenue building where he lives in the penthouse suite?"

"He doesn't live in a penthouse suite!" Maya snapped her mouth shut, but it was too late.

"Oh, so you know, eh?" Shaking her head, Angie moved back to the hot counter to check her saucepans and adjust the heat. "You know where your lover lives, Maya? So you do indeed hang around outside his house, like a love-lorn teenager, and then you preach to me about freedom and choices? And only because you want designer shoes we can't afford?"

A hot blush flooded Maya's face, and Angie nodded. "Yes, I did notice. I'm not stupid, Maya, and not blind. Just because I've chosen to be a cook doesn't mean I don't read magazines. I know what those red soles mean, trust me, and I wonder why you needed to spend five hundred bucks on a pair of black high heels." She shrugged. "But, well, it's your money, and you worked to earn it. So if it's shoes you want, go buy shoes. I'll even give you the money for a second pair if that will make you happy and stop whining." Her blue eyes flashing, she banged the lid on the pan. "Because that's what you're doing, Maya; you're whining, and you're making me and everyone else miserable with it. If you hate us that much, move out. Go and get that life you want so badly. Go and hang out in nightclubs and limousines, pimp yourself out to rock stars and actors, if that's what you need to be happy. But stop flouncing around the house as if we're vermin. We're not. We're your family, and we love you. We love you without designer clothes and manicured hands."

"Mama…"

It was warm inside the shop despite the open door, steamy from the hot food on the counter. Angie had made samosas and pakoras, and there were deep-fried pastries right beside them, waiting to be sold. Four huge pots with curry and korma simmered gently behind the pane, their aromas mixing into an enticing, golden fragrance. Beside them was the vat with rice, saffron-tinted basmati, a treasure all by itself. There was chai, and coffee, and some fruit juices, and even a stray can of soda.

Karim believed in purity, and that meant no Western food or drink. Angie had been the one to bend the rules, saying they had to cater to people's wishes. If they wanted soda, then soda they would get. They were a deli and not some kind of food temple. For once Karim had caved, and now there was Coke on the menu.

"I don't know what else to tell you, Maya. You make me feel ashamed of my life, and I'm starting to resent that. I'm happy. I love your father, and I love my cooking. I don't look like one of the sleek women you'd like to hang out with, but I know who I am and what I want. I don't think you can say that much for yourself. A pair of Louboutins and a Gucci purse don't define a person. What you love, what you do, those things are important."

"I love," Maya replied, her voice brittle, "you and Papa and my sisters. I really do. I love you more than you know, Mama. I love you so much that I wish you could lead a different life, have it easier, and not have to stand in the kitchen all day. I love you so much, I wish you could live like Jon Stone's wife, like a queen. I wish we all could."

Very gently, with a slow, deliberate movement, Angie picked up one of the samosas and bit into it. The flaky crust crumbled onto her apron, and she ignored it.

"I made these," she said. "They are delicious, perfect. They are the best samosas this side of the Pacific. They are so good, I got mentioned for them in a number of travel and gourmet magazines. I'm proud of them. I'm proud of getting the dough just right, and the filling too. I've experimented and tried for many years to get them just this way. Manhattan restaurants have asked for them, and I have declined. I'm not a caterer; I'm my own boss; I have my own shop. Whoever wants to eat my samosas has to make their way to Brooklyn, to Atlantic Avenue."

Karim entered the store, and they fell silent, both turning toward him.

"I've been thinking," he said, "maybe now, with winter coming, we should add some soups to the menu."

Angie smiled.

THE BED STOOD exactly where she had imagined it.

The windows were open, letting in a cool, damp breeze from the river; and Maya had the distinct feeling Sal had done that just for her, to show her that the curtains around the bed would indeed move, would flutter and billow the way she had imagined.

It was a wonderful place. The colors were just right, with the cream and white upholstery and fabrics complementing the dark wood floor and red brick walls.

"Now all we need is a good stereo." Sal was in the kitchen, rummaging in the fridge for milk to put in her coffee, which muffled his voice. "Then this will feel like a real home."

He hadn't even tried to touch her yet. They had been meeting for weeks, going out for meals, taking walks, shopping for the loft; and always there had been the pretense that she was helping him.

"Sal."

His head came up, the gray locks bobbing on his brow. "What?"

"What am I doing here, Sal?"

He wiped his hands on his jeans and shut the fridge door. "You're helping me with the loft?"

"You know that's nonsense. If it were true I could leave now and never return; the loft is finished." She had no idea where she had found the courage to speak up like that. "You must have realized by now that I won't sue you and Jon for that accident, so that's not a reason for me to be here either. Why am I here? Why do you keep asking me to come?"

His gaze drifted to his cigarettes on the coffee table.

"I need a reason to be here."

At that his eyebrows came up, and he gave her a tiny grin. "You do? Isn't it enough that we like spending time with each other? That we enjoy each other's company? I know I love having you near. Anyway, I'm taking you out now; I'm in the mood to buy you a new purse. How do you feel about that?"

Maya sighed. "Don't you see," she plodded on, "how improper this is? I'm in your home, in your…" She gestured at the huge, canopied bed behind her. "I'm in your bedroom! And you talk about purses? I can't accept a purse from you!"

"Oh, nonsense!" He slapped the kitchen counter. "Of course you can! I can buy my girlfriend a purse if I feel like it. End of discussion! Now can we go out and grab some milk on the way, and lunch?"

The moment the words had left his lips his face changed, as if by saying it out loud, something changed, something settled into place, and a veil was lifted from the air.

"Yeah, that's it, isn't it?" Smiling, he came toward her, his step all of a sudden easy, relaxed. "You're my girlfriend, in a very cool and old-fashioned way. We haven't even kissed! No embrace, and yet I know you're my girlfriend. Not one of the girls passing through for a few hours of mutual fun, but mine."

She took a step back, only to be stopped by the foot of the bed and the quilt hanging over it. He was standing before her, laughing, a kind of happiness in his eyes she hadn't seen there before, making him look young, handsome, fun.

"I know what you're doing here, Maya," Sal said. "I know why you're here. You're here because I love you, and because you love me back. Isn't that so? Tell me it's true!"

Her mouth opened to reply, but he didn't let her. Gently, tenderly, he reached out for her, and Maya stretched out her hand to place it in his.

chapter 17

OLAF HAD SENT people from the hotel to do the Christmas decorations, saying that she probably didn't have anything on hand, and he knew how much she loved to have everything perfect. They showed up with a truckload full of wreaths, ornaments, and even a live tree, and turned the house into a fairy place.

Red, she wanted red, and some gold, not too many colors, nothing too fancy, just enough to make the house festive and cozy.

Jon watched in amusement—well out of the way—a cup of coffee in his hands. He'd never cared about these things. All the years he'd lived on his own in LA, there'd never been a trace of Christmas in his house, let alone planning or preparing for a big feast. It was true, he had celebrated, but celebrated at one party or other, where people like himself met: the lonely and lost, those who could not muster the energy or hope to travel home to their families for the holidays. His mother had asked him often enough, had even come out to California one year; but she had given up and left him to stew in his misery after that, tossing at him that it was his choice, life was moving on, and he had to snap out of it or go down. And as always, he had turned to the pictures on the shelves, to the images of Naomi, and brought out a bottle to drown his sorrow.

BUT SHE WAS here now, in a blue wool dress that showed her belly nicely, standing in the middle of the hallway, telling the two men carrying the tree exactly where she wanted it and to please be careful of the floors. His wife, decorating their house for Christmas, and Jon could hardly wrap his mind around it.

From the doorway to the studio he looked on as the tree went up, and the lights were meticulously draped around it, the ornaments hung, and a red velvet cloth wrapped around the trunk. The tart scent of resin filled the air, and that more than anything else brought back memories of peaceful holiday seasons at his parents' house.

He put down the cup and went over to Naomi, laying his hands on her shoulders. "Now we need some presents, don't we?"

Her hair smelled of flowers and spring when she leaned into him.

"What would you like, my love? Is there anything you'd like for Christmas?" It was a stupid question, Jon knew it, and she would respond that she really wanted nothing at all, nothing; but he had to ask anyway. Somehow he needed it, needed the idea that he would go out and buy something for her, have it wrapped up in tissue and pretty ribbon, and place it under the tree. But she surprised him.

"You're right," Naomi said. "We need presents. If we're going to throw a Christmas party, we need presents for everyone. That's a brilliant idea, Jon!"

He groaned. That wasn't what he had meant, and he was sure she knew it. "All right, but I swear, I'm not going to buy anything for Sal's girlfriend."

That made her turn around and gaze at him thoughtfully.

"Don't look at me like that!" He raised his hands in defense. "Seriously, Naomi, I'm not having her here at the house. That's where I draw the line. It's my house, and I decide who I invite and who I don't."

She opened her mouth to speak, but he shook his head. "Don't ask. I don't know why. There's no good reason. I just can't. It seems so wrong. She's what? Half his age? And really, you should have seen her, she's pathetic."

"You are such a snob!" Naomi slapped his arm. "She's a nice enough girl, I'm sure. It's none of our business, Jon!"

"That's exactly the point; it's none of our business. And that means she's not coming here,. Or at least not until they're married or whatever."

Taking her wrist, he tugged her away from the decorators. "Don't you realize? We let her step into our private lives, Naomi, if we invite her here, Sal or not. And if they break up in a couple of months, she'll be able to tell all the world how Jon Stone lives, and what toilet paper he uses. That can't happen. I won't let that happen just because Sal thinks he's in love."

"Good grief, aren't you conceited."

But he could see by the look on her face that he had made a point and that she agreed.

"How…" Naomi toyed with the hem of her sleeve. "So how did you handle these affairs back in LA? Before; when you were still alone?"

"That was different." He didn't want to talk about it, let her know how rough and incidental his life had really been.

"That girl, Eva," she said gently, "she reminded me of Sophie. Don't you think?"

Jon walked away, left her standing there in the hallway, and went into the studio, where he stopped by the window, his hands in his pockets, to stare out at the city.

Slowly, Naomi followed. "It was like a mirage, seeing her up there on the stage," she went on. "For a moment my heart stopped. Maybe that was the reason why I picked her out, and, Jon, I saw in your face that you were thinking the same thing. So tell me, how did you treat the girls you were with, after me, before me?"

"That was different." He shook his shoulders, uncomfortable now with the way the discussion was going. "They knew they were one-night stands, nothing more. There was never any thought of getting serious. Yeah, we took them home, they stayed overnight, but then it was mostly good-bye. Quick and easy."

With a sigh, he turned around. There she was: Naomi, a fragile woman with very white skin and black, curly hair; big, dark eyes; and a lovely mouth. The vision of all his dreams, the heart of all his songs, Naomi was his reason for being alive. He could close his eyes, and his hands would be able to trace her shape in the air, every curve and angle, every breath.

"I don't want to talk about Sophie. I don't want to talk about any of them," Jon said.

He didn't want to be reminded. The memory was still too fresh, the scar too tender. Sophie, who had fired those shots at Naomi and who had died in a mess of blood at the Oscars, she had been the only one, other than Naomi, who had stayed for more than a few nights.

"I don't ever want to talk about her again. She's dead. Good riddance, I say, the stupid slut; she tried to kill you."

"Jon!"

He waved her away, tired of the discussion. "Anyway, we weren't talking about my old affairs; we were talking about Sal and his Oriental beauty. And here's my decision: she's not coming here. End of story."

"Jon."

There was no other way to put it. He loved her. He loved her with every cell of his body, with every thought flitting through his mind; and now as she came toward him across the room, that soft smile on her lips, he knew he would lose again, would give in, no matter what she asked of him.

"Jon, I see your point. I see what you mean about our privacy, and keeping it. But, darling, if Sal is really dating her, if she is his girlfriend and he wants to bring her, we can't very well tell him not to. We also can't force him to ask your approval when he falls in love."

She put her arms around him, and how wonderful was that, the fact that she could not mold herself into him anymore, that her belly was between them like a statement of their love.

"You didn't say anything when Russ fell in love with Solveigh. You were happy about that. You accepted Solveigh!"

"Ah, but that's different." His fingers pushed through her hair. "Solveigh was not someone he picked up on the street; she was part of your life, your friend. Of course I'm happy for Russ and her!"

"What a snob you are."

How he loved to kiss the crinkle of her smile in the corner of her mouth and feel the warmth of her lips against his.

"If we invite all of them, and Sal says he wants to bring her, then the girl is welcome," Naomi stated when he let her go. "That's part of living a normal life, Jon, letting new people step in. And I have to tell you, I'll be glad to deliver the invitation to her in person if that makes Sal a happier man."

He felt like grumbling, like muttering grumpy, half-baked sentences filled to the brim with evil words, and the thought made him smile.

"Besides," Naomi tossed at him, returning to the hallway to see what was going on, "we can buy extra-special toilet paper for that night so she'll never know what brand we really use."

"As if you care," he called after her, but it was halfhearted. He knew he had lost.

SHE WAS OUTSIDE, on the steps, discussing the decoration of the entrance and the garden path, when Jon made his way upstairs. Driven by a need he could not name, he wanted to visit the room they had set aside for the nursery.

It wasn't too close to their bedroom, but on the same floor, so that Naomi would have a feeling of control. The window looked out on the footpath leading from the street to the Promenade. It was a quiet room, light, airy, and big, as yet unfurnished. Right next to it was the room for the nanny. It was more like a small apartment, well away from their room, safeguarding her and their privacy.

Jon ran his hand over the sill as he gazed at the bare, cream walls.

He had gone to the checkup with her, and how hard that had been. How he had hated entering a hospital and walking through those hallways again, a nightmare reminder of the many hours he had spent beside her bed after the shooting. The smell alone was enough to make him reel. But Naomi had not wavered and led him straight to Julian's office, and moments later Jon had witnessed the wonder, the miracle of the new life they had created. Tiny, a tiny creature, floating on the screen of the ultrasound machine; and he had bent down to see the baby better, count those limbs and look for something human in the shape of the head.

"Looks great" had been Julian's verdict, and he had handed Naomi a wad of tissues to clean off the gel from her belly, "Everything is just the way it's supposed to be. So far, you're doing great!"

The printouts in hand, Jon had sat in the office while they did other things with her, things where she didn't want him along, and he had wondered if it was at all possible to tell the gender yet. Naomi hadn't asked, and he had not dared to, afraid of looking stupid, afraid he was supposed to know.

He had stared at the rows of books on the shelves behind the doctor's desk, recalling how he had first seen Julian, on the steps of their house, his arm around Naomi's shoulder, and how he had fled from that vision, his beloved, in another man's embrace.

How silly he had been, how stupid. How much misery he had caused himself, and her, over that. The photo of his unborn child on his knee, he listened to the sounds from the hallway, typical, dreary hospital sounds, and then, suddenly, out of the blue, there had been Naomi's laughter, the silver tinkle of her voice, and she had come into the room, her eyes happy, her lips smiling at him, and all had been well.

DOWN BELOW, ON the path, a couple of young women strolled past, pushing baby strollers. One was holding a paper cup of coffee that she sipped as they walked, chatting idly, enjoying the winter sun.

For a second he was tempted to throw open the window and shout down to them, let them know that he lived here, and look, even Jon Stone was capable of leading a normal life with a family and all; but he shook himself out of it and retreated back downstairs and into the Christmas fairy house Olaf's people had created for Naomi. She was still busy with them, directing them through the living room and pointing out the large, arched windows, so he went into the studio and closed the doors behind him.

The piano beckoned.

There was an empty coffee mug on top, carefully placed on a stack of music sheets and not on the wood, a pencil beside it, his glasses.

In the corner, on the pillows of the window seat, sat her laptop. It was the same one he had bought for her in Hamburg in that almost forceful attempt to make her write, use the talent she had, break free from the notion that it was useless to even try.

Naomi hadn't noticed, but he loved to watch her write. She had a way of losing herself in her words, of not even looking at the screen as she typed but into a space that only she could see, as if the ideas and phrases were laid out there for her, and all she had to do was copy them down.

He had never seen her take notes or plot. Every morning, after breakfast, when they drifted here for a few hours of work, she opened her computer, read what she had written the day before, and began typing, just like that, as if she didn't have to even think about it. He had tried to ask her, tried to pry her secret out of her; but she had given him one of her distracted, puzzled glances and replied that it was easy—all she had to do was write.

It had always been like that for her he knew, and yet it seemed like a mystery that he badly wanted to unravel, and perhaps gain a piece of it for himself.

"But how?" he'd asked just a few of days ago. Naomi had given him one of her small, dismissive shrugs and replied, "Just do it. It's easy," and he'd been ready to throw his cup at the wall because it wasn't.

It wasn't easy. For him, writing was work, a battle with his muses, a yoke he couldn't get rid of, a drive he couldn't ignore. And once again he had felt the awe, the admiration, and the envy of her gift, at the innocence and ease of it.

Jon sat down at the grand and laid his hands on the keys, let them glide over the smooth ivory.

A song. He had written so many songs, little stories told in three or four minutes, most of them about a love that had once been true then lost, but he had always shied away from larger, more involved composing, afraid of the commitment, afraid of failure. Now, with the musical well under way, he felt an urge to move on.

She had done it. She had opened that door for him with her usual magic, with the ease of her trust.

Jon picked up the phone. He had wanted to talk about this to Sal, but the presence of that girl had kept him silent. There was no way he was going to discuss work with her around.

"Come here," he said when Sal picked up, "and please, this time, alone. I want to talk about work."

Sal didn't answer right away. Then he replied slowly, "You're mad at me. I know you are. Why?"

"Not now." Jon wondered how Sal, the savviest of all Hollywood managers, could be so dense about this. "Just come, and then we'll talk about that movie deal. Naomi is in a Christmas mood and decorating the entire house, and I need a break. Move your ass over here now."

"It's about Maya, isn't it?"

In the background, Jon could hear street noises, a passing truck. Sal was somewhere outside.

"Yeah, it's about that girl. I'm surprised I have to tell you, Sal." Anger welled up in him. "You bring a stranger, a fan, a strange girl to a lunch meeting with me? Are you out of your frigging mind? What am I, your trophy, to get someone in your bed? Is that it, Sal?" There was no reason not to shout. He was in his own house.

"It's different, Jon." Sal sighed. "I know it was a mistake. I saw it the moment you walked in that door. And I'm sorry. But that's not how it is at all."

"That's not how it is? You're not trying to…" Jon broke off, tired of the sordidness of it all. "I don't even want to know. Take her to bed if you want to, but leave me out of it. I'm done with that."

"I'm in love, Jon."

He was sure he had misunderstood. He was certain those words had never crossed Sal's lips, much less in that tone.

"I think I love her. Maya. It's different. And I'm sorry. I didn't bring her along to impress her or anything, but when you called we were out together, and so I thought…it sort of seemed natural. I wanted her with me."

"You've lost your mind." It was the only thing that came to Jon's mind to say. "You're utterly out of your mind. That girl is, what? Twenty? A nobody? She doesn't even know how to dress, or pick the right purse."

"My God," Sal breathed, "I never knew you were such a snob, Jon. Look what marrying into Canadian nobility has made you; you care about a woman's handbag? She doesn't have our kind of money, all right; she's just a normal, regular girl, not a princess like your wife. Not everyone has the luck to win someone like Naomi."

They were, and in an incidental phone conversation, on the brink of speaking truths that no one wanted to hear.

Jon took a calming breath and let the air seep out of his lungs.

"Just come here," he said, "and we'll talk."

chapter 18

IT FELT WEIRD waking up in a strange bed.

She'd never stayed away from home like this before, to sleep with a man, to wake up by his side.

Her clothes were on the floor, in a heap, where Sal had dropped them after peeling them off her, one piece after another, kissing each new spot of exposed skin. He had undone her braid and draped her hair around her shoulders, wrapping the ends around his fingers in a vain attempt to make them curl. He knew what he was doing; Maya had expected nothing less from a man like Sal. His lovemaking was considerate, patient, gentle, and she had enjoyed it. And yet it felt strange to wake up and see him beside her.

Carefully, she got up, collected her clothes, and made her way to the bathroom. She had no toothbrush with her, and she balked at using Sal's. This struck her as funny. They had shared more than just kisses during the night, and yet she couldn't bring herself to touch his toothbrush. Rubbing toothpaste across her teeth with her finger, she scrutinized herself in the mirror. Somehow, she thought she should feel differently. Her first night with her lover, and Maya was vaguely disappointed that there was no elation, no joy in her heart, just the desire for a hot shower and a cup of good coffee.

She let the water run over her face and head, savoring the warmth and the soft drumming on her shoulders and neck, and felt better.

"I want to take you out today," Sal greeted her when she returned. "I want to spoil you."

Her heart skipped at the thought of buying clothes and shoes, and maybe a purse, but then the guilt took over.

"I have to go home. I'm supposed to work today."

"Call them!" In his shorts, Sal went to the kitchen to start the coffee machine. "If you have to, call them and tell them you're staying with your lover, and he's taking you out today. You deserve a day off now and then, darling."

Darling. The word hummed in her mind like the flutter of a butterfly's wing: fragile, shimmering, and very lovely. The trepidation she had felt in the shower blew away.

"My father will give me hell."

"Hasn't anyone ever told you that as a grown-up, you pretty much can do as you please? You can even change jobs! You're not your family's prisoner."

He smiled at her while he measured out the coffee. "So, what would you like to do today? Where can I take you to make you happy?"

Her cell phone in hand, she made a decision. "I'd like to try that caviar thing again. But this time without Jon staring at me in disapproval, please."

She knew she'd said the right thing when his smile widened.

"WHATEVER YOU LIKE," he said, but then when she named a designer she'd always wanted to try, he suggested, "Why not Valentino. Let's go check out Valentino."

So Valentino it was. She liked the clothes, but it seemed to her as if he was picking things meant for someone else, someone more graceful, and with a different skin tone. Maya didn't care for rose or blush. She had never carried a clutch. She wasn't used to holding a purse in her hand and would likely forget it at the first possible moment.

"I can't take these things home," she said as they sat at the Russian Tea Room.

Sal, busy ladling sour cream on his blini, looked up. "Why not? They're yours."

She hadn't touched the little mother-of-pearl spoon yet, and now she folded her hands in her lap. "There's just no room."

"Oh, come on." He stuffed the morsel into his mouth. "You don't have room for a few more dresses?"

"Sal." She could hardly say it. "Sal, I share a room with my younger sister, and a closet too. There isn't a lot of room in our apartment."

For the longest time he didn't respond and just ate, gesturing for her to do the same.

The fishy little things weren't the best thing she'd ever eaten, even with the champagne. When the tiny bowl was empty, and all those little pancakes gone, she still felt hungry, unsatisfied.

"You own that building, don't you?" Sal asked when they were ready to leave. "It has more than two floors? What's upstairs?"

"It's rented out." Saying it, this occurred to her for the first time ever. "There's a family living up there. But yes, my parents own the building."

Holding the door for her, Sal shrugged. "So toss them out and use those rooms yourself. The deli should make enough money without that, I should think."

"I've never asked." Thoughtfully, she followed him.

"I need ice cream," he announced. "Caviar is all well and good, but somehow it never fills me up. Or maybe cheesecake?"

Maya hooked her arm through his. "Or both?"

He gave her a radiant grin.

BACK AT THE loft, Sal went straight to his closet. It was a big walk-in space, and there wasn't a lot in it yet.

"Here" He pointed at the unused side. "You can put your things here if you want."

"In your closet?"

"Well, why not? You're not going to wear those to work, are you; but you will when we're together, so you might as well keep them here."

Slowly, carefully, she stepped closer to where he had put her shopping bags on the floor, right next to the rod he had indicated.

"I won't spoil it by unpacking them myself," he added, waiting.

"I can't move in with you." The words dropped from her mouth before she'd even thought them, and yet she knew they were the right thing to say.

A single, bare truth, a conviction deep in her heart, and even as she stood there, waiting for his reply, she wondered why this was so.

"No one is talking about moving in." There was a subtle trace of disappointment in his voice. "I'm only offering some closet space."

Outside, it had begun to snow. The other side of the river was no longer visible; the flakes were fat and wet. A ship passing by on its way to the ocean, blared its horn.

"And what if I want something and you're not here, away on some errand for Jon?" Maya wanted to slap herself. This, she was certain, was not at all what she had meant to say; her mouth bypassing her brain, leaving it dumbfounded.

"I'll give you a key." He was busy picking out spare hangers and putting them on "her" side, neatly, in a row, each one exactly the same distance from the other. They sounded a little like castanets when they met, though slow and inexpertly played.

Maya wondered if it really could be this easy, this simple.

"Next time," Sal said, "we'll buy you some things for evenings, for when we go out."

HE NEVER LET her go home on the subway anymore. There was always a car, and not a cab but a car service, a black Lincoln with a small, discreet number somewhere in the back but otherwise unmarked. They sped her across the bridge and down the Brooklyn Queens Expressway, the drivers discreet, the seats comfortable and deep. She always made them stop a block away from home so no one would notice. The questions would be too much to deal with.

Her father threw her a venomous glare when she entered but said nothing. No one else was in the store, no customers, and none of her family either.

"I'm sorry," Maya said, and he shook his head.

"No, you're not." He kept sorting credit card slips. They still had one of the old, manual card readers, not an electronic one, of course. In one of his better tirades, Karim had surmised that air conditioners, coffeemakers and credit card machines were all manufactured by the same conglomerate of companies, out to gain control of the entire world by rationing electricity at some point and making them all dependent. "If something happens" had been his rationale, "if a plane crashes into Manhattan and everything goes downhill, people will still be able to come here and buy food." Angie had given him one of her long-suffering but loving glances and gone to make coffee with the new espresso machine.

"You're not sorry at all, as it happens," Karim was telling her now. "You were away all night. Don't think I didn't notice. I know you're grown up, and of age, and all that; but you're still my daughter, and I want to know where you were, and with whom."

With a sigh, Maya placed her new Valentino purse on the counter. This one piece she'd not been able to leave behind at Sal's. She could hardly believe she owned one; it was the prettiest thing she'd ever seen.

"I was with my boyfriend, Papa. He lives in Manhattan, and it was too late to come home last night. I'll do this more often from now on."

He grunted in response and shuffled the papers into a drawer, effectively destroying all the work he'd done a moment ago. "I can't stop you from doing that, can I? But, Maya, you have a job here, and I expect you to show up for your shift. You'd have to do that for any other job too."

He was right, of course, and she hung her head, but only for an instant.

"I want my own room," Maya said.

Karim slammed the drawer shut.

"I'm twenty-four, Papa, and I want my own room, my own space. Otherwise, I'll have to move out. And I won't stay in Brooklyn, that I can promise you. I can find a job in Manhattan, and a place to live. I'm tired of this cramped life. We need the upper apartment for ourselves. Soon Uma will want some privacy, too, and she and I could share it. We need more space. All of us."

To her utter surprise, he nodded. "Yes, I know. I've been thinking much the same thing. I'll talk to them. But Maya…" He leaned forward on his elbows, his bushy eyebrows drawing together. "I want you to make up your mind. This secret coming and going, it's not good. I want to know where you spend your time, and I want to be able to rely on you."

For the first time in her life she felt as if he was treating her like an adult, like someone worth listening to. "I promise." She nodded. "I promise I'll always be here in time for my work shift, even if I spend the night somewhere else. Is that good enough?"

"I guess it will have to be."

Nothing else came from him. He turned away as if the conversation was forgotten already and went to sort the tomatoes.

chapter 19

SHE HAD CHANGED.

How beautiful she was now, once again glowing, lush, her hair glossy, and her eyes radiant. She was a fairy creature, the most beautiful woman on Earth, and she moved through his house as she had done in Malibu: a mystery, a magical being come to rest in his care.

Jon, from his seat at the piano, kept gazing at Naomi, his hands motionless on the keys, the pencil between his fingers. The score sheet propped up in front of him was empty, not a single note written down. She was sitting so quietly in her window seat, the new couch ignored, her head turned away from him as she watched the snow drift down from a dark gray sky, clouding the view of the skyline as if it were a dense curtain hanging over the river. Her hair was pinned up; it had grown back enough for that, but a few wisps drifted around her neck, blurring the line of her cheek into a soft curve. Just like in Norway, during those still winter months they had spent there, she had taken to wearing woolen things, combining a riot of colors that made her look like a bird of paradise against the drab winter background. He loved seeing her like that, in those short skirts and square-cut sweaters, her legs in thick tights that brought out their shape so well.

His love for her was a tight coil around his heart, a living entity that wove itself into his body with every breath he took, every movement he made. Sometimes, in an unsuspected moment when he tried to turn around too fast and he lost Naomi from sight, he could feel those tendrils slide and slither over the beating muscle and grip them even tighter, burrow into his flesh. He welcomed it. He wanted to feel the ache, wanted his whole being possessed by this loving alien.

"You're not working."

Her voice: the music of his life, the one sound that made everything right, the tone that would soothe his wildest and scariest dreams.

"Jon, you're daydreaming."

He blinked.

"Jon, I'm talking to you. We need to decide who we want to invite, and what we're going to serve. Could you please listen to me?"

She had turned toward him, she was speaking, and he hadn't even noticed. Mortified, Jon put down the pencil and sat up.

"I haven't seen you compose anything at all since we moved here. All you do is stare at me. I'll have to leave the room so you can work."

She moved, rose from that seat in one graceful movement, like the selkie, like a mermaid, carrying her growing belly easily.

"No, see, I'm working!" Jon patted the empty sheet. "See, I'm really thinking of music. Only…I love looking at you. You're so beautiful. Why should I do anything else when there's you to look at."

Naomi threw up her hands. "You're useless. I thought I was marrying one of the smartest men in show biz, and what do I get? A sentimental, aging singer."

"Don't call me aging. Don't do that." The beast around his heart loosened its grip marginally, as if taking a breath, as if sighing in longing, only to pull even tighter. "I'm not old yet. I'm going to be a father in a few months; I can't be old. And you, my dear, you're…" He couldn't say it. On impulse, he wanted to whisk her away, take her back to Norway, to the quiet and innocence of their solitary months, or maybe to Malibu and their house there, so they could go for a walk on the beach at sunrise, like they used to do. For a moment Jon felt restricted, his life narrowed by these surroundings, elegant and comfortable as they were. He wanted her for himself, and in the lonely spaces where no one else had bothered them.

"You're healed," he said softly, trying on the words, tasting them on the tip of his tongue.

"Yes." Her hand came to rest on her belly, the diamonds on her finger glinting at him. "I think I am."

As if with this act of love, the one that had created this new child, they had driven out the demons of the past year, and had reshaped their lives.

"I think it's over now, Jon." She came to him and stood between his knees, in much the same way as always, letting him wrap his arms around her hips. "I think we're finally in calm waters."

And that, he knew, was true. Their life was as sweet as molasses, peaceful, quiet, and slow. No one was pushing them into anything. They had at last mastered their own time.

Christmas, and he remembered how a year ago everything had still been strange, new, he with a wife at last, trying to settle into something like domesticity. How his sister had made fun of him for that, for putting up the tree at their mother's house, for even going out and buying it in the first place. He'd never done anything like that before, not since he had left New York to move to LA; and here he'd been, with a wife and a grown son, celebrating a family Christmas.

As if reading his thoughts, as if she knew what he wanted, Naomi said, "We really should make this a very special Christmas. We need to go out and buy gifts for everyone."

Jon laid his hands around her waist. At least he tried. Before, only a few months ago, it had been nearly possible for him to span it, but now it was impossible. "Again, dear heart? Again in the shopping mood? You really want to raid the stores, like last year?" He groaned a bit. "And FAO Schwarz, that too?"

Her smile was so gentle, so sweet. "You wanted a doll, remember? You wanted to get a doll to convince this little one to be a girl. Are you wimping out now? Afraid you can't deal with two women in your house? I'll tell you, little girls want everything pink. You'll be swamped in pink. And oh!" An impish grin replaced the smile. "Daddy. You'll have to watch your princess go out to dances and proms, and boys will be coming to pick her up! You'll have to hand her over to other men!"

"Not so!"

She laughed, ruffling his hair. "Yes, so. You'll have to bear the thought of her smooching with a boyfriend in the car while you pace the floor, waiting for her to come home." With a new sparkle in her eyes, she bent down and kissed him lightly. "She will fall in love with some rock or movie star and put up his posters; and you'll tell her that she has a different destiny, that someone better than a useless singer is waiting for her and not to throw her life away on romance. You will be just like my father, Jon. I bet you will."

The thought alone was enough to make him swallow in fear. "No, I won't! I won't be like Olaf, and I know this because I even pried Joshua out of your and Olaf's scheming fingers and let the boy go his own way, and what a good thing that was! But…" That other thought, the one where a teenage daughter began to show interest in young men, that was just too dire even to finish. "But surely we can keep her away from any danger until she is grown up."

"And when do you think that will be, Jon? When do you think girls start dreaming of that one man, the one they want in their bed, the one they want to make love to?"

Jon looked up at her, at the sweet curve of her lips, and shook his head. "And you, my dove. When did you first feel that yearning, when did you first lie awake at night and dream of a lover to come to you and ease that ache? How old were you? And who was on your posters? Who was your secret passion?"

And here they were, once again drifting off into their past.

"You know very well," Naomi whispered; "I don't have to tell you. There was no one else, and you know it. I wanted you before we ever met, and all my life. Every single night of my life, all my dreams were always about you. There is no room for any other man."

"When we first met, when you walked into that hotel lobby in Geneva…"

Naomi laid her fingertips on his mouth. "Not again, Jon. Really. It's all over now, all the turmoil, all the sadness, and all the loneliness. Look at our new life, and all we've achieved, and please stop dwelling on those memories. You should know by now that I love you. You should be able to accept that I won't leave you, ever."

"You say that so easily." He nodded grimly, his grip tightening. "You say that, but then you're gone again, and I'm left alone. You skip across the world as if it means nothing and you let stalkers abduct you to New Jersey."

A shiver ran through her; he could feel it. Her glance drifted away from him and toward the rings she was wearing, new rings, bought only a few months ago. Putting them on her finger had felt like marrying her all over again, like renewing the vows he had said in the church in Halmar; only this time it had been done in the privacy of their bedroom, the aftermath of the abduction like the debris of a tsunami at the edges of their life.

It had been a narrow escape. Jon carried a deep love for Jane in his heart, that cool-headed little woman who had picked Naomi up without a second thought when she had managed to slip her captor's surveillance for a moment. He had given her diamonds to show his gratitude, the best he could come up with. Jane had accepted them, but with an ironic smile on her lips.

As if, she had said, as if he needed to pay her for saving his wife. As if that required payment, and wouldn't he have done the same thing?

"Everything happens for a purpose," Naomi was saying, dragging him back into the here and now, "And if Parker hadn't done that, who knows. We'd never have met Jane. I wouldn't be going to lunch with her and letting her talk me into writing."

She sat down on his knee, and he smiled. "Again, perched on the piano bench, even though we have that big, comfy couch right there. We never learn."

Jon shut up when she kissed him, her touch as gentle as the mist of dew on thirsty flower petals.

The doorbell rang.

It still confused Jon, this possibility for others to just intrude, just step up to his door and knock. It almost felt as if here, in Brooklyn, people felt entitled to treat him like a normal human being in a way they never would have in Malibu.

"Sir." It was LaGasse, here to tell him that they had visitors and did they want to see them? She stepped aside to let him see Olaf and Lucia, and behind them, wide smiles on their faces, Ferro and Gemma. From a second car, Naomi's uncle Cesare and his wife, Angelica, were emerging.

Naomi's Italian family. The artist Ferro, and here he was, a crate propped against the car, waving, calling out to them in a way that made the people on the other side of the street turn their heads while Gemma slapped his arm to shut him up.

"We arrived last night," Ferro let the world know. "And here are your paintings, Jon. I can't wait to hear what you think!"

Instantly, the house turned from the quiet solitude into a copy of her uncle's house in Positano.

Helplessly, he watched his living room transform into a lounge, with Lucia taking over the kitchen while Olaf and Ferro began opening the crates. Naomi, still standing in the door, gazed at him around Gemma's adoration of her stomach and the many questions she was firing off, her voice trembling with happiness.

"You all," Jon said, "you're all staying for lunch, of course. I'll call my

mother and sister over, we'll have a family lunch. It's great to see you."
He broke off, tasting the words, and then added, "It's really wonderful.
What a wonderful Christmas surprise."

And so it was. He could not say why, why this storming of his house
seemed like a wonderful gift, like a treasure to add to his happiness.

"Of course we are staying," Lucia called. "And we're going to cook
for you too. I'm betting you're not getting any Italian food at all right
now, are you, Jon? We brought everything we need. Angelica, come
here, help me. This kitchen is so useless. Only my daughter would have
all these appliances and all of them in the wrong place!"

LaGasse and Alan appeared, bearing bags and baskets loaded with
groceries, and left again to bring in crates of wine and fruit.

"We brought all this yesterday, on the plane," Cesare explained,
picking out a bowl of fresh figs. "Here, Jon, from your favorite tree!"

Once again, the velvety skin of the fruit made him think of human
flesh, of soft, secret, erotic encounters, breathless sighs in the dark of
the night.

Clearing his throat, he returned the fig to Cesare. "How?" Jon asked.
"You're not allowed to bring groceries into the US. Did you smuggle
all this food here?"

"Stupid boy!" Olaf straightened. "We run a hotel business! We import foodstuffs from Italy and France all the time! What did you think?
That we serve American wine and ham in our restaurants? Or Californian champagne? Really, Jon."

Jon raised his hands in defense, but Olaf went on, "They even
brought their own bread. As if we'd touch your soggy stuff. Go, have
some, with homemade butter too!"

"Bread!" Those words seemed to wake Naomi from her trance.
"And olives, uncle? Did you bring me olives? And oil?"

Cesare went over to her and wrapped his arms around her shoulders.
"My sweetheart, your father made us fill the entire plane with food for
you. Everything is here, and in plenty. We will have a feast, and you will
have a lot left over to nibble on during the next weeks. Had I known
earlier that you were pregnant and homesick for our food, I'd have sent
you all you want weeks ago! You need good, homegrown food, our food,

to make you strong and give the baby all it needs! Your family is coming to your rescue."

"It's not as if we shop at Walmart," Jon growled, but his heart was singing as he watched Naomi tear off a big hunk of the golden bread and angle for the pot of butter. Lucia, wordlessly, had handed her a plate and a knife and was even now opening the jar of olives for her.

"You can't have wine," Cesare added, "so we brought you grape juice. You will drink it; it will make your blood red and healthy!"

"There." Ferro's voice made them all turn around.

Yes. There she was. There was Naomi, the way Ferro had portrayed her, sitting on a rock in the surf of the Mediterranean, flowers floating around her feet. The selkie, gazing in wonder at the blossoms, while the wind played in her hair.

"That dress!" Naomi broke the enchanted moment for Jon, pointing at the painting. "It was way too large back then! I'm sure it would fit me now! What a lovely day that was! We had that picnic down on the beach. Oh, I want to go back!" She was holding a thick slice of bread, butter slathered onto it liberally, and strawberry jam.

Jon shook his head at her. "Ferro," he said, "come to my office. I need to write you a check. It is wonderful. It is just the way I wanted it."

"The painting is a gift from me." Olaf took off his jacket and dropped it on the couch. "We never gave you a wedding gift. This is it, now. Welcome to your new home. Actually, I'm giving you both."

"Both? What both? Is there another one?" Naomi left her spot by the kitchen counter to come over.

Jon, slightly overwhelmed by her family, held out his hand for her, and she grabbed it. Her fingers were sticky, and it made him smile. She had not been this animated, this hungry, in a good long while.

"Yes, another one," he replied, and gestured at the second canvas Ferro and Cesare were busy unwrapping, "It's for you. I bought it from Ferro when we were in Positano, after..." His words fell away, seeing the expectant faces around them, seeing them wait for him to explain. Jon sighed. "After seeing you pray in Ferro's chapel, praying to the Virgin for a child. I wanted you to have it. I know you loved that mural, and here it is, in small."

Pleased, he was so pleased with the way her cheeks flushed and her lips parted at seeing the painting.

"The Annunciation," Naomi whispered.

"Yes." How he loved this picture. How he loved the soft shine on the Virgin's face at the sight of the angel, the gentle acceptance, the quiet wonder. A deep happiness settled in Jon's heart at seeing it again, remembering the hours they had spent in that little church in the meadow, visiting Ferro to see his work. That afternoon, so many things had seemed finally to come right, finally to settle into a kind of peace.

"If this baby is a girl," Naomi announced, her hand firmly in his, "I want to call her Allegra. I want her to be all the joy and laughter we can have." She turned to him for a kiss. Sadly, it was not a deep or long one, with her family standing around and watching; but its taste lingered on his lips, flavored as it was with butter and strawberry jam.

chapter 20

OSSO BUCCO. HE remembered the aroma from Positano, and now it was wafting through the entire house. In a way it was archaic, nearly ritualistic, how the women had congregated in the kitchen and the men in his studio, as if family bonding happened within the genders.

Helen and Valerie had come over; and now, a couple of hours later, Kevin and his wife were on the way to join them for dinner. There was a trace of regret that Joshua and Ethan couldn't be there, but Valerie's two girls had arrived and were chatting away with Gemma while helping set the table.

The dining table in their new dining room, so far a virgin, never used for a dinner party before.

Lucia had thrown up her hands. "You have this wonderful house," she had exclaimed, "one of the most beautiful mansions on the Promenade. And almost the only things in it are that Steinway for Jon and the coffeemaker I bought for you! Where are your plates, where is your household? And you, Naomi, running a hotel for so long! Everything was perfect at the Seaside—you were so meticulous—and here? Empty cupboards!" Accusingly she had pointed at the shelves in the kitchen where a couple of mugs sat beside a small stack of breakfast plates, but that was all. "What is wrong with you; you have a state-of-the-art kitchen, the best appliances money can buy, and you shy away from some decent dishes and cutlery?" Rolling her eyes in a very good show of Italian temper, she picked up the phone and fired off a rapid list of orders into it.

"There," she said to Naomi, "it won't be Spode, but it will be good enough for a while. Good thing we own hotels."

"Where do you want the painting, Jon?" Ferro was looking around in the big space of the studio in appreciation. The guitars were there, in a neat row along the wall—five of them, in their stands—the Steinway gleamed in ebony arrogance. "The light is very good. This would be a great atelier. This is a wonderful house! Can we see the rest? It's huge!"

So Jon led Cesare, Ferro, and Olaf through the entire house, from the library next door, his office, the living and dining rooms, and the kitchen from where they were expelled quickly enough by the women, and then up the stairs. Here was Naomi's study, right next to the bedroom, with the grand view of the city and the river, even all the way to the Statue of Liberty in the distance. It was furnished in pastel rose and cream, a soft, feminine boudoir-like space, a room for a princess.

Jon saw the tiny smile on Olaf's face, saw how he glanced at the jewelry cases on the table, the Oscar statue and the flowers, everything just the way it had been back in LA. Here, too, was a large walk-in closet filled with lovely dresses, rainbow colors with designer labels, silks, satins and lace, gossamer cotton and finest linen.

Everything. Jon wanted her to have everything, every beautiful thing in the world, exclusively, utterly hers. It was a rare day he came home from town, from the theater, and didn't bring something back that had caught his fancy, had seemed to have her name written on it: a shawl, a purse, sometimes just a single rose.

They stopped in the nursery, and the apartment next to it, discussing security, Naomi's health, hospitals, even baby names.

"Allegra," Olaf said softly, "I really like that. I like the thought. And I'm glad there's so much joy in your life. In Naomi's. Yes."

They had never discussed names, and he was pleased with her choice, loved how his daughter's name flowed over his lips like a melody.

"She'll end up being an Allie, you know," Olaf burst his sentimental bubble. "Are you sure you want your child to be called Allie?"

"I can deal with Allie." And that was true too. The name reminded him of the movie, *Contact*. He'd been there for the opening night and enjoyed it very much.

He also remembered how he had listened to the soundtrack, how Alan Silvestri's sweeping score had gripped his heart and made him wish he could fly away with Jody Foster, see those far and mysterious realms and those wheeling galaxies in the darkness of space. It had been one of those moments when he'd felt the yearning to soar, to be more than just himself, and it had nearly made him cry.

"Allie is a good name. And I'm sure we'll give her more than one name, so she can pick her favorite." His heart was humming. The music was filling it; the wish to go and lock himself up with the piano was overpowering. The urge to compose had not been this strong in a long while.

His mouth tightly clamped, Jon took them up the stairs to the third floor, into the unused and empty spaces of the rooms under the roof. They seldom came up here. There was the space Joshua had claimed, but it was still empty; waiting for him to finally decide how he wanted it furnished.

"It is a wonderful, old house," Cesare stated. "You did well to buy it."

Jon did not reply right away. There was still that weird feeling that if he opened his lips, music would come forth instead of words.

"I think Naomi bought it," Olaf answered instead. "It was her wedding gift to her husband."

Cesare stared.

"Yes." Olaf nodded. "I know. She hasn't lost it. She's still a mighty fine businesswoman. I think she knew right away what this property would be worth. I'm sure she struck a really good deal too." The old anger, the bitter regret, stung in his words, but it was a lot better contained than it used to be.

"I'm sure," Cesare said, peering out of the window at the skyline of Manhattan, "that business didn't play a role at all. I'm sure she just wanted to live here with her husband. It would appeal to her, wouldn't it: the grand view, the quiet, the closeness to Jon's family. She's like that, Olaf. She'd cut out her heart to make him happy."

"Don't even go there." There was steel in Olaf's voice now.

Jon wondered if they had forgotten that he was there. In a way it was amusing. No one else, no one in the world, treated him like this. No one would even dare to attempt it, knowing he'd not tolerate it for a second, and here he stood and took it from his wife's family. Here he stood, the world-famous rock star, the icon, the Master, and for Olaf and Cesare he was nothing more than that: Naomi's husband. The man she had chosen, the prince consort, second to her.

And yes. Jon shifted his shoulders, trying on this title. It fit well. Indeed, it fit him so well he shrugged a little more, nestling into it.

With the scent of dinner drifting through the hallway, the laughter of women coming up from the kitchen and these men judging his life, Jon let go.

It felt a bit like standing on a dock, on one of those narrow, wooden ones where sailing boats would moor, and seeing the water stretch away on all sides, the vista widening with every breath—he could step away from the need to be famous and celebrated—he could stop being himself and embrace this new feeling.

"Yes," he said, and it sounded normal enough, "we are like that. We'd do anything to make each other happy."

Olaf grinned mirthlessly.

"ACTUALLY," GEMMA HANDED Naomi a small bowl of olives. "I've come over to help you with the baby. You'll need someone, and why should it be a stranger when there's family to help." She shrugged as if it had already been decided. "Right?"

"Yes!" Naomi, olives forgotten, laughed. "Yes! Why in the world didn't I think of that? Yes, Gemma!"

And as easily as that, as if it had been planned ever since they'd been in Italy, the thing was settled.

"You'll stay here with us, of course! We have rooms for you! Heck, we have half a house for you! I'm so glad! The rooms aren't furnished yet, so you'll even get to pick out whatever you want, decorate them any way you like!"

Gemma waved her hand at Naomi in a fluid motion. "Calm down, cousin, or that baby will be born before its time. For now I'll stay at the hotel, and enjoy New York a bit. You need all the peace you can get, and to be alone with your husband. I also want to help Ferro with the exhibition."

"We are going to set up Ferro's art at the hotel," Olaf called from the table, where he was busy carving wafer-thin slices from the ham Cesare was holding for him, "He needs to make the jump from his chapel to the art world of New York, and high time too. Now he has enough paintings to make it worth a big exhibit."

"I'm not done buying your paintings, Ferro," Naomi said around the olive in her mouth. The aroma was so intense and overwhelming that she had to suck back the juices. Home, it tasted like home, and she stopped talking to ponder this thought for a moment: she thought of Positano as home, for the first time in her life. The long time in Norway, all those long years running the Seaside, alone, lonely, and sad, seemed to slip away from her as if time was bending and putting her back into the heart of her family, only this time without the pressure of her inheritance, free.

Imperiously, she held out her plate to her father, and he piled ham on it, carefully removing all the fat and giving her only the choicest morsels.

"Which one do you want?" Ferro was busy opening wine bottles and sniffing them, but he looked up at that. "We can mark down any painting you want, but I'd still like to show them."

"Nothing, mark down. I'll buy them. And then you can show them all you want, but I'll own them first."

"I'm having this totally outlandish idea." They all turned to Jon. He was standing in the door to the studio, a box of cigars in his hand, pointing toward the terrace, and the men moved. "I'm having this thought, and now that I'm thinking about it, I have to say I wonder why it never occurred to me earlier. Ferro, why don't you do the set paintings for the musical? Why aren't you the art director? Why did I never think of that? I mean, who could do it better than you, with the wonderful murals you produce? I'll have to make some phone calls later, and tomorrow we're going to the theater together. I want to introduce you to some people, and I want you to do this."

"Ah." Olaf put down the knife. "What an intriguing thought, indeed. And when I offered to buy into this venture, you said I was…"

"That was different. You had just insulted me, and I was angry at you," Jon cut him off. "If you really want to throw in some money, be my guest. Not that we need it. The investors are standing in line." He grinned grimly. "I know it doesn't mean a lot to you, Olaf, but my name does attract them. I do have a reputation."

"Yes, I bet you do." Olaf's blue eyes sparkled icily. "And it doesn't have anything to do with your profession either."

"It's all served on one plate, Olaf." Jon gave him his most brilliant stage smile. "You have to be a certain kind of man to make your way to the top. You should know; you're there too, aren't you?"

"Oh, shut up, both of you." Lucia dumped the bread basket on the dining table. "Your growling at each other is getting so old. Just go and smoke, and stand in the rain while you bark. Go, go!"

"You look even more alike now, you and Gemma." Angelica patted Naomi's cheek. "When you were in Positano, you were such a pale waif, thin and wan, and now look at you! Rosy cheeks, gleaming eyes, and these pounds you've gained are doing you a lot of good! I've never liked that super-slim look on any woman, and even less on one of my family. Now, if you came home, you'd fit right in. I'm very happy!"

"Thanks, Aunt Angelica," Gemma said. "I thought Naomi looked wonderful, as slim and pale as a fairy. I was so envious! Now she looks just like one of us."

"I think she looks a lot better now," Lucia agreed; and Helen nodded, adding, "Yes, you look the way you did when Jon first brought you home." She smiled. "I remember how surprised I was, seeing you. There he was, my famous son, the superstar; and he drops by, as casually as you please. Says he's getting married, and here's his fiancée. So I expect one of those Californian Barbie dolls, but no. He presents a real, live woman, a beautiful woman too. I never thought he had it in him, had the guts to fall in love with someone like you, Naomi."

"I wonder why." Naomi shook her head at them. "I wonder why you all see Jon in such a warped light. He's a normal man, with a normal life, and normal dreams."

Their laughter made the men on the terrace turn around and curiously peer inside, which made them giggle even more.

"Yes, sweetheart, I'm just glad you see things that way," Helen replied; "I love you for loving him like that. He needs it too. You are a saint."

"So what are you doing with your time these days?" Angelica asked, "beside wait for the baby to be born? I know Jon is busy with that musical, but you?"

Suddenly shy, Naomi pressed her hands between her knees as she hunched down on one of the stools at the kitchen counter. Lucia was giving her an encouraging smile, even nodded at her, but she still blushed and didn't answer right away.

"You can't go shopping and strolling around Manhattan every day, can you now?" Angelica pushed. "Even that must become boring after a while."

"I'm writing a book," Naomi said, her face hot with embarrassment, waiting for a reaction, but none came.

"Ah," Angelica said, and went on cutting tomatoes. Gemma pulled down the corners of her mouth, Helen and Valerie didn't react at all.

"I don't know how it happened," she went on. "It just...happened. I woke up one morning and knew I wanted to write a book. So, I started.

I've been wanting to do it for a while now, and then one morning, it just seemed right."

"Is that how it works?" Curious, Gemma leaned forward on the gleaming top of the counter. "I've often enough sat for Ferro, and while I had to sit still, I watched him paint. It sometimes seems as if he isn't even looking at me but at something else, something that's under my skin. He creeps me out with that. Is that how it feels to you, too, when you write? What are you writing about?"

"I wanted to write a story that's enmeshed with New York." Naomi took a deep breath and let the air flow from her chest. "About a life that's entwined with the city or maybe several lives. Something contemporary, romantic. I don't know. It's just tumbling out. I don't think about it a lot."

"That's what Ferro says too. He doesn't think while he paints. My, don't I have talented cousins." Gemma tapped on the jar of strawberry jam in front of her. "All I know how to do well is family stuff. Bake bread. Make jam. Cook, and look after babies. And I don't even have children of my own."

"Not yet," Angelica amended gently. "You are still young, Gemma. And granted, there aren't many eligible men in Positano who would attract your attention."

"Auntie, I'm not young!" With a deep sigh, Gemma pushed away the jam. "I'll be thirty-five in a few months. And not a man in sight."

The doorbell rang, and she jumped up. "I'll go!"

"That will be Kevin and Sarah." Helen grabbed a cloth from the rack to help Angelica remove the meat from the oven. "They are a bit early."

Gemma opened the door.

Sal stared at her. "Hello," he said.

chapter 21

HE BLINKED, BUT the mirage didn't disappear.

There she was, walking in front of him, the same swing to her step as Naomi, the same hair, only hers was long and tumbled down her back. She was sturdier, but not in an unpleasant way. Her shocking beauty was better grounded than Naomi's; she was more of a rose than a fragile lily, but just as stunning.

"Who are you?" he asked before they reached the living room, "Are you Naomi's sister? I didn't know she had a sister."

She turned around and threw him a smile. It hit his heart like an arrow, that smile. There was the same curl in the corners of her mouth, the same glint in her eyes; even the way she glanced over her shoulder was the same.

"I'm her cousin." Said in the sweetest lilt, the Italian accent warm and sweet like heated syrup. "My name is Gemma."

"Gemma." Sal tasted the sound on his lips.

She wore a red dress that alone was almost too much to bear. He loved red on Naomi.

"Jon." Gemma threw open the door. "You have a visitor."

Surprised, Sal stopped in his tracks. The house was full of people, and he hadn't even noticed. They were just sitting down around the large dining table. He would have sworn he'd never seen a meal that opulent laid out anywhere, ever. It was like walking into some kind of food-style show, or a magazine page.

There was Jon, still standing, a carving knife in hand, flanked by Olaf and another man, a tall, formidable man with a head of thick, black-gray locks and Naomi's dark eyes; and they were debating the best way to cut what looked like an entire ham, while Naomi, a plate in hand, looked on.

"Just give me more," she was saying, and quite impatiently, to which Olaf replied, "I'm sure you've had enough. It's a bit salty."

Jon nodded, which made her huff at them and flounce away in a show of temper, but with a small grin on her face.

"Ah, Sal." Wiping his hands on a napkin, Jon came to meet him halfway across the living room. "Come in. The family is here."

"So I see." He held out the folder he had brought. "The contracts."

That woman, Gemma, had joined Naomi at the counter that separated the kitchen from dining room, and between them they were pushing around a jar of jam as if it had a deeper meaning. His head was spinning, seeing them there together, like mirror images, copies from the same mold and two flowers on the same branch.

"Naomi's cousin Gemma." Jon glanced their way. "You wouldn't believe what I saw in Italy, Sal. That family…so many of them. And they all look alike. I thought my head was going to explode. It was beautiful beyond words."

Sal, though, had a good idea how that must have felt.

"It's good that you're here. You can have dinner with us." Jon opened the folder to read through the papers.

"What are you doing, working now?" It was Olaf, peering their way curiously, and Sal took a step back. His respect for Jon's father-in-law had not diminished, and seeing him now in these surroundings somehow made him more threatening, not less. Sal had never figured out why exactly. Olaf just seemed sinister.

Jon didn't even look up. "It's a new contract," he replied. "I'll just sign it. Give me a sec."

"What, sign and not even read?" Olaf came over; the knife Jon had put down earlier was in his hand. "What's it about? What did you buy?"

"Didn't buy anything. It's just a work deal. I'm going to write a movie soundtrack. Again."

"Ah." Peering over his shoulder, Olaf looked down at the papers. "Is the pay good? Are you asking enough?"

"Pay?"

Sal loved how Jon said it: dry, arrogant, amused, in command again, the Master.

"I don't work for a pay, Olaf. I get a share of the profits. The music is an important part of the movie, just as important as the script and the directing. I'm not going to be paid like one of the technicians; I'm in on the profits. Always."

"Risky," Olaf mumbled. "What if it fails?"

"Fails?" Jon handed the papers back to Sal and indicated for him to follow. "The things I touch don't fail, Olaf. I won't let them fail. Not a film with my score, not a musical I stage. The word 'fail' is not in my dictionary where my work is concerned. I thought you'd figured that out. It's all a matter of control. I may be the wuss you think I am over your daughter, but I'm certainly not in my work." And he strode off, walking out of the room as if leaving a stage, without turning back to make sure of the applause, with the utter conviction that all eyes were on him.

Sal loved him for it.

HE COULDN'T HELP himself; he kept staring at Gemma and Naomi. They were sitting next to each other, chatting away as if nothing else mattered, as if the world had not just been turned upside down and he was in free fall. In fact, the vista was so disturbing, Sal was fighting a headache. Not even the wine the man introduced as Ferro poured for him could get his brain sorted. The plate set down before him was heaped with steaming meat in a lush, red sauce, poured liberally over a melting mound of polenta. He hadn't seen anything like it in a very long time. The aroma was enough to make him drool, and it made him a little homesick for something he didn't even know he missed, something he'd never had.

"Have some bread." Helen was holding out the basket to him. "I swear, Sal, I wish I could eat like this every day and not regret it. Jon has done the most amazing, wonderful thing marrying Naomi, bringing this family into my life. Eat." She smeared butter onto a piece and handed it to him. "I know you guys have seen a lot of wonderful places and stayed at many grand hotels, but this, Sal, this beats it all. It's their own stuff, homegrown. And I swear to God, I'm going to visit them soon. I'm in heaven."

Surprised, Sal took the bread from her and bit into it. Helen was the sanest person he knew, and here she was, raving about Italian butter.

His head was spinning.

"Sal has a girlfriend," Naomi's voice woke him from his trance; "She is Indian. Now Indian food. That would be something. We should all go tomorrow and check out her father's deli." She was smiling at him, but he was certain there was a trace of mischief lurking in the corners of her eyes. "Her father owns a deli, isn't that right, Sal? And not very far from here. I'm in a mood for samosas for lunch tomorrow!"

"She's not really my girlfriend." How that lie tasted, how it grated in his throat. "We're just friends. I'm looking after her. She was in an accident…" His words died.

Naomi, still looking his way, had her chin propped on her hand, her elbow on the table. Even though nothing had changed in her face and the smile was still the same, it seemed to have frozen, a memory of the real thing only seconds ago.

"I took her out a couple of times," he plodded on, "and she helped me decorate my apartment. But girlfriend…that's taking it a bit far."

Jon was even worse than Naomi. He had put down his fork and was talking to Ferro, but Sal knew he had heard. His own words rang in his ears, when he had told Jon on the phone that he was in love; and here he was, staring at Gemma, and everything was falling apart.

"An affair." He was babbling again. It seemed like a terrible new habit, one that he had developed since coming to New York, and it made him feel very old. "It was just a short affair."

"Are you saying it's over?" There was a trace of regret in Naomi's voice. "I was going to invite her to the Christmas party, along with you. I'd even thought of going down to the deli to deliver the invitation myself, to get to know her a little better. You seemed quite in love, Sal. What a shame. She's a lovely girl."

"Yes, she is nice too. A bright young thing." Said that way, it sounded abysmally patronizing and cold. His neck and face crawled with sweat.

Strangely enough, no one but Jon and Naomi seemed to notice, or care, and Jon didn't seem in the mood to comment. His gaze slid past Sal when Helen addressed him, in the way someone chose to ignore a person he wanted nothing to do with at all. Never before, not in their most terrible moments of disagreement, had Jon ignored him like this.

"I have to go," Sal said, and rose.

Naomi followed him out into the hall.

Like a fairy, she stood in the warm light from the Christmas tree, her hands folded in front of her in the same still manner he had always loved about her, watching him, waiting.

"I wanted you to love someone." Her voice, and Sal closed his eyes, the pain a claw ripping down his back. "I was so happy for you, Sal. I was happy to see you happy at last."

"You look well." He waved in her direction. "That color looks good on you."

She laughed, and it sounded as if a breeze had gone through the tree and made the glass ornaments tinkle softly. "Which one?"

It was true; she was in blues and greens, with some violet thrown in: peacock colors.

"Sal."

If she came two steps closer, he'd be able to smell her perfume.

"Sal, what happened? You brought that girl to lunch with Jon; he told me about it. He was so upset! And now you sit here and tell us she was no more than a flirtation? What happened?"

Again, he wondered how it could be possible that she didn't know. To him it felt as if he were wearing a tattoo on his forehead, a banner on his chest, proclaiming his love.

"Nothing happened. Nothing. It's as I said. We go to lunch together sometimes. She helped me with the loft. And I made sure she'd not sue Jon for the accident."

"But Sal, that was two months ago. There were many people, including the paramedics, who could testify to the fact that she was unharmed, and standing where she wasn't supposed to be in the first place. That can't have been the reason."

From the dining room they could hear Cesare's voice booming as he told an amusing anecdote about a peach tree, and the answering laughter of the others.

The scent of food was heavy, delicious, making Sal's mouth water. He had hardly touched his plate.

"It was a stupid idea, coming here like this. I should have called first. I apologize." He moved into the entrance where he could see the falling snow through the glass panes in the door. Loneliness was waiting for him out there in the dusk. Loneliness and a long evening alone in his new loft. He could go home now, step out onto the roof garden and look across the water back at this house, at the beckoning lights behind the curtains, and feel the loneliness seep into his bones, the snowflakes melting on his face. The idea of walking across the bridge came to him. He could stroll down the Promenade all the way to the ramp and then walk across in the night and cold, toward the glittering city, the tall fingers of the World Trade Center guiding him home.

She was standing so quietly, waiting for him to talk, waiting for him to explain his life to her.

"Nothing happened." His hand on the doorknob, he turned back to her. "Yes, we're dating. It's more than just a friendship. But…"

Naomi moved forward. It was a small, slow step, and she stopped right away when Jon appeared behind her from the dining room. He looked at the tableau silently, waiting, his hands in his pockets, his shoulders arrogantly relaxed. Even now, in such a dire moment, Sal could appreciate his build, the well-balanced, tall body and good profile, so important, such an asset.

Jon stepped behind Naomi, putting his arm around her; and she leaned against him, her face softening, her entire attitude changing.

"I'm going home," Sal said. Pathetic, it sounded pathetic. He didn't move, realizing he was hoping for another glimpse of Gemma before he left.

"Let Alan drive you. It'll be tough to catch a cab now." Reaching into his pocket, Jon brought out his cell. "Have you thought about getting a car and driver? Or are you going to use a car service? It's quite a stretch from your loft to the theater."

"And do you need me there at all?" It popped out before he knew better, before he could stop the whiny plea.

Those hands on her belly, Jon's covering hers, made him stare and swallow. With an effort he pushed away the image of her in his arms, Naomi in love.

"I don't know what you're talking about, Sal," Jon was saying, his voice dropping those calm, sane words into his thoughts like ice cubes into a drink. "We've been over this. You know I need you. Why should things change? You came here today so I could sign that contract, didn't you?"

"Yes. Yes." His heart didn't feel quite like a brick anymore.

"You need to snap out of the blues, and fast." Jon was still talking, even though his attention was turning back toward the dining room and their guests. "Right after the holidays, work starts in earnest. I've been thinking about this score, and there are some other things I want to talk to you about. We need to find studio space here, and musicians; we need to get set up."

"Or we go to LA," Naomi interrupted. "It doesn't make much sense to reinvent the world when you have everything you need there, Jon. This is silly, and a waste of money." They both looked at her, surprised, but she shrugged and went on, "I love the Malibu house. I feel secure there. It would be warm too."

"But I thought you wanted to be here for the musical production." Sal dropped his hand from the doorknob and took a step back toward them, toward what made him want to live. "God bless your little nomad heart, Naomi; how did you ever manage to spend so many years in Halmar, in one spot? You're like one of those migrating birds."

"We aren't going to LA. You're not going to traipse all over the world, my little bird, not until this baby is born; and not for a while after either. Flying isn't good for babies. We're going to stay put. If you get a hankering for the beach, we'll find a house in the Hamptons. I've wanted to settle down for so long, and now that we have, we're not going to change it again." Jon waved at Sal. "Come on, Sal. I don't know what bit you, but your plate is still on the table, and you haven't seen Naomi's portrait yet either. Let's finish dinner!"

His jacket was in his hand, and he was still standing between the entrance and the hall, undecided.

But there she was, her hair shining in the gleam of the fairy lights, her smile so sweet, and she was gazing at him patiently, knowing, waiting.

"A portrait, eh?" Sal cleared his throat. "Yes, I'd like to see that. And yes, we can go and have breakfast at Maya's place tomorrow, if you want. It's a restaurant, after all."

"I think not," Naomi replied. "We'll stick with the Italian fare. Why should I eat samosas when I can have Parma ham and fresh figs?"

chapter 22

THIS WAS MORE fun than he had expected.

This was a real life. Jon had never before realized how much he had missed being part of a family, of a larger group of people who belonged together, people he knew he could trust without having to think about it. People who would let him be himself without questioning him.

There was a residue of derisive irony in Olaf, but even that was getting better by the minute, as they walked through the huge halls where the stage was being constructed.

"I didn't want just plain old set paintings," Jon said. "I want it to look real." They had stopped to watch how huge slabs of metal were rolled past them into the depths of the warehouse. "I'm imagining something on the scale of Cirque de Soleil—you know, moving stages, multiple levels. Naomi won't have it. She says it would distract from the music and make it nothing more than a backdrop to the visual impact."

"I think your wife is very clever," Olaf replied.

"Yes." What else could he say; it was the truth.

The others, the women, guided by Naomi, had vanished upstairs, into the costume workshop. He could hear their laughter, and wanted to go after them; but it would seem soppy, following her everywhere.

"So you want Ferro to create the imagery for this musical of yours?"

Olaf's voice shook him out of his thoughts, and Jon turned to face his father-in-law. "You can't fool me, Olaf. You might as well drop the act; I saw through you a long time ago. Stop being the cynic, will you? We're alone and don't have to play the alpha for any woman; we can say what we really mean. And yes, I want Ferro to do the imagery. I don't know anyone who could do it half as well; beside, why not keep things in the family if we can."

"You would have made a great Mafia boss, you know." A smile slipped across Olaf's face.

"Yeah, people keep telling me that. It's nonsense, of course. Just because I have a good business head and know what I want to do with my talent doesn't mean I'm a criminal. It just means that I have good instincts." He pulled out his cigarettes, ready to light one, and then stared at the pack. How many of these had he needed during his lonely years, and the drinking too? A good glass of Bourbon still tasted nice after dinner, but those bottles lasted a good while longer than they used to. In fact, they were hardly touched if there weren't any guests at the house. The only thing he needed, wanted, was to see her there in her window seat or on the couch, and life was good.

"I'm not one of your hungry, starry-eyed artists, Olaf. I want the success." Thoughtfully, Jon nodded to himself. "Success, yes. Naomi understands what I mean. Creativity means nothing without success. It's not an end in itself; it has to reach somebody, be worth something to an audience. That's the validation I need."

"Validation." Olaf seemed to chew on that word. "An interesting point. I don't think I've ever looked at it that way. I really like art; don't get me wrong!" He took one of the cigarettes and lit it with Jon's lighter. "But I also think a man has to make a success of himself. Can't deny the fact that you've done that. Only I've always thought of showbiz as something ephemeral, glitzy, useless, an empty life."

"I'm a bit tired of people thinking creativity is something that has to happen, no matter what. That artists will be artists, regardless of pay. Creative people like to eat too. I like the good life. I've worked hard for it. I've always worked hard. It's cool being able to give beauty to the world and make money from it. I don't think I'd still be in this business if it hadn't been a success for me." The cigarette didn't taste good, and Jon dropped it to step on it. Olaf watched with raised brows.

"And then?" he asked. "What would you have done instead? Somehow I can't see you going to work somewhere in a suit and tie every day."

"Hey, I look great in a suit and tie." Slightly embarrassed, Jon tucked his shirt back into his jeans. "Only, you know."

Olaf grinned and adjusted his silk tie before buttoning his jacket. He was immaculately dressed, as always, as if he was about to go to a meeting with investors, or was on the way to buy a new hotel. A little enviously, Jon eyed the fine cut and material of his suit, wondering what Naomi would say if he started dressing like that on a daily basis, and deciding she would probably love it. It would give her another reason to shop the designer stores she favored. The thought made his heart expand. How he loved taking her to Valentino and to the other stores she liked, watching her try on all those wonderful creations. He loved to pamper and spoil her.

"I have no idea. I can't tell you. There is enough obsession in me to be quite driven. The music spills over. Not so much the words, but the melodies." Jon waved at the air. "All around me. In the wind, in the sounds from the street. Naomi says, she says…" His head swiveled toward the stairway. "She says every town has its own music, she can hear it too. Only with her it comes out in poetry, in words; and the way she says things, the way she can grasp things and put them into words brings me to my knees. She is incredible. It's as if she lives in my mind." This made Jon smile. "Well, she does. She lives in my heart."

Olaf cleared his throat. "Well, it's nice to know my daughter is cherished in such a way. I have to admit, I hated you, Jon. When Naomi came back home all those years ago, so broken, so desolate, I wanted to go to LA, find you, and smash in your face. I wanted to lie in wait for you outside your house and run over you with a car, buy a gun and shoot you. My lovely, wonderful daughter, abused, made to suffer, and tossed away. You have no idea how much I hated you. And when you showed up in Geneva, searching for her, God, I wished I had owned a gun. I would have shot you, right then and there in my living room. My poor, sweet Naomi, and you were the bastard who had made her so unhappy. The thought was enough to make me want to vomit."

Jon fished out another cigarette, and this time he took a couple of deep drags, really deep ones, and wished there was a stiff drink to go with them. This had been meant to be an outing, a fun day showing the family the workshop and introducing Ferro to the musical, and here he stood with Olaf, bearing this torrent of bitterness and old fury.

"Pregnant," Olaf went on, "she was pregnant, and she wouldn't hear of an abortion. We really tried hard to convince her, bribe her; we would have done anything to wash away anything that reminded her of you, but she wouldn't listen. All she asked was for me to hide her away, hide her in a place where you would never find her. So we took her to Norway." He held out his hand for the cigarettes, and Jon handed them over. "When Joshua was born and I saw that sweet little face, I was glad she had been so stubborn. We loved him instantly."

"I didn't abuse her." His voice sounded rough, and Jon had to clear his throat before he could go on. "Never, I never abused Naomi. It's true, I neglected her; I didn't care for her the way I should have. But I never abused her, or did her any harm. Never."

"I know." The answer was so dry and curt that Jon blinked. "I know, and I knew that all along. She never said anything bad about you, and she never permitted us to either. You were not discussed. She wanted you cut out of her life the way I wanted the child cut out of her womb. Only neither one happened." His teeth showed in a mirthless shark's grin. "You're hard to avoid. That voice of yours is quite recognizable on the radio."

"I loved her the entire time." A simple truth, and easy to confess. "I loved Naomi all the time, every day of my life. Every morning, all those years, when I woke up, for an instant I let myself drift and believe she was there, next to me. But I was alone." Jon closed his eyes and rubbed his brow. "Love can be so cruel. Once it has its hooks in your flesh it'll never let you go. And if you lose the one you love, you will compare everyone new to the love you lost. Everything will be a small, sad replica of the real thing. And it's strange, other memories grow stale after enough time has passed. They dim, grow into a sepia print of themselves; but this, real love, it burns in your heart like a bright flame."

They both turned when they heard Naomi's voice from upstairs. A moment later she appeared, a length of gossamer fabric draped around her shoulders.

"Look at this, Jon," she said, coming down to them. "This is just what I meant when I said peacock colored. Isn't it wonderful? I'm wondering if I should ask them to make me a dress from it as well."

They were staring at her, both her father and her husband, suddenly silent, and she stopped in her tracks. "What? What now? Why are you looking at me like that?"

It was so funny, Jon thought, how they loved her, each in his own way, and so fiercely that each wanted to protect her from the other.

"Nothing, baby," he replied, "nothing at all. You're right; it's lovely."

SHE STOPPED AT the gate. It was high, a solid metal slab, and the walls on each side were like the sides of a bastion. No one would enter these premises without being invited first.

Sal rang the bell as if it was nothing, as if this was the house of nobody special at all. The camera on the wall was watching them like a little one-eyed metal owl, and Maya wondered who was sitting at the screen right now, ready to let them in. She felt awkward. Sal had insisted on buying her clothes for the occasion, even new shoes and a purse; and even though she had loved it, had enjoyed the half hour at the Blahnik store for the shoes, it somehow made her feel guilty.

And now, outside Jon's house, the feeling of trepidation was back. As if he had been ashamed of her, as if he wasn't ready to take her to this Christmas party as herself, the way she was, but had to dress her up to meet expectations, and not even in the clothes he'd bought her before, but brand-new ones.

"I have no idea who's here," Sal said. "You're not nervous, are you?"

She noted that he was fiddling with the box of cigarettes, opening and closing it as if he couldn't make up his mind.

"How can I not be nervous, Sal? I'm about to be a guest in Jon Stone's house. Do you even realize what that means? This is something that only happens in romance novels!"

"Yeah, but there's no grand love affair waiting for you here." He gave her a brilliant smile. "Jon is as disgustingly married as anyone can possibly be, and you're my girlfriend."

The door buzzed open, and Sal entered ahead of her. A front yard greeted her, with a garden path leading up to the house. Maya could hardly believe her eyes. A front yard, in the middle of Brooklyn. She had a good idea how much money had gone into buying this house and the ground on which it stood.

"Jon grew up two blocks down the street from here," Sal was telling her, but she was barely listening. "Maybe you even went to the same school. Did you know he's a local boy?"

As if he wanted to diminish him, wanted to make him seem more ordinary. Maya wondered if it was to calm her fears; and she was about to say that it was okay, she wasn't nervous, and please remember she had seen Jon in his undershirt before the show, so it wasn't really that intimidating at all, but Sal gave her a critical look and nodded. "Good. You look good."

"What did you think I'd look like?" She stopped in her tracks.

"What do you mean? All I said was that you look great!"

The door to the house opened. Light and music spilled down the front stairs, closely followed by the scent of food and coffee.

"Sal," Gemma cried in greeting, "you're just in time. Naomi is complaining because we won't give her any champagne, and she needs distraction."

"Oh, good grief, then give her some," came Sal's reply. "Just a teeny bit, she's just trying to make a point."

Maya watched how she kissed Sal on the cheek, rising on her toes to do so, and how he grasped her around the waist without even thinking about it to return the kiss and say, "You smell nice. Cute perfume," and her flippant reply, "Bought it in Naples, before we got on the plane. I have a passion for these English scents, but they are hard to get in Positano." Then she laughed and added, "Actually, not at all. I love exclusive things."

"And so you should," Sal agreed. "A lovely woman should have things that are beautiful and unique to her own style. Your cousin is a great example of that; she follows this credo with verve."

"Oh, Naomi!" Gemma waved him away. "No one is like Naomi. She is unique all right. And thank God she has found the right husband to take care of her!"

IT WAS LIKE stepping into a magazine, into a perfect Christmas setting.

Maya had never seen anything like it in any house she had visited, but then she had never been in any house like this either. While she waited for Sal to take her coat she gazed around at the large hall with the fireplace and the tall Christmas tree, the mound of gifts under it, all of them wrapped in red or gold. A garland of greenery wound around the banister of the stairway leading upstairs, and in the window on the landing hung a holly wreath with a big red bow. The entire place seemed to gleam festively.

A movement made her swivel around.

There he was, Jon, and her heart stopped for a moment. He was coming toward them from another room, and he looked nothing like he had that day when they had met for lunch. Now he smiled at her and even pecked a kiss on her cheek in greeting, as if she belonged, as if she was a member of this extended family.

"The accident girl," he said, and her knees turned to mush at hearing that voice. "Welcome, and Merry Christmas!"

She was going to swoon. She was going to faint in his arms and make a fool of herself, Maya was certain of it. He smelled so nice, of cigar smoke and an aftershave with the scent of cedar, just the way she thought a man should. His arm was still around her while he chatted with Sal, and guiding her, they entered the living room.

At least Maya thought it was a living room.

It was more like half the ground floor turned into a living space, with couches and chairs and small tables, an open arch leading into a large dining area, and beyond that, a huge kitchen, separated from the rest by a marble-topped counter. Everything was airy, generous, spacey, and elegant in a cozy way.

It was hard to imagine anyone actually living here. The setting was that perfect, that lovely, and the people in it fit there as if it were a painting. Some faces were familiar; she remembered them from the concert night. Art, Russ, and of course, Naomi.

Naomi, who was even now waving and moving across the room.

"Welcome," she said, kissing her on the cheek much like Jon had done a moment earlier. "Welcome to our home. I'm glad to see you."

And those, Maya thought, were words she had never dreamed of hearing from Jon Stone's wife. She tried to smile, but it came out rather crooked, and hidden by a wild blush.

chapter 23

IT WASN'T THAT anyone was unkind. They filled her plate, offered her wine, asked her if she had everything she needed, and then they ignored her.

Maya was certain it wasn't intentional—there was no maliciousness to it—but the talk flowed around her and over her; the subjects they touched were so far beyond her, there was nothing she could contribute. She had never heard of places called Positano or Kleinburg, and she had never been inside the Shubert Theater, let alone the Met.

Utah, the gray-haired man was saying, the one who had been introduced as Naomi's father, when Joshua had suggested the idea of a hotel with rooms open to the sky. What did they think of that? A place in the desert where people would be able to sleep under the stars but with all the comforts of a luxury resort.

Jon didn't think too much of it and said so without hesitation, but Naomi sat back thoughtfully and took her time replying.

"The rooms would have to be big," she then said, "so they don't seem like cells when the ceiling is missing. And you would have to have retractable ceilings that could be quickly moved back in place when the weather is inclement."

"I think it's an intriguing idea." Olaf reached past Maya for the bowl of Brussels sprouts. "Innovative. We'd have to do some solid marketing, of course."

The talk drifted away again, back to the musical and the work on the stage, the costumes, the story.

"Who edited the script?" Olaf asked Naomi, and she smiled.

"Jane" was her answer, and he pursed his lips in appreciation. "Jane did it. That was a fun experience, and now I know what's coming my way with the book."

And with that they began talking about her writing, and again Maya listened, hearing the words but hardly understanding their meaning. It was an astounding experience, almost as if all these people around her were talking in code.

"No, it's really easy," Naomi was saying. "I think all it takes is a good sense of observation. The stories are all there. All you need to do is write them down."

"It's the same with painting." Ferro nodded at her words. "Everything you ever want to paint is there. You just need to see it first. Most people don't really pay attention to their surroundings. They follow the path they have laid out for themselves and don't ever stray left and right. But that's where the images and stories are."

"Like when you're at a restaurant. Every person around you has a story. The young businessman, eating with his mouth open, talking with food in his mouth, and you know no matter how much he spent on his suit, his upbringing sucks. Or the other day when I had lunch with Jane. There was this author with a host of publishing people around her, and she had no idea what she was doing there or what they expected of her. It was weird to watch. And it made me wonder how she came to be an author in the first place. She looked as if someone had dropped her into the role, and the clothes were still too big for her."

"So what do you do? Are you in the music business too?" Gemma had asked this, and she was now looking at Maya across the platter of grilled birds.

Pheasant, Sal had told her when she'd been uncertain if she wanted any, and they were delicious. She was not sure she agreed with that. The meat tasted gamey, and she actually abhorred the yellow, creamy pulp they called polenta.

"No, I'm not." She hadn't prepared for this question, she realized, and fell silent, thinking.

"Maya's family owns a deli on Atlantic," Sal answered for her. "They specialize in Indian food. It's excellent!"

As easy as that. He had spoken nothing but the truth; and yet in her mind she saw a well-kept place, with linen napkins and nice, wooden tables, simple but elegant, stylish, and not her father's dingy shop. A hot wave of shame washed over her.

"It's not big," she said, "just my family work there. Nothing fancy."

"Oh, but if the food is good size doesn't matter," Gemma smiled at Sal. "I love Indian food! Maybe we should all go there and have lunch someday soon. I need to explore this part of New York anyway if I'm going to live here in the future, right? Maybe Maya's deli is a good place to go for a walk with the baby, have a bite there and turn around."

"You're always welcome." Maya balled her sweaty hands together in her lap. She didn't feel like sitting here anymore, and she certainly didn't feel like eating.

Chestnuts. She only knew chestnuts from the street vendor at the corner who sold them in a paper bag—hot, steaming, the skin black from the fire—but not this brown mush in the bowl right in front or her. Baby poo. It looked like baby poo, and she couldn't stand the thought of eating it.

A yearning for one of her mother's samosas came over her. She wanted to be in the steamy kitchen, where she could sit on the windowsill and hold Selma in her lap while they nibbled nuts, samosas, and fried potatoes.

"So how did you meet Sal?" This from Jon's mother, she could hardly believe it. She was sitting down for dinner at one table with Jon Stone's mother as if it meant nothing. And the strange thing was, these people were pretty normal. Totally different, living in a totally different world, but in their own way just as much a family as her own.

"At a concert," she began to reply; but Sal quickly said, "We literally ran into Maya. She's the one we nearly hit with the car."

"Oh." Helen gave her a small, shrewd smile but didn't pursue the topic any further.

The talk drifted away from her again, this time to Ferro and his art, to the contract he had just signed with Jon and his partners for the stage design, and how this would keep him in New York for an indefinite time. He shrugged their concern away; for now he was fine at the hotel, and he'd start looking around for a loft or something. He had always wanted a loft in Manhattan, he stated, but so far there had never been a reason to move here.

Just like that. He said he wanted a loft in Manhattan, and everyone around the table nodded, as if it was the most normal thing in the world.

Maya remembered only too well how much Sal had paid for his and how she'd wondered how it could be that anyone, anyone at all, could go out and spend that kind of money in the blink of an eye. Just like he hadn't thought twice about taking her to the expensive shops on Fifth

Avenue to dress her for this occasion.

"Nothing fancy" had been his words, "but classy."

And so here she was, in a red dress with a small jacket over which she had worn a new black coat, and there was a matching purse, too.

She liked the Valentino label in the back of the dress, but somehow it hadn't felt right. Somehow it felt as if he'd have been ashamed of bringing her here in anything else.

"I have a nice loft," Sal said, "a really great place, and in a fabulous location, right on the river. The one below mine looks empty."

She needed to use the bathroom. Excusing herself, she got up, and instantly there was a maid by her side, indicating she would show her the way.

They returned to the hall, where the girl pointed to a door near the top of the stairs and left her to her own devices.

Maya climbed the stairs and looked around. The doors were all open, inviting her to step closer and have a look inside. Furtively she looked around, afraid someone would catch her and throw her out of the house, but she moved to the doorway of a corner room and stood in the light spilling into the hall as she glimpsed inside.

Her breath stopped.

Here it was, the sanctuary, the heart of all the music: a Steinway grand, highly polished, open, and on the stand above the keys a sheaf of paper with staff lines, a pencil, reading glasses. Farther into the room stood a couch, a cashmere throw balled up in one of its corners and a book open on it. A laptop sat on the small table beside the couch, open, with an image of Jon onstage on the screen. He was caught in a beam of blue light, the microphone in one hand, the other one raised, pointing at Sean, who was waving back at him. A coffee mug stood beside the computer, and a pair of woolen socks lay on the carpet, as if someone had taken them off there and had been too lazy to pick them up.

On the wall, in a spot that could easily be seen from the piano bench, hung a large painting. Forgetting herself, Maya stepped closer to look at it more closely.

It was, without question, Naomi, and it was the most beautiful painting she had ever seen. She wondered where it had been done, with that brilliant blue water and the backdrop of green mountain slopes. Even the flowers drifting in the surf seemed strange, as if picked in another world. The dress, Maya adored the dress. It was too large, slipping from Naomi's shoulder, the skirt trailing in the water, but that only enhanced the romance of the portrait.

"My cousin painted it."

The blood drained from Maya's head. "I'm sorry, I didn't mean to intrude," she began, but Naomi waved it away.

"No worries, the door was open; you're welcome to look around. Even though—" With a laugh, she pointed at the socks. "I should have cleaned up, right? Lazy!" She went over to the couch and with some effort bent down to pick up the socks and roll them into a ball. "This is where I work. It's a cozy niche, and I can watch Jon at the piano."

Maya could imagine it very well. One composing, one writing, sharing the space. It would be very quiet, except for the music Jon created. A quiet, tranquil room—no food smells, no shouting, graceful, lovely.

"I like that dress," Naomi said, tossing the socks on the couch. "I was looking at it myself the other day, but right now it doesn't make any sense to buy normal clothes." With a smile, she patted her stomach. It wasn't very big yet, but clearly visible under the rose dress she was wearing. "Valentino is my favorite designer. I'm glad you got it. The dress, I mean."

She sounded, Maya thought, as hare-brained as she imagined the wife of a wealthy man like Jon Stone to be. As if nothing but fashion and the interior of her house mattered.

"I'm so glad Sal found you," Naomi went on, "He needed someone in his life. It's so nice to see him happy, and I like you for that. A lot."

Surprise washed over Maya, and she opened her mouth to reply, but Naomi said, "He's a wonderful man—gentle, generous, and very kind—even though he hides it behind his cynical shell. If anyone deserves to find the right woman and some peace, it's Sal."

Naomi waited for her response, her hands folded over her belly in that ancient gesture of all pregnant women. She was beautiful, very lovely with her large, black eyes and the fair skin, her dark hair curling around her face and shoulders. Compared to her, Maya felt like a clumsy giant. Diamonds glittered around her throat, big marbles caught in filigree metal, really much too large to be real; but Maya was sure that there would be no fake jewelry in Naomi's possession.

"It's not really my kind of dress," Maya said. "Sal picked it. He said it looked good on me, but I don't know. I'm really more accustomed to wearing simpler things, nothing with lace and bows, and certainly not velvet." She gestured at Naomi, and the wide folds of chiffon flowing around her body. "It would look really good on you, though. It's your style, totally."

Naomi's lips drew together. It was only a fleeting, marginal thing, hardly noticeable; but it was there.

"Yes, it is my style," she agreed in a slow, meditative tone. "As I said, I was looking at it myself a few days ago."

For a moment silence settled over them, a nearly tangible web of thought and memory. They could hear the voices of the others from the dining room, a cork popping, and a snatch of Christmas music, Jon falling in and singing a verse with the orchestra, which brought him a round of laughing applause.

"It's a lovely dress, and it looks lovely on you," Naomi said. "I'm happy to see Sal care for you. And yes, velvet does look good on you. It's very festive! Don't worry, it suits you just fine."

The words were there, but somehow Maya had the feeling that something was hidden under them, a current like a trickle of water under a cover of leaves or in the fold of a meadow.

"So…" Maya gestured at the computer. "This is where you work? Don't you feel the need for a space of you own, where no one will interrupt you?"

A fine smile appeared on Naomi's lips, a dreamy, gentle curling of her mouth. "Oh, there's so much space in this house, Jon and I could live here and never meet. And yet we like to share the same room. We both have been lonely and without the other for much too long in our lives; we both feel the need to make up for that. Yes, this is where I work. I'm a writer now. Who would have thought?"

"A writer." She'd never thought about it, never wondered what someone like Naomi did, if anything at all. She didn't talk a lot, and mostly it was about simple, everyday things. It seemed as if everything centered on Jon for her.

"Sounds crazy, I know." Astoundingly, a faint blush tinged Naomi's cheek. "And presumptuous. But…there it is. I'm writing a book, and I have a friend who's a publisher, and she loves it. We'll see how it turns out." She shrugged. "It's not as hard as I thought. All I have to do is write it down, sort of. It feels too easy to be honest. I don't know. But it also feels right." Her slim hand waved through the air as if to catch the words she wanted to say. "It's funny how you know what to write."

"I don't know. If you say so…" This was awkward. A trickle of sweat ran down Maya's back.

"Oh, don't worry." The moment was over, the strange vibe drifting away like a wisp of smoke. Naomi smiled again; there was nothing left of the pensiveness of a second ago. "I have no idea what I'm doing myself. But it's something I've always wanted to do." A small shrug, a tiny wave of her hand.

Maya wondered how someone like Naomi Stone could be so full of doubt, so uncertain of herself, and even ready to admit to it.

"And now I have the space to do it, and the freedom." Naomi added, and it sounded like an afterthought, like something she'd just realized.

"I would have thought you could do whatever you wanted, and all the time." It had slipped out before she'd thought about it. In an attempt to take back the words, Maya pressed her fingers on her lips, but it was too late, of course.

Naomi's lips quivered, and then she laughed. It was a lovely sound, like gentle drops on petals. "Lord, no. If you come from a family like mine, duty is woven into your first onesie and never leaves you, not until you either accept and master it or get rid of it by drastic measures. I chose the second option, and it brought me many years of bitter estrangement from my family. It's only now, only after my son decided he loves our family business better than music, that some peace has been found. It's a high price for me, but everyone else is happy. And without Jon…" Her gaze drifted toward the door. "Without Jon, I don't think I'd ever have found the courage to start writing in earnest. He practically forced me to it. He believes in me more than I do, God bless him. I'm not a very brave person."

Now that, Maya was sure, was the lie of the century; and again she wondered about this woman, and how it could be that she had this strong hold over someone like Jon Stone.

"Here you are!" And there he was, the Master himself, a trace of worry on his face, replaced right away by a smile when he saw them.

"What are you doing here? Dessert is about to be served."

Three big strides, and he was by Naomi's side, his arm around her waist, holding her close.

"We were looking at the portrait," she replied, leaning into him.

"Maya likes it. And I do too. It doesn't look a bit like me, but it's a lovely painting."

"It does so look like you, my love. That was just the way you looked that afternoon, a selkie, a lovely mermaid; and you were complaining that we weren't feeding you." His lips were on her hair as he gazed up at the picture over her head. "And yes, it really was a lovely day."

As if she wasn't there. As if she was just a piece of furniture, something bought and placed there, and now of no further consequence.

Softly, Maya retreated, left the big room with the Steinway, and the people who belonged there.

chapter 24

SHE WOULDN'T HEAR of it.

Of course, Naomi said, ready to toss the coffee in his face, of course, she would come along to the theater and watch the first rehearsal. There was no way he was going to keep her home. She was not going to be locked up for another three months in the house; this was her musical, and she wanted to be there.

"I'll get premature gray hair over you," Jon said, carefully removing his cup from her reach; and she replied, "At your age, hardly premature."

In the night, she had woken him by taking his hand and placing it on her belly. Tired as he'd been, he'd cradled her and rested his head against her neck, ready to fall asleep again, but then he had felt it.

A tiny tremor, like the knocking of a chick inside an eggshell, like a tentative try to get into contact.

He had spread out his fingers, cupping the curve, and there it had been: like a sea creature caught in a net, a movement, a turning from one side to the other, reshaping Naomi's body for a moment, taking complete possession of it.

"She's wide awake," Naomi had mumbled, "ready to play. Go to sleep, little one," and had settled back into sleep herself, her shoulder against his chest, soft, warm, loved.

But Jon, he'd lain, his hand still in place, and pretended he was holding that squirming, kicking thing in his arm, gazing into a real face, tiny lips and tiny nose, black curls on the tiny head, and fingers so small they hardly counted.

So soon now, only a few more months, and Naomi was holding up well. Kevin had once again told him what to look for: the swelling ankles, shortness of breath, or, even more ominous, a persistent, liquid cough—he hadn't even asked. He didn't want to know. He'd just nodded and promised to take her to the hospital right away, against her protest if need be. She went for her checkups regularly, and he went along. There wasn't an ultrasound every time, even though he'd have loved it; but Julian always sent them away pleased, actually pleasantly surprised, saying she was doing better than he had hoped.

"Your medical history made me very uncomfortable," he had admitted the last time, "but it seems you're doing everything right, and getting enough rest."

"Rest, rest, rest." Back in the car, Naomi had tossed her gloves and purse on the seat, muttering. "Yes, I'm getting enough rest. What does he think, that I go to a party every night, the way I'm looking now?"

It was just bravado and Jon knew it. He never responded to her outbreaks, but now, over breakfast, he knew that she was serious.

"You'll have to promise me," he said, "at the first sign of feeling tired, we come home."

"No."

Surprised, he turned to her from the coffeemaker, where he had gone for a refill.

"I will go home," Naomi added, "and rest, rest, rest. But you will do your work, Jon. We only have until September to make this show spectacular, and we've just started. You can't let this go downhill while you sit here and hold my hand. There's a lot of money involved, and I want this to be a success."

She was in wool leggings and a big sweater, her feet in thick socks, nothing like the glamorous beauty of their Christmas party; and he was sure he loved her even better this way. Somehow it seemed as if she was just his: private, relaxed, showing her true self, trusting him to love her even with uncombed hair.

And what that said about them. They had come so far, through so many trials; and here they were, in calm waters, as if every song of the storm had been sung, only a memory now.

"I can't let you go alone!" He couldn't even imagine it. Naomi, not feeling well and being driven through town by herself, and what if something happened and she needed help...

"Stop it, Jon." She bit her lip to keep from laughing. "You are such a drama queen. I can see what you're thinking, and it's not going to happen. Nothing will happen. You'll see. It will be a perfectly boring day." Taking a bite of her toast, she added, "I'm really curious to hear

Eva sing today. I wonder if Stan will let her. Do they start singing at the first rehearsal?"

Jon had to admit that he didn't know, and hadn't asked. He was comfortable being a watcher, much more so than he'd thought. In fact, he enjoyed seeing what others did with his music, giving it a new meaning, putting their own mark on it.

"I wonder," he said, and it sounded a bit out of the blue, "if this is how it feels when you release a book. You had your own thoughts writing it, wanted it just that way, and expected everyone else to see it like that too. Only they don't. They read it totally differently, interpret your words like you never thought they would."

Naomi brushed the crumbs of her toast into a little heap, waiting.

"If you insist on coming, get dressed," Jon said. "We have to go."

IT WAS ALWAYS the smell that fascinated her most.

She wondered where it came from or how it had grown to be like that: theater. Walking into that auditorium was so different from the venues Jon used. It was large and yet intimate, built only for this one purpose, to focus on the stage. No ghost of sports events or others spectacles, just the performance on stage and the audience.

To Naomi's disappointment, there was no music.

"No, no, no, no," Stan cried in his usual, dramatic way, "first the play, then the music! First the roles, then the singing. Don't you know anything about staging a play?"

"No," she replied quite candidly, "and I don't have to either. That's your job, isn't it?"

Mumbling, cursing, putting on another show for her, he trotted off toward the stage, where the actors were waiting.

It felt strange to see a blond man playing the fisherman. She had always envisioned him to look like Jon, and here was a stranger, someone fair and tall but wiry, a dancer, and with a tenor voice instead of Jon's baritone. He looked good with Eva and her red hair, she had to admit. They made a striking pair.

There were no sets yet. She could see all the way to the back of the stage, where it seemed to dwindle into darkness, ominous ropes hanging down from a ceiling hidden by curtains and light riggings. The piano was gone now, the boards empty but for some chairs and a single bottle of water, forgotten there, lost.

Someone had drawn marks on the stage, indicating things, maybe the beach, maybe the fisherman's hut, Naomi couldn't make it out.

The door to the outside world opened just as Stan broke out in a harangue about some script or other not being there, and Wilfred flitting out the backstage entrance to run and get it. For a moment the street noise of Manhattan in midmorning spilled inside, calling, teasing as always, trying to lure her into its bloodstream and take her away, and Naomi turned.

Sal was there, Maya in tow.

Naomi hadn't seen her since the Christmas party, six weeks ago now, and she drew back in surprise.

This was hardly the girl from the concert night. This was a stranger, an elegant, well-dressed stranger. Her hair had been cut and layered, there was makeup on her face, and she was in fine clothes. The purse she was carrying matched her boots and gloves, and her scarf was the finest cashmere.

The funny thing was, everything she was wearing looked like something Naomi would gladly have bought for herself. That rose coat with the narrow waist and wide, swinging skirt gave her twinges of envy and made her resolve to ask where she'd got it; and the purse was another Valentino, mauve, with a big leather bow, and to die for. She wanted it.

"You look wonderful!" Naomi said, and meant it. "Really gorgeous! Are you going out for lunch or something?"

And it was true, even Sal looked different, as if he had put on some weight, the worry lines around his mouth gone, his hair groomed; and he was in a new leather jacket.

"Yes, we are, but Sal wanted to drop by first." Maya tossed back her glossy mane, looking down at the stage where Jon was talking to Stan, Sal moving down the aisle toward them. Jon raised his hand in greeting when he saw his manager and smiled.

"This is exciting. I've never been inside a theater during rehearsals." With a crooked smile, she shrugged. "I've never been inside any of the Broadway theaters before."

"Do you like opera?" This piqued Naomi's interest, and she rose to stretch, her hands pressed against her lower back. It was beginning to hurt. The memory of that pain during her pregnancy with Joshua came back, and how she had often done the same thing then to ease the stiffness.

"I'm not sure." The purse came to rest on the seat next to Naomi's. She wondered if she could talk Jon into taking her to Valentino's to get one for herself but then dismissed the idea regretfully, knowing it would look silly if she ran around with the same bag Maya was carrying.

"I'm not sure I like opera," Maya was saying, "But I'd certainly like to see the Met from the inside, and see a performance someday. Maybe ballet would be more my thing." She sighed, poking at the purse. "I hate this thing. It's way too flouncy for me. But Sal loves it; he says it goes well with the coat. Oh, well, if it makes him happy." Unbuttoning the coat, she added, "It's not really my choice of a coat either. But, well…" Her head swiveled to where Sal and Jon were standing, their backs turned toward them as they debated something on the stage. "If it makes him happy, I'll wear it. See, if I could pick a designer it would be Lauren. He's more my style. Valentino is so frilly."

A dark, dangerous suspicion rose in the back of Naomi's throat, a thought so dire that she had to force it back down like acid reflux, like bile. She sank back into her seat, her hands limp on her knees, hardly hearing what Maya was saying. The bag sat beside her. She would have bought it immediately, would have veered toward it in the store as if drawn by a magnet and clutched it to her chest until someone came to wrap it up for her. It had her name stenciled all over the fine leather for all she knew.

The same went for that rose coat with the wide skirt and the pleated lapels. Rose—how she loved that color, and how Jon loved it on her too. Valentino, one of her favorite designers. How well she knew that store, and its sister in London.

Jon and Sal were coming their way, laughing together about something, pleased, relaxed; but when Jon saw Maya he stopped, a crease between his eyes. It lasted only an instant, then he smiled again and even pecked her on the cheek, which made her draw back and blush furiously, and not prettily.

"Maya would like to go to the Met," Naomi said, looking at Sal.

His face lit up. "Really? What would you like to see, darling? When do you want to go? We need to get you a lovely dress for that, right?"

"Sal…" it was little more than a sigh, then Maya shrugged and nodded.

"I'm thinking of going back to LA for a few days." Sal rubbed his palms together in a show of glee. "And I'm taking Maya with me. Just for a few weeks, for a break. I'm sure she'll love the beach. And I can use the time to get rid of my old apartment."

"Are you going to stay there? At your old apartment?" She had no idea what made her ask, but Naomi wanted to know.

"Nah, we'll stay at a hotel." Slinging his arm around Maya, Sal looked down at her. It wasn't with the usual intensity, though, and not the tenderness she knew only too well.

"You can stay at the Malibu house," Naomi replied, and then clamped her lips together, confused by her own words, bewildered by what she had said. She could see the same puzzlement on Jon's face, but he remained silent. "There are plenty of guest rooms, and Amparo is there. Just, you know, not my bedroom. That's private."

For a moment the old Sal was back, the one who'd cared for her before anyone else. The memory of the long weeks of recovery traveled across his face, quite open to see, and how they had all traipsed through that room to get to her roof garden, where she was languishing, so hurt from the shooting.

"Of course." The old gentleness was back, the soft smile he'd always reserved for her. "Of course, Naomi. You know I'd never overstep like that. Thank you for the offer. It's very generous."

"Well then." Jon's voice sounded gravely with thoughtfulness. "Have a good time. You can drive the Porsche, if you want."

And just like that, it was settled. She would let Sal take a stranger to her house, see how they lived when they were in Malibu, let her tread along her path to the beach, comb through her surf for treasures, maybe even sit on the stone bench in the arbor and dream of kisses by moonlight.

"While you're there," Naomi added, "you can go visit my favorite designer in the world. He made the dress I wore to the Oscars, among others. I'm not sure he's quite your style, but maybe you'll find something you'll like. Please say hello to Jamal for me, will you? He's a very nice man. From Lebanon. The fashion is exquisite, very unusual, and he sure loves color."

She would, Maya said, and thanked her, delight and surprise in her face, the idea of the adventure taking her away before they had even left. With regret Naomi watched how she picked up the purse and hooked her arm through Sal's, ready to go.

"What a brilliant idea," she heard Sal say to her, walking away. "I'm sure we'll find something for you at Jamal's. Those colors, those silks, will look amazing on you. Oh, and you'll love the garden of the Malibu house! It's so romantic..." His words drifted away as the doors fell closed behind them.

NAOMI FELT SICK.

She couldn't even muster the energy to answer Jon's questions, to explain why she had so freely offered their house without even asking him, without at least informing him. Her hands shaking, she pushed herself up and stood, rubbing her back again.

"Jon."

He stopped, waiting for her to talk, his fists on his hips.

"Jon, something very weird is going on." That was about it, almost all she could say.

"Let's go." He took her elbow to lead her outside despite Stan's cry of protest. The car was waiting, and he ushered her inside, patiently waiting for her to speak first.

"Home," Naomi said, her tone wavering, and then changed her mind right away. "No, to my parents'. I don't know. I'm so freaked out. Just... let's drive around. I don't know."

The big limousine glided up the road toward Lincoln Center, silently navigating the early-afternoon traffic.

"I wanted that purse Maya was carrying," Naomi said, still shaking. "The minute I saw it, I wanted it. It was one of those moments when you see something and you know you just *have* to have it."

Jon laughed. "Is this what this is all about? Baby, we can go to the store and buy it right now. Really, Naomi."

She turned to him. "No, Jon, that's not it. That coat, the gloves, the purse, even the haircut. The dress Maya wore for the Christmas party. The shoes. I don't even know what to say."

"She likes the same things you do, it seems." He took her fingers between his palms to rub them, cold and stiff as they were.

"That's not the point, Jon. She keeps telling me that she doesn't care too much for these things, that her taste is different, that she only wears them to please Sal because he likes them on her. She told me that she thinks these outfits would look much better on me." Pensively, she pulled up her shoulders. "And it's true. I'd gladly wear any of them. They are lovely."

Jon let her fingers slip out of his as he leaned back. He looked out of the window at the passing buildings, his mouth a narrow line.

"It's as if…" She had to start again; it was so preposterous and wild. "It's as if…"

"As if he wants to turn her into a copy of you," Jon finished the sentence for her, his voice hard and dry. "As if by dressing her the way you do, he'll have a copy of you."

"It's even more than that." She had to swallow hard before she could continue. "That day when we saw them at the hotel, do you remember? The day after the concert? In the lobby, when…"

"Yes."

"And…you know, Jon, I offered the house to test this assumption." A tissue, she needed a tissue to wipe her nose. The tears were taking a strange path. "That's why I told them to go to Jamal."

"Yes. I see. Now it makes sense."

Naomi leaned forward and tapped against the pane to tell LaGasse that she had changed her mind. She wanted to go home; she couldn't face anyone right now, least of all her father and his dry comments.

"We can't do anything, can we?" Jon asked.

"I don't think so, no."

The bridge loomed up before them like a gate to safety, a pathway to a sanctuary. Gray, dark clouds hung low over the river; a cold drizzle drifted from them toward the water below. The skyline of Manhattan behind them, the double towers of the World Trade Center, shimmered through the haze like fairy lights.

"We could talk to Maya," Jon said it slowly, uncertainly, and Naomi shook her head.

"No, we can't, Jon. It's not our business. What would we say? 'Listen, Sal is trying to turn you into a copy of Naomi'? Maybe she wouldn't even care or worse, love it. It's so creepy. It makes me sick." A sob like a hiccup escaped her. "And it scares me. It reminds me of Parker."

"It does."

The car stopped outside their house. The lights were on, welcoming them, bidding them to come inside and be safe.

"I'm tired" Naomi sighed. "And very sad. I think I need to lie down."

chapter 25

"IT'S A GIRL." Julian handed Jon another of those cryptic images. "Congratulations!"

"But how can you tell?" As hard as he tried, he couldn't make out much more than curves and angles, and the five fingers of a tiny hand. That, at least, was clearly visible, and a great relief.

Julian grinned. "Well, it's obvious, something is not there." He tapped at the ultrasound photo, somewhere on a shadowy spot that didn't seem any different from its surroundings at all.

"Allegra." Naomi sighed. "Thank goodness. It's so much easier to think of a girl's name than a boy's. I would have been stumped trying to find one." The mound of her belly was covered in glistening goop. It was a good-size mound by now, round and hard, and she had some trouble cleaning herself off with the tissues Julian handed her. A nurse came over to help.

"Is that the name you chose? Lovely!" Julian printed out another image. "Look, we got lucky! She is smiling at us!"

And this time Jon did recognize something. There was a face, a real face, eyes scrunched up, a nose no more than a tiny bulb, and lips that already had the same curve as Naomi's. He felt as if he might faint. He'd never felt like this before, never, not even that day when the call came to tell him he'd gotten his first gold record, not even when he had kissed Naomi for the first time. This was different, elemental, truly awesome. It was poetry and magic, and the most inspiring moment of his life.

"Allegra," he repeated softly.

Julian was busy examining Naomi's legs and ankles, prodding and poking them. "You're doing fine. Way better than I'd hoped. Just, you know, at the smallest sign…" He brought out his stethoscope and set it down on her chest, where he listened with half-closed eyes and an open mouth, which made him look slightly dopey. "Your heart sounds good, too, and your lungs are clear, no edema. Good!"

The old worry was like a scar, or a painful wound, and it would never, Jon knew, go away. The price they'd paid for their happiness, her health.

"Get plenty of rest. You only have a few weeks left; don't start stressing yourself now, okay?" Julian perched on the corner of the exam table. "Let your husband pamper you. Use this opportunity to get everything you want out of him, just as long as you do it from a couch." He laughed at her when she groaned and rolled her eyes.

A girl. A girl. The words rang in him, he had to keep repeating them to make them real.

In a short while, in weeks, less than he could count on two hands, he would be holding a daughter in his arms. This made him realize that, except for his nieces and nephew, he'd never held a baby. He'd always refused, too scared to break or drop them, but mostly, and this was hard to admit, too detached to care. Infants had nothing to do with him. He'd not been a father to a small child, owned a family, not even someone to love, and so he wasn't entitled to hold a baby.

ALONE IN HIS studio on a cold, gray morning early in March, staring through drizzle at the Manhattan skyline, Jon recalled his old life, the life he had led for so many years, after she had left him, before he had found her in Norway. Looking back, it didn't even seem like a life anymore. It had been a mere existence, daily survival. So famous, so adored and so successful, and yet, inside, he'd been nothing but a dried and deserted husk.

His head turned toward the hallway, toward the stairs.

She was asleep in their bed. He had made her an omelet for lunch, with fried mushrooms, her favorite, and had watched her wolf it down, three eggs, nearly a pound of mushrooms. She had been ravenous and asked for more, asked for fried potatoes and pastrami, and he'd sent Lourdes out shopping.

By the time she'd returned, Naomi had been tired and announced she would take a nap, and gone upstairs. He'd watched her, watched how she slowly, ponderously, climbed the stairs, her hand pressed into her back, her belly big now; and his love had felt like a huge wave of hot syrup; delicious, sweet, burning. When Jon had gone to check on her a while later, he had found her slumbering under her quilts, her body curled up around her middle as if protecting it, and he'd softly drawn the curtains and left.

His wife. Naomi, his wife.

There was a wild impulse to pinch himself, to make sure he wasn't caught in a long dream, maybe even in a drunken delirium, passed out somewhere in the beach house in LA.

Slowly, he made his way upstairs again, drawn to her, needing her close, needing to feel her touch, her breath on his face, anything to make this real.

He would lie down beside her, watch her sleep, and be there when she woke up. No more than that. No more than the assurance that she was really there, really his.

Carefully so he wouldn't wake her, he lay down, her head under his chin, inhaling her scent and warmth with each breath. She fit perfectly into his arms. Her body, even now, even the shape it had now, fitted his: her shoulder into his palm, the form of her back and hips against his body as if they were carved from him. Never, not once, had another woman felt like this, and no other had ever given herself to him like Naomi did.

"Jon."

He woke from his sublime reverie.

"Jon, do you remember when I told you about when Joshua was born?" She stirred, moving closer into him.

Of course he remembered. He remembered so well it felt to him as if he'd been there that cold, snowy night, had been waiting with her for the taxi and then inside the hospital lobby for a nurse to come and take her to the labor room.

"Did I also tell you how a woman knows when it's time? How your body tells you, how you get restless before the pains even start and you feel like prowling, like looking for a safe niche where you can huddle and hide?" Her hand, covering his on the ball of her stomach, was cool, soft.

The small hairs at the nape of her neck tickled his throat.

"Something feels different, like something is shifting inside your body, getting ready to go to work, collecting itself for the task ahead." She sighed and moved again. "There's an enormous pull. As if the entire Earth is using its gravity to help you give birth, as if it's holding its hands open under you to catch the baby." Again she sighed. "And then the pains start. While the Earth is pulling, your body is pushing. And you're caught in between, helpless, and nature does its thing." A tremor ran through her.

"You don't have to be afraid. You're not alone this time." The baby was moving. Jon could feel a ripple run through her belly, like surf, like waves, one following the other.

"I'm not afraid, Jon." Her voice sounded distant, quiet, as if she were standing on the other side of a river, as if she was turned inward, listening. "But I think I should get up now."

"No, stay. It's warm and comfy here; why go anywhere else? I'll stay with you; I promise." And it was true; he was ready to doze off, the cocoon under the blankets was so soothing.

"I'm afraid I can't, my love." With an effort, she was sitting up, freeing herself from his embrace. He looked at her, his heart breaking at the sight, at her loveliness, the loving smile she gave him.

"I think," Naomi said, "we should go to the hospital now and have this baby."

IT WAS TOO early. The baby was five weeks early, and yet Naomi was as calm and serene as he'd ever seen her.

Standing in the hall, waiting for the car, she had her eyes closed and her hands on her belly, humming softly, humming "Secret Garden" of all songs.

"We should have called an ambulance," Jon muttered nervously. "We shouldn't go on our own. What if we get stuck in traffic and something happens?"

But she shrugged without opening her eyes. "Nothing will happen. Calm down, Jon."

They were not, he wanted to say, in Halmar, where there was only one proper road, no rush hour, and only one taxi for the entire population. They weren't going to a hospital where the lobby was smaller than the hall they were in just now, at their own house; and she wasn't a girl of twenty-one anymore either: healthy, strong, young.

Jon gazed at her, looked at her pale face and the closed lids, veins shining through the fragile skin, at the jacket she had wrapped around herself, once again one of the old things she'd brought from Norway. He wondered if it maybe was the same one she'd worn that night too, that winter night so many years ago when Joshua was born, and he so far away, so clueless, and probably drunk and in bed with some girl or other, even at the same moment she went into labor and had their son.

"We should go," she said softly. "We really should go, Jon."

"That does it. I'm calling an ambulance." And he did, against her protests, and for good measure he called Julian, announcing they would be there soon.

It was weird to do these things without Sal, without someone else making those calls for him, arranging everything; but he wanted it this way. He wanted this to be private, theirs alone.

"So strange," Naomi whispered, by now sitting on the couch near the fireplace, her breath measured and deliberate. "So strange to have a baby in the daytime, and not alone."

"You aren't alone." Jon wrapped his arms around her. "Not for one single moment will you be alone this time. I'll be by your side every single second. They'd have to carry me away, Naomi. I love you. You're not alone." His tone was so anxious and fierce that she opened her eyes and smiled at him.

"It's only a baby, Jon. Stop fretting, darling; everything will be fine. You'll have a daughter soon." She gasped. "Sooner than you think."

Carefully he settled her back onto the couch and went to the door to open it, shout out at LaGasse to watch out for the bloody ambulance, and where the hell was it anyway?

Sweat was stinging between his shoulder blades, cold; sheer panic made his heart hammer.

"Jon." Her voice sounded pained, and he rushed back to her. "Jon, I think…" Again she gasped for air. "Maybe you should call Helen. And help me. Help me, Jon. The couch in the studio. I need help. It's coming too fast."

When she was stood, water ran down her legs and collected in a puddle on the floor. Naomi moaned. "We need to clean that; it will leave a bad stain. Jon, it needs to be wiped up. Oh, damn…"

"Forget the floor." He picked her up and carried her to the studio, where he put her down on the couch and helped her remove her shoes. Fluid was pooled in them, her sweatpants were soaked.

"The baby, Jon." She cupped her belly with her hands as if that would keep the child inside. "She wants out, and now. Please, Jon. Help me. Call Helen!"

His mother answered the phone right away, and when he said, "The baby is coming, and the ambulance isn't here yet," all she said was "I'll be right there."

THIS WAS NOT the way he had imagined it at all.

He had always thought everything would be civilized, orderly, happening in a clean and luxurious hospital suite, doctors and nurses dancing attendance on Naomi while he held her through the labor pains, massaged her back, and let her squeeze his hands to pulp while she brought their child into the world.

But now here she was, stretched out on her couch, while Helen and Valerie peeled off her sodden clothes and put towels under her.

"Too fast, too fast," Naomi kept repeating, trying to sit up, while Valerie tried to keep her reclined.

"Come here, Jon, dammit," Valerie finally shouted at him, and he moved from where he was watching anxiously. "Sit behind your wife and hold her, calm her down. And where is that frigging ambulance? When did you call for it, Jon? It should be here by now. Call again!"

"I did!" It was the only thing he could say in his defense. "They said there was a big accident, and they'd be here as soon as possible."

"I hope you sue their asses off for this," Val said. "I'm a music teacher, for crying out loud. I've never delivered a baby."

"But you've had them," Helen cut her off. "Shut up, Val. Let's get this baby born. She's really anxious to see her daddy."

It was ridiculous. Here he was, one of the wealthiest men in Hollywood, married to the daughter of one of the wealthiest families in Canada, and they were having their baby at home because there wasn't an ambulance to be had in Brooklyn. The thought that there had been no time to call Naomi's parents made him sweat even more. Olaf would have his head on a silver platter and probably eat it for dinner if something happened to her or the baby.

Not that he would care, in that case. Not that he would need a brain or heart ever again if something happened to her.

Naomi's head was against his shoulder, her back against his chest, her hand clamped around his wrist. He could feel every cramp, every shot of pain that went through her as if it radiated into his own body.

From the hallway, they could hear commotion, voices, the metallic noises of a stretcher being unfolded.

"Oh, thank heaven," Helen breathed.

"She's coming now," Naomi said through stiff lips. "And if you let those strangers in to see me like this, Jon Stone, I'm going to pull every tooth out of your mouth, one by one. They can bloody well wait until I'm done."

chapter 26

SHE WOKE IN the middle of the night.

For a moment she lay, disoriented, confused, before a vague fear crept up in her, the memory of another night when she had woken just like this, in a similar bed, with monitors beeping around her, and she had nearly died after the shooting.

The light in the room was dim, but it was a kind, warm light, not the greenish glow she remembered from the ICU in LA. This bed was much more comfortable too, wide, with enough pillows to sink into, a colorful, soft blanket, and crisp linen sheets that smelled of lavender. In fact, it reminded her more of a hotel than a hospital.

A small sound made her turn her head and look toward the window. Jon was there.

She knew it was him; his silhouette was cast against the backdrop of the lit high-rise buildings visible through the panes, and for a minute she lay, gazing at him, loving the figure he cut standing there, halfway turned toward the view. He was talking, his voice as gentle and melodic as a forest brook.

"All this will belong to you, my darling princess," Jon said. "The entire world, and every heart in it. I promise you'll never get hurt and never have a sad moment. You are so loved."

He was holding their baby. Jon was holding Allegra in his arms, and he was talking to her.

"I didn't believe your momma, you know." He bent his head to bring his face close to the baby's. "All this talk of baby smell, she drove me nuts with it. But she was right. You're delicious. You're the loveliest thing I've ever seen." A low chuckle escaped him. "Well, besides your momma, of course. My Allie. My baby. My daughter."

It was just the way she had imagined it, just the way she had wanted it. This, this was the one dream she had held on to, and here it was now, real: Jon, with their newborn child. The one thing she had wanted to give him more than anything else, the one thing she had wanted for herself, the redemption she had needed.

That night in Halmar returned to her, when she had been alone after Joshua's birth, alone in that hospital room looking out at the snow and the Norwegian winter storm, and her heart had hurt from the bitter loneliness. A sigh escaped her, and Jon turned to come closer.

"Naomi?" he asked quietly.

Sitting up was more than she had bargained for, but she managed.

"You're supposed to be asleep." He perched on the edge of the bed, the baby safely tucked into the crook of his arm, the other hand resting on the little body to keep her safe, as if he'd done this all his life, as if it was the most natural thing in the world.

Naomi gazed from one face to the other, father and daughter. "She looks like you."

Jon smiled. "No, she looks like you. She has your lips, and your black curls. She is lovely." He went on to tell her that he'd been allowed to give Allie her first bath and that he had also dressed her—with the help of the nurses.

"They were so excited," Jon said, and a small, ironic smile crept over his face. "The one and only Jon Stone, putting a diaper on his newborn daughter."

Reluctantly he handed the baby over when Naomi held out her hands for her. "Careful, okay?"

That made her laugh. "Yes, Jon, I'll be careful."

"Would you believe it, they even asked me for autographs, right there in the baby room. Took some photos and asked me to sign on those cards they hang on the cribs because there was nothing else around. It was quite something." He rubbed his hands on his knees. "It was like a henhouse."

Naomi looked down into the tiny face. She removed the cap from Allie's head to see her hair and run her fingers over the downy, black curls, which made Allie purse her lips. Her eyebrows drew together in the frown Naomi knew only too well from both Jon and Joshua, and her fist came up the same way Joshua's had, imperious, demanding.

"I was wrong, you know." There was a trace of pain in Jon's voice. "And you had it right. Last summer when you were nearly killing me with all this baby talk, when I kept telling you it didn't matter, I didn't care about having another baby. I was wrong. You drove me crazy with it, when you went on and on about the sweet smell and that I deserved to hold my own child: do you remember?"

He was breaking her heart. Naomi nodded, cradling the infant close to her chest.

"I've never felt anything like I did when they laid Allie in my arms. I thought I was being given the most precious jewel, a fragile flower, given into my care and mine for the keeping." He help up his hand, the palm open, as if he wanted to cup light, catch an elusive blessing. "A wonderful, magical gift, something I can't ever hope to repay. I had no idea. I had no idea what you meant, and I had no idea what I was refusing so lightly. Now I understand why you were so driven, so obsessive about this, my love. And I understand why you were willing to take any risk for it." With a sigh, Jon laid his hand over hers where it was around Allie's head. "I love you for this, Naomi. I've always loved you—you know that. But what you've done, what you've taken upon yourself for my sake."

"Oh, shut up, Jon."

A surprised laugh escaped him.

"You get so dramatic in hospitals." Naomi handed the baby back to him to push the pillows into her back and open her gown.

Spellbound, Jon watched as she put Allie to her breast and settled down comfortably, her eye half closed, humming to herself and her infant. Allie's little fist opened and came to rest on Naomi's skin. She made little sounds of contentment as she nursed, something between a gulp and a sigh.

"You are the most maudlin man in the whole wide world," Naomi said softly. "I didn't do anything. I wanted another baby with you, and I got it. That's all."

"Like hell that's all, and you know it." All the emotion, all the love he was feeling seemed like big pearls in his mouth and throat, and he was having trouble talking around them. "You were willing to risk your life just to give me this, to let me know how it is to see a new baby."

Naomi opened her eyes to stare at him.

"You were willing to give your life just so I could have this moment." His fingers brushed over her cheek and chin. "How I adore you."

Gently, she detached Allie from her breast and switched sides. There was a small cry of protest until she had found the nipple and happily latched onto it, and Naomi grimaced. "She's just like Joshua. She's just like your son. Ouch."

It was the most beautiful thing he had ever seen. It reminded him of Ferro's paintings of the Madonna—she was that lovely in the dim light of the small bedside lamp.

"I love you, Jon." Her voice woke him from his reverie. "I love you so much. I'd do anything to make you happy."

"I know." And it was true, he did. "And that's what scares me about you. You have this way of doing things, of really pulling them off no matter what the cost, and you scare me with that. From now on, no more risks, and even less without telling me about them, okay?"

Her eyes were large and very dark. "I promise," Naomi said. "From now on we'll be as sedate and careful as any other middle-aged couple."

She asked him to put Allie in the crib and push it next to her bed so she could touch it, and to then lie down beside her. Just like always, like they did in their own bed, they lay, curled into each other, his arms around her. Dawn was creeping over the buildings, swallowing one star after another, a big blue bird spreading its wings across the darkness of night. The last thing Jon heard before he drifted off to sleep was the nurse coming in on tiptoes and leaving right away, softly closing the door behind her.

And that was how Joshua found them in the morning when he dropped by to see his new sister.

THEY WERE HAVING a late breakfast on the terrace when Art phoned.

"The baby is here," he announced, "and in true Stone fashion, she arrived with drama and fanfare. A pretty little thing too."

Sal's chest felt as if the ocean had crushed it, all those huge waves, all the debris, even some whales, all of it crashing on his chest.

"And you call me now? When was she born?"

"Oh, yesterday afternoon." Art sounded as if the sun had just risen. "A bonny lass, spitting image of her mother. The cutest little poppet." He snickered down the line. "Of course she is. Jon Stone's new baby, she'd be picture-pretty like a porcelain doll, right? Allegra, they named her. Allegra Lucia Helen. Poor little mite, that's quite a heavy load; but they're calling her Allie, which is simple enough."

Allie. Allie. Sal let the name roll over his tongue, and it felt like a pebble, a chunk of ice, coiled barbed wire, a drop of bitter poison.

"How is Naomi?" He could hardly say it. He could hardly go there with his imagination, seeing her struggling and in pain, again. Those weeks after the shooting had been bad enough, when he had watched her waste away and sink into depression, every day a little more. Somehow something had changed at some point, somehow Jon had pulled her out of it, but Sal had never figured out what had been said or done.

"She's fine! Had the baby at home, can you believe it. The ambulance wasn't fast enough for her. Helen and Valerie delivered her, right there in Jon's studio. Now if that isn't right and fitting, eh? What a news release that will make! His fans will gobble it up. Drama, baby, drama!" Art laughed, and it sounded like an old woman's delighted cackle. "Those two are natural-born stars. You couldn't make them any better if you tried."

"I'll be home tomorrow," Sal replied, his voice as raspy as sand grating on a stone floor.

"Yeah, if you want to experience Naomi as queen-in-residence at the hospital, you'd better." Art laughed again. "She even does that really well. You should see her, sitting in that bed, receiving visitors, and my, she's as beautiful as she ever was. Motherhood really suits her, wouldn't you know. I swear, she doesn't look a day over thirty, and as lush and healthy as she did at…at…when she was very happy in LA, right before…you know."

Sal knew. He turned away from the breakfast table and Maya, and let his gaze drift into the house, recalling that day more than a year ago when they had stood in the foyer, all of them—Art, Russ, Jon, and he—waiting for Naomi, waiting for her to come down and go to the Academy Awards with them.

Jon had poured them drinks and doled out some of his precious Cuban cigars, and there they had stood, four men in expensive tuxedos, waiting.

And then she had appeared, had flowed down those stairs in that cream silk-and-chiffon creation of Sayed's, and Sal's heart had stopped. It had stopped as if someone had driven a knife through it, nailed it to his spine with one swift, deft movement. He recalled how Jon had almost lost it for a moment, probably thinking the same thing, thinking she had decided not to go at all and was only here to tell them she was on her way to bed, but no, that wasn't a bed sheet wrapped around her; it was a gown, and what a glamorous, suggestive thing it had been. Her long hair had been down, the curls tumbling over her bare shoulders and back, her makeup had been so subtle it was almost invisible, and there had been no purse, no jewelry. It was as if she'd just climbed out of bed, as if she'd just been loved and was now searching for a cup of coffee, some breakfast, her lover.

Jon had been ready to sink to his knees, Sal had known it, because he himself had been ready to lie down and die.

"Jon has presented her with the most amazing piece of jewelry," Art was saying, shaking him out of that memory, "and she's wearing it, right there in her hospital bed. I think that diamond must have cost millions. It's as large as the baby's fist, and the smaller ones surrounding it aren't small either. You should have seen Olaf's face when Naomi opened that purple velvet box. Even Olaf was impressed, for once. And Jon, the sentimental sod, tells her it's nothing, nothing compared to the gift she's given him, nothing at all, just a bauble, when she has given him the world. Oh, those two."

He would never need a heart attack, Sal realized. He would never need a real, painful death, and he hoped God knew that. The pain he was feeling now was quite enough. It felt like dying, and in a slow and very creative way too.

"Yeah, yeah"—he cut Art's ode short—"I'll be back, and see the wonder of it all for myself. Getting on a plane tomorrow morning."

"Whatever you say, Sal." Again, Art cackled. "You're the boss. Only remember, that's not your baby, and you better not show up with diamonds. Your head would look great on a spike adorning Jon Stone's garden wall."

He put down the phone on the table, right next to the jar of mango jam. "We're going back. You should start packing."

Maya nodded. Silently she rose and went into the house. Sal watched her leave. She was in a light-blue dress, a flimsy, light thing just right for the warmth of LA, and barefoot, her hair streaming down her back. Seeing her like that, in the dimness of the house, if he really screwed up his eyes and didn't look directly, he could almost imagine it wasn't her at all, wasn't Maya, but someone else.

chapter 27

HE HAD TAKEN her to that designer.

He had taken her many places, but that one day stuck in Maya's mind as if it had been nailed there, and the memory hurt like that too.

Jamal had welcomed them with spicy mocha and a platter of cakes that had made her homesick. The baklava had been outstanding, and while Jamal went to find gowns that he thought would look good on her, she had nibbled the fluffy pastries and thought of her mother. Angie's baklava, she had to admit, was even better, fluffier, and the butter taste was more intense. She had a suspicion that these had been sweetened with syrup and not honey at all, and the filling was more brown than green, which showed it was heavy on walnuts and they had been stingy with the pistachios. For a minute she had an impulse to pick up her cell phone and call Angie to tell her about it, but then Jamal had returned with an armload of dresses.

"You are slim and tall" had been his words; "I want to see clean lines on you. Russet colors! Naturals!"

But Sal had dismissed all his suggestions and picked out colorful, lacy things, extravagant gowns of a kind she would never have chosen.

"When would I wear these?" she'd asked, and he had shrugged.

"All the time" had been his answer.

She could see herself at the deli, serving curries and pakoras in that rose dress with the big satin bow in the back, the skirt so wide it would swipe the menus off the tables when she turned, and a near hysterical laugh had bubbled up in her chest.

"You should buy that for Naomi," she had suggested, and Jamal had nodded, running his hand over the silk folds.

"Yes, yes, Mrs. Stone would buy this one," he had agreed. "I think Sayed even designed it with her in mind. He's quite a bit in love with her, and her style. Naomi knows so well what looks good on her, and she's not afraid to wear extravagant clothes, like so many others. But you, no." A stern crease had appeared on his forehead. "No rose and chiffon for you. Silk, yes. But wild silk. No lace either."

Sal, though, had disagreed and bought the dress for her, and a gossamer shawl shot with pearls and gold threads to wear with it.

In the car, Maya had taken it out of the shopping bag and let the long fringe run through her fingers. It was lovely, wonderfully precious; it had cost a fortune. She could just see Selma stealing it to play princess.

Sal had dropped her off at the house and told her he needed to see to some things at the office, after all he was still Jon Stone's manager, and for her to have a good time.

"You could take a walk on the beach," he had suggested, "and collect some shells to show me later."

Like a good girl she had nodded.

She had never seen any sense in collecting shells. They looked pretty on the beach; but once they were dry and taken from their natural surroundings they seemed to lose their luster, as if their souls were left behind in the surf, and that gave the word *shell* a totally new and very sad meaning.

Nor could she understand Sal's obsession with the little stones on the beach, and why he wanted her to pick them up and take them back to the garden. They were, after all, only stones.

HE HAD, SAL told her, one more meeting, one more thing to wrap up, but then they were free to go home. Standing in the entry of the Stone mansion, the keys to Jon's Porsche in his hand, he smiled at her. "You should start packing. We'll leave first thing tomorrow. So if there's anything else you want to do in LA while we're here, we should do it tonight."

And with a kiss on her cheek he left her.

She was alone in the house. The housekeeper, Amparo, had gone shopping, and the security man who lived over the garages was busy polishing his SUV. The silence was overwhelming even though it was framed by the sound of the ocean and the occasional call of a gull.

The sun shone from a flawless sky when she stepped out onto the patio, the bushes rustled in the lazy breeze and, beyond them, the dark crowns of the cedars swayed gently.

A cedar grove in a private park, a cool, fragrant nook that made Maya wonder what they used it for, if it was Naomi's personal forest for her to take strolls in. She had been there only once, at Sal's insistence, after he'd told her how lovely it was, in a dell of its own, with a brook running through it too.

So she had gone, but it had been the spookiest place she'd ever seen. Everything seemed dead and mute under those big trees, as if they ate up every noise and sucked the breath right out of her lungs. Their smell had stung in her nose and made her retch, and the shadows had moved in the corners of her eyes, ghosts flitting across the bed of dead needles on the ground, mocking her.

Maya sighed. The dishes from their breakfast were still on the table, the butter in its dish beginning to melt from the rising heat of the sun. She carried it inside and put it in the fridge.

Her back against its door, she looked around the wide space, every surface gleaming and clean, and the marble floor spotless. So much room, so much luxury, and it was unused, waiting for its owners to come back on a whim, for a week or two, before their fancy took them away again, maybe to Paris, or London, or the Maldives.

Slowly she made her way upstairs to start packing. Every time she climbed the stairs to their room on the third floor she had to pass that one door, the one Sal had told her never to open, to leave alone at all costs. It was calling to her, singing a whispering invitation, and this time she could not refuse. Listening to the house, Maya laid her hand on the knob. Her heart was beating out a warning in a fast, panicked voice, but she ignored it. Her last day, and she wanted to know more than anything else why she was forbidden to enter this room.

She had never figured out why they all called it "Naomi's room" when in fact it was their bedroom, hers and Jon's; but now, entering it, she understood. It was like stepping into another world, into the boudoir of a queen, with the soft colors and fabrics, the closet full of lovely gowns, and shoes, and purses, the fresh flowers on the table, the silk quilts turned down to reveal rose linens and lace pillows. It was waiting for her to return, waiting for its mistress to bring it back to life.

There was a terrace door leading out onto a roof garden, and here, too, everything had her name written on it. It was truly her realm, her retreat; and Maya wondered again how Naomi could have given it up in favor of the Brooklyn house, this paradise, this view of the balmy Pacific and of the hills with the palms.

On the table, right next to the vase, was an open jewelry case, a diamond bracelet negligently tossed into it, and she stopped to stare at the thing.

As if it meant nothing, as if Naomi owned so many that this one piece had been happily forgotten. As if, with a shrug of her shoulder, she would go out and replace it once she noticed it was missing.

Maya stretched out her hand to touch it.

"What are you doing?"

Her heart stopped. Her hand, only a second ago hovering over the diamonds, hid behind her back.

"Nothing," she replied, her voice shaking in time with her fingers. "Nothing. I just wanted a look. I was curious."

Sal didn't take a single step into the room. He stood in the doorway; his fists on his hips, and every trace of kindness or love were gone from his face. Hard, his mouth was a hard line in his face, his eyes as cold as dark-brown eyes could ever be.

"I told you not to go in here. Naomi told you. It was her explicit wish, the condition under which we were invited here. And we are guests in this house, Maya. I don't know if you were brought up without learning this much courtesy, but as a guest you abide by your hosts' wishes. Now, get out of there. You have no right to be in here. It's her room. It's Naomi's."

Maya opened her mouth to apologize but instead she said, "All the things you're buying me. They look as if you really meant them for her. For Naomi."

Something changed in his face. It was only a second, less than a heartbeat, but it was there: guilt.

"Of course not." Sal waved it away. "Utter crap. I buy things for you because I like to see you in fine things. And in my opinion Naomi has the best taste in the world, and so I let that guide me."

It was a lie. Maya knew it was a lie, but she had the eerie feeling that even Sal realized this only now. He looked away from her, the anger flowing out of him.

"What you're saying, Maya. That's not true."

"But you never let me pick anything myself. You always tell me what you'd like me to wear." She didn't know what to do. He was blocking the doorway, so she couldn't leave the room, and yet she wanted out of it more than anything else. All the beauty, all the finery, seemed to stare at her, seemed to be baring fine, white, sharp teeth that were only hidden under satin and lace.

"Because those things are lovely. They are beautiful! Why wouldn't you want to look like her, look like Naomi?"

And here was a truth, a bitter and dangerous truth, and it had slipped from his lips without him realizing what he had said. Maya, watching him, thought she could almost see those words drop down his chin like vile, rotten pieces of moldy flesh.

"I need to pack," she said, and he stepped aside.

IN THE END, it was that easy.

Gray mist was hiding the skyline of Manhattan when they approached LaGuardia at dawn, soft drizzle hitting the windows of the plane.

She had fallen asleep somewhere over the plains, stretched out on the couch of the Gulfstream, her eyes on Sal; but he had not seen. His mind had been far away. She had a good idea where his thoughts were.

Now, back on the ground, on the way to the waiting car, she said, "I'm going home, Sal. Drop me off at a subway station, will you?"

He stopped walking and turned to her. "What do you mean subway? We're going to the hospital, aren't we, to see Naomi and the baby?"

"No. You are going there. I'm going home. Home to my family."

"And I'll see you later today?" Holding the car door for her, he waited for her reply.

"No, Sal." She wished she had packed her own things into an extra suitcase so she would not have to untangle them from what he had bought for her. That shawl, though, the one he bought at Jamal's shop, that one she would keep. It would be her memento. And the first pair of shoes. "No, Sal, you won't see me later today, or any other time. I'm going home."

"What? Are you breaking up with me?"

This nearly broke her heart. He really seemed hurt, shocked, as if he meant it.

"Yes, I think we should break up." How calm her heart was. How fearless and numb it felt, letting her say these words. It had clearly been waiting for her to do this for quite a while now. "I don't think you love me at all, Sal."

Sal did not try to touch her but sat, his hands folded over his knees, listening, as the limo pulled out onto the street.

"I don't even know why you thought this would be a good idea,"

Maya went on. "You don't love me; you never did. You love someone else, another woman, and it's so obvious, I wonder why I had to go all the way to LA and into her bedroom to realize that." She cradled her purse against her chest, a terrible, silly habit she knew she had to get rid of, and quickly. She wasn't a child anymore.

"You love Naomi." There, she had said it, and a sad satisfaction filled her when she saw him flinch. "You love her with a desperation that is painful and embarrassing to watch. During these past weeks, in Los Angeles, you've done everything to…I don't even know what to call it. Only I'm hurt beyond my ability to bear it."

He had the good sense not to protest, which made her love him just a little, and relent somewhat.

"I'm not like Naomi," Maya said, and her voice wavered on the words. "I'm not like her, Sal; and no matter how many beautiful dresses you buy, I'll never be what you want me to be. I'm sorry. I'm Maya. I'm not Naomi. You don't love me for myself."

For the longest time he didn't speak. Then he leaned forward and told the driver to go to Atlantic Avenue first, please.

Only when the car had turned and was speeding toward her home did he take her hand in his. She let him, let him play with her fingers and lay them on his knee.

"I'm so sorry, Maya."

She had, in fact, Maya admitted, come to love the sound of his voice. She had come to love quite a lot about him.

"It's hard to take, you know, what you're saying, that's hard to take. I don't think anyone has ever had the guts to put it to me like that, quite that bluntly, but…" Sal looked away from her, looked out at the buildings flitting by in the rain. "But you're right. It's the simple truth. I love her."

And this, now this hurt. Hearing it from him was different.

"I've always loved her, since the moment I first saw her. So many years ago it was, in Geneva. She walked across that hotel lobby toward Jon, and they didn't know I was there. Jon had insisted on meeting her alone, the poet, the lyricist. And you know what? It was my own fault. I let him have those lyrics she'd written in the first place, let him determine how he was going to meet her. I could have kept it a secret, could have traveled to Geneva on my own, met her myself; and who knows, who knows what would have happened then, if she'd seen me first and not Jon." A pained sigh escaped him.

Maya stared at him. "Do you really think that, Sal? Do you really think you ever had a chance, even for a second? Don't you know anything about those two? Don't you *watch* them? Don't you see they are like one person, one soul? I don't think Jon would ever have loved anyone else if he hadn't met her. And Naomi? She is like his extension, the original Adam's rib, a piece of his heart and soul living outside of him. Sal, no one could take his place for her. You've wasted your life on a hopeless dream."

"I know, I know." His shoulders came up.

There was nothing else to say. They passed the street that would, if they turned left, lead them to the Stone house. With a sigh, Maya waved good-bye to it, knowing well she would never cross that threshold again.

"It's not true, you know," Sal said. "I didn't try to turn you into Naomi. It's just…everything about her is so beautiful. I wanted that for you too."

She even believed him. "But her kind of beauty isn't mine, Sal. You tried to shape me into a replica of her, even down to the beach walks and the restaurants you took me to. We never had a chance to be something else, something new. Be honest, tell me: during our time in LA, what did we do that you either didn't do with Naomi or wished you'd done? One single thing?"

There was no answer.

The car stopped outside the deli. She had forgotten to tell the driver to stop a block away; and here she was now, in a big, black limousine, and there was her father, staring, a crate of peaches in his hands that he had just unloaded from the truck.

"Will you come and pick up your things from my place?" Sal asked. "I'd really love to take you out for lunch one last time."

Maya was fumbling for her key chain in the purse. She removed the one to the loft from it and handed it to Sal. "No. I don't want those things, Sal; I never did. I wanted to love you just for yourself. I thought I wanted you because you were my ticket to a different life, to wealth and comfort; but it wasn't true. Over the past few weeks I've come to realize that there are things I want even more than pretty dresses and going to the Russian Tea Room for lunch."

He nodded, his lips pressed together, and she clasped his hand. "It's okay, Sal. Don't feel bad. We used each other. I have to apologize to you too. What I did wasn't really fair either."

"That stuff is yours; don't be ridiculous, Maya. I'll have it packed up and sent to you. I really like you, darling. It wasn't all a lie. I tried."

That made her lean toward him and kiss his lips. It was a friendly, chaste kiss, one of good-bye and peace making. "Do come by and have breakfast if you feel like it, okay? I'll make samosas for you." She smiled. "Or rather, I'll have my mom make them. She is way better than I can ever hope to be."

"I will."

They both knew it was a lie, but it didn't matter.

"And I'll have your stuff sent to you. Silly, you not wanting it. Tell me you don't want the purses and shoes?"

Maya shrugged. "You should give that mauve Valentino purse to Naomi. She was ogling it when she saw it at the theater. But then, I bet she wouldn't really accept anything used."

"You're wrong about her," Sal called after her when she got out of the car. "Naomi isn't like that at all. She's really very nice. She lived a really simple, quiet life for many years."

"Yeah, yeah." Maya waved at her father. "Sure, Sal. It's easy to lead a simple life when you know you can actually step out of it at any moment, and all you have to do is raise your little finger. That's a bit like Marie Antoinette playing shepherdess in the Versailles gardens. You never have to worry about the sheep shit, and you always have hot water at the end of the day. It doesn't count."

That made him laugh despite the dire moment. "I've changed my mind. I'll bring your things over myself in a few days, including the mauve purse. Naomi can bloody well get her own. If you don't want it, give it to your sister."

And that made her nod. Uma would love those dresses.

The car pulled away.

"Hello, Daddy," Maya said to her father. "I'm back from my holiday. Did Mom make samosas? I'm starving."

chapter 28

HE MADE THE driver take him straight to the hospital. It was still early. The sun spilled over the buildings in a shower of light, making them shine and sparkle. Like sentinels, as if they were the mother and father of the city, the World Trade Center gleamed above all others; and for a moment, seeing that magnificent skyline from the bridge, Sal felt safe, protected, and welcomed. In that instant he understood Naomi's feelings about New York, about its grandeur and uniqueness. It was a fabulous place. Only it wasn't his place. He was certain of that more than ever now, after having returned from LA.

Sal sighed, mourning his old life, the life they had led before Naomi had reappeared and everything had changed.

Things were better for Jon now, that was true; but for the rest of them it meant change, uprooting, and new beginnings.

AT THE DESK in the hospital lobby, they gave him a blank stare when he asked for Naomi's room. He saw the security man standing close by shift in his direction when he pushed his hand into his pocket to get out his cell phone, and that made him smile grimly.

"Jon," he said, "what's Naomi's room number?" and began to move toward the elevators when he got the necessary information. On her floor there were more guards; among them, right outside Naomi's room, stood LaGasse herself. Her gun barely hidden by her black suit jacket, and Sal loved her for it. She opened the door for him, but he stopped when he heard voices from inside. One was Naomi's, silver-clear and light, and the other sounded familiar, but it took him a minute to recognize it.

"He is so cute," Gemma said. "He's the cutest man I've ever met."

"Cute? I don't think anyone has ever called him that." Laughter was swinging in Naomi's reply. "But if you say so!"

"He's a sweetheart, and I'm going to win him, just wait and see. That bit of a girl he's running around with, I'm telling you, he'll get tired of her in no time."

Naomi's answer came slowly. "I have a feeling you're right about that, you know. That is a mismatch if ever I saw one."

Sal's hand felt sweaty.

"On the other hand, I don't know if I should get involved with a man right now. I'm here to look after you and the baby, after all." It was said with some regret, but Naomi laughed. "Oh, Gemma, don't worry about that for a second. Of course you can. Look at me—I'm fine! No one ever thinks I can do anything, least of all Jon. But I can! I love the idea of having you around, but you need to live your life too. And if you're in love, go for it. I'm serious. You deserve it. And don't worry about me."

"Cesare and Olaf said my job was to take care of you."

There was the sound of a zipper being closed and a bag being set down on the ground, and he took that break in their conversation to knock and push the door open.

Both of them turned toward him, and once again it was like being slapped, like being hit with a different kind of reality, one that mocked and hurt him.

"Sal." The voices. Those were different. And the expressions on their faces. Naomi was smiling at him in friendly welcome; but Gemma, she stared at him in a mixture of surprise and boredom, her black eyes distant, the corners of her mouth drooping.

"Hey," she said, and it sounded almost like disappointment.

The flowers in his hands felt silly. He had picked white roses, tied with a pink satin ribbon; and here he stood, the bouquet held in front of his chest like a shield, facing the two women.

"Give me those," Gemma said, waving her hand impatiently at him. "What a shame. Let's hope someone else enjoys them."

"Naomi could take them home," Sal offered, but she shook her head.

"You never take flowers back home from the hospital, Sal, and you should know that. It's bad luck."

This made him snap out of his stupor and snatch them out of her way. "Really, Gemma, that's Italian superstition and nothing more. Flowers are flowers, no matter where you put them!"

"It's not superstition, you stupid man; it's belief, and that's something totally different!" Her dark eyes sparkled like finely polished onyx.

"Yeah, you'll have to come and take them from my cold, dead body if you want them. I'll give them to the next nurse who crosses my way, but you won't throw them away!" His soul soared, and he had no idea why. He had no idea why all of a sudden, from one minute to the next, it felt as if a switch had been pulled and his heart was beating in a lighter, sweeter rhythm than it had in a good long while, in fact in as long as he could remember.

Gemma shrugged. "Please yourself. As long as you don't take them out the entrance door of this building."

"I could give them to you. You're not a patient."

That made her pause. Taking a rapid, deep breath she said, "Oh, nonsense. They would be secondhand roses then. Toss them already!"

Naomi sat down on the bed, looking from one to the other. "Where is Maya? When did you get here? Weren't you in LA?"

She had this way of cutting right to the heart of things; she had always done that. As if he'd been caught stealing candy, Sal drew his shoulders together.

"I just got here. We…I came as soon as Art called and told me the baby had been born."

Her hand wandered to the crib beside her bed and came to rest on its side.

"So…" Sal pointed. "May I have a look at the princess?"

There she was, Jon Stone's daughter, as pretty as an expensive doll in her rose suit and cap, her little face framed in lace. A black curl had escaped and lay on her forehead, her skin as smooth and white as her mother's. Her lips had the same exquisite shape he knew so well from Naomi, and Sal was sure if she opened her eyes, he would see the dark brown both her parents had too. It seemed only right and fitting that Jon should have the perfect baby, to go with his perfect wife.

"Lovely," he said, swallowing against the raspy dryness in his throat, "really cute. Congrats again. I heard it was quite dramatic, the birth and all."

"It was exciting, yes." That voice. How he loved that gentle and amused tone in it. "But everything went well."

"And how are you?" This, surely, was not overstepping.

"I'm fine, Sal."

He stepped back from the infant and looked at Naomi.

"I'm better than they expected me to be." A trace of defiance had crept into her words.

"Yes."

"So where is Maya?" Naomi asked, with a glance at the clock.

"I dropped her off at home." Somehow he knew he would not get away with it. They were both watching him, Gemma and Naomi, waiting for him to go on, ready to ask if he didn't. "She…we've broken up." There, he had said it. The strange thing was that he didn't even feel sad. He didn't feel anything, only numbness, and the beginning of jet-lag. Sal wondered why that was, why he wasn't heartbroken at having lost his girlfriend after almost six months, but there was nothing.

"I'm so sorry, Sal." Of course Naomi would say that, would say it in her soft, melodious voice and put in all the sorrow he didn't feel.

"Yeah, it's okay." He wanted a cigarette, and badly. "She wasn't happy. I don't know why. We just…parted. I still have all her stuff at my house. I need to pack it up and get it to her somehow. I don't know. I've never packed a woman's clothes."

Naomi was gazing at him quietly, waiting.

"I need to find boxes or something, to pack those things in."

"You can't be serious," Gemma said. "Boxes? You can't dump those dresses in boxes, you idiot. Here, I'll go with you and do it. Honestly."

Sal wondered why Naomi was biting her lip and lowering her head over her folded hands.

He needed, Gemma went on, a trunk. Did he have a trunk? He couldn't just pack designer evening gowns into boxes or suitcases, they would be ruined—and didn't he know that by now, with all the traveling they had done in their lifetime? How much was there to pack?

"Go buy a trunk," she ordered. "And I'll meet you at your place."

Gamely he nodded, and stopped at the door when she called after him, "And Sal? A nice trunk. Not a cheap, ugly thing. Do this in style, do you hear me?"

Strange, it was strange, how he'd come to see Naomi and the baby, and now he was being sent off to buy a trunk for Maya.

But his heart was suddenly light, the weight he'd felt blown away by Gemma's terse orders. In fact, as the elevator doors closed behind him, he smiled, thinking of Gemma.

He'd buy her lunch.

AS PROMISED, GEMMA showed up a few hours later. She stepped out of the elevator into his loft and looked around, and he let her, standing aside.

"It's a nice place" was her verdict. "A bit undecided, no? As if the people living here didn't really care how it looked, or if it's comfortable to live in."

She put her purse on the kitchen counter. "Everything is so…unrelated. It's not harmonious. Not a place where a heart lives."

He gazed at the loft and tried to see it through her eyes, through the eyes of a visitor, and realized she was right.

"It's as if you collected all the pearls," Gemma said, "and then dropped them here instead of stringing them into a necklace. If that makes sense."

It made perfect sense. In fact, it made so much sense that he felt like blushing and mumbling excuses.

"Well, then." Gemma pulled a hair clip from her purse. With a quick twist she pinned her hair up into a pile at the back of her head and then pushed up the sleeves of her shirt. "Where are the things you want packed? And where's that trunk?"

She had, it was quite obvious, done a lot of packing. The dresses were zipped up into their plastic covers and stowed into the waiting trunk with deftness, and in an order that made sense even to Sal.

Holding up the red dress Maya had worn on Christmas, Gemma said, "You know, I love this dress. It's one of the nicest dresses I've ever seen. But on Maya it somehow looked wrong. It would be lovely on Naomi—it's her style. But on Gemma it looked pathetic. She's too tall for this kind of dress. Too bad, that girl has no taste." She pointed at the mauve Valentino purse. "Naomi would adore that purse. On Maya it looks kitschy. You should have taught that girl some style."

"Actually, I picked out that purse for her." There, he had admitted to his weakness, and this, too, made him feel better.

Gemma looked up at him from where she was crouching to pack up the shoes. "Aha," she said.

"I thought what looks good on Naomi would look good on her."

The trunk was closed with a snap. Well pleased, Gemma gave it a loving pat. "You picked a nice one, Sal. Now, a cup of coffee, please, and then we'll take it around to Maya. Nothing like doing these things right away. And then, I'm sure, you'll want some rest. You must be so jet-lagged."

"I need to order a car," he began to say, but Gemma shook her head.

"You don't need to. I borrowed Naomi's. LaGasse will be here in thirty minutes." She moved over to the kitchen and without much ado began making coffee, handling the machine as if she'd used it all her life. "We don't want to embarrass Maya, do we? Her family will be there, I'm sure, and they don't have to know you're dumping off her stuff after a breakup. So we're going to deliver them in style and give that neighborhood something to talk about."

The machine hissed, spreading the aroma of espresso.

For a moment, closing his eyes, Sal could imagine being back in LA, back in his old apartment and life, but then he heard Gemma say, "If I didn't know better, I'd think you wanted to turn Maya into a replica of Naomi. But they aren't alike at all, so that's utter nonsense."

He grabbed the cigarettes from the table and went out to the roof garden, but she followed, two cups in her hands. Handing him one, she leaned on the wall and looked out over the river.

"My lovely cousin," she went on, "she is like no one else I know."

"Yes, she is very lovely." That much he could surely say without raising suspicion.

"I wonder, though." Gemma placed her cup on the rim of the wall and turned to look at him. "I wonder what would have happened to her if Naomi hadn't met Jon. I mean, can you imagine any other man being able to cope with her? What would a normal man do with her? What would someone who isn't Jon Stone do with someone like Naomi Carlsson? She needed someone who is larger than life: special, beautiful, more than just a man." She pointed at the loft behind them. "Can you imagine Naomi living here?"

"She lived a pretty quiet life in Halmar," Sal muttered, "and for a very long time."

Gemma laughed. "Is that what you think? Is that what she made you believe? Yes, she lived in Halmar. But she lived the pampered life of a wealthy daughter, well protected, without wanting for anything. It was playing at being poor and lonely, nothing more. One wave of her little finger and both families, ours and her father's, would have been there to take her away and give her back her princess life. And on her way to the jet, two dozen suitors would have stood in line, hoping for a smile from her, dropping flowers in her path. Olaf would do anything for his only child, anything. If she wanted the World Trade Center, he'd buy it for her. If she wanted a house in the middle of the Brooklyn Bridge, he'd build one. He hated Jon with a passion for taking her away from him."

"Yeah, because he wanted her to run the hotel business, I know." They'd been over that often enough.

"Oh, the hotel business." Gemma waved him away. "Olaf doesn't give a crap about the hotel business. There are enough people to run it, as long as there's a Carlsson to own it. He keeps saying that to impress people like you and Jon. What he really wants is to protect Naomi from any harm, any hurt or pain at all. She's his precious princess. He wanted to handpick a husband for her so he'd know she would be cherished and treated with respect, and what happens? She runs away with a bloody American rock star and ends up in the drug-and-sex hell of Hollywood. And then she returns pregnant. We could hear Olaf bellowing all the way from Toronto to Naples!" She tilted her head. "But you know all that, don't you? I mean, everybody knows it."

"Yes, yes, of course." He needed more coffee. Something stronger than coffee perhaps, and lots of it.

"But Naomi had better instincts than Olaf, and she found the right man for herself. Jon is perfect. Music, good looks, charm, patience, all the romance she can take, and enough money to satisfy even her exalted desires. And, most important, he understands her. That can't be said about everyone."

With a quick glance at her watch, Gemma sighed. "We should get ready. The car will be here any minute."

"You aren't like Naomi at all. You look so much alike, and yet you aren't like her at all."

Gemma laughed at him. "There are nine of us, nine female cousins, and we all look alike. But not one of us is like Naomi. It would be way too exhausting."

chapter 29

"I'LL DO THE talking," Gemma said as the car pulled to the curb outside the deli.

Her purse clamped under her arm and her sunglasses dangling from her fingers, Gemma followed Alan, who was carrying the trunk, inside. Maya's father was there, serving tea to a couple sitting at the same table where Sal had sat that Sunday morning last fall. Behind the counter stood Maya, once again dressed in that traditional Indian suit of pants and a long shirt, her hair in a braid. She looked tired and pale, which made Sal realize that she must be just as exhausted as he was and yet here she was, working.

"Miss Ansari." Gemma pointed at the trunk. "We're pleased to deliver samples of this winter's collections to you, with the best wishes of Jon Stone's management. We wish you all the best for your future and thank you for the valuable work you have done for us."

A deep blush flooded Maya's cheeks. Her lips moved, but no words came out. Karim, suspicious now, came over to them, the tray still in his hand.

"What's this?" he asked.

"Thank you, sir." With a wide smile, Gemma turned to leave. "We wish you a lovely day."

On an impulse, Sal got out a business card and handed it to Maya. "Call me if you ever need anything. Okay? Take care."

She nodded but did not reply. The tiniest smile softened her face as she looked after them, lightening his heart. He stood for a moment before leaving the deli and gazed around, trying to memorize the smells and colors, and then dismissed it. There was nothing here to remember, nothing he needed to carry away, not even a pull on his heartstrings. It was as if she had never really resided there at all, as if she had never made her way into his heart. He could look back at her as she stood behind that counter, raise his hand in a final salute, nod at her father, and walk out into the street without any pain.

On the sidewalk, Sal took a deep breath. It was over. Just like that, it was over.

Gemma was ready to get into the car. "Bye, Sal," she said. "I'm sure we'll meet again soon enough."

Confused, surprised, he watched as the Rolls pulled out into the traffic and left him there on the curb of Atlantic, forced to find his way home alone.

"Sal." Maya had followed him. She was standing in the door, her hands folded in front of her body.

"Oh, hey." Listless. That was how he felt now, there was no other way to put it. "Your stuff."

"Thank you. You needn't have done this." How different she looked in that outfit, how strange. Like a stranger, like a different person, not at all like the girl he had spent so much time with during the past few months. It almost seemed as if, by wearing these traditional clothes, she had stepped away from everything they might have shared; and in a convoluted and painful way it reminded him of Naomi and her old life in Norway, where she had worn that black dress to work. Jon had hated it, had hated the stiff linen pleats. It had vanished soon enough, to be replaced by lovely colors and softer things, as she blossomed and bloomed with her love for Jon.

"They are yours," Sal said; "I have no use for them. You're welcome." A cab. He needed a cab, so he moved closer to the curb to hail one.

"I'm sorry, Sal." A gust of wind blew up her shirt, and she quickly held it down. "I wish I could have been the way you wanted me."

"No. No." A cab had stopped for him, and he waved to the driver, asking him to wait. "No, Maya." Gently, Sal took her hands in his. "It's me who has to apologize. I really wanted to love you."

"I know."

There was nothing left to say, nothing. Sal got into the taxi and watched as she returned inside, the door closing slowly behind her with gentle finality.

ALONE. ONCE AGAIN he was alone. The loft seemed curiously empty, as if with her clothes a part of its soul had left, as if it now was once again a dead, empty space waiting to be inhabited. Sal had made coffee, glad he had remembered to buy some, and sat by himself at the kitchen counter, staring at the furniture scattered around the large room. It stared back at him in boredom, uninspired, disenchanted pieces not really comfortable with their lives, but resigned to the fact that they now belonged here. The cleaning woman he had hired had wiped away the last remnants of Maya's chalk marks around the bed and tossed away the almond milk she had preferred to real milk, and with that, every trace of her was gone. She might as well have never existed.

He had tried to find a remnant of love, a blossom of sorrow some-where in the corners of his heart, but there was nothing. Not even the act of deleting her number from his cell phone had moved him, and it made him wonder if maybe he wasn't able to love at all, if maybe his adoration for Naomi was the only thing that mattered, would ever matter.

Almost two months had gone by since the breakup, and he had done nothing. A couple of times he'd gone to the theater, just to show his face and assure Jon that he was still alive, but that was it. The rest of the time he'd spent wandering through New York, measuring the island of Manhattan from top to bottom with his steps. One day, he had walked all the way to Harlem, always following Broadway, curious how far that street would lead him. It hadn't ended there, but his feet had given out. He'd stopped at a corner coffee shop for a sandwich and a big mug of coffee, the only fair-skinned person in a restaurant full of Spanish-speaking people, and then taken a cab home, only to step back into the lonely silence of the loft.

Every day there were messages on his phone, but he deleted them without even looking at the numbers, unwilling to deal with them. He didn't turn on his computer either but just sat, mostly out in the roof garden, watching the ships pass by on the river and the cars down on the street.

Sal was just about to get up and refill his cup when the doorbell rang.

This was so unusual; he just stood and tried to find the source of the sound for a minute before he went and pressed the buzzer for the door of the building. Only then it occurred to him that he hadn't used the speaker to ask who it was. From below, he heard the elevator moving, and he stepped back, nervous now, wondering who it might be.

"Good morning," Jon said, "you look like shit."

The same could not be said for his boss. Jon looked as dapper as ever: well dressed, well groomed, rested, healthy, and wide-awake even this early in the day.

"Naomi and Gemma sent me. They are worried about you and wanted me to check on you."

Sal, muttering, went to get his coffee. Jon followed and held out his hand for a cup.

"If you want some I'll have to make a fresh pot."

"Or we could go out for breakfast," Jon suggested. "After you've taken a shower, shaved, and dressed properly."

"Aren't you busy with your wife and baby?" It came out a little snarky and wasn't at all what he had wanted to say.

"My wife and baby are just fine, Sal. When I left them, Naomi and Gemma were having croissants with butter and honey, if I remember correctly, and that's just what I want too. So get moving."

Sal hated how Jon seemed so fresh and alive, so calm and collected, as if he had his life and day well under control.

THE SUN WAS shining brightly—it was warm. The end of May, and it seemed like summer. Sal was sure he would never get used to the humidity in New York. Naomi had told him it was even worse down near Washington DC, that she'd thought she'd die in the sweltering heat of the eastern shore; and that made him wonder, while he waited for Jon to unlock the car, how people could live even farther south, in Alabama or Tennessee. He vowed never to find out. Once again he felt homesick for the mild weather of LA.

Jon took them straight to the hotel that belonged to Naomi's family, up near Lincoln Center; and when Sal threw him a questioning glance, he shrugged and said, "The parking is free, and their croissants are really good. You know they make everything themselves. I think they even import the flour and milk from France. Not sure though."

As if there had never been any strife, as if he and Olaf hadn't been at each other's throat only a year ago, after the Hollywood shooting. All was bliss and peace in the Carlsson-Stone household these days.

Seemingly reading his thoughts, Jon added, "Olaf has created a trust fund for Allie. As if I can't afford to pay for my daughter's education. But, hey, I'm not going to complain."

It was so strange. Only two years ago, it had been Jon who had wasted away his days in a stupor, who had to be pried out of the shack by the beach he'd been living in. Often enough Sal or Russ had more or less broken into his house by climbing the steep wooden stairs up from the beach and entering through the deck door to find their friend in bed at noon, still asleep from a drinking bout the evening before.

Strange, it was strange to see their roles reversed, when he wasn't even pining for Maya the way Jon had pined for Naomi. Jon had been broken over his love, had wasted away from his loss; but that had been different, so different. Sal was certain he wasn't missing Maya.

They entered the restaurant where Jon was greeted as if he owned the place and were led to a table in a niche next to a window looking out at the Met.

He didn't even have to ask; within seconds a silver coffee pot was brought and their cups filled, and a second waiter asked what they wanted to eat.

"It's must be nice being the owner's son-in-law," Sal grumbled, and Jon smiled.

"I'm the owner's husband," he replied pleasantly.

This was new.

"Naomi wrangled this hotel and the one in Positano out of her father last fall. I don't know why, but she wanted to own them. Olaf handed them over as if they were playing Monopoly. Don't ask me, Sal. I'll never understand these people. They toss property at each other like tennis balls. I think Olaf was happy that she wanted anything to do with the business at all, and Naomi was actually not taking anything from him but giving in a little. Or something like that. One way or the other, he was more than pleased about her demand. And a demand it was, I can tell you."

"Aha."

Their breakfast appeared. In a silver basket, wrapped in a linen napkin, they were offered the freshest and most fragrant croissants Sal had ever seen. There was white bread with a heavenly crust, golden butter, and honey as dark as resin, and on a silver platter, ham and finely cut, fragrant salami, some olives, a couple of figs.

"I don't come here often enough." Jon sighed as he bit into his croissant. "I love this family. They really know how to do food."

Sal didn't reply. He didn't feel like eating either.

"Life is good," Jon went on; "I never thought I'd be this happy. I never thought anyone could be this happy."

"Yeah." All this talk about family and food and happiness made Sal feel queasy. He wanted a brandy and a cigarette with his coffee.

"Gemma is such a dear to have around. She and Naomi get along so well, and she's so sweet with Allie. I'm really glad this worked out." One of the figs wandered into Jon's mouth, the whole thing, and he chewed with his eyes closed, savoring the aroma.

One more statement about marital bliss, and, Sal was certain he'd puke right across the table. "Great," he croaked, "wonderful."

"But I'm not here to talk about me. I have everything I ever wanted, now that my Naomi and I have finally settled down and found peace. I'm here to talk about you, and your botched love affair, and how you're hiding yourself away."

"Yeah, you should know all about that." It sounded a lot angrier than Sal had intended, but Jon didn't take the bait.

"No one knows better about hiding away than I do" was his calm reply. "And I was probably even worse off than you. I wanted to die, Sal. Every night when I'd drunken myself into oblivion, I went to bed and prayed I wouldn't wake up the next morning. I wanted my life to waste into nothing, into that state where you stop feeling anything. And the worst thing was, it didn't lessen with time, this desperation. It only gripped me harder. As the years passed, the loneliness and sorrow accumulated. It was like crawling through an endless, black tunnel, with no light at the other end in sight. And I'm not going to let that happen to you."

Bitter laughter bubbled up in Sal's chest. He tried to drown it with a big gulp of coffee and a bite of buttered bread, and for good measure popped a slice of ham into his mouth too. "But I'm not crawling," he said around the food. "Maya and I parted peacefully; there was no fight, nothing. I'm just taking a break. That's all."

Jon pushed away from the table and brushed a few crumbs from his shirt before he answered. "Just this once, Sal, let's talk straight. You haven't had a decent relationship in years."

"Not unlike you," Sal mumbled, but Jon waved him away.

"Yeah, like me, and for the same reason. I know, Sal. I've always known, ever since that day in Geneva. We've been together for too long for me not to see what's going on. But you know…hell, I don't even know how to say this. You know there's not a chance in the world…I mean, some things will never happen. I'd never give her up, and I don't think she'd ever…Well, Sal, you know what I mean." Angrily, Jon tossed the napkin on the table and got up. "I need a cigarette. Come on, let's go outside."

"Aren't you going to pay?" On the point of plucking out some bills, Sal stopped when Jon said, "We own the place, Sal. We don't have to pay for a meal. How ridiculous would that be."

They crossed the street to sit on one of the park benches in the small, green square between the hotel and the Met, in a spot where they could see the fountain and the big, open space in front of the opera building.

"I love this place." Jon brought out his cigarettes and offered one to Sal. "It's like the heart of Manhattan, isn't it? The place where all the music comes together. I'm so glad we have that box at the Met. Makes me feel like I'm a part of it, a part of the real music."

"What do you mean, 'real music'? You create real music, Jon. You always have."

"Yes, but not…" Jon shrugged. "We're not here to talk about music, Sal. We're here to talk about Naomi."

Sal's blood turned to icy slush. The smoke of the cigarette tasted like burned horse dung, and the green of the trees seemed like poison darts.

"You've forbidden yourself to love anyone. You've locked up your heart. And then Maya comes along, and you try to change her into a copy of Naomi." Jon slapped his shoulder hard when Sal turned away from him. "Look at me, you silly sod. I'm your friend, and I'm here to help you out of this!"

"How can you, Jon. I feel like a fool. And some things should never be said aloud."

"It has to be said aloud, even if only this once, Sal. If we don't talk about this, you'll drown. I know how it is. Trust me. I've been there, and I don't want to see you go that way."

A couple of minutes passed while Jon finished his cigarette, watching the traffic. Then he said, "Naomi says there's a symphony in the sounds of New York. The longer I live here, the more I think she's right. I'm getting to love this place more than I ever did before, more than I love LA. She puts magic in things, my wife does."

Misery, and the fateful knowledge that it was time to let go. "Yes, she does. It's a huge part of her charm." There, he had as much as confessed to it, but Jon didn't react.

"She is so very special, such an amazing, wonderful woman," he said instead, and as calmly as if he were talking about the weather.

"I know that." Anger was replacing Sal's cold shock. "I've never, ever attempted anything, Jon. I've never overstepped."

"I know. And that's not the reason why I'm here, Sal. I want you to let go of this infatuation. It's nothing more than that. Naomi is your Holy Grail; you adore her, but I don't think you love her in any real way. You must let go of this, Sal, and allow yourself to love someone else." He took out another cigarette. "Now, Gemma. Gemma loves you as if you were the last man on the planet. She's mooning and sighing over you all day long, and it's the only thing I can't take about her. Couldn't you please find it in your heart to fall in love with Gemma? That would really be a great favor."

Sal thought he'd misheard. "Gemma? But she's Naomi's cousin!"

"Yes, that's the Gemma I'm talking about." Amusement made Jon's voice go dark and gravelly, made him sound as if he was onstage and flirting with his audience.

"But she's Naomi's cousin," Sal repeated stupidly.

Jon rose and stretched, ignoring the glances of a couple of women walking by with their dogs. "Yeah, she is. And? You haven't shown your mug at our house in almost two months, and the girl is going crazy. I told her to give you a call, but she's too scared of being brushed off by you. So, Sal, do yourself, and me, and my household a favor and take her out for dinner, please?"

"I can't."

Jon turned back to him, his eyebrows raised.

"Jon, how would you ever believe that I loved her for herself, if that should even happen? She's Naomi's spitting image, and if you think I tried to turn Maya into Naomi's copy, how would you not think that with Gemma?"

Jon laughed. "Because, my dear friend, Gemma isn't Maya. She'd give you hell if you tried to manipulate her like that. I mean loud hell. She is nothing like Maya, and she only looks like Naomi. She's her own person, and quite a handful. She's perfect for you. Come on, give it a try. Come by for lunch tomorrow. And take a walk on the Promenade with her."

Suddenly, the leaves on the trees looked more like precious jewels blinking in the sunlight than poison darts.

chapter 30

SHE NO LONGER appeared frail.

Watching her from their bed, Jon admired the curves of her body, so healthy, so luscious, so delicious. Naomi was still slim and lithe, but now she looked the way she had when he had found her in Halmar more than two years ago. Her cheeks had a natural glow, and her eyes hadn't lost their happy sparkle despite the sleepless nights and demands of having a new baby in the house.

He loved that she had decided to let her hair grow out, giving in to his argument that he missed wrapping it around his hands when they were making love and how it clung to their skin.

Nothing had paled, nothing. In fact, the more time passed, the more they grew into a family, the deeper his love grew. There was nothing better, no better moment in his day than sitting on the terrace for breakfast, Allie on his knee, and Naomi beside him. That hour, while he fed the baby her first spoons of soft egg from a mother-of-pearl spoon that had belonged to Joshua, watching her slurp the yellow mush and lick her lips, were precious beyond words. He had tried writing songs about it, but he couldn't find the lyrics, and Naomi refused to write them. She was, she told him, too busy editing her book with Jane, and the publication date was drawing close.

She had really done it. While he had been taking walks with the baby, working on the musical and the soundtrack, she had finished her book and submitted it, and Jane had signed her. It had been that easy. No fuss, no discussions, from one day to the other, his wife had turned from writer to author.

He'd taken her out for dinner to celebrate and bought her a car. Her face, when he took her down to the Porsche dealer and handed her the keys for a red 911, had been priceless. It wasn't a convertible, he couldn't bring himself to do that; and he made her swear then and there never to go out on her own, to always take either LaGasse or him along, or Sal, if no one else was around. And absolutely no jaunts with

Gemma and the baby, that she had to promise.

Olaf had taken them out for dinner and given her a gold pen with her name engraved on it, a useless and luxurious thing that she would never even use to write, she was that comfortable on her computer. But she had accepted it and embraced him, blushing and with swimming eyes, understanding that finally he could show her how proud he was.

"COME BACK TO bed," Jon offered, and she gave him a smoldering glance over her shoulder.

"I can't. Have to take Allie off Gemma's hands; she wants to go out with Sal today. Something about a trip to Coney Island, I think. Those two, they drive me crazy. I think I need a new nanny."

"Come here. Just ten minutes."

"Ten minutes, Jon. I know what that means." But she dropped the dress she was holding onto the couch and came to him in nothing more than her panties and bra, and he knew exactly how to get those off her in less than ten seconds. Ten seconds, and she would be naked and lovely in his arms, and he could sink into that embrace and forget the world. Her perfume, mixed with the sweet scent of her body, invaded his senses when he dug his face into her hair, his hands tracing the shape of her body, his lips touching her mouth. She sighed a bit under his gentle assault—just the way he liked it—and softened against him.

Nothing, nothing had paled.

"GEMMA AND SAL are hitting it off, then?" Jon didn't have to ask, but he needed to talk about them. It had taken Sal a month after his talk with Jon to make up his mind, and then he had shown up at the house out of the blue. For an hour he'd sat with them over breakfast, just the way they used to in Malibu, chatting about the news, work, weather, and nonsense things, his eyes on Jon and Allie as she sat on his knee and tried to turn over his cup and grab the toast. It had been hot and humid that morning, almost too hot to sit outside at all. Summer in New York was so different from the dry heat of LA.

Then when Gemma had come back from the kitchen with more coffee, he'd looked up at her and asked, "I have to go to Amagansett today, out on Long Island, to see a friend. Want to come along? We could have lunch somewhere along the way, maybe on the beach. They have fabulous lobster there, I've been told."

She had gazed at him, her head titled, the coffee pot in her hands forgotten, and said, "Can we go to the beach and look for seashells?"

And that was when Jon had known Sal's heart had taken a turn away from Naomi and toward Gemma. With that one sentence, she had won him. They had gone off together and not returned until late that evening, Gemma sporting a straw hat and a linen tote bag with a kitschy painting of the shore and Montauk lighthouse on it, filled with stones and shells and one smelly starfish. With Sal's help she had lined them up on a board along the garden wall, where they sat through July and August, reminding Jon of Naomi's collection on the railing of the beach house where he had spent those lonely years without her.

"They're hitting it off." Naomi's gentle voice woke him from his thoughts, and he clasped her tightly to him. "Well, more than hitting it off. They are courting."

Life was so good. Life was so smooth and perfect; it felt as if it were coated with honey, as if the sunshine were honey dripping from the sky, right onto his hungry lips, and all the way into his heart. It felt like a time between times, between the long and lonely sadness of his exile and something that was yet to come, a change, a new beginning, something that would take them unaware. Softly, his body wrapped around Naomi, he hummed one of the songs for the soundtrack, the one he had come up with only the night before, when he had crept out of bed to write it down.

"That's a sweet melody," she whispered, "like a fairy light in a dark forest."

Jon opened his mouth to ask but instead kissed the corner of her mouth, sighing. She would refuse anyway.

"Have you written the lyrics yet?" She shifted against him. "Or aren't there going to be any?"

His pulse quickened. "No, I haven't attempted any lyrics yet. But yes, I do want to sing this."

He could see the song. He could see the hero of the movie lost in that dark wood, searching for the love that had fallen from the sky for him, and to keep the shadows of the trees at bay he'd sing to himself. And there she would be, a light in the night, a lovely creature of star shine and morning mist, waiting for him under a blooming jasmine tree. Yes, it would have to be jasmine, the scent of the flowers surrounding her like a cloak, like her long, golden hair.

"Can you play it for me? Can we go down and you can play it for me?" Her fingers were curled in his hair, tugging to draw his attention back to her from where it had wandered.

"Yes, yes." She hadn't done this in a long time. She had refused to write for him, stating that he was the songwriter and she the novelist, and he had to learn to do it on his own again, the way he had for so many years when she hadn't been around.

"You're so lazy" had been her verdict. "You really like to shove that part of the work on me, don't you, just so you don't have to mess around with words. Forget it!"

Every time she taunted him like that he wanted to kiss her hard, kiss her until she begged for mercy and yielded to his fierce embrace, and she knew it. He could see it in the gleam of her eyes and the set of her lips, and he loved her for it.

"Can't you hear the words, Jon?" Naomi freed herself from him and sat up, pushing her hair behind her ears. "I can hear them. I can hear them dance around the music. Why can't you hear them?"

"Because I'm not you." She made his heart break with the beauty of her talent. "I can't hear the words. I only hear the music."

GEMMA WAS IN the kitchen with Lourdes, Allie on her lap. There was the scent of coffee and scrambled eggs, of frying mushrooms and fresh bread. Walking in, Jon could hear the giggles of his baby daughter, the young women's voices as they chatted, and he had to stop and take a deep breath. Naomi, just behind him, took his hand and squeezed it, peering around him.

"Oh look," she cried, "Lourdes, you lovely girl, thank you!"

Mushrooms, how she loved them fried in butter, with a little onion, and wrapped inside a fluffy omelet.

He had cooked that for her the day she had decided to leave him, after the shooting, when life had folded in on itself like a battered cardboard box. The day he'd been sure everything was over, and yet here they were, in a haven of happiness and bliss.

Only six more days until the musical's opening night, a date carefully selected—well away from the lazy weeks of August but before the craziness of the winter holidays started. September 16th a new chapter of his life would open. Then he would see if he was made for this kind of work or not. It still felt strange not to be on the stage himself instead of those young, fresh-faced kids singing his songs.

Naomi was taking Allie from Gemma's arms and dancing around with her, humming the short phrases of the new song and making up nonsense words to it, while Allie tried to grab her hair and stuff it into her mouth.

Jon loved those baby legs. He'd never expected to be in love with something like that, but here it was: there was nearly nothing sweeter than those tiny toes and the soft feet that fit into his hands so well, nothing more dear than the little fold of flesh on Allie's thighs. The same was true for her arms and hands. He loved her, loved his daughter in a painful, tender way he had never known existed. Her chubby baby face was an echo of Naomi's, the same features but still rounded and blurry; but everything was there: the shape of her eyes, the fine line of her brows and the curl of her lips, even the color of her hair. Naomi had wanted to cut the thick locks, but he had forbidden it, had implored her not to touch them, to let them grow, just like her own; and she had given in, sighing and muttering, calling him a sentimental, romantic fool who would make his daughter suffer for the sake of his dreams, but she had smiled as she said it.

Almost six months, half a year, and Jon wouldn't have missed a single moment, not the long night hours when he'd sat with Allie in the studio, soothing her through a case of colic while Naomi and Gemma slept; not his early-morning walks with her in the baby stroller—Alan two steps behind him—to get a fresh baguette or croissants and a newspaper before breakfast; not even the stinky diapers that he had learned to change.

THE DOORBELL PULLED him from his musing and the sight of Naomi in her swirling skirt.

Sal strolled in. He'd changed so much from the wan, oldish man sitting beside him on that park bench in May; he'd returned once again to his happy albeit cynical, lively self.

"Good morning," he nearly sang, and patted Naomi's arm in passing without even looking at her, his eyes and attention already fastened on Gemma, his stride firmly in her direction. "And how are you today, my dear? Ready for a day in the sun? I want to go on that roller coaster.

We'll buy ten tickets and spend all morning on it until we're hungry for lunch." Looking her up and down as she sat there, in cut-off jeans and a gingham blouse, her hair in a ponytail and her feet in flip-flops, he added, "You look perfect. A perfect girl for a perfect day!"

Naomi rolled her eyes at Jon behind Sal's back, and Jon shrugged back at her, a wide grin on his face.

"We're off," Gemma said, with a cautious glance at Naomi. "Are you sure I can leave you? I mean, I've been away a lot recently." She blushed and added, "I'm really neglecting my job, I know. I feel bad."

"What nonsense, Gemma." Naomi pulled a strand of hair out of Allie's fist. "You're not an employee; you're my cousin. Off you go!"

And in a way, Jon loved it. He loved to see Sal and Gemma walk out of the house, and he loved that Lourdes announced she had to run some errands, go to the cleaners, the grocery store, and visit her dentist. They were alone with the dirty dishes and the baby, just a regular family, just the way he remembered it from his own home. Only Naomi didn't put on an apron like his mother used to but wandered into the studio, a cup of coffee in her hand, still humming that elusive melody.

"I'm going to start a new book soon," Naomi said, setting her coffee on the windowsill. "Jane wants me to write a sequel. She says readers are suckers for series, and if I can think up more books with the same characters, it would be a good thing. So that's what I'm going to do." She sat down in the window seat and pulled up her legs, settling Allie in her lap. "She'd like me to finish it by Christmas so it can be released next fall. My hobby seems to have turned into real work."

"It always was." Jon marveled how she still couldn't understand, how she didn't see herself the way he—and the rest of the world—did. "It was work the moment you sat down all those years ago to write those very first lyrics for me, the ones you sent to me before we'd ever met. You've always been a writer."

"Play for me. Play that melody for me, Jon."

So he did, watching her with the baby while his fingers glided over the piano keys and the music unfolded.

Naomi's lips were moving with the slow rhythm, her head turned away toward the greenery and the view of the city. She was singing, singing words under her breath that came to her as she was listening to him play, as if the rhymes were right there, woven into the fabric of his composition, and he was just too stupid to hear them.

Allie's head rested against her chest; she was nestled into her mother's arms, sharing the song with them.

It was a perfect day.

chapter 31

SAL AND GEMMA returned from their excursion late in the afternoon. Lourdes had brought back curries and samosas from her shopping trip, and Sal, seeing the containers on the kitchen table, felt no regret at the name on them.

Olaf and Lucia were there, happily eating from paper plates, helping themselves to iced tea and beer. Allie, riding Olaf's knee, tried to snatch food from him, making little smacking sounds as she watched the adults eat until Naomi relented and made her some baby cereal. Olaf insisted on feeding her, stating that he'd never had the time to do this with his own daughter. He had always been on a plane, or in some business meeting, when Naomi was growing up, but now he would enjoy every moment with his granddaughter to make up for that. His hand cupped Allie's curled head as he said this—she had his full attention. He didn't even care when she dipped her fist into the bowl and then smeared cereal on the front of his shirt.

It took Sal a while to get Jon's attention away from the loving family scene and get him into the studio where they could talk alone.

"What?" Jon asked, his head turned away, back toward the kitchen where the others were.

"I've been thinking." Sal wondered if he could convince Jon to go outside with him. This strict no smoking policy inside the house irritated him. They had spent so many days and nights smoking and drinking in LA, and no one had ever bothered about the overflowing ashtrays or empty bottles. Here everything was neat, orderly, pretty.

"I've been thinking," he repeated, "I don't want to waste any more time. It's now or never. I want to ask Gemma to marry me."

Jon patted his jeans pockets, and that made Sal grin. "Do you mind?"

"What do you mean, do I mind?" With a wave of his hand, Jon indicated that he should follow.

They stood on the front steps, just outside the entrance where they could look across the front yard and toward the buildings across the street. They smoked in silence for a few minutes. The sun was setting and cast a mellow, golden light on the old brownstone houses and the trees lining the sidewalk. It was quiet, a moment of tranquility in the lively city.

"Why should I mind? I pushed her in your face, didn't I? I made you date her. This is what I'd hoped would eventually happen, Sal. It's going a bit faster than I thought, but I'm very happy about it." The cigarette was only half gone when Jon dropped it. Carefully he stepped on it to put it out and then bent down to pick up the butt. "Naomi would kill me," he explained with a shrug.

"So I was wondering." Sal cleared his throat. He ran his hand through his hair, scratched an itchy, sweaty patch at the back of his neck, and tugged his shirt sleeves. "Will you come with me when I buy a ring for her? I think it's only fitting since you'll be my best man if she says yes."

"I am?" But Jon laughed saying it, and Sal didn't take the bait.

They had only a handful of days until the opening night, and now, standing in the evening light, Sal felt the old spark of excitement, the same quickening of his pulse that always came just before they'd embarked on a tour. There was a good measure of anxiety, the nervous running through mental lists to make sure that nothing had been forgotten, that everything was packed and in the right containers. That the hotels, buses, and planes were the way they wanted them too, and that everyone stayed healthy.

"Who else?" His cigarette finished, Sal walked down to the gate and opened it to toss the butt out into the street in a show of defiance that made Jon shake his head. "Who else would be my best man?"

"All right," Jon said "Let's go buy a ring tomorrow. And while we're at it I can pick up Naomi's anniversary gift. I had an idea with some diamonds, had it custom-made for her."

"Diamonds, diamonds." It was more of a sigh than a laugh. "Why does it always have to be diamonds?"

"DON'T GET UP," Jon said softly. "It's still early. Even Allie is still sleeping."

Naomi tried to snuggle up to him, but he wasn't there. She opened her eyes to see him dressed, sitting on the edge of the bed.

"I have a breakfast date with Sal and that friend of his, the one with the management company at the World Trade Center. After that we'll hop over to the theater and take a look at things. They should be done installing the set today, and I want to get a feel for the stage."

"You're not going to be on that stage." She wanted to get up and go along, wanted a day on the town, with a hotel breakfast, and she really wanted to go inside those towers if only once, to look down at Manhattan. They'd always talked about it but never gone. Half asleep, she imagined how tiny the deep, shadowy veins of New York must seem from that height. "I want to come."

With a gentle laugh he drew her into his arms, his fingers pushing against her hairline and gripping her locks, forcing her to offer her lips. "Not today, my lovely. Sal has secret things to do, and he doesn't want women along for that. Maybe later." He sighed. "Why don't we meet for lunch? I'll buy you lunch. Hey, why don't you come in your cute little Porsche and I'll take you out for lunch, just like any other New York businessman and his girl, and then we'll spend an hour or so browsing a couple of stores, and you can buy something from the new fall collection, just because."

He was warm, solid, and he smelled wonderful. The muscles in his back moved smoothly under her hands, and she wanted him back under the sheets, not going anywhere.

"Don't need more clothes," she mumbled. "Come back to bed. Just ten more minutes."

Jon laughed. "Yes, and I'd love to. God, you are so lovely. But I promised, baby. I promised to meet Sal for eggs Benedict."

"Where?"

"I think he wanted to go to the Marriott near the Battery. Said they made a fabulous breakfast. I don't know. We'll see." His lips brushed hers, his tongue pushing against the corners of her mouth. "I wouldn't mind some fried eggs and a good cup of coffee." The kiss was deep, promising, but he drew away again after a moment. "Don't do that. Don't tempt me like that. In a minute I'll be back in bed with you and stand up Sal. I love you, Naomi. You make me so happy, every day."

She watched him move through the room in stocking feet while he put the shirt she had tugged out of his trousers back in order and ran his hands through his hair, humming under his breath. Almost forty-eight, and he was as handsome as ever. Little laugh lines had appeared around his eyes recently, fine traces of a good life etched onto his skin. It seemed as if time was taking care of them, gracing them with some extra years of youth to make up for their lost time together.

"Stop that." Jon threw her a smoldering glance that traveled from her face downward to where her breasts were barely covered by the sheets. "Stop looking at me like that. One more sigh from you and I'll drop my clothes. And there'll be no breakfast, no Sal, and no…" He caught himself, grinning. "You vixen. You nearly made me tell you!"

"I don't care what you're up to with Sal." The covers slipped just a little bit more.

There was a subtle change on Jon's face, the amusement and joking becoming something more attentive, more alert, and almost predatory. Like a jungle cat, like a tiger who'd located his prey, he slowly came closer. "You really want me to stay here with you and forget about the outside world. And I can tell you, I'm sorely tempted. The way you look right now, the way you're looking at me… That's desire in your eyes, sheer desire. You want me."

"Go." The word felt like an ice chip on her tongue, but she managed. "Go, my love, and face the world. But come back to me, and hold on to that feeling for tonight."

Again he shifted toward her, but stopped at the end of the bed. "No kiss. I'm not going to kiss you good-bye. If I get any closer to you now I won't be able to leave; I know it. Love you, baby. I'll call you later, and we'll meet for lunch. Promise?"

"I promise."

With that he was out the door, and there was nothing left but the imprint of their passion.

LOURDES WAS MAKING coffee when Naomi came down a while later. There was a loaf of fresh bread on the kitchen counter, butter, and strawberry jam; and that was all she really needed. Those omelets with mushrooms that Jon loved to cook for her were really more of a ritual, something that reminded her of dire moments in their lives.

She missed Andrea's cinnamon rolls. For the longest time she hadn't thought of those, or of her old life in the small coastal town in Norway. They had moved so far away from that now, from the quiet, slow days they'd lived there before she was ready to go out and face the world again at Jon's side and share his public life.

Standing in her kitchen, a mug of coffee in her hand, Naomi gazed at her contorted image on the polished surface of the fridge. Older, but not a lot. Damaged, but healing. In love, and happy, and at peace. Safe, too, in a safe place, protected by Jon's love, and by high walls and security, even by her family's vigilance.

From the hallway she could hear Gemma come down with Allie.

Normally she always looked after the baby in the morning, but today she had decided to have coffee first, secure in the knowledge that Gemma would bring her down any minute.

"It's a lovely day," Lourdes was saying, moving toward the terrace door. "We should let in some fresh air. It's not hot at all, not humid, just right, and there's a light breeze. If it was like this all the time I'd never miss California."

Birdsong drifted in with the scent of flowers and wet earth, and for a second, if she closed her eyes, Naomi felt as if she were back at the Malibu house. The radio was playing an old song, one she had always loved but Jon had never sung; and now, listening to Matt Monro croon about a secret love and how he would even tell the daffodils about it, she stepped outside and decided to ask him to sing it for her. She could hear his voice wrap around it, strings and the gentle strumming of a bass, a melody like a satin ribbon with words as poetic as a sparkling dawn.

She looked up at the sky, the blue flawlessness punctuated by a stray puffy white cloud. She drew a deep breath of the fresh fall air. Taking another sip of coffee, ready to turn back inside, she glanced over at the city and the twin towers, thinking how Jon was there now, also having coffee, and discussing obscure future plans, forging a path for their lives.

There was smoke.

Somewhere up in one of the towers there was a blazing fire, and smoke pouring from the windows.

"Something's happened at the World Trade Center," she called. Gemma and Lourdes joined her.

"Must have been one of those little planes," Gemma said, disdain in her voice. "Those should really be forbidden over the city."

"It's an awful big fire for a small plane," Lourdes replied. She had a paring knife in one hand, an apple in the other.

There was no TV in the living room, but they had a small set in the kitchen so Lourdes could watch her favorite show while she cooked. They turned to it. There were some commercials running, and on the news they were talking about baseball.

"Jon is there." Naomi put down her cup. "Jon is at the Marriott near the World Trade Center."

"Call him!" Holding out the phone to her, Gemma added, "Sal is with him, isn't he?"

Yes, he was, Naomi admitted, and that was all she really knew. Guilt crept up her neck at the memory of her morning with Jon, at the mindless lust that had made her forget everything else.

He didn't pick up the call. Jon had, after repeated badgering, created his own outgoing response on the mailbox, and she could hear his voice telling her that he was not available and to please call the office if it was urgent; but that was all. No music, no funny remarks, just a couple of terse sentences. He didn't, he had told her, want anyone who dialed his number by mistake to know who they had called. This was his private line.

She sank onto one of the stools by the counter, the phone in her limp hand, wondering what to do.

If she leaned back just a little she could see the smoke rising from the tower. Actually, it wasn't really rising. It was standing there, like a plume of feathers around a very tall hat, undecided, as if it was waiting for something, waiting for someone to tell it where to go.

Helen.

Naomi picked up the phone and dialed Helen's number.

"I think," she said, "maybe you should come over. There's something happening at the World Trade Center, and I know Jon and Sal are near there right now. And I can't reach Jon on his cell phone."

THE IMAGES ON the television screen changed. A second plane had swooped down on Manhattan and struck the other tower of the World Trade Center.

She had never before felt this, even though she'd read the phrase in so many books it had become a trite standard: her eyes refused to take in what she was seeing. Her stomach in an iron knot, her breath refusing to pass her throat, Naomi returned to the terrace.

The television wasn't lying. Clouds of smoke were now poisoning the lovely September sky like ugly gray clouds rising from the heart of Manhattan.

"I can't reach Sal either." Gemma was standing behind her, phone against her ear, Allie on her arm. Her face was as white as the lace on the baby's dress. "He didn't tell me what he was up to today, only that he wouldn't be around until late this afternoon, or possibly tonight, and then he'd take me out for dinner. Now I'm scared, Naomi."

Scared. The thought hadn't occurred to Naomi yet, as if her brain had forbidden her mind to go there.

Lourdes appeared in the door, Helen right behind her.

Her hands were folded in front of her body, her head lowered. "They say two planes have crashed into the World Trade Center. Not small planes but big, commercial aircraft. There are videos. Someone flew those planes into the towers on purpose." It sounded like a prayer, like a sad litany, the way she recited it. "Something terrible is going on!"

"What do you mean, Jon is there and you can't reach him? Why is he there?" Helen's face was as ashen as the sky. "What's he doing there?"

"A business meeting. They were meeting someone for breakfast." Naomi put her arms around her, but Helen did not return the embrace. Her body was rigid with panic.

Gemma was pacing between the TV and the terrace, the phone firmly in her hand, dialing Sal's number over and over again.

"I love him," she said after her tenth attempt, "I loved Sal the moment I opened the door to him that night when he dropped by and the whole family was here for dinner. I wanted to push a big fat knife into Maya, chase her into the river, sell her into slavery, make her disappear from his life. I want Sal."

Her words fell into the silence of a world ending.

chapter 32

THIS WAS HOW Art found them: a tableau of women, as still as stone angels caught in the immensity of the moment. It had seemed the right thing to do, to bring Sue and call Russ and ask him to come over with Solveigh and the baby, to gather at Jon's house just the way they always did when something happened.

They were all upstairs in Naomi's bedroom, out on the balcony, where they had a better view; and for a moment he had this crazy image of fishermen's wives watching a storm, watching for the boats and their men to come home from the sea—they looked just like that.

Naomi was on the phone. Olaf had called. "Daddy," she was saying between sobs, "Daddy, I'm so scared. Daddy, what is happening?"

Art could hear Olaf's voice on the other end but couldn't make out what he was saying.

"Daddy, I'm so scared," and, more like an afterthought, "are you and Mama all right? Where is Ferro? Where are you?" She listened to him, again facing toward the burning towers and the expanding cloud of smoke. It hung over Lower Manhattan like a dirty duvet.

"Terrorists." LaGasse had come up behind Art, her face set into a grim, rigid mask. "They're saying these are terrorist attacks. They've flown a plane into the Pentagon as well." Her hand dropped to the gun at her back, as if by touching the cold, heavy metal she would have more control.

"Coffee," Lourdes said, "I'll go and make coffee. We need coffee." She left, almost walking backward, her eyes locked on the display of horror across the water.

"Daddy."

Art tried very hard, but he couldn't recall ever hearing Naomi use that tone before.

"The line died. There was some crackling, and then the line died." She sank down on the unmade bed. "My father said he's going down to the Marriott to try and find Jon and Sal."

Down on the Promenade, only a few yards from the house, people were gathering. There was an eerie silence. Their attention was directed at Manhattan, at the horrible thing happening there. Along the path leading from the street to the park, more and more spectators slowly came in a ghostly procession, needing to see this with their own eyes, needing the confirmation that this was real, not something dystopic.

"I don't know how they will fight that fire," Russ said softly. "God, I hope no one was up there. They'd never make it out." Seeing the expression on Naomi's face, Art's mouth snapped shut.

"It's still early," she replied, sounding almost defiant. "No one will be in those offices yet."

He turned away. One day in January, he and Jon and gone to visit Sal's friend at his office in the World Trade Center on the seventy-ninth floor. It had been weird seeing how small and cramped those suites were, and how they had gotten off the elevator a floor below and then taken an escalator to reach their destination. They'd been offered bad coffee and stood, gazing out the huge windows at the panorama of the Brooklyn Bridge and the river, and the land spreading away into the distance.

He had wondered how it would be to work there, to see that view every day, and if they even looked at it after a while.

But yes, Bill had told them, yes, he did look every morning when he got in. He thought it was a privilege, the best workplace in the world. With a shrug he had added, "It's small, and no longer really up-to-date. We need new carpeting and furniture, but I'd not trade this for any other place. I'm proud to have this address on my business card."

That had been well before nine in the morning. The sun had just risen beyond Long Island and was shining right into their eyes, right across all the other buildings of the city, like a brother, as if it was looking their way and sending out its rays for an early-morning hand-shake with the kings of the world.

That office was still there, Bill still worked in it, and all the others in his company; all of them were early starters.

WITH NEITHER JON nor Sal here, Art felt the weight of responsibility settle on his shoulders. The towers were burning. For a crazy, almost insane instant, this image flitted through Art's mind: a picture of Olaf and Jon with their Cuban cigars and how he'd always thought they looked so vulgar, so ostentatious with the clouds of smoke they produced. Those cigars, Jon had always brought them out for special occasions, like that evening before they had left for the Academy Awards. That day had ended in disaster.

He shook his head to get rid of it and turned his attention to reality. Only there wasn't any reality. The city was screaming. The noise of its agony rose from it in layers, in the screeching of fire engines, the sirens of police cars and ambulances, and again a manic, second view appeared on the back side of Art's eyes, that of a wild beast tied to the ground, captured and bound and tortured, bellowing in pain.

Lourdes returned, a tray with the coffee pot and mugs in her hands. She set it down on the bed beside Naomi.

It was funny, Art thought; they were bystanders, watching this tragedy unfold like witnesses called together to observe and memorize, and later retell.

He glanced down at Naomi, as still as marble, Allie on her lap, and wondered what to say, what to do, to reassure her that Jon and Sal would be fine, everything would be fine, those were just two burning buildings, albeit very high buildings, and nothing terrible would happen.

"Those were planes." Naomi wrapped her arms tightly around her daughter. "Those were commercial flights, with passengers. Those people, all those people on those planes." Her lips were as white as her skin. "All they wanted to do was fly to wherever. And now they're dead. Murdered." A small sob escaped her, a strangled, tiny sound, a crack in the dam holding back the flood of terror. "Dammit, where is Jon?" She wrapped her fingers around Allie's fist.

"Madonna." Gemma's anguished cry made them turn back toward the city, away from their own troubled thoughts.

It was so fast, as if the beast that was Manhattan had shaken itself to get rid of an irritating itch: the first tower came down. It left behind a column of dense smoke and an expanding circle of dust like a billowing skirt of gray tulle.

Russ stepped forward and pulled Gemma inside. "Close the doors. Lourdes, run downstairs and close all windows and doors. Turn off the air-conditioning. Seal the house!" He pointed at LaGasse. "Go over to your building and do the same. Lock the place down. We don't know how far that dust will travel, or what's in it. Check how much bottled water we have. No one leaves until this has calmed down. We need to find out where Jon and Olaf and Sal are. That's the most important thing now. There's nothing we can do except stare and cry, and we have to look out for our own. I want to know where those guys are, and now."

"But surely, Russ," Solveigh began, and he raised his hand to shut her up. She was holding Marisol, standing in the corner of the room, as far away from the balcony as she could.

"No, Solveigh," he replied, gentler. "We don't want to take any risks. If it were up to me, I'd load you all on a bus right now and drive you up to Canada, to Naomi's family place, out of the US. But I'm sure Naomi would never leave without Jon and her parents, so that idea is moot."

"What are you expecting, Russ, what?" Marisol on her hip, Solveigh called after him as he was about to leave the room, and he stopped in the doorway.

"I don't know, but I have a very bad feeling," Russ said.

THE PHONE WAS beside her on the sheet, a stoic statement of the silence that had begun with the explosion of the planes plowing into the towers.

Naomi stretched out her hand to touch it. She ran her fingers over the cool linen, over the same piece of fabric that she had clasped to her breasts only this morning, letting it slowly slip to tease Jon. She had to keep swallowing, had to keep the bitter juice of panic from rising into her mouth and spilling out in a torrent of screams and tears.

She wanted to lie down on that unmade bed, her child in her arms, and close her eyes on the world until she could hear the door opening downstairs and hear Jon's voice calling for her. Fear was a monster with very sharp teeth, and it was eating her heart with big bites.

They were still in the same places, even in the same postures, when the second tower imploded, showering Lower Manhattan with another rain of debris, ashes, and death. The city vanished under its shroud of agony, wrapping itself into it, hiding the terrible destruction. From the crowd on the Promenade rose a sigh, a chorus of lament, a dirge of desperation, clearly audible even through the closed windows.

Naomi closed her eyes. The tears behind her lids felt as gritty as that heavy, deadly dust, the grief in her chest like the hot shards of metal.

Again she picked up the phone, this time to dial a different number, but the line was dead.

Jane, she wondered if Jane was all right. She'd only been to her office once, to sign her book deal. It was so close to the towers, it had seemed close enough to touch, and now buried under that cloud. The thought of Jane being caught in that maelstrom was almost too much to bear. "My father, Jon, Sal, Jane." She could hardly say it. Speaking it made it seem more real. "They are all somewhere over there." There was no need to say more; the others knew what she meant. It was clearly visible in the way they turned to her, moved closer, in an attempt to provide comfort.

"We need food. We need to do something. I'm going to cook now." Gemma rolled up her sleeves. "Come on, all of you, to the kitchen. There's no sense sitting here and staring at that catastrophe. We can't do a thing. But we can carry on."

SHE SET THEM all to work. Solveigh was ordered to look after the babies while the men were sent to the cellar in search of wine and grappa. She wanted, Gemma stated, a big glass of Cesare's grappa, and right now, while she chopped onions and garlic. She wanted them to bring up a dozen of the dried hot sausages he had sent a couple of weeks ago. And the ham.

"And the curly pasta in the blue bags," she shouted after them, wiping her eyes with the back of her hand. It was shaking, and Naomi, seeing it, was quite sure she wasn't weeping from the onions.

"My grandmother," Gemma went on, speaking to no one in particular, speaking as if by doing it she would keep the terror and the panic at bay, "my grandmother would tell me stories about the war, about how she, and her sisters, and her mother, would start cooking for the men, for the entire village, when things got really bad. They'd bring everything they could find down to the church, gather at the priest's house, and start a cooking orgy. And it wouldn't be light food either. It would be lasagna and pasta, anything that was fatty and golden and melted into bliss in your mouth. Huge amounts of it too. And everyone would come and sit in the churchyard and eat, their plates on their knees. And that food, it gave them the strength to go on. It was a symbol of life, that life would go on, no matter what." Her black curls danced around her face as she chopped, the tears dripping onto the vegetables, mingling with the onion juice. "They suffered, some died, some never returned from the battlefield, some were just plain lost. But those women and children and old men in the churchyard, they had their bellies full of pasta and cheese, and they knew that despite everything, life would find a way. Yes."

The aroma of olive oil and garlic filled the big kitchen, the dining room, and drifted down the hallway and through the entire house; and it was true: the scent distracted Naomi from the thoughts that were crowding her mind and made her realize that she was hungry.

In fact, she wasn't just hungry, she was ravenous. She wanted that pasta sauce, wanted to sit in a corner and slurp it right from the bowl, and maybe, by filling her body with it, she could dispel the iciness in her limbs and put some warmth into her frozen heart.

She had turned her back on the view at Gemma's orders, but the images were burned into her mind, and there was no evading them.

Lourdes had refused to turn off the TV; she was glued to it, fascinated by the unspeakable terror of what had happened. It was, she commented, like one of those really spectacular movies; and why, please, did they always destroy New York? Why did it always have to be New York; why couldn't one of those movie directors decide to destroy Detroit, or Chicago, for a change?

Naomi couldn't take it.

Gemma and her frantic industriousness; Lourdes, entranced by the catastrophe; and Solveigh, her oldest friend, playing with Marisol, following the lively toddler as she explored the room, ignoring it all. This more than anything else struck Naomi, how Solveigh was so detached when normally she would have been the one to take control.

She looked up now, straight at Naomi, sensing her scrutiny. "I'm thinking of all those people who are dead or dying," she said in a very small voice. "All those people who were just on their way to work. Innocent people. And about all those who are right now missing someone, afraid that they might have been caught there."

It was too much.

"My husband." Naomi could hardly say it. "Jon is there, Solveigh. I'm standing here like a salt pillar; I feel like I'm going to crumble any moment in fear and desperation if I turn around one more time to look at the city. I can't even say how scared and desperate I am. I'm one of them; I'm missing someone. And if Jon...if Jon..."

Russ was there and caught her when she swayed, and settled her on the couch. He offered her the grappa bottle, just like that, no glass, nothing, the cork still in it, which made the corners of her mouth twitch into a ghostly simile of a smile.

"Jon and Sal can take care of themselves," he said, and that woke the memory of another day when she had feared for them, when they were still in Norway. That night, when Jon and Sal had flown to Geneva to see Olaf and force him into accepting Naomi's decision to marry Jon. There had been a terrible storm, and just like now, no one had known where they were. Jon and Sal—it was always the two of them.

"They'll be safe and dry in some bar or other, you can bet on it. They're just waiting for everything to settle down, and in a couple of hours they'll waltz in here and make fun of us for acting as if the world had ended."

Naomi opened her mouth to reply, but the phone rang. In her haste to pick it up she dropped it, and so it was Russ who heard Joshua ask if they were all okay and should he come down from Harvard? He wanted to be with his family now, and he'd drive down immediately. He'd been trying to call them forever, he added, ever since the second plane hit the World Trade Center, only somehow it was impossible to get through.

"No!" Again panic nearly inundated Naomi. "You're not coming to New York, Joshua. I want you to call your uncle Carl. And then I want Kurt to drive you up to Canada. I want you out of the US now. And I promise, as soon as I know what has happened to your father, I'll join you there."

There was an unbelieving snort on the other hand, a "But, Mom!" that made him sound like a teenager again; and for some reason she couldn't name, this made the dam break, made the steel ribbons that had held her emotions inside for so long snap.

"You're going to do what I tell you to, Joshua," Naomi shouted at him. "And you'll do it now! I want you to drop whatever you're doing and go to Toronto! I have no idea what's going to happen next, and at least you, I want at least you to be safe!"

Russ was staring at her when she put down the phone. "You sound as if you really think this is the start of a new war."

"Yes." Again a wave of sadness washed over her. "Yes, Russ, if this was a terrorist attack, there will be war. Not here, and not today, but there will be a long and terrible war. America will never, never let this pass without revenge. But I want my family out of harm's way when that happens."

chapter 33

NAOMI WAS CERTAIN there was at least two pounds of cheese in
the lasagna. They could hardly spoon it onto the plates, it was that rich
and runny—a golden, oozy mess, with threads sticking to everything
they touched.

At Gemma's orders, Russ had poured grappa for them all. She had
brought out glasses, not shot glasses but whiskey tumblers, all the
while deploring that a house like Naomi's didn't have anything to hold
a proper drink.

The babies had fallen asleep in the nest of cushions Solveigh and
Naomi had built for them on the couch, both girls napping side by
side, blond and black curls like halos around their little heads. Solveigh
was sitting with them, her arm on the back of the couch in a protective
gesture, and she refused to come to the dining table. She couldn't see
the window from where she was, only the children and how peacefully
they slept, and that was all she wanted to see. There was no need for her
to witness the agony of the city. The world was staring at Manhattan
right now, so she would stare at her daughter instead and wish she were
back in Norway, in the quiet safety of Halmar.

Sixteen years. That was how long they had been friends, had shared
every day, working at the Seaside Hotel there; and never, not once, had
Solveigh retreated like this. Not on the worst or stormiest night, not
when they had kept the hotel restaurant and bar open all night for the
families of fishermen out at sea waiting for them to return through
the gale, had she ever faltered. Not even when the news came that one
of the boats had gone down and there had been women to comfort.
But here, now, she was nothing more than a withdrawn, weeping,
frightened girl. Not even Russ could make her snap out of it.

Naomi herself was drawn to the destruction as if it were calling to
her. Still—two hours after the final act of the disaster, the destruction
of the second tower—no word from Jon. Against the men's wishes she
had again opened the terrace door and gone outside in a vain attempt

to be closer to him. Standing alone out there, she marveled how a day could be so lovely, so balmy, so disinterested in humankind's pain. The planet didn't seem to care. It turned and traveled through space, did its eternal dance around the sun, not at all impressed by the hurt the creatures living on its back were inflicting on one another.

She tried to go to that place in her head, that dark chamber in the lowest reaches of her mind where only a narrow, rickety staircase led and look down at that pit. It was pitch-black, filled with roiling, stinking slime and a sound like a steady moan of sorrow.

This was the world without Jon. This was what she knew the world would look like if he did not return to her. There would be nothing left, nothing. No love, no song, and no words for her to write.

She needed to call her uncle in Toronto and make sure Joshua arrived. And their family in Italy, Naomi had no idea if Gemma had thought to call them. She was sure they wanted to know that Gemma and Ferro were safe, one with them and the other with Lucia.

It was like trying to climb out of a vat filled with molasses. Her limbs felt leaden, her body unbearably tired. And yet Naomi managed to raise her head, give the mountains of dust hanging over the city one last glance, and then return inside.

Shutting the door, she said, "Please make more coffee, Lourdes. Gemma, we need to try and make some phone calls." Pushing up her sleeves, she added, "We've sat and mourned; it's time to talk to our families."

EVERYONE WAS ACCOUNTED for, except for Jon, Sal, and Olaf.

And Jane—Jane's cell phone was dead. The landline was either busy, or when Naomi got through, no one picked up.

Kevin and Sarah, Helen informed them, had called. They were safe; Sarah in their home, Kevin at the hospital, where he had phoned to tell her that he wouldn't be able to leave anytime soon. Their son, Ethan, had gone to Toronto with Joshua, and they were very glad about that. Lucia and Ferro were at the apartment in the hotel. Naomi tried to phone Olaf, but he didn't answer. She hoped it was because the lines were down. She hoped it with every fiber of her heart, seeing the dense clouds of the explosion hovering over Lower Manhattan.

Valerie and the girls had opted to stay at home. Val had asked Helen to tell Naomi that they didn't need the big family gathering right now.

Instead, they would be baking cookies, sheets and sheets of them, and they'd bring some over later, or maybe tomorrow. But for now they wanted a small, safe ritual in their own surroundings.

"I want to know where Jon is," Helen said, looking around in the living room where they had all gathered.

Naomi couldn't speak. She tried, she opened her mouth, but the words just sat there like stones and wouldn't pass her lips.

The phone rang. All of them stared at it as if it were an alien intruder, something that they'd never seen or heard before.

It was Lucia.

Yes, she said, she and Ferro were safe and staying inside, not venturing out onto the roof garden. They had opened the hotel for rescue volunteers, had offered rooms and food for anyone who needed it; and right now the lobby was full of people who had fled there, unable to leave Manhattan.

"They are herding everyone out of Lower Manhattan." Lucia sounded as tired as Naomi had ever heard her. "On foot, across the bridges. Ferries and boats have been commandeered too. This is like war. All these people, refugees. Your father and Jon." Her breathing stopped for a moment. "I haven't heard from your father. He left right after he talked with you. He drove down to the Marriott, and..."

There was no need for her to go on. Naomi knew. He would have been very, very close when the first tower came down, and she had sent him there.

"I want to go and search for them," Lucia said.

"No!" The sweat of panic gathered on Naomi's neck. "No, Mama, you can't go down there! Stay where you are, please! It's too dangerous, and anyway, I don't think they'll let anyone near there. Mama, please! We don't even know where to look! If I knew I'd go with you!"

"But you said the Marriott. I could take a cab and go to the Marriott." Her reply sounded sullen, desperate. "We can't just sit around and wait, Naomi! I can't just sit here and hope Olaf will come home. And Jon! We must do something."

Allie was waking up. Her fists were waving in the air. She looked as if she were directing an orchestra that only she could hear.

"All right." Naomi caught one of the baby's hands in hers, which made Allie open her eyes and look straight at her. "All right, Mama. I'll come over, and we'll search for Jon and Daddy and Sal."

"You aren't going anywhere." Taking the phone from her hand, Gemma walked away with it. "Neither you nor Aunt Lucia are going anywhere near there, not as long as I'm alive. I'll lock you up if I have to; I'll lock you in the wine cellar! I won't take the responsibility for this when Jon comes home and you are gone, trying to make your way into that destruction where anything can happen! And the same goes for you, Lucia! Olaf wouldn't want you to go search for him!" She pointed toward Manhattan. "Look at the TV. The bridges are full of people! No car could ever get through there, not even Naomi's fancy-schmancy Rolls!"

THERE WAS A sound from the hallway, the sound of a key turning in the door.

Art was the first to move, but Naomi was faster. She was out of the living room before anyone else.

Jon looked at her across the hall through dull, tired eyes. "Baby," he said, and his voice was that of an old man, of someone who was ready to lie down and die. She rushed into his arms, heedless of the dirt and sweat, the white dust on his face and hair; and he held her tightly, kissing her hard. It was a very long kiss, one that nearly drowned her. For a second it made her forget everything that had happened, forget everything but his embrace and love, but then reality returned in the form of the stench coming from his clothes.

"You saw." More wasn't necessary. He nodded in reply.

Sal was right behind him, still standing in the same spot, dazed, exhausted, and just as filthy as Jon. "We walked," he said. "We walked across the bridge, with all the others. And then, once we were across, it didn't seem to make much sense to look for a cab. There weren't any anyway. All those people, they all wanted a ride. So we walked here."

Gemma was by his side, stroking his shoulder, waiting for him to notice her, to shake off the stupor.

"The only thing we could think of." Sal drew her into his arms. "The only thing that mattered was to get back to you and find you safe."

"We were safe, the whole time," she assured him. "We were so worried about you. You didn't pick up the phone."

Sal's glance met Jon's over her head. "Yes. The lines were all jammed and then they went dead."

They needed a shower, Jon said; more than anything else they needed a shower and clean clothes. "I can't stand the smell," he added. "God knows what we were breathing."

Naomi watched as they walked up the stairs, two tired, bowed men: ghosts, survivors, shadows of themselves.

There had been no sense in asking. She was sure that Jon would have told her if they'd seen Olaf, that he'd gladly have given her the news that her father was well.

Her hand pressed to her throat, she stood alone in the dimness of the hallway, choking back the panic.

The day didn't want to end.

THERE WAS SO much food.

They sat, Jon and Sal, at the dining table, mute and exhausted, and ate what Gemma and Naomi put on their plates, and drank a lot of water, while the others waited for them to unwind and begin their tale.

Sal was in clothes Jon had loaned him. The things they'd worn were in trash bags, set outside on the doorstep by Lourdes.

Neither of them, neither Jon nor Sal, had ever been silent types. They were talkers; they needed to verbalize their thoughts. But now, poking at the steaming lasagna with their forks, they had a hard time finding words.

Jon refilled his glass and took a long drink of water. They had, he said, been so close. There was this jewelry store on Broadway, near the corner of Fulton, a very nice shop. His hand wandered into his trouser pocket to bring out a small box.

"The last time I was down there I saw that store and walked in, on a whim, to have this made for you as a gift for our wedding anniversary. Today seemed like a good day to pick it up. Only I can't give it to you for our anniversary anymore now. It would always remind me of today, and not of our wedding day."

His voice, that was worse than anything else. Not even after Naomi had been shot, not even then, when she'd woken from her coma dreams in the middle of the night to find him crying and praying at her bedside, had he sounded like this, so broken, so defeated.

He pushed the box across the table toward her but didn't even look to see if she opened it or not. Instead he reached for the grappa bottle.

"Be a good girl," he said to Lourdes, "and get us some Bourbon. I have a feeling we will need it."

His hand shook so badly when he tried to pour it that Naomi took the bottle from him and did it herself, careful not to fill his glass. That made him give her a tired grin, but he didn't protest.

"We'd just had breakfast at the Marriott," Sal picked up the narration. "We had just reached the jewelry store when we heard the noise of the explosion and then…" There was no need to go on, they'd all seen it happen. "We told Bill to stay with us, and to stay away from the towers; but when the second plane hit, he was dead set on trying to find the people who work for him." He threw a longing glance at the Bourbon bottle Lourdes had brought. "So we parted, and he returned to his office. I don't think he could have made it. Everything was burning, and people…" His voice faltered on the last word. "I have no idea where he is."

Safely inside the store, they had watched the ambulances, and fire engines, and police race toward the World Trade Center, and how people had fled from it. The owner had suggested that they stay and wait inside until it became clear what had happened and they could safely leave.

At some point Jon had lost his patience and insisted they leave the store and try to get back home. They had been two blocks away when the first tower came down, and they had run from the wave of dust and dirt like all the others.

Sal took the bottle from Naomi and poured. He didn't look at any of them as he downed the entire contents of his glass in one gulp.

"It was my fault. I wanted to go shopping today. And I asked Jon to come along. He wouldn't have been there today but for me."

"What did you want there?" Gemma had sat down across from him, her elbows propped on the table, chin resting on her fists.

"Not now."

It was interesting, Naomi thought, how that innocent question made him blush. It was interesting to see Sal blush at all. She couldn't remember having seen it ever before. Some animation had returned to Jon as he watched the exchange between Sal and Gemma. Pushing away the Bourbon, he said, "Go on, Sal. Tell the girl. It's now or never."

"You first," Sal said, pointing at the unopened box sitting on the table in front of Naomi.

She wasn't sure she wanted to open it. "It will always be a reminder.

Whatever it is, it will always remind me of today."

Jon reached out and took her hand. "Yes. It will always remind us of today; there's no way to change that. Even if I'd given it to you on our anniversary and you'd never known I picked it up today, it would still remind me. So let's turn it around. We will use it as a reminder. It will always remind us that we survived today and that the world will go on, one way or the other. We won't give in to fear and terror. We're alive. We have reason to celebrate."

It was a ring. He had, Jon explained, wanted something to symbolize their family, something that would look like the love they felt, not only between the two of them, but with their children. His voice cracked a bit on that word, and he repeated it, like an echo, as if he loved the sound so much that he wanted to hear it again. So here it was now, the design more or less his own, and he brought it out of its box with a shy, boyish grin.

"See, it's me, and Joshua and Allegra."

There was no need for him to explain though. There were two interwoven strands of diamonds, one rose and one blue, and clamped between them like a flower, a big white one.

"Though I don't know that I deserve the white," Jon went on, and pushed the ring on her finger.

Naomi closed her hand around it. It felt good. It felt as if she could, with that simple movement, hold her little family in a tight clutch, safe from any danger.

"You picked just the right stones, just the right gift. I'm so glad you're back home, and safe."

The words she really wanted to say wouldn't pass her lips with the others around, but she could see in Jon's eyes that he knew only too well what she thought. A small, secret smile passed between them, the promise of other things later, when everyone else was gone and peace had returned to the Stone house.

"Marry me." The way Sal said it, it sounded almost gruff. "Marry me, Gemma. I'm tired of waiting, and hesitating, and wondering if it will work out. I want you, and I want a life together. So far, I haven't had one. But if you marry me, then I might find the happiness and peace I've been dreaming of. So please, marry me."

Gemma didn't wait for him to put the ring on her finger; she did it herself, and quite quickly.

"And I was afraid you'd never ask," she replied.

chapter 34

THE CALL CAME as the others were leaving.

Helen was still standing in the hallway with Jon, listening as he told her over and over again that he was okay, and to stop worrying; all he wanted was another long, hot shower and some rest. He hadn't, he told her, walked this much since he was a kid, and his shoes today certainly hadn't been the right kind for long hikes.

Ruefully he thought of the fine Italian loafers he'd been wearing, ruined now by the dirt and dust.

It made him smile. Despite all the terror, this made him smile. He had destroyed more expensive shoes since he'd found Naomi again than he had in the many years before. First the ones he'd worn on his flight to Norway, only to step off the plane and into a snowstorm, and then the pair he'd worn the night he'd gone to Solveigh's house, to learn that she was pregnant and wanted to leave Russ. Oh yes, that had been a terrible night, with a storm raging over the Halmar bay, and Naomi, she had scolded him for going out without a jacket. It had been the day after their wedding. One day after she'd at last promised to be his forever and ever.

And here she was now, watching him with his mother, watching patiently and silently until the fear and worry seeped out of Helen's face and was replaced by fatigue and wrinkles of relief.

"Everyone is fine," Jon said again. "We are lucky. We survived."

That was when the phone rang. Naomi picked it up.

"I'm off." Helen pecked him on the cheek. "Please be careful, Jon. Don't venture into Manhattan. Stay away from there. Who knows what else will happen."

"The preview for the musical starts in four days," he replied. "I'll have to go, Mom. But don't worry, the theater isn't close to…to the…" Jon couldn't say it

He couldn't call it by its name anymore, and he wondered why that was. The place was the same, only the buildings were gone.

"My father." Naomi's voice brought him out of this black pit. For a second, for an instant, he felt the sweet rush of relief, but then he saw her face.

"He's at the hospital." A sob caught in her chest, and she slapped her hand over her mouth. Two deep breaths later she added, "He had a stroke. We have to go."

"There's no way we can get into Manhattan today." He tried to say it as gently as possible, but every fiber in his body and mind balked at returning to the city. He wasn't even sure it was possible to get back into Manhattan at all, and part of him didn't want to find out, not even for Olaf's sake.

Naomi was still on the phone, listening. "But, Mom," she cried, and then fell silent as Lucia spoke again. Tears were dropping from her eyes onto her blouse.

Jon went over to put his arm around her shoulder.

"Mom, I can't just stay here. I want to be with you now! And Daddy!" She sounded like a child, like a hurt and frightened child, and it broke his heart. It reminded him of the day his own father had died, and how he had wailed like a baby to be suddenly alone, suddenly the adult, the next in line. Nothing had made Jon feel old like that, like the death of his father. He took the phone from her hand to talk to Lucia himself.

The police had found Olaf, she told him; and at first they thought he was dead. He'd collapsed while fleeing from the collapse of the towers. He was paralyzed. He couldn't talk. But he was alive.

"Please don't come," Lucia said. "I'm glad to know you're all safe and well, and I need this knowledge to keep my sanity. If you drive into Manhattan and something happened to you or Naomi, it would be more than I could take. I need to know you're in your own house, and safe. Please, Jon. I promise to keep you informed."

For him, it was an easy promise to make, but Naomi refused to accept it.

"He went there because I was so worried about you, Jon. Otherwise, he wouldn't have been in the vicinity of the World Trade Center at all. I have to go. What happened to him, it's my fault." She was shaking so badly that he led her to the couch and made her sit down.

"It's not your fault, baby." Her hands were icy cold, limp, trembling. "You were worried, and you did what you had to do. Believe me, if you'd been down there instead of me, I'd have sent an army after you; and your father, no one would have been able to keep Olaf from storming into the devastation to find and rescue you." The thought alone was enough to bring the food and grappa back into his throat, where it burned like vinegar. "What happened today, it's no one's fault, least of all yours."

"Don't tell me it's no one's fault, Jon." Naomi pulled her hands out of his to clamp them into angry fists. "Someone was flying those planes. Someone hijacked them, probably killed flight attendants and pilots to get them under control, and then flew them into the towers with all the passengers on board. Yes, it's someone's fault. And the fact that my father was harmed today, that's my fault. It's my fault because I was being egotistical and panicky, because I cared more about your safety than anyone else's, even my father's. And he went himself to search for you. He went even though he knew it was dangerous and he might get hurt."

"Of course he did." Helen, already half out of the door, returned to them. "Of course he went, Naomi. He did what he had to do for his children. Don't you think I would have done the same for Jon if you'd been caught there and I was close? I love Jon enough to want to see him happy. He would never be happy without you, so I'd do everything to make sure you're okay."

Jon drew Naomi into his arms. "I promise, darling. We will go just as soon as it is safe."

"My mama is all alone. She's at that hospital, and she's all alone. How can I let her be there, all by herself, while they try to save my father?"

The irony of it. After the Oscars, when Naomi had been in the hospital, shot down by Jon's former lover, it had been Olaf who had stormed in and demanded his daughter, demanded that she be taken to Canada right away, to the safety of their ancestral home. And now it was Naomi who was living through the same fear for him. This, more than anything else, made Jon realize how deep their love for each other really ran, despite all the battles they had fought.

"She's not alone, Naomi, your cousin Ferro is with her. I promise I'll find a way to take you to him," he said softly. "We'll go as soon as we possibly can. Hell, I'm not Jon Stone for nothing." When she smiled at him through her tears, he knew he had said exactly the right thing.

JON WANTED TO draw the curtains and shut out the burning city, but Naomi begged him to leave them open.

"There's no way I can't think about it," she said. "And if I have to think about it, I might as well see it."

A greenish glow hung over Lower Manhattan. In its own way, it was beautiful, cruelly, horrendously beautiful. It could have been a gigantic art installation, one of Christo's monumental projects. She recalled going to Berlin a few years ago, on a whim, just to see the wrapped Reichstag; and what an otherworldly experience that had been. The last time she'd been there it had still been a torn city, divided by that gruesome wall, but by then, nothing had been left of that. She had walked under the Brandenburg Gate and into what had formerly been the east, and there was no trace, nothing. In a way, this felt sad. History had been wiped out; there was nothing left behind. In their haste to merge the two parts of their country into one, the Germans had erased every trace. There was a monument, a few feet of the wall left in a different place, ogled by tourists. But from those few pitiful stones it was hard to tell how sinister the border had once been.

SHOWERED, FED, AND rested, Jon came to their bed and made love to her in an almost feral way. It wasn't really making love at all; claiming her, he was claiming life, asserting that life still existed, and she held on to him, tears running down her face, as they tried to drive out the nightmare of the day.

"Will everything change now?" Naomi asked later, when they were resting against the pillows, looking over at the city. "Will the world really be different?"

Jon too his time replying. Then he said, very slowly, "Yes, I think so. I think there will be war. There will be retribution." His fingers combed through her hair. "And the world will be on our side. This attack was totally, utterly senseless and cruel. Even if you hate America, you don't attack a city, kill innocent people. This is barbaric, utterly sadistic. And we need to fight back."

The way he said it made her stomach knot up in dread. "But not you,

Jon? You're not on the point of signing up with the army, are you?"
A rumble of bitter laughter ran through his body. "Ah, no, babe. I'm
too old for that, and I've never served. They'd laugh their butts off
at me. But I'd sure like to, I can tell you. I wouldn't mind getting the
people who planned this in front of a gun and blasting them into hell
myself. Yes."

"And respond to violence with more violence." She sighed and freed
herself from his embrace. Despite the heavy meal Gemma had served
them, she was hungry again.

The day had been so strange, so different from their normal routine.
Sal had stayed. There was no way for him to get back to his Seaport
loft, and Naomi had offered him one of the guest rooms. She was
quite sure, though, that he wasn't using it but sleeping in Gemma's bed
tonight. Just like she and Jon, they would need to be close.

"How else? How else would you want to respond to something like
this, Naomi? They need to be hounded down and brought to justice.
Every single one of them. Every terrorist who threatens America.
We can't have our people killed like that!" He sat up. "Don't you see?
If we let them get away with this, then there will be more attacks.
They'll think America is weak, and they can bash us now. No, darling.
Retaliation must come swift, and harsh."

"Yes. Yes." She knew that everything he was saying was true, but it
left her feeling queasy, and very scared. "I'm just so glad we won't be
here then. I don't want to be here when America goes to war."

"Where will we be, then?"

In her bathrobe, her hair pinned on top of her head, Naomi went to
the door. "I'm hungry; I want something to eat. And a cup of hot tea.
Are you coming?"

He climbed out of bed and grabbed his jeans. "Where will we be,
Naomi? We've just settled in here. Are you telling me now you want
to leave?"

Her hand rested on the doorknob. "I have to take my father home,
Jon. I have to take him to Kleinburg. And I want to stay there for a
while too." She waved at the burning city. "I don't think I can live with
this view right now. And I need the feeling of safety the family house
will give me. I can't stay in New York right now."

Without waiting for his reply, she made her way down to the kitchen.
Everything had been cleaned up; it looked just as always. Even the

trash had been taken outside.

In the fridge were a dozen bottles of water. Naomi stared at them for a minute, letting this image sink into her brain. This, more than anything else, even more than the view from her window, brought home the immensity of what had happened. They never stored water in the fridge. Jon drank tap water, and she didn't like hers cold.

"What do you want to eat?" Jon came up behind her, yawning. "Do you want me to cook for you, now, at this time of the night?"

It wasn't that late. They'd all gone to bed early—exhausted, drained, and at some point no longer able to be around company.

"I'll just have toast." Her appetite had disappeared when she saw those bottles.

"Let me make you grilled cheese."

"Oh goodness, no more cheese today. We had so much with that lasagna...which reminds me; there should be some left over." She peeked into the oven, and there it was, nearly half a pan of it. Naomi brought it out and set it on the kitchen counter and got a fork.

"Cold? You're going to eat that cold? Here, let me pop it into the microwave for you!" But she nudged him away when he tried to grab it.

Jon sat down on one of the stools and watched her eat. "You really want to go back to Canada? Are you serious about that? I remember all too well your blistering hate for everything connected with that house. You said you never wanted to go back."

Naomi let the fork sink. "I want to be where we are safe, Jon. And the Carlsson house is safe." She poked at the congealed cheese on the lasagna and put the fork down.

Jon sat silently for a moment, digesting her words. Then he said, "What you're saying, Naomi, it sounds unbelievably dire. Your haste to get out of the US, your sudden decision to return to Kleinburg...I don't know, but this scares me just as much as being caught in that dust wall this morning. What do you think will happen here?"

He didn't get a reply.

There were steps on the stairs, and a moment later Sal and Gemma showed up. Sheepishly, Sal grinned at them and opened his mouth to apologize, but Jon just went over to the cabinet and brought out a bottle and two glasses.

"Let me go put on a shirt," he said, "and then we can heat up the rest of the lasagna and eat and drink and talk a bit. Naomi here, she thinks the world is about to end, and she's scaring the shit out of me with her dark thoughts. Let's have some booze and talk about better things. Like your wedding."

"Bring some wine from the cellar," Naomi called after him.

chapter 35

JON COULD HARDLY stand it.

The smell, the sounds, even the lighting—everything reminded him of those terrible nights and days he'd spent sitting beside Naomi's bed after the shooting. He wondered how she could walk into the ICU like that, without balking.

Lucia came to meet them. Her face was gray and lifeless, her clothes wrinkled, and her normally glossy hair tied back into a ponytail with a rubber band.

Olaf was awake, she informed them, and stable. But that was about it. He couldn't move or speak.

"The only things alive in him are his eyes," she said, and tears spilled over her cheeks. "His eyes look at me, and they are trying to tell me what he can't say. I have no idea what to do."

"I do," Naomi replied, trying to look around her mother to where Olaf was. "I know what we have to do, Mama. We have to take him away from here, have him flown to Kleinburg, and take him home. We'll hire doctors and nurses for him, but he will be home, and safe."

Safe. That was a word she had used often during the past twenty-four hours. It had become a sort of mantra, as if by repeating it she could will her family into the quiet waters they needed now.

The city was still singing its song of the storm. They were still searching for survivors. Jon had invited Sal to stay—the house was big enough. He'd been thinking more of Gemma than Sal when he had extended the invitation, knowing very well how she would feel if Sal went back into the city.

Awestruck. That's how he had felt when the first images of the destruction. There was nothing left, nothing. Just a mound of rubble, a few steel bones reaching for the sky in a pathetic reminder of its former grandeur. It was as if it had never been there, never existed; and yet that gap in the skyline felt as painful and as raw as pulled teeth.

"You want to go to Kleinburg?" Lucia's voice woke him from his thoughts. "You?"

"Don't be silly, Mother." Naomi took her by the shoulders and made her turn around. "It's our home. It's the one place where we can all go when things get rough in the world. If you remember, that's where I went first when I fled from LA. Not Positano, not anywhere else. Home, to Kleinburg."

"Yes. Yes, you're right." It seemed as if a tremor of relief went through Lucia, and as if with Naomi's words, she sagged a little, letting go of worry.

"I called Carl," Naomi went on. "He's taking care of everything. We'll transfer Daddy right after the preopening of the musical."

This made Lucia turn and look at Jon. "You're going through with it? You're going to open the musical despite what happened?"

"Because of what happened." He was so proud of Naomi, his chest felt like bursting. It had been her idea, which had made him change his mind about this. Stan had been ready to faint, but no, Jon had told him, Naomi was right. The people of New York needed this. They needed to know that life was going on, that the routine would be back. "The show must go on, right. We are show people. We play and sing, even amid the ruins." It came out more cynically than he had intended, and so he added, "It's a small measure of relief. A spark, no more. But maybe a spark that will bring life back."

Olaf was looking at them. It was a ghostly sight. Those steely blue eyes, that gaze that had made Jon furious so often, was now nothing more than a silent plea for relief.

"Daddy." Naomi sank down on the edge of his bed. "Daddy, I'm so sorry. It's my fault, I know. I asked you to look for Jon, and you did because you love me. Anything I can do, I'll do it. We're going to take you home soon. Is that what you want? Do you want to go home, to Kleinburg?"

The eyes closed briefly, and he sighed.

Naomi took his lifeless hand in hers. "Daddy, we'll hire anyone you need to help you get better. And I'll be there. I won't leave you. I promise."

Panic coursed through Jon at those words, but he did not interfere.

"I want my family out of here," she was saying, "and I think the only really safe place is the family house. So we are all going. Right, Jon?"

He nodded when she looked up at him imploringly. They had not talked about it really—he had not made up his mind—but this wasn't the time to discuss it.

A single tear pooled in the corner of Olaf's eye, and she gently wiped it away with the tip of her finger. "You don't have to worry about anything. Joshua and Ethan are in Canada already. They are with Carl. I'm taking everyone with me who wants to come. We'll relocate the entire troupe, if they want to. We're getting out of here."

Olaf's lips moved. His face turned white, and a sweat broke out on his forehead; but he didn't give up.

"Allie," he whispered.

Naomi pressed his lifeless hand. "Everything is all right, Daddy. She's at home, with Gemma. Everyone is okay and accounted for."

Again he sighed, and closed his eyes briefly.

Except for Jane, Jon thought; that little puzzle piece was still missing. He had a feeling, though, that they were going to find out soon if and how she got away. Naomi was too fond of her to let it pass.

"Yes," he said aloud, bending over Naomi's shoulder so Olaf could see him better, "Naomi is right. We're going to leave New York for now and go to Toronto, all of us. We haven't talked to the others yet, and of course it's their decision. I don't know about Sean, but I think he'll want to stay and go on conducting the orchestra. But I'm pretty sure Sal and Russ will come, with their…" No one had told Lucia and Olaf of the engagement yet. "Sal has asked Gemma to marry him! We're going to have a wedding soon, Olaf. Your niece hardly let him finish his proposal; she even put the ring on her finger herself."

As if a gray veil was lifted from his soul, as if suddenly life was returning to him, Olaf smiled. It was a weak and wan smile, but a smile it was, and it made Naomi laugh in surprise and delight. "You do want to go home, Daddy? You want to be taken to Kleinburg?"

"Yes." Another whisper from trembling lips, but clearly audible.

"He's talking."

Jon turned around to Lucia. She was crying softly, her hands folded over her chest.

"He's really talking, isn't he?" she asked, and Jon nodded, drawing her into his arms to give her support. Her hair smelled stale, of sweat and hospital, but he didn't care.

"He is talking, Lucia. Everything will be fine. We'll take him home." And curiously, once he had spoken those words, a yearning for the cool, green estate in the forest west of Toronto rose in him, for the tranquility and solitude. Naomi was right; she was right. The sight of New York was unbearable.

THEY MADE LUCIA leave with them, after promising Olaf she would be back in a little while. She needed a break, needed sleep and a shower, and hot food. Olaf tried to talk, but this time only a dribble of saliva ran from the corner of his mouth, which Lucia cleaned with the corner of his sheet.

"I can't stand to leave him like this," she sobbed in the elevator. "Oh, God, this is such a nightmare."

"Mama, we'll find the best doctors for him, as many nurses as he needs, and we'll see to it that he gets the best physical therapy. If money can buy it, he'll get it." Naomi took her mother's hand in hers and held it.

"Yes, but he was always so full of life, so full of energy, and in command. And now this, this is almost too much to bear. He hates this. He might as well be dead."

"Don't say that! That's nonsense, Mama! He will get better, just wait. We need to take good care of him and be very patient." Imploringly, Naomi glanced at Jon, but he shrugged, helpless. "You'll see. He'll get better!" She paused, the raw feel of guilt in her throat. "And it's my fault. If I hadn't been so upset, he wouldn't have gone after Jon…"

"Shut up, both of you." In his fury, Jon hit the aluminum wall with his fist, leaving a shallow but clearly visible dent. "Stop this right now. None of us is guilty of anything. I've so had it with all this guilt in this family! None of us flew those planes into the towers; none of us left the house yesterday intent on harming anyone. We are not the murderers; those frigging terrorists are. And I'll tell you something else." He had to take a deep breath before he could go on. "No one in our family died. We are all here, all alive. But out there, thousands died, and many more lost loved ones." Again he heaved a heavy sigh. "So please, let's count our blessings. Let's be glad we're alive." Seeing their pale, shocked faces, he added, "We will do what you said, Naomi. We'll take the family to Canada. No one is interested enough in Canada to plan terrorist attacks there. We'll be safe. The children will be safe."

He could hardly bear the thought of Joshua going to school in New York right now. For the first time he was truly grateful to Olaf for having lured him away to Harvard. But then Harvard too—Jon could see Harvard as a potential target. An elite place, a place where America's future was formed. If he was planning an attack on America, he would hit there, were the young ones were. The thought was enough to make his blood freeze.

On an impulse, he embraced Naomi tightly. "Thank you. Thank you for sending Joshua to Toronto right away. You did the right thing."

"PACK EVERYTHING," NAOMI ordered, and that's what they did. Even Ferro's paintings were taken off the walls and were returned to their crates.

It was scary. It felt like an exodus, like fleeing forces that couldn't even be identified yet, and watching how their new house was being dismantled made Jon sadder than he had been in a long time.

Like a curse, it was like a curse. The moment they had settled into one place, had found peace and happiness, something happened to uproot them again and send them wandering, in search of a haven.

He'd asked her how she felt about going back to LA for a while, spending the winter there instead of Canada, where it would be cold and dreary, but Naomi had declined. First, she wanted Olaf settled and a new routine established, and then, after a while, when it became clear that America had the situation under control, then they could think about returning.

"I love this house," she said as they walked through all the rooms. "I love living here. But I can't bear to look out the windows. They've hurt New York." Standing by a window, her arms wrapped around herself, she watched the grey cloud still hanging over the city, now, three days later. "What they did to it. I can't bear the pain. Can't you hear the city weeping?"

For once he had to admit that he indeed could hear the lament. The joyful din, the cacophony of Manhattan, had turned into something sad, bitter.

Jon had been to the theater, where work had resumed, where the last rehearsals were even now under way; and once the heavy doors had closed behind him and there had only been the music and the stage, he'd been able to forget for a short while. Here, everything seemed as always. But once Stan called a break and the actors sat together for a snack and a drink of water, the talk drifted to the attacks, and one question came cropping up again and again:

"Where were you? Where were you when the towers came down?"

No one had been harmed. This was their good luck that they were actors, musicians, artists, who didn't get up early in the morning to be at an office or other workplace. Their jobs began when others were returning home.

Stan sat down beside Jon, handing him a mug of coffee. "We're going to see this through."

"Yes." The coffee was excellent. Naomi would have loved it. But she was at home, packing.

"I think it's a good thing to see this through," Stan said after a moment; "I think we need to make a statement. New York will not bow to terrorism. Life goes on. The frigging show must go on."

Jon heard the echo of his own thoughts in Stan's defiant words. "Yes. We will not give in. I agree. In fact, if I could, I'd give a concert, just to show them."

Silently, Stan sipped his coffee. The rehearsals started up again.

Eva, what a great choice for the role of the selkie she was. Her lush, red hair flowed down her back like a torrent of rusty water, contrasting nicely with the peacock costume of her fishtail. Her voice was lovely, too, a mellow soprano that sounded like a wooden instrument, like a flute; and it reminded him a lot of Kiri Te Kanawa's. She had the same quality, the same softness. Eva would have a long and good career if she took care of that voice, he was certain of it. He made a mental note to talk to Russ and maybe give her a little push, offer a record deal. Something like that. Something to turn her into a star and give her more than just a musical stage.

"You could, you know." Stan tore him from his musings. "I mean, give a concert. You could have it here. Granted, it's not Madison Square Garden, but it would be a nice enough venue for an impromptu show. I think all it needs is a note in the newspapers. You could even give a free show! Now that would be patriotic."

"Or I could do it in Central Park." The idea was intriguing. "But no. My band isn't here, Stan, and I'm not going to make them come to

New York right now. Sean..."

Sean was even now in the pit, conducting the orchestra. He wasn't coming to Toronto. Jon had talked to him, and Sean, giving him his gentlest smile, had replied that no one had any use for him in the Carlsson mansion. He was staying. He loved his new job.

"Well, you and Sean are here," Stan argued. "And there's the entire orchestra! I mean, it's not as if they couldn't play your songs!"

He couldn't do it. Deep down inside, Jon knew he wouldn't be able to do it, and he wasn't sure how Naomi would feel about it either. She wanted out. She wanted to leave New York so badly, she was counting the days and hardly interested in the musical at all anymore. All her thoughts were of Olaf and his health, and her family's safety.

"No, this will have to be enough. We'll be here, Naomi and I, and it has to be enough. Naomi can't bear the sight of New York without the towers. This is breaking her heart. And now her father..."

He had promised to take her to Jane. She wanted to go. They'd talked on the phone, Naomi and Jane, but very briefly, and it wasn't enough for Naomi. She wanted to see her friend.

"No one can bear the sight of New York right now," Stan said. "It's a nightmare. And it will never be the same. Never."

"Naomi thinks there will be a war. She's convinced of it." Jon shifted in his seat. "She thinks the US will retaliate."

Stan barked a dry laugh. "Hell, yeah! I want to go and knock those bastards out of their lairs! If I wasn't too old I'd sign up today! We're going to get them—make no mistake, Jon. No matter how long or what it takes, we'll get them. And they'll be made to pay for what they did to us."

Wild fury bubbled up in Jon at Stan's word, a helpless, intense wish to lay his hands around a throat and throttle it. He could see himself facing one of those murderers, pressing the ligaments and muscles of his neck and screaming at him, screaming this single word: Why?

Why attack an innocent city; why wreak havoc on civilians, on innocent men, women, and children? The irony of it: the World Trade Center was the one place in New York where so many foreign companies had their offices.

The Pentagon, now that, in a weird, twisted manner, made sense. The

White House would have made sense, too. In the same weird and twisted manner.

But New York…

He shook himself out of it, but barely. It didn't feel right to leave his country. It didn't feel right to turn his back on it, and leave it to its own devices, when there was surely something he could do, something, anything.

"You could do a tour in spring. Take your music out on the road again, just to show people that everything will be all right. I think you should do that." Stan got up, stretched, patted Jon's shoulder, and sighed. "You may consider retiring, Jon, and I can see why. But you're who you are, and not for nothing. You're one of the few people who can really bring solace to this wounded world."

chapter 36

IT WAS A long drive.

Jon had LaGasse drive them across Staten Island and then down toward where Jane lived. Once they were in New Jersey, and away from the coastline, things changed.

He noticed that everywhere, in every yard, nearly every window, the flag was flying. The country was showing its soul in a solemn, quiet way, gathering its strength, trying to cope. Jon felt pride blossoming in his chest.

THEY HAD TO ring twice before Jane responded. She stared at them through her glasses for a second before opening the door wide enough to let them in. Jon had the impression that she wasn't too happy to see them but was too polite to send them on their way after they'd come all this way to check on her.

Nothing had changed in the small house. The big dog was still there, curiously watching them from the den but too lazy to get up and come over for a greeting.

"Would you like coffee?" Jane moved away, toward the kitchen. "I'll make some coffee." She sounded fatigued, muted, not at all like herself; and she didn't really look at them at all. It was late morning, around eleven, and yet she was in yoga pants and a too-large sweatshirt, her hair uncombed.

"We just wanted to make sure you're okay." Naomi had followed her and was standing in the kitchen door, where she could see both Jon and Jane.

Jane pushed her glasses up on her nose. "I'm okay. And you? Is everyone okay? How is your father doing?"

"Yes. Yes, we're all okay. And Daddy, he'll be better once we get him home to Kleinburg." Naomi threw Jon a beseeching glance, but he shrugged.

"I was so worried." Carefully, Naomi took another step toward Jane.

"Your office, it's so close to…" Her lips moved, but she couldn't say it.

Jane nodded but didn't respond. She poured the coffee into mugs, quite unceremoniously and without asking them if they wanted milk or sugar. Her own cup in hand, she returned to the living room and sat down in an armchair in the corner, well away from the couch. Nursing the hot coffee, she waited, her head bowed, her fingers trembling. Jon realized that they should leave, leave her alone to digest her impressions and fears, that maybe she wasn't ready to talk about it yet.

"We should go," he said out loud. "We shouldn't bother you any longer. I'm sure you've been through a lot and need some peace."

Jane looked up, but she said nothing.

"I'm sorry, Jane." Naomi moved to rise, and that was when Jane seemed to shake off her stupor.

"The worst thing," she softly said, "the worst thing was those people jumping. I'll never get over that sight, or the sound. I don't think I can ever go back there. It was so close; they were so close." Another sigh shook her. "After the second impact, my husband called and told me to get out of the city, and immediately. They were going to lock down the city." She put down her coffee and combed her fingers through her unruly hair. "I tried, but all the trains and subways were closed. So I went back to the office, and we just waited. And then, and then…"

They sat, all three of them, reliving those hours, each in his or her own way.

"After the dust had settled, some of us made our way up to Penn Station. We figured if there was any way to get out it would be there. But the main entrance was surrounded by National Guardsmen. I remembered there was an access through Madison Square Garden, and so we walked around that huge building and rattled all the doors. One of them, miraculously, was unlocked." As dry and unemotional as her tale was, the feelings were clearly visible on Jane's face. She was barely holding herself together. "We made our way through those empty hallways, down, down, down…" She shot Jon a brief smile. "And I recalled how different it had been when we were there for your concert. So many people, such a happy crowd. And now, no one. The guts of that beast are creepy when no one's around, I can tell you." Carefully she picked up her mug and took a sip of coffee. "So we finally made our way to the New Jersey tracks, and there were all these people…" She broke off and looked away, looked to where her dog was stretched out in a spot of sunlight on the carpet. "The security guys were sort of herding them onto a train. I just got on. Didn't care where it would take me; I just got on. My husband, he works in a TV newsroom. I knew he wouldn't be able to get away for days, they'd be working twelve-hour shifts to cover the situation. I had no idea when I'd see him again. But at that point, all I cared about was getting out of that hell."

Again she sipped some coffee. "Those people with me on the train. It was so quiet. No one spoke, no one cried or laughed or anything. Many of them were covered in that white dust. They looked like the living dead. We just sat there, like zombies, glad to have escaped. The train raced through the tunnel; it went so fast I was afraid it would jump the tracks. And it didn't stop until we reached Newark." Her hand waved in the general direction of New York, somewhere to the north, invisible from where they were now. "Normally, when you're on the train from Penn Station to Newark, once you get out of the tunnel, you can see the tallest buildings of Manhattan. But this time there was only smoke and dust."

"The city is hiding its hurt," Naomi murmured, and Jane and Jon gazed at her in bemusement until she blushed. "It seems that way. Don't mind me."

"I got off in Newark," Jane continued, "and took a cab from there to get home. It cost a fortune, but I couldn't stay on that train. And I didn't want to arrive at my station and see all those cars still in the parking lot, wondering which ones would sit there gathering dust, waiting for drivers who never returned." She sighed. "And here I am, waiting to hear from my husband, trying to understand what has happened."

Silence fell while they sat and contemplated what they had been doing when the towers fell. There was hardly a sound: the dripping of the kitchen faucet, the faint hum of the air-conditioning, a soft whine from the dog, dreaming in his sleep. No cars, no noise from the ball field across the street. It was if the world had turned in on itself, was hiding and licking its wounds even here, twenty miles from Manhattan.

For a while, a kind of late-summer serenity descended on them, the drowsy peacefulness of a mild September day.

Jane stirred. "It's so kind of you to come all the way from Brooklyn.

That can't have been an easy trip."

"Jane, why don't you come for lunch with us? You look to me as if you haven't eaten a whole lot the past few days, and it would do you a world of good to get out."

She was, Jon could see, on the point of refusing but then nodded. "Yes, okay. Let me change."

It didn't take her long to return, now in jeans and a plain white shirt. "Lunch is a good idea," Jane stated, and saying it, her face seemed to look fresher and more alive than it had when they'd gotten there.

There was, she said, a café not too far away, nothing fancy, nothing like they were used to, but it was clean and they made good food. She shot Jon a dubious glance, but he chose to ignore it. The days when he'd never shown his face in public without an entourage and careful planning were long over, in fact since he had flown to Norway to find Naomi. He'd walked out of his LA home alone that morning, determined to bring her back into his life, and hadn't allowed anyone to go with him, had even gone to the airport on his own and arranged his flight himself, just to prove to himself and the world that he was still a human being, still had it in him to take care of himself.

There had been obstacles, a couple of huge stumbling blocks, but never, not once, had he been on the brink of reconsidering. This was the life he wanted. This was the freedom he needed.

"Let's go," Jon replied. "I hope they have decent cheesecake."

chapter 37

SAL FOUND HER in the studio, a blanket wrapped around her legs while she sat in the window seat staring out at the smoking city. So lovely, like a picture, and for a breath or two he stood staring, probing his heart for all those feelings he had held.

He found them, too, right where he thought he'd left them, in a neat little bundle, folded together like faded love letters, tied with a frayed ribbon. Hidden away in a treasure chest all their own, but one that he'd locked up and left behind.

Naomi noticed him and smiled. "You're going to be my cousin. You'll be family. I'm so happy for you and Gemma, Sal."

"Thanks." One more step toward her, and another one, but this time she didn't retreat into herself as she had in the past. "I have a strange need to talk to you about this. I have to justify it. I have to justify it to myself too. I know it looked as if I dropped Maya like a hot potato the minute I met Gemma. But that's not all of it. Maya…"

She waited for him to go on.

"I did something very wrong with Maya. I treated her very badly. I didn't mean to, but I did. In fact, it was downright sordid." Sal glanced back over his shoulder as if he were expecting her to show up as soon as he said her name. "I love Gemma."

Amusement crossed Naomi's face. "Yes, Sal. That's quite obvious."

"But it's not…" Again he stopped, awkward, unable to say it to her.

Dropping the blanket back on the couch, Naomi came over to him. "Sal, you don't have to explain or apologize. I know things were terribly wrong with Maya. You were struggling so hard to love her, but you didn't. You didn't love Maya for herself."

This was more than he had bargained for, and he took a breath to reply, but Naomi went on. "Sal, we don't have to talk about this. I know what you're trying to tell me. Everything is all right. Just be happy now." Something else occurred to her, and, more thoughtfully, she added, "I need you now, you know. I may ask you to leave Jon and work for me instead. I may need someone to help me run the Carlsson estate. And since you'll soon be family, I'm turning to you. I trust you."

A wedding. The thought alone was enough to make him sweat. His whole life, as far back as he could remember, he'd pined for a woman he knew he'd never get, and now he was on the verge of getting married to someone else.

"I want you to know," he said, "I love Gemma for who she is. There's no…there's nothing…" Losing patience with himself, he blurted out, "Dammit, I love her even though she's not you!"

There. He'd said it, and to her face. He waited, embarrassment and fear creeping up his spine like a herd of little spiders, but Naomi only smiled softly.

"You'll have a lovely wedding, Sal. A day you'll never forget. I'm really looking forward to it. And I'm very happy for you and Gemma."

The craving for a cigarette was more than he could take. A drink wouldn't have been half bad either, but it was too early in the day, and Jon wasn't around. He'd never ask Naomi for Bourbon.

"Oh, I don't know. I was thinking of getting married here, before we leave…" he began, but stopped when she laughed.

"Darling Sal, you're marrying my cousin, a DeAngeli. There's no way this will happen anywhere other than in Positano, in their church. This family is huge, and they won't let her marry away from home. And Gemma, she'd never pass it up either. You, my friend, are going to Italy. We all are!" She was about to move past him and leave the room, but then stopped and added, "Oh, and it won't be a hasty affair either. The way I'm seeing this, your wedding will be in the spring. Let's say March. Yes, that would be a solid guess."

Her silver laughter left with her, fading into the fragile tinkle of raindrops on leaves as she walked up the stairs.

Sal was left to stare at the bare spot where only a couple of days before her portrait had hung; it was now on its way to Toronto.

Nothing was the way it was supposed to be.

ALLIE WAS THERE when Jon came out of the shower.

She'd woken up, Naomi said softly, and she'd brought her to their bed so Gemma could sleep. She didn't add that it gave her solace to have the baby close, to feel her solid little body in her embrace.

He stood, watching how Allie was playing with Naomi's fingers, gurgling, giggling, her arms and legs waving, making her look like a precious beetle. Jon stretched out beside Naomi, drawing her into his arms, curling his body around hers.

It was so sad. Here they were. They had everything they'd ever wanted: the house, the love, the baby. And yet they mourned and wept.

"Stan suggested that I do a tour soon, to show I care, and to bring solace to people." Her hair, as always, had that faint rose smell. Jon closed his eyes and sank his face into it, breathing in peace and comfort.

"You just did one, Jon. We've just returned from a tour."

"Yes, but that was a year ago." So peaceful, it was so peaceful in the room, he wanted to close his eyes and drift off to sleep.

"Well, if you feel you must." Her hand cupped his where it was lying on her stomach. "But a tour isn't the only way to show America how you feel, Jon."

How he loved that voice. How he loved when she talked in that low, gentle tone, the one that was almost always reserved for him, for private moments such as this.

Jon took a deep, calming breath and felt the tension and sorrow flow out of him with the air he exhaled.

It had always been like this: everything centered around her. Everything good came from her, and all he had to do was calm down and listen to what Naomi said and the world would be restored to order.

Order, yes. They had managed to create order from all the chaos, and if he was honest, most of it had been done by Naomi.

They were ready to leave for Toronto. The only thing left was the preopening night of the musical, just a few hours away now; one more night to sleep and then they'd be gone. "So what do you think would be better than a tour?" he asked.

Naomi stirred. "Jon, you never really said what happened down there the other day. It seems as if you can't talk about it, as if it was so bad that you can't verbalize it. You are a composer, a songwriter. If you can't put it into words, put it into music. All of it. The horror, the fear, the loss, but also the heroism, and the valor of the rescue teams. Relief, hope, joy…put it into music. Write an American symphony. I think that would mean so much more to your audience than another tour with old songs. This is your moment, Jon. Take that experience and use it to create something people will never forget."

There it was.

There was the source of his deep love for her, the reason why life had never been really life without Naomi. He lay silent for a long time, so long that she turned to look at him, to check that he had heard and not fallen asleep.

"I love you," Jon said softly, "love you more than life, more than anything in this world."

That made her smile and close her eyes, and relax into his embrace. They didn't talk.

Jon's mind wandered back to those moments of terror when that wall of dust had hit the store's display windows, when it seemed the universe had been swallowed by blackness and destruction. Somber. Somber and slow. A dirge, a lament; a woman huddled on the ground, rocking with fear, crying, wailing, mourning.

A flag, fluttering in the afternoon breeze in New Jersey, fluttering on its mast in a front yard, while a little boy raced down the road on his bike, and children played football on a school field.

A nation, pulling together to heal the wound it had been dealt. Finding strength and hope on a smoking mound of rubble, finding a new awareness.

And a family, his own, safe and well.

All these came together in the melodies that began humming in his head. Jon felt the prickle of excitement on his skin, the itch to write down the notes in his fingers, felt the song vibrating on his lips.

His muse. That's what she was. His beloved and his muse.

With a sigh, he moved to rise.

"Come on," Jon said. "It's time to get ready. Life goes on…."